heart
of
the
frontier

heart of the

of

the

frontier

a western romance collection

BRITTANY LARSEN ✶ JEN GEIGLE JOHNSON

JENNIE HANSEN ✶ CAROLYN TWEDE FRANK

Cover image: *Historical Woman with Cowboy Hat Walking in Field* © Magdalena Russocka / Trevillion Images. *Seamless Pattern Based on Ornament Paisley Bandana Print* © Labetskiy Alexandr / Shutterstock. Cover and interior design by Kimberly Kay

Cover design copyright © 2021 by Covenant Communications, Inc.

Published by Covenant Communications, Inc.
American Fork, Utah

Printed in Mexico
First Printing: July 2021

28 27 26 25 24 23 22 21   10 9 8 7 6 5 4 3 2 1

ISBN: 978-1-52441-814-4

Covenant Communications, Inc.

OTHER BOOKS AND AUDIOBOOKS

BY BRITTANY LARSEN

Pride and Politics

Sense and Second Chances

The Matchmaker's Match

PRAISE FOR BRITTANY LARSEN

"A story that promotes the concept that wealth and position are not as important as independence and doing your homework before making assumptions based on surface impressions. There's a strong Regency flavor to this tale set in Wyoming Territory."

—Jennie Hansen, author *When Tomorrow Comes*

"Brittany's characters are vivid and engaging. Who wouldn't love an English baron and a New York school teacher escaping their pasts and falling in love in Wyoming? This fresh storyline combines with a touching romance, easily engaging the reader."

—Carolyn Twede Frank, author *His Accidental Bride*

"A blunt, bold woman meeting a proper, well-mannered gentleman promised to be a fully engaging story. True to form, Brittany Larsen did not disappoint. I was hooked from the beginning."

—Jen Geigle Johnson, author *A Torn Allegiance*

the gamble

BRITTANY LARSEN

CHAPTER ONE

The Western Union Telegraph Company
Dated: SS Britannic 30 Nov 1878
To: Sir Thomas Clayborne
30 Herefords lost to storm. Drowned in pens or washed overboard. Remaining will arrive in New York 3 Dec.

SIR THOMAS CLAYBORNE SET DOWN his fork, leaving the bite of steak untouched as he read the telegram his valet had handed him.

"Troubling news, sir?" Smith stood behind him, and though Thomas couldn't see his valet's face, the concern in his voice reminded him to keep his composure, much as he wanted to sink into his seat.

"Very troubling." He crumpled the telegram and shoved it into the inside pocket of his tuxedo jacket before pushing away his uneaten meal. "It seems I've lost a third of my investment," he added as he stood. Any appetite he'd had for beef was gone.

His appetite still hadn't returned the following morning as he stepped off the ship and paused. His next steps would be the first into his new life in America, a life already off to a start as wobbly as the rocking gangplank under his feet. The telegram had thoroughly shaken his confidence that his venture into cattle ranching was bound for success.

"Ready, sir?" Smith asked gently.

"I suppose I'd better be, hadn't I?" Thomas straightened his hat and finished his shaky walk to the solid ground of New York City.

It was dirtier than he'd expected. When Jasper Howe had spoken to him of America, he'd done so in such glowing terms that Thomas had imagined the entire country as sunny and as warm as the Italian countryside. He shouldn't have been surprised that New York had the same murky air and factory odors that plagued London. The cities, it turned out, were not only comparable in size, but also in filthy industry.

As though to reiterate Thomas's epiphany, Smith guided him around a steaming pile of manure. "Shall I hail a cab, sir?"

"Yes, please." He hated to think what the inside of a New York hansom cab looked like, but it couldn't be worse than the city itself.

Smith was careful in selecting the driver he waved down, and the cab was remarkably clean—not as comfortable as the carriage or hansom cab Thomas had left behind in England, but adequate enough to take them to the Windsor Hotel on Fifth Avenue. Mr. Howe had procured rooms there for Thomas and his valet while they awaited the ship carrying Thomas's Herefords.

The ride from New York Harbor to the hotel was rather long, allowing Thomas plenty of time to contemplate the demise of a significant portion of his investment. He'd been informed that the *SS Britannic* had encountered strong winds, during which the ship had lost its rudder chain and been hammered by waves that flooded the main and spar decks holding the cattle pens. His Herefords had been tossed to and fro until thirty of the one hundred had been overcome with exhaustion and died, their carcasses to be thrown into the sea.

The carriage rolled past many-storied buildings and under the newly opened elevated railroad, but Thomas could only focus on what had brought him thus far and what lay ahead.

He had considered he might lose some of his cattle before the animals reached Wyoming and had calculated that into his estimated earnings. Unfortunately, he had never considered he could lose a third of his herd before even reaching America. None of the figures Mr. Howe had shown him of his own earnings had included such losses.

Or perhaps Thomas had been so distracted by another figure—that of Mr. Howe's daughter, Clara—that he hadn't paid as close attention to Mr. Howe's proposition as he should have.

Thomas found himself thinking back to that day at the Doncaster Cup and lost himself in the memory. Though he had lost a good portion of his inheritance at the race, he'd had the good fortune to meet the man who could not only restore what Thomas had lost, but double—or even triple—the amount, and the greater fortune to meet the man's daughter.

Thomas spotted Clara Howe on the green with Edward, Duke of Leinstar. The duke was an inveterate gambler, and Thomas had won a number of bets against him just that summer. That alone would have been enough for Thomas to approach

Edward, but the beautiful, honey-gold-haired woman with him made it impossible for Thomas to stay away. She was a bright spot on an unseasonably cold and blustery day, wearing a yellow dress that glowed against the gray sky.

He caught the duke's eye, and the duke promptly waved him over. "I was hoping to see you here," Edward said to Thomas after shaking his hand. Then he turned to the young lady and the older gentleman with her. "May I introduce Jasper Howe and his daughter, Miss Clara Howe?"

The sun had peeked from behind the clouds, illuminating Clara like the saints in paintings done by Italian masters. She was regal in stature, and her eyes were the same blue as the rare cobalt those artists had used in their masterpieces. Lifting her delicate chin to see him from under the brim of her yellow hat trimmed in red roses, she smiled in such a way he thought he might lose his breath.

"And this, Mr. Howe and Miss Howe, is Sir Thomas Clayborne, son and heir to the seventh Baron Northbrook."

Edward had a marvelous way of presenting partial truths in such a manner that they couldn't quite be called fact or fiction. Mr. Howe's eyebrows rose almost high enough to meet his receding hairline while Clara's smile grew. Thomas's own smile faltered, but only for a moment, as he took Miss Howe's hand.

"Lovely to meet you." Clara paused, allowing her hand to linger in his. "I'm not sure how to address a baron."

"Call me Thomas, please." He bowed over her hand to keep from looking into her eyes. In truth, he was the fourth of the Clayborne sons, the others of which had sons of their own, making him ninth in line for the barony. He knew he should correct the misconception, but before he could, Edward clapped him on the back.

"Which horse do you like? I'll take the other, and we'll make a real sport of it." Edward's mouth pulled into a tight grin, daring Thomas to refuse.

Thomas hesitated only a moment, feeling Miss Howe's eyes boring through him with the intensity of light piercing glass. "Hampton." He swallowed the worry clawing its way from his stomach to his chest and gathered courage from Miss Howe's steady gaze. "I have it on good authority he's favored to win, so name your price, Edward."

"Five thousand pounds."

Thomas's courage faltered. A loss that high would decrease his inheritance by a fourth but would barely make a dent in the duke's fortune. The duke's life would continue unchanged, but Thomas would be forced to seek gainful employment.

The warning words his father had given him about gambling echoed in his mind, almost swaying him to say no. Though nearly a year had passed since his parents' unexpected deaths, Thomas felt their presence, along with their disapproval, each *time he placed a bet. Their youngest son was not living in a manner that would have pleased them.*

Thomas glanced from the duke, who waited expectantly for his answer, to Miss Howe, who batted her eyelashes.

Despite his father's warnings, Thomas had won nearly five thousand pounds over the summer with a few lucky bets. If his winning streak continued, he'd be in a comfortable enough position to hold off finding employment for another season.

"If Miss Howe will act as my good-luck charm," he answered, "I feel I cannot lose." Thomas held his bent arm to Miss Howe, and as she slipped her hand through it, he felt certain of his success.

Thomas followed the duke and Mr. Howe to the duke's box with Clara by his side. She kept close, cheering loudly with him as Hampton took the lead right out of the gate. They continued to cheer as the horse kept his lead during the first mile, and their excited shouts grew louder the closer Hampton got to the finish line, still in first place.

They went silent in the last hundred yards as Hampton, who had performed so admirably, tired and came in third.

"I'm so sorry, Thomas, but oh, what excitement!" Miss Howe's cheeks were the same pink as the prettiest sunset, and her lovely smile helped him hold his.

"Well done!" Edward shouted.

Bile burned his throat, but Thomas kept his composure and shook Edward's hand.

"I believe I've earned everything back I've lost to you this season. And in one race." The duke blew the smoke from his cigar over Thomas's head. "How remarkable."

"Indeed." With a smile frozen on his face, Thomas's cheeks felt stiffer than his collar.

The hansom cab hit a hole in the street, jolting Thomas back to the present. He looked out the window at the endless brownstone buildings and the snow dusting the sidewalks in white. New York didn't look so different from London, but America was a very different place. With its more fluid class system, America was the place for Thomas to make his fortune. A man could move up or down through his own volition—or lack of it—rather than because he'd been born first in line.

His fate, including his journey to America, had been sealed in more ways than one on the day he'd met the Howes. Mr. Howe, impressed with Thomas's willingness to not only take chances but also to face loss with such composure, had taken an immediate liking to him and issued an invitation to dinner.

At that dinner, Mr. Howe, or rather Jasper, as he'd asked Thomas to call him, had an opportunity for him.

"I've two thousand head of cattle I'm looking to double," he'd told Thomas. "I can buy the cows for pennies on the pound and sell them three years later at a twenty-five percent profit."

Thomas had often doubled his earnings at cards and horses, but he'd just as often lost more than that. Jasper's description of ranching in Wyoming sounded like a much surer bet.

"You bring me a hundred Hereford bulls, and I'll soon be able to double my herd. I'll give you a cut of the profits when we sell," he'd offered Thomas.

"I'll take some of your herd until then along with a percentage of the earnings," Thomas countered, and the deal was done.

Over the course of the following month, Thomas had spent as much time as possible making plans with Mr. Howe before the man's return to America. Thomas felt confident from their conversations that his prospects for making a fortune were sure.

From October through November, when Thomas hadn't been preparing for his move to America, he was writing to Clara Howe. Though she'd answered his own frequent correspondence rather infrequently, thoughts of her beauty propelled him forward. His brothers were all married with families of their own, and he wanted the same.

Clara Howe had many of the qualities he longed for in a wife. She was well bred, beautiful, and encouraging. However, a woman raised with such wealth that, as her father bragged, "she'd never had to tie her own shoes," would want a wealthy husband. Thomas's claim to a title he likely would never inherit would not be enough to win her hand.

But with Thomas's move to America, riches were within his grasp, and he hoped Miss Howe's hand was also. Fortunately, he would have the opportunity to renew his attentions to her that night. He'd sent her a telegram before leaving London, asking her to meet him at Delmonico's for dinner once he came into port. He had every hope they would share sparkling conversation over their steak and champagne. It seemed the perfect introduction into his new life.

America's taste for beef was only growing, and if they could find a way to get the beef across the Atlantic, Howe had assured Thomas that his profits would be even higher than what he'd predicted. The Northbrook Barony might be out of his reach, but the title of cattle baron was so close he'd be tasting it that night at Delmonico's.

"We're here, sir," Smith said as the carriage came to a stop in front of the Ionic columns of the brownstone Windsor Hotel, one of the finest in New York and Miss Howe's current residence.

"This will certainly do for a few days." Thomas stepped from the carriage and tilted his head back to see the seventh floor, Clara Howe's floor. His lip pulled into a half smile as he imagined Miss Howe's lady helping her with her stockings and latching the tiny pearl buttons of her boots.

His smile vanished, however, when the clerk at the front desk handed him an envelope with the elegant, curling letters of Miss Howe's fine hand. He tucked it into his coat pocket until he'd been shown his room and Smith had left him for the servants' quarters. Then he made himself comfortable on the velvet upholstered sofa and unfolded the letter.

My Dear Mr. Clayborne, she began. He hoped her *my dear* was an encouraging sign of things to come.

> *Please accept my apologies in being so negligent in answering your last letter. I fear I am an unworthy correspondent.*

He smiled as he read her list of excuses, which ranged from a busy social season in New York, wherein she needed a number of gowns that required an inordinate amount of fittings, to making travel plans to join her father in Cheyenne. Thomas understood the demands of busy social seasons and promptly forgave her but did wonder why she'd taken the time to write him when he'd be seeing her that night.

I do hope you'll forgive me, but I'm afraid I have to cancel our dinner at Delmonico's, he read next, feeling less forgiving than he had moments before.

> *Father has asked me to return to Cheyenne as he will be entertaining the Earl of Lambeth—perhaps you know him? Father is in dire need of my assistance as I am always so confident amongst the superior classes. I confess, I don't quite understand the ranks of royalty and can hardly keep straight whether someone is a duke or an earl, but the British system fascinates me. I think I should fit in quite well amongst your titled friends.*

Thomas's lip twitched, and his smile faltered. She might very well fit in with the nobility, though he hoped not too much. He often found their self-importance exhausting.

Thomas read on with less enthusiasm.

> *Of course, we will be dining together often once you're settled in Wyoming territory. Until then, I do have one slight favor to ask*

of you. I hope it won't be too much of an imposition, but I believe when I lay my case before you that you won't have the heart to refuse my request. Particularly as the task will allow you to act the hero in rescuing a poor damsel in distress.

Was Miss Howe in need of rescue? His enthusiasm returned.

I have a dear little friend—the niece of Mrs. Merriweather with whom I boarded and received my education in New York— who has lately been left an orphan. Mrs. Merriweather recently died in somewhat "unfavorable" circumstances, and poor Ella cannot possibly stay in New York. It seems Mrs. Merriweather was insolvent and, upon her death, made no provisions for her niece. The poor dear has no other family to speak of.

I have arranged for her to come to Cheyenne, but it would be improper for her to travel such a distance unattended. Thus, I'm appealing to your tender heart to let her accompany you on your journey here. Knowing you were acting as her protector would put my poor heart at ease. She is such a dear.

Thomas read on, losing confidence in the sincerity of Miss Howe addressing him as *dear* with each repetition of the word. It seemed to be a term of endearment used rather casually. And yet, as Miss Howe laid out the plans she'd already made for her young friend Ella Merriweather, Thomas understood he couldn't say no, as unconventional as the task may be. The child's ticket had already been bought. The plans had already been made.

Even if a ticket hadn't been purchased for Miss Ella Merriweather, Thomas could hardly afford to refuse Miss Howe. Her father held Thomas's fate in his hands. Furthermore, though he didn't know the Earl of Lambeth personally, he knew of him. The man was a rapscallion. Thomas had been mistaken in thinking Clara would have few suitors in Wyoming, and now he could not allow the earl to weasel his way into Miss Howe's heart. For that reason alone, Thomas was willing to play chaperone to a child, despite the fact he was neither a governess nor an old maid.

As a matter of fact, if escorting an orphan across the country put him in Miss Howe's good graces, the task was certainly worth whatever inconveniences might arise. Thomas didn't have much experience with older children, but they had to be easier than his brothers' children still in the nursery, and he was quite good with them. In truth, the dining cars had plenty of desserts he could use to coax Miss Merriweather out of any ill temper, and he happened to be very good at cards. He could teach her any game she wanted to learn.

With the matter settled in his mind, Thomas called for Smith and dictated a telegram to send to Miss Howe.

> *Happy to assist with Miss Merriweather. Will do my utmost to protect and care for the girl on our journey to Cheyenne.*

With that, Thomas put Ella Merriweather from his mind.

CHAPTER TWO

December 1, 1878
Tarrytown-on-Hudson, New York

ELLA MERRIWEATHER TOOK THE LETTER from the messenger boy standing on the steps of Mrs. Merriweather's Seminary, then gave him a penny. The small change wasn't enough, but it was all she could spare. She recognized the handwriting of Clara Howe on the envelope and was tempted to toss it on the sideboard. Curiosity, however, got the best of her, even though she knew the words were likely what she'd already heard from Miss Howe.

Ella opened the letter and scanned the short, elegantly scrolled note: *Father has arranged the job for you in Cheyenne. I've arranged your passage. A member of the British nobility will accompany you.* A train ticket accompanied the note, and Ella scowled as she read the date on it. *December 4.* As though she could prepare that quickly even if she were inclined to take help. She had no need of rescue, particularly not from the likes of Clara Howe or any of her "noble" friends.

"Anything else you need, Miss Merriweather?" a young girl asked, interrupting Ella's thoughts.

"Thank you, Maggie." She tucked the envelope into her apron pocket. "You can go home now if you like. I'm afraid I've come to the end of my limited funds."

"That's okay, miss. I don't mind staying to help you pack." Tears threatened to spill on the ten-year-old girl's freckled cheeks. "You've been so good to me."

Ella laid a hand on Maggie's blonde hair. "Thank you, Maggie, but I think your mother will mind if you come home from a full day's work without the wages she's expecting." Wages that would likely go in her father's pocket just long enough for him to hand them over to whomever had won them from him.

Maggie's chin quivered, and she threw her arms around Ella's waist. "I'm going to miss you, ma'am."

Ella patted the girl's head, resisting the urge to hold her close in order to avoid the pain of letting her go. "I'll miss you too." She unhooked Maggie's hands from behind her back and held them while bending her knees to meet Maggie's downcast eyes. "You must keep reading every day. Take great care with the books I've given you."

Maggie sniffed and raised her gaze to Ella. "I will, ma'am. I'll treasure 'em like they was gold."

"They're worth more than gold, my darling." The books had brought Ella comfort on more than one occasion. She'd often found refuge in them when the other girls at Mrs. Merriweather's excluded her. They took their cues from her aunt, Beatrice Merriweather, who resented not only the responsibility of raising Ella, but also the necessity of educating her alongside the wealthy girls whose families paid her handsomely to do so. "A young lady can have the best education in the world and still remain ignorant. Stories will teach everything you need to know about people."

A tear dropped from Maggie's eye. Ella wiped it away and tenderly held the girl's face in her hands.

Since becoming a mathematics teacher at Mrs. Merriweather's, Ella had taught many young ladies, but she'd never received the same level of satisfaction as she had from teaching Maggie to read. Ella's students would likely never have need in their high-society lives of the algebraic concepts she had taught them. But Maggie could rise from poverty simply by being able to read.

Perhaps it was Ella's experience teaching Maggie that had her still thinking about Clara Howe's suggestion that she come West to work at the private school in Cheyenne funded by her father. Ella wouldn't be able to teach there—Clara had made that very clear—what with Aunt Beatrice's scandalous death, but Ella knew many rural schools were looking for teachers. Perhaps Ella could endure working as a maid until she was able to get a job teaching at a school outside Cheyenne.

Ella felt no guilt at the thought of allowing Jasper Howe to pay for her passage West, then walking away from the job he'd procured for her. She suspected Mr. Howe had known exactly what he was doing when he'd convinced her aunt to invest in his floundering cattle business and now wanted to keep Ella close in order to keep her quiet.

Aunt Beatrice had lost everything, including the money Ella's father had set aside for her to inherit at the age of twenty-five. Clara Howe, in the meantime, still kept rooms at fancy hotels and wore the finest clothes.

And while Clara had talked of Wyoming Territory as being backward and uncivilized, Ella remembered the news about women voting in the 1870 elections there. That sounded more forward-thinking than New York where she'd had little recourse against Mr. Howe.

Ella took hold of Maggie's hand and walked her to the door. She waved goodbye from the stoop as Maggie trudged the gravel drive toward the street. When Maggie had disappeared around the corner, Ella went inside and latched the heavy doors shut. She leaned against the door and tipped her head back. The faux-castle mansion let in little light, and the darkness of the foyer pressed upon her.

Her years living at the school had not been happy ones, but Mrs. Merriweather's Seminary was the only home Ella knew. Hundreds of girls had come and gone in the fifteen years since eight-year-old Ella had been dropped on the doorstep after her father had contracted typhus while fighting in the war and died shortly thereafter. Her mother had succumbed to the same disease after nursing him. Ella had no other family to go to other than Beatrice Merriweather.

Beatrice Merriweather had not been a blood relative to Ella, having married the brother of Ella's father. Ella had few memories of her uncle, who'd died even before her own parents had. Though Ella had never found a family with Aunt Beatrice or her wealthy pupils, she did find a family in the servants and other teachers who'd worked for the old lady.

She had been very sorry to say goodbye to them after it had been decided the school would have to close. Upon her aunt's death, it had been discovered that Beatrice Merriweather was deeply in debt. The school and everything in it had been sold, and the new owners would take possession of the school in the coming weeks.

Ella pushed away from the door and went back to the library. The new owners had said she could take whatever books she liked as those that remained would be donated to the new Lenox Library. Of course, Ella had nowhere to put the books, but she was determined to take her favorites with her wherever she might end up. The characters in them had also been her family.

She packed as many books as possible in her luggage while thinking through her options. The one thing her aunt had given her of value was an outstanding education, which should have made it easy for Ella to get a teaching job anywhere. Unfortunately, the outstanding reputation of Mrs. Merriweather's Seminary had died with her aunt when the woman had been discovered dead in an opium den in Chinatown.

Ella had been the only one who was unsurprised by the manner of Beatrice Merriweather's death. Though Ella had never been in an opium den herself, she'd smelled its sticky sweetness every night when she'd helped her aunt to bed. When she pictured her aunt dying, she imagined it as something akin to drowning in honey. As uncaring as Aunt Beatrice had been, Ella did not like the idea of her suffering in death as much as she'd suffered in life from her dependence on opium.

A soft knocking pulled Ella out of her reminiscing as she realized it came from the front door. She set down the books she'd been considering packing and walked to the dark foyer. Since Aunt Beatrice's death, very few people, other than reporters, had dared knock on the wooden door, and Ella debated whether to answer.

She rose on tiptoe in order to peep through the small window in the door. A young man wearing a charcoal bowler and clutching a fashionable walking stick stood on the other side of her door whistling a tune she didn't recognize. His clothes were too fine to be those of a newspaper man, and the cane was most certainly an accessory rather than a necessity.

Ella lowered her heels to the floor, crouching below the window so he wouldn't see the top of her head. She contemplated sneaking away, but at the last moment, she cracked open the door and asked, "Can I help you?"

He startled at her question, then leaned toward the door. "I'm looking for a Miss Ella Merriweather." His accent was decidedly English but not like Maggie's. Like his clothes, his voice belonged to a man of means.

What could such a man want with her?

"Who shall I say is calling?"

"Thomas Clayborne." He stood straighter and tucked his walking stick under his arm. "We have a mutual friend in Clara Howe."

Ella did not open the door any wider than the inch she'd allowed. He was sorely mistaken if he thought knowing Clara Howe was introduction enough for her to let him in.

"She's asked me to accompany Miss Merriweather to Cheyenne." He leaned closer to the door, but when Ella made no reply, he continued, though with less confidence. "I thought we should meet before leaving in order to put her at ease about our journey."

Ella shut the door, shocked—though she shouldn't have been—by Clara's audacity. She'd never agreed to the plan, and Clara's certainty that Ella would agree only made her want to refuse the offer. Furthermore, Clara had sent a *man* to accompany her across the country. The gesture was an insult disguised as a kindness that—no matter the man's rank among the British upper class—clearly communicated Clara did not consider Ella a lady in need of an actual chaperone.

The gentleman seemed genuine in his concern about any nervousness on her part.

"Are you her guardian?" his muffled voice asked from the other side of the door.

Ella cricked her neck to the side. *Her guardian?* What in heaven's name had Clara Howe told him about her? The two women were the same age, though Clara had always treated Ella like a child. A child to be petted and molded when Clara wasn't giving her orders. An inferior who would be a reflection of the image of charity and kindness Clara wanted to project in public. In private, Clara was quite a different person, demanding "favors" in exchange for gifts Ella had unwillingly accepted from her.

But had Clara actually told this man that Ella was a child?

She flung the door open so quickly the man stepped back in surprise, nearly falling off the step. "I'm Ella Merriweather," she announced while he struggled to regain his balance.

He blinked twice. "My apologies, but I meant the young Ella Merriweather."

In a flash of annoyance, she let out a sigh. "How many Ella Merriweathers do you think there are?"

"I, uh . . . don't know . . . precisely." His cheeks pinked under his blond whiskers. He had no beard, a point which gained him favor in her eyes, but he had far too much mustache.

"Well, there is only one in this house, and you are speaking to her." She softened her tone. After all, he was hardly to blame for her irritation with Clara.

"You're Miss Merriweather?" He frowned.

"I believe that's been established." She tugged at the hem of her blouse, then smoothed it over her skirt waist.

He blinked again, his eyes a pleasant blue.

"My *sincerest* apologies again, Miss Merriweather. I was expecting someone much younger . . ."

Her eyebrows went up.

"A child," he clarified. "Which . . . you . . . certainly are . . . not."

Ella waited for him to go on. He did not.

"Did Miss Howe tell you I was a child?"

He looked thoughtful for a moment, then laughed. "No, I suppose not. The mistake was entirely mine."

Ella pinched her lips to keep from smiling. The man's eyes had a playfulness to them that put Ella at ease. "How can I help you, Mr.—?"

"Clayborne. Thomas Clayborne." He held out his hand, and she shook it.

An awkward silence followed wherein she should have invited him inside but couldn't. With Maggie gone, they'd be alone, and even if the girl hadn't left, Ella had no interest in letting anyone see the inside of the house in its current condition. She'd not been able to keep up with the cleaning after she'd had to let the servants go. In fact, she'd just noticed her dark-green skirt was white with dust.

"Mr. Clayborne," she said, brushing at her skirt. "I appreciate your coming here, but I haven't yet decided whether or not to go to Cheyenne." She wasn't sure where she would go, but at the moment, she'd rather it not be anywhere near Clara Howe.

"Oh." He took his cane from under his arm and tapped it on the stoop. "I'm sorry to hear that. I'm sure Miss Howe will be too."

Ella doubted that very much but held her tongue. "You can tell Miss Howe she has gone above and beyond any duty she may feel she has toward me." She rested a hand on the doorknob, expecting Mr. Clayborne to leave.

He didn't.

He tapped his cane again, then cocked his head and looked at her from under his bowler. "May I ask why?" He took off the hat and met her gaze. "Miss Howe was very determined in her instructions that I accompany you. I would hate to disappoint her."

Ella sighed. Apparently, he would not be easily put off. She considered how much to tell him. "It was very kind of Miss Howe to think of me, but I would rather stay in New York until I've earned the funds to leave myself." She wasn't sure why she'd been quite so honest with him except that there was something sympathetic in his smile.

"Ah." He nodded. "Lack of funds. That's something I know a thing or two about."

His herringbone overcoat and gold watch chain said otherwise, but then she still wore the clothes of better times.

"What will you do until then?" he asked.

Ella chewed on the inside of her lip. "I'll tutor or . . ." She had no other options, and though she'd said *tutor*, there was no one who knew her aunt's history who would hire her. Those who would look past the fact that all of Ella's teaching experience was at Mrs. Merriweather's Seminary would not pay her enough for Ella to support herself.

"I don't mean to pry, but if you already have an offer of a job, why not take it?" His concerned tone loosened the tightness in her chest, leaving her defenseless against his logic. "From what I hear, opportunities abound in the

West. If you don't like the job in Cheyenne, surely you can find another in the Wyoming Territory."

She tried to be careful in her words, but she didn't like the feeling of being a trapped animal whose only escape depended on her captor. "I'd rather not be indebted to Miss Howe for her charity. I've been in that uncomfortable position before, and the price of it is too high."

"I see." Mr. Clayborne cocked his head to the side, and his brow creased. It took him several seconds to answer. "I suppose, then, you must decide where you would be most uncomfortable, here or there." He moved his walking stick from one point to another as though showing her Cheyenne and New York on a map. "If you decide a short time with Miss Howe is the lesser of the two evils, I will be waiting for you at the station two days from now. Perhaps we can buoy each other up on our journey to a new start." He tipped his hat to her, then went down the steps, looking back when he reached the gravel drive.

He didn't say anything more but turned again to continue on the path to the street. Ella went inside but could not resist the temptation to watch Mr. Clayborne through the small window. He'd made it only halfway down the drive before he turned again. This time, he walked a few steps back, and she wondered what more he had to say to her.

Apparently nothing because he took only two steps before turning back toward the street.

She watched him until he'd disappeared, but his words stayed with her for the rest of the night. Facing a new life with a fellow traveler in the same position certainly made the prospect more appealing. And as little as she wanted to consider Mr. Clayborne's point that a job already awaited her in a territory abounding with opportunity, she couldn't put it from her mind.

In fact, the idea had already been there before he'd put words to it. The practicality of taking the one job available to her was indisputable. Ella had no desire to stay in New York for another two days, let alone another few months, when her chances of finding a good-paying teaching position were remote. The sooner she started working, the sooner she would be an independent woman.

But was independence worth being dependent on Miss Howe's charity?

CHAPTER THREE

Thomas cut into the prime steak the waiter set in front of him. His enthusiasm for dining at the famous Delmonico's had been somewhat diminished by having to do so alone, but the first bite of the tender steak almost assuaged his disappointment.

Almost.

As he chewed the meat, Thomas thought about his recent disappointments: the empty seat that should have been occupied by Miss Howe, the loss of thirty bulls, the loneliness of being in a new country, the opportunities he might have had if he hadn't gambled away so much of his inheritance. Obviously, he'd be disappointed about each of those. What surprised him was his disappointment that Miss Merriweather likely wouldn't be accompanying him to Cheyenne.

In fact, Thomas found his thoughts of Miss Howe drifting more and more to Miss Merriweather, but he didn't understand why. Miss Merriweather's beauty didn't compare to Miss Howe's. She had neither Miss Howe's statuesque figure nor her deep blue eyes.

In fact, although not a child, Miss Merriweather could easily be mistaken for one. While Clara stood eye to eye with him, Ella Merriweather barely came to his shoulder. Her eyes were brown and not even an attractive shade of brown. He'd describe them as muddy if asked. And her hair? Her hair—for all that was good and holy—was *red*.

How could an Ella Merriweather ever occupy a space in his heart when there was a Clara Howe?

Perhaps because the clearest memory of Clara Howe that had taken hold in his mind was the fact that she couldn't tie her own shoes. Ella Merriweather, on the other hand, was determined to make her own way in the world. If he were still a betting man, he'd put money on Ella Merriweather becoming an independent woman while Clara Howe would need to be cared for and petted all her days.

"More wine, sir?" A waiter held a decanter over Thomas's glass, interrupting his thoughts.

"No, thank you." He needed a clear head to sort out what he was feeling about Ella Merriweather.

Curiosity? Perhaps.

Admiration? Possibly.

Attraction?. . . Certainly not.

Clara Howe was the type of woman who would look nice by his side as he took on the title of cattle baron. Cheyenne had more millionaires per capita than any city in America. She'd be the kind of wife who could move among the wealthy with ease and confidence.

He suspected Ella Merriweather was not that kind of woman.

Yet Thomas could not put her out of his mind as he ate nor after he returned to his hotel. He thought of her over the next two days, wanting to know more of her story. What was the misfortune her aunt had suffered that had so affected Miss Merriweather she had to leave New York? His own banishment to the wilds of Wyoming was due to his own mistakes, and thus, he was deserving of it. But it was unfair that Miss Merriweather should suffer because of her aunt's choices.

He had wondered often if he should try again to convince her to go to Cheyenne. At one point, he'd found himself on the same train he'd taken to Mrs. Merriweather's Seminary but didn't have the courage to ride it all the way to her stop. Instead, he got off at a stop along the way and switched to the train returning to Manhattan.

On the morning of his departure, he and Smith were among the first passengers on the platform for their train, but they did not board. After giving his luggage to the porter to stow in the private car Jasper Howe had hired for him, Thomas waited on a bench in the depot. He knew the odds of Miss Merriweather showing up were against him, but he'd taken bigger gambles and won. He was willing to take his chances.

Thomas waited until the conductor's last "all aboard" before he stepped onto the treadboard.

That's when he heard his name echo off the tiled walls and floor of the depot. He leaned back, holding the bar to keep his balance, and saw Miss Merriweather waving her hat at him. His lips twitched into a smile at the porter trying to keep up with her bags.

"I've decided to come," she said, a bit breathlessly, when she was close enough to be heard over the whistle of the locomotive and the crowds waving goodbye to their loved ones.

"Better hurry, miss! Train's leaving!" another conductor on the train yelled.

Thomas took the carpet bag she carried and handed it to the porter onboard their car. Then he wrapped his hand entirely around her much smaller one, pulling her onto the treadboard with so much force that they nearly toppled over. He caught her about the waist to regain his balance and held tightly to keep them from falling again as the train rattled to a start. The porter shut the door, the train picked up speed, and Thomas breathed in the smell of lavender and soap, holding on to Miss Merriweather longer than necessary.

"I hope my bags made it on," she muttered and stepped out of his arms.

Thomas cleared his throat. "I hope my valet did."

"He won't be traveling in our car?"

Thomas was somewhat taken aback by her question. "No, he's in the second-class carriage." As befitted his station. As much as Thomas valued Smith's service, a man and his valet didn't travel in the same carriage in England.

Did servants travel with their employers in America? This was certainly something to consider if he were going to embrace the "all men are created equal" vision America promised.

"May I show you to your seats, sir?" the porter asked, then led them down a narrow corridor and through a door into a compartment with plush swivel chairs and sofas. Though much smaller than the London drawing rooms he'd spent many nights in, the area was equal in luxury.

"This will be the lady's room," the porter said, tucking Miss Merriweather's bags into a space under one of the sofas. "My name's Elias, and I'll be taking care of you. Mr. Howe has hired me special for your journey."

"Thank you, Elias." Miss Merriweather smiled at the porter and sat in the tufted velvet seats nearest the window.

As she arranged her dress, Thomas happened to catch a glimpse of her very small, dainty feet. His eyes drifted involuntarily from her foot to her ankle, which peeked from beneath her skirt, before he quickly looked away to respect her privacy.

"Your room is through here, sir." Elias directed, and Thomas followed him to the opposite end of the room. There Elias opened a small door, and Thomas peered through it into a small closet-like room with a washstand basin and another door. Elias opened the door to reveal a second drawing room identical to the first. "I've already stored your bags in here. You have it to yourself until Chicago."

Elias walked through the room and out the main door, leaving Thomas alone. It took only a few moments for the monotonous clacking of the train's wheels to convince Thomas how unappealing sitting in the empty compartment for the rest of the day would be. He turned around and went back to the first drawing room.

"Might I join you?" Without waiting for Ella's reply, Thomas took the chair across from hers. "Perhaps we can enjoy the scenery together."

Her eyebrows rose as if the idea of enjoying anything on the journey hadn't occurred to her. The longer she kept silent, the more heated his face became, but he could hardly leave her alone without feeling awkward.

He cleared his throat and looked around the room for something to talk about. "It's quite lovely, isn't it?"

"The car?" She looked around as if seeing it for the first time. "Yes, I suppose so."

The luxurious surroundings apparently didn't have the same effect on her as they did on him. The heavy curtains and green velvet seats reminded him of White's, and he experienced a moment of nostalgia as he thought of his club.

Thomas had made many friends at White's but also lost a fair amount of his fortune at its tables. Before leaving London, he'd committed to never gambling again—the money he'd asked his friends to invest with him in the cattle industry was so sure that it didn't count as gambling. He looked forward to the day he could return to White's having made himself and his fellow club members rich through his investments.

If Thomas had needed any more convincing that the cattle business was guaranteed to make that day a reality, his current surroundings would have done it, his view of Ella Merriweather being no exception.

He scrambled for something else to say as she took off her gloves and smoothed her hair, removing a hairpin which had come loose.

"Have you traveled by Pullman car before?" It seemed a silly question, but it was all he could think to ask.

"The last time I travelled by rail, Mr. Pullman hadn't invented his sleepers. I was only eight years old, but I remember the journey was very uncomfortable. I hadn't anticipated this one being any better, but it seems I underestimated Clara's generosity." She put the hairpin between her lips while she twisted the loose hair back into place, then spoke around the pin. "I don't often admit to being wrong, Mr. Clayborne. This day is momentous in more ways than one."

Miss Merriweather's hair, Thomas realized, was not just red but the same color as the rich cherry wood of their carriage. Her eyes, now that he saw them in a better light, were the color of a dark cognac, a favorite of his at White's.

"It seems we'll have some time to become better acquainted. I hope you'll allow me to join you for meals. Perhaps I'll have the opportunity to admit to being wrong also, though that, too, is an infrequent event," he said, hoping to get a smile from her.

She took the hairpin she'd held between her lips and stuck it back in her hair, her cheeks flushing pink. "You're certainly under no obligation to entertain me, Mr.—"

"Please call me Thomas."

"Thank you, Thomas." She paused. "I have plenty of books to read, and as we've established, I'm not a young girl. You don't need to play chaperone."

He should have been put off by her response. Instead, he found her more intriguing because of it. Thomas had never run from a challenge, even when running might have been the wiser choice. And as he had no books himself, Miss Merriweather seemed a better source of distraction than the scenery.

"If I promise not to 'play chaperone,' as you say, will you answer one question for me?"

Her jaw softened, and if he was not mistaken, she was doing her utmost to keep from smiling, though she answered with the slightest of nods.

"What changed your mind? You seemed quite resolved against Cheyenne."

She studied him carefully before answering. "I suppose I came around to your point of view that the West is a land of opportunity."

"I certainly hope it is." His eyes flicked from her face to his fingernails, which he examined briefly before working up the courage to say what he was feeling. His eyes met hers, and he blurted, "I admire you for striking out on your own." He smiled in hopes he would get one in return. Ella Merriweather's lips had a certain heart shape to them that he very much wanted to see in a smile.

"I had little choice." She offered no smile, just a serious look that dared him to show her any pity.

"Miss Howe indicated as much, but I disagree. Not every woman would take action in the way you have, Miss Merriweather." The car had become suddenly warm, and he slipped off his coat.

"You may call me Ella," she answered softly, her voice having lost the sharpness it had carried since their first meeting on her front stoop.

She stared out the window for a few moments before turning back to him. "And what about you? According to Clara, you are British royalty. Surely you had

far better choices than settling in a place so uncivilized as Wyoming Territory."
She lowered her chin and burrowed to the heart of her question. "Or perhaps
there's an arrangement between you and Clara?"

Thomas laughed and shook his head. "We have no arrangement, and I'm
afraid she's greatly exaggerated my connection to royalty." Though perhaps
with good reason as he'd never corrected her misconception about his dismal
position in the ever-increasing line for the Northbrook Barony. "The uncivilized
Wyoming Territory, as you call it, seems to be my best chance of making my own
fortune. The untamed open range offers more than a clerkship or the church.
And certainly more than farming with the current agricultural depression."

She narrowed her eyes, and the smile that had crept onto her face disappeared.
"So, you plan on going into the cattle business?"

"Precisely. As a matter of fact, I already have." He crossed his legs and relaxed
into the sumptuous chair.

"You're a gambling man, aren't you Mr.—Thomas?" The corner of Miss
Merriweather's mouth pulled into a smile, but it lacked warmth.

Thomas shifted in his seat and straightened his collar, unsure how honest
he should be with Miss Merriweather. "I've won—and lost—my fair share at
the tables but not anymore. I've vowed not to gamble again. Why do you ask?"

Her lips formed a stern line that he imagined her students received after
giving a wrong answer. "Because only a gambler would take his chances on
making a fortune on cattle."

The disdainful way in which she said the word *cattle* brought to mind the
image of his Herefords at the mercy of the waves that had crashed onto the
cargo ship. He felt his confidence being rocked in the same way.

"And what does a woman know of investments and cattle?" he snapped.

Miss Merriweather stiffened. "You might be surprised." She clamped her
mouth shut, but her leg shook as she bounced her foot up and down. She
was holding something back, and Thomas braced himself in case she let
loose the anger radiating from her.

"I will give you the same warning I gave my aunt before she turned over
her savings—and, unbeknownst to me, mine also—to Mr. Howe and his Great
Western Cattle Company. His projections are fantasy. At best, you'll get back
what you put in. At worst . . ." she took a deep breath. "You'll end up as penniless
as I am."

"What . . . why . . . ?" Thomas sputtered trying to recover from the blow
her words delivered. "That can't be true." He cleared his throat and regained

his composure. "Even if it were, your misfortune doesn't mean I'll have the same experience. As I said, women know little about investing."

She let out a bark of a laugh, then leaned forward, gazing into his eyes with such force he couldn't look away. "Do you know what the weather is like in Wyoming Territory, Mr. Clayborne?" Her return to formality stung as much as her words. "Cold. Freezing cold. Some of your animals will not survive the winter. Did Mr. Howe tell you that?"

Thomas pinched his lips closed and did not answer her, but he felt another piece of his confidence slip away. Mr. Howe had said the weather was similar to that of England in the springtime. He did not specify what *time* of year Wyoming felt like an English spring.

"Others will die of disease, and still others will be killed by wolves, mountain lions, or bears." Her tone softened, and he knew he had failed at keeping doubt from creeping into his eyes.

"Just because you want your cows to bear calves, that does not mean they will. Paper projections are very different from real life." This she said even more gently, then waited some time for him to respond. When he didn't, she went on. "You aren't entitled to success simply because you're a *man* who believes his plans will come to fruition. Thomas, your sex doesn't guarantee your fortune any more than my aunt's sex guaranteed her failure." Her words landed hard even with her softened tone and return to his Christian name. "The only thing your sex does guarantee you is more opportunities. Opportunities that will likely go to waste if you refuse to listen to anyone other than hucksters promising riches."

It was only after Ella Merriweather had finished her speech that Thomas became cognizant of his mouth hanging open. No one had ever spoken to him so bluntly. He did *not* like it. Not in the least.

"As I suspected, you know little of the cattle business," he sputtered, even though she'd clearly demonstrated that she did. "Your negative views of the opposite sex seem to influence every aspect of your thinking, so that even if you were capable of understanding investment projections and figures, you could not see the assuredness of my financial prospects in Wyoming."

She sighed, then picked up his hat, which had rolled to the floor, and handed it to him. "You won't be the first Englishman to be taken in by the cattle barons of Wyoming. Jasper Howe and the other Cheyenne millionaires didn't get rich by cows alone."

He snatched his hat from her and stood. "I think I'll retire to my own room and leave you to your reading."

With that, Thomas crossed the room and went through the water closet to his own room. He sank into a seat close to the window, determined to enjoy the American landscape they were passing through.

Unfortunately, neither the scenery nor the two doors separating him from Ella Merriweather were enough to keep her words out of his mind. He gave up staring out the window and buried himself in his newspaper, avoiding the financial section and the story about falling beef prices as studiously as he intended to avoid Miss Merriweather for the rest of the trip.

CHAPTER FOUR

ELLA HAD DONE IT AGAIN—OFFERED her opinion where it wasn't wanted. She'd been harder on Thomas Clayborne than she needed to be when he had been nothing but polite. Or at least he had been until he'd made that comment about women not knowing about figures and investing. She'd likely studied higher mathematics than he had, and judging by how white his face had gone as she pointed out the perils of cattle ranching, she'd also studied the financial pages more thoroughly than he had.

She thought about apologizing and would have if she'd had the opportunity. However, despite their being the only two passengers in the car, Thomas successfully avoided her for the rest of the twenty-four-hour trip to Chicago. Occasionally, she heard him using the washbasin or talking to Elias, but she didn't see him again until Chicago.

Things did not get better as they changed trains and took on the promised additional passengers. The two men leered at her from the moment they boarded the private car, so she shut herself in her room in order to avoid them completely. She heard their laughing, and occasionally their swearing, as she ate her meals and looked at the scenery alone.

As they neared Omaha, however, Ella knew she'd no longer be able to stay in her room. Not only would they have to change trains again, but the dining car would also be left behind. She would either have to buy her remaining meals at depot restaurants along their way—an expense she could hardly afford—or she would have to purchase enough food in Omaha to get her through the remaining twenty-four hours to Cheyenne.

After counting her money, Ella decided to take a meal at the Omaha depot in the hope she could share a table with Thomas before buying the rest of her food necessities. A meal together would provide her with an opportunity to apologize.

Unfortunately, though he helped her from the train, Mr. Clayborne joined the Chicagoans for dinner. Perhaps he'd thought she would sit at the same table, but she preferred to sit alone than with the other men. Thus, the men drank and smoked while she sat a few feet away by herself, but not without their notice. The gentlemen—Mr. Perkins and Mr. Lassiter—made frequent inappropriate remarks about her traveling alone.

Though he looked uncomfortable, Mr. Clayborne said nothing.

Ella poked at her muttonchops and boiled potatoes knowing she should be enjoying the food. The meal would be the last substantial one she'd have before Cheyenne, and it had cost her dearly, both financially and emotionally. The cook at her aunt's had made this same dish as often as possible because she'd known it was Ella's favorite. But as the men's comments grew from inappropriate to outright rude, she found it impossible to eat.

The more they drank, the more they forgot their manners, Mr. Clayborne being the exception. He didn't laugh at their comments, but when he finally did reprimand them for their behavior, it was too quiet to have any effect. The men laughed so heartily at him that he stared into his half-empty glass, not meeting their eyes or Ella's, which was fine by her. After all, she'd told him very plainly she had no need of a chaperone.

She could, however, use a friend.

Since Mr. Clayborne had proven he was not her friend, she determined then that he deserved no apology from her. Ever.

When she could no longer swallow the food or the impolite behavior of the men, Ella pushed away her plate and stood. The only exit took her directly past the men, so she lifted her chin, determined to walk by them without a glance.

She didn't make it past the first man before she felt a hand on her bustle. Though she flinched, Ella congratulated herself on not showing any other reaction. She would have liked to slap him, but these men were friends of Jasper Howe, who currently held her fate in his hands. She couldn't afford to lose the job he'd promised her. At least not until she'd secured another.

After exiting the restaurant, Ella walked quickly to the first vendor advertising "lunches put up for people going West." There she purchased enough food to last her until Cheyenne. She would not need to leave her room or see Mr. Clayborne or any of the other gentlemen again.

With bread and sausage tucked under her arm, Ella followed the placards pointing the way to her Cheyenne train. She wove in and out of the hordes pushing their way to their own cars and held her breath against the smell of them. A dozen different languages flooded her ears, reminding her of the streets of New York.

When Ella reached her train and was able to leave behind the noises and smells of the depot, she couldn't help but be grateful to Clara. They would never be friends, but without Clara, Ella would have been riding in a crowded car elbow to elbow with strangers. She would have had no place to lie down and sleep, nor would she have enjoyed meals brought to her.

Ella had hoped to make it to her room before the other men boarded the train, but as she climbed aboard, she heard their voices. The door to their room was open, and one of the men called out to her as she walked by.

"You're a pretty little thing." His words were slurred with drink. "Why don't you join us? Isn't that why Howe put you in a car full of men?"

Ella didn't stop or respond, but she heard Mr. Clayborne answer the man. "I'm acting as her attendant, Lassiter. I'd advise you to leave her alone." His words were not slurred, and the threat behind them was unmistakable.

Ella hurried the short distance to her room and shut the door behind her. Her hands shook too badly to lock the door, but the latch seemed to be broken anyway. She sank into her seat and took as deep a breath as her corset would allow. It felt even more restrictive than usual.

Her breathing returned to normal as the train left the depot, but just as she relaxed into her chair, she heard the door to the washbasin open.

"I thought you might like some company in here since you refused my invitation to my own room." Mr. Lassiter's voice sent chills up her arms.

She swiveled in her chair to face him. "I'm not sure why you would think that, Mr. Lassiter. Had I wanted company, I would have extended my own invitation."

A snake's smile slid across his face. The chandelier above his head clinked softly as its crystals shook with the rattling of the train. "Sometimes a lady needs some convincing she could use some company."

He continued his approach, and Ella pushed herself out of the chair to better stand her ground. Her brain pounded, and she couldn't choose which thought to follow. Was it too soon to scream or should she try to reason with the man?

A knock at the door stopped Mr. Lassiter, and before Ella could say, "enter," Elias came in the room.

"I've got your bags, Miss Merriweather." He did not look at Mr. Lassiter, and his stony face told Ella that it was no accident he'd chosen that moment to bring her bags. "I'll just get them stowed, then I can make up your bed if you'd like."

"Yes, thank you, Elias."

Then he did look at Mr. Lassiter. "I've brought some nightcaps to your room, sir. I believe your companions are waiting for you."

Lassiter glared at him, then at Ella before leaving through the washbasin corridor.

Ella took a deep breath as Elias crossed the room and locked the door behind Lassiter. "He shouldn't bother you again, miss."

"Thank you, Elias." Her heart swelled with gratitude. His race and her sex left them at the mercy of the men in the next room, but he'd found a way to help her. With him by her side, she'd be okay for the rest of the trip.

"Miss Merriweather . . . *Ella.*" Mr. Clayborne's voice came from the outer corridor just before he walked through the open door. "Did Lassiter hurt you? Are you okay? I went to check on my valet, and when I came back, Lassiter was leaving your room."

He moved quickly toward her, glancing at Elias as he did. Elias returned his glance with a look of warning.

"I'm sorry. I was supposed to protect you, and I've done a poor job of it," Thomas said as he neared her, then reached out as though to touch her.

He stopped short of doing so, and Ella, to her dismay, felt the loss of it. She quickly brushed off the thought of his warm hand on her arm. While she was touched by his concern, he could have stopped Mr. Lassiter much sooner. Yet he'd chosen not to because, she could only assume, he didn't like being told by a woman to be careful in his business.

"I'm quite all right, Mr. Clayborne." She took a step back from him and felt Elias inch closer to her.

"I promise they won't bother you again." He said the words as much to her as to Elias. "I won't leave your side until we arrive in Cheyenne, and I will report their behavior to Mr. Howe."

She balked at his mention of Jasper Howe. "Do you honestly believe he will care? That he will side with someone he views as a 'servant girl' over the men who put money in his pocket?"

Thomas drew back from her. "Jasper Howe is a gentleman. And Clara is your friend. Neither will tolerate this sort of behavior." He straightened to his full height—a full head above her own—but his voice rang with uncertainty.

"Oh, Mr. Clayborne," Ella said gently, though not without some unintentional condescension. "You really have been taken in by them. I'm certain Mr. Howe believes I have evidence he swindled my aunt and wants only to make sure I don't release that information to the papers in New York." Ella kept her eyes locked on Thomas's even as color crept into his cheeks. "As for Clara, she has never seen me as anything more than someone to wait on her."

Thomas returned Ella's stare, his jaw working back and forth like he was chewing on the words he'd like to say.

"Would you like me to make up your bed, miss?" Elias interrupted with a pointed gaze at Mr. Clayborne.

"Yes, thank you, Elias." Ella moved away from the sofa and Mr. Clayborne in order to allow Elias room to lower the back of the sofa to make a double-width bed.

It was only then that Thomas looked away from her. "I believe you're mistaken about the Howes, but nonetheless, Mr. Perkins and Mr. Lassiter won't lay a hand on you or they will have me to answer to."

He walked out the door, and she shut it behind him. The window in the door allowed her to watch him walk down the corridor, but she couldn't see whether he'd gone back into his own room. She didn't hear a door close.

"All ready for you, miss."

Ella turned back to Elias and the bed made up with pillows and quilts. After the day she'd had, it looked more inviting than ever.

"I'll hang the curtains over the windows and be out of your way," Elias continued. "Door's locked to the washbasin, so Mr. Lassiter won't be able to return through there."

"I don't think the lock on the main door is working."

"I'll take a look." He hung the curtains over the door and the windows facing the corridor, then checked the lock. "I'll need some tools to fix it. Be right back."

He went out the door, but she heard his voice outside. "Can I help you, Mr. Clayborne?"

"I would be very appreciative if you could bring me a pillow and blanket," Thomas answered.

Ella walked swiftly to the door and pulled open the curtain. "You need not stay, Mr. Clayborne. I can take care of myself," she said firmly through the window.

"I'm aware of that, Miss Merriweather, but I'm a man who keeps his word, and I've given mine that I will see you safely to Cheyenne," he answered with a smile in his voice. "I'll be right here should you need me."

She pulled open the door and faced him. He'd removed his coat and wore only his shirtsleeves and unbuttoned vest, causing her to blush. "Surely you're not going to sleep on the floor all night when you have a perfectly good berth."

"I'll sleep better here knowing the so-called *gentlemen* in the next room are aware of my presence outside your door." He lowered himself to the floor and leaned against the wall.

She glanced at Elias who stood nearby. He offered her a gentle nod that reassured her.

"That lock's been meddled with," he murmured softly. "I don't know if it can be fixed. I'd feel more comfortable myself knowing Mr. Clayborne was out here in case . . ." His eyes drifted to the door of Mr. Lassiter's room.

"Good night, Miss Merriweather." Thomas's eyelashes feathered across his cheeks as he closed his eyes.

With no other options, Ella returned to her room. Mr. Clayborne was determined to protect her, and as much as she wished she didn't need his protection, her encounter with the gentlemen from Chicago had proven otherwise. Elias had also proven determined to protect her, but his job—and perhaps his life—would be endangered if Mr. Perkins and Mr. Lassiter attempted what they had alluded to in the dining room or that Mr. Lassiter had implied in her room. She felt sure Elias would do what he could to stop them, and he would pay the consequences for it.

In that sense, Mr. Clayborne was ensuring both her and Elias's safety. He could stop the men before they acted. Despite their earlier disagreement, Ella couldn't help but appreciate and respect Mr. Clayborne. She'd seen too many people care little for their words and promises for her to disregard a man who didn't.

But she did not appreciate being indebted to someone. She had to provide some service to him in return for his sacrifice of sleep and comfort, but there was only one thing she could offer.

Ella undressed quickly, discarding her restrictive corset with a sigh of relief and a deep breath—the first one she'd been able to take all day. Then she put on her best nightgown with the French-knotted roses followed by her heavy dressing gown to keep out the cold.

Once she was comfortable, she pulled out her lap desk. It had been Aunt Beatrice's and one of the few things Ella had wanted to keep of her possessions. Unfolding the writing slope, she took a sheet of paper from inside its drawer and readied her pens to write.

If Mr. Clayborne was so determined to invest with Mr. Howe in his cattle business, he would need to ask the man some serious questions about the odds of the venture's success. Ella remembered well the ugliness between Aunt Beatrice and Mr. Howe when she'd discovered he'd lost her savings and the money she'd borrowed against her home.

Ella had listened at the door as her aunt had lobbed allegation after allegation at Mr. Howe when he'd come to take Clara from school. Beatrice had accused him of misleading her into investing in cattle with inaccurate projections.

From her perspective, with her ear pressed to the door, Ella thought her aunt had made a very good argument. Beatrice's subsequent suicide had sealed Ella's certainty that the woman had been ill-used by Howe. She had gone on to read whatever article she came across about the cattle industry. It hadn't taken much research to conclude that investing in cattle was far from the sure thing men like Jasper Howe portrayed it as.

With her aunt's demise in mind, Ella wrote Mr. Clayborne a letter. First, she thanked him for his attentiveness to her safety, then she offered an apology for her brusqueness. Lastly, she offered him a list of questions to ask Mr. Howe.

How many cattle had Mr. Howe taken to market year after year?

The articles she'd read speculated that only one of every four cows made it off the ranch. She added a note that every cow that was not sold would cost him, rather than make him, money.

What percentage of Howe's cows successfully calved each year?

It was a delicate question for her to write but perhaps the most important one for Mr. Clayborne to ask. Many projections she'd seen in publications heralding the financial virtues of cattle breeding said herds would double within seven years with plenty of steers to sell along the way.

This, she explained gently to Mr. Clayborne in her letter, *is statistically impossible unless one could guarantee more female than male calves would be born—another statistical impossibility.*

The last question she urged him to ask was what percentage of his herd Mr. Howe had lost each year to weather and predators. She'd heard Clara complain enough about the weather and wildness of the Wyoming Territory to understand that it was nothing like England, though she'd never been to either place.

After signing her name to the letter, Ella peeked through the curtain at the door. Mr. Clayborne lay asleep on the floor with a pillow under his head and a thin blanket covering him. She opened her door and looked both ways to be sure the Chicago men were nowhere to be seen, then tiptoed into the corridor. She tucked the letter into the inside pocket of Mr. Clayborne's coat, which lay at his head.

Ella was about to return to her berth when Mr. Clayborne shivered and pulled his knees to his chest. She studied him for a moment: the whiskers that followed the honed outline of his jaw, the determined brow that creased even in sleep, the slenderness of the fingers tucked under his cheek.

With quiet steps, Ella walked past him and picked up his coat. She cradled it in her arms for a moment while listening to his soft breaths. Then she gently laid the coat over his shoulders and torso.

The sharp scent of tobacco and soap followed her back to her room where, despite her exhaustion, she lay for many hours before falling asleep.

CHAPTER FIVE

THOMAS BLINKED HIS EYES OPEN, letting them adjust to the dark. As the fog cleared from his mind, he remembered why he was asleep on the floor rather than a bed. He sat upright, rubbing the stiffness out of his neck as he tried to recall when he'd covered himself with his coat.

He stood slowly. Though he'd slept soundly for much of the night, his body preferred feather beds to hard floors. Gray morning light peeked through the window, and Thomas drew the shade to see the sun's first rays making their way over the prairie. The landscape was so different from the rolling green hills of Northern England. He'd never seen so much snow or such a vast area with only a few solitary trees. The emptiness of it blinded him with loneliness.

Turning from the window, Thomas faced the door to Ella's room. No light peeked through the curtains still covering her windows. He shouldn't have expected there would be—it was hardly dawn—but that didn't stop him from feeling disappointed. He slid back to the floor to wait for her to awaken.

Mr. Perkins and Mr. Lassiter hadn't caused any more trouble, but Thomas was glad he'd slept outside Ella's room anyway. His gesture, he hoped, would go toward repairing the damage he'd done to his reputation as a gentleman by letting his concern over his investment keep him from more firmly defending Ella's honor. He hadn't known either of the Chicagoans long enough to determine how dangerous they really were, but he would take no further chances with her safety. He would take no chances with any woman's safety.

As the sun continued its ascent across the plains of Nebraska, light filled the car, and Thomas stood again to gaze out the window. The landscape was still barren, but in the distance, he saw small, brown mounds. He squinted to get a better look, and as the train drew closer, he saw the shapes were actually large animals.

Elias entered the car, and Thomas pointed to the massive humps. "Are those bison?"

Elias leaned over Thomas's shoulder to look out the window. "Yes, sir. Probably why we've slowed. Have you got a rifle you'd like me to get from your room?"

Thomas turned to Elias in surprise. "A rifle?"

"To shoot at them."

"For what purpose? Surely the beasts can't be skinned and butchered quickly enough to avoid delaying our journey."

"We've got skinners aboard." Elias shrugged. "The bison are a nuisance to the railroad—tearing up the tracks and blocking the trains—so passengers are allowed to kill them. Workers get fed some of the meat—most of it gets left behind. In summertime, you can smell the carcasses a mile away. The robes get shipped back East."

As if on cue, a shot rang out, startling Thomas. Elias shook his head. "Can't drop nothing from this distance, but they'll keep moving closer. If they weren't such dumb beasts, they'd run every time they heard that noise. Ain't hardly any of them left, but they never run from the guns," he murmured as he walked toward the exit.

Thomas worked open the window latch, then lowered the pane and stuck out his head, the cold air biting his cheeks. The bison were close enough for him to distinguish their huge heads from their massive humped shoulders. As the train continued down the tracks, he had the urge to reach out and touch one of the beasts; they seemed that close.

The report of another rifle made him jump just before he saw one of the beasts fall. A loud whoop was followed by another shot, then a whole bevy of them. A bison bellowed and fell, then another and another. The animals at the front of the herd panicked, but with the train ahead and more bison pressing from behind, the only escape for the herd was to run next to the train, which was no escape at all.

Bison after bison went down, their blood turning the white snow red.

"What's happening?" Ella's voice asked from behind him, and he understood from the trembling in her voice that the scene he found so interesting she would find shocking.

He moved in front of her but was too late to protect her from the scene of slaughter. Her hands went to her mouth, and her eyes grew wide. But the tears he expected never came. Instead, her face grew red with anger, and she pushed past Thomas for a better look.

"Indian babies will be starving again this winter," she stated as the train came to a stop, allowing even more gunmen—and women—to hit their marks.

"What do you mean?" Almost as soon as he asked the question, her meaning became clear. He'd been part of many hunts: fox, pheasant, even deer on occasion, but the meat had always been eaten or used. The buffalo meat would be left behind to rot while the Indians who had hunted buffalo for centuries in order to feed their families would go hungry.

"Killing the buffalo is the army's way of forcing the Indians onto reservations. If the tribes don't have food to follow, they have to stay put and farm," Ella explained.

"Is farming so bad?" He hated the thought of anyone going hungry, but there did seem to be another solution.

"You tell me, Thomas. I believe you are the one who said there is an agricultural depression. Isn't that part of the reason you're here rather than England?" She tipped her head and waited for his answer.

Thomas's lip pulled into a smile. She had bested him again, which should have irritated him, but he'd always been more attracted to a challenge than a sure bet. "Miss Merriweather, I've never met anyone quite so quick-witted as you."

Ella's mouth twitched, and he thought for a moment she would smile. "I'll take that as a compliment and sincerely thank you for not taking offense to my quick wit."

"Quite the opposite. I—" He was interrupted by the yelling of Mr. Perkins and Mr. Lassiter. They came from their room with their guns at the ready and opened the window at the opposite end of the car.

Thomas glanced at Ella, noticing for the first time that she was in her dressing gown. He stepped in front of her to block their view. They were only interested in what was happening outside the train, but unless Thomas escorted her, they would see her undressed state before she could return to her room.

Taking her by the arm, Thomas continued to act as a barrier to their potentially leering eyes as he led her to the room and the davenport there, which was still unfolded into a bed. Just as he helped her sit, the train lurched forward as it began its journey again, causing Thomas to lose his balance and topple onto the bed with Miss Merriweather under him.

"I beg your pardon." He scrambled to right himself, a task only accomplished by rolling off her and onto the floor. Once on his feet again, he bolted to the opposite side of her room. Her cheeks glowed pink, and she clutched her dressing gown closed over her chest.

Heat rushed to his face, and he turned his back to her. "Please accept my apologies, Miss Merriweather. I did not intend for that to happen."

"It's quite all right." Her voice shook, and he was mortified by the thought that she might think he'd tried to take advantage of her. "I believe I'll stay in my room until the shooting stops."

Thomas nodded and walked back into the corridor. He pulled her door closed without looking back at her.

The train picked up speed, and he couldn't stop himself from looking out the window. The sight that greeted him was one of the worst he'd ever seen. Bison carcasses lay bleeding at the side of the tracks while those who'd escaped a similar fate stampeded past. There was nothing left of the unending whiteness he'd been greeted with that morning. Everything was dirt and the acrid smell of death.

Thomas shut his window and sunk to the floor again. He stayed there for the next hour, listening for any sound coming from Ella's room. Occasionally he heard some movement, and he was tempted to try apologizing again, but he couldn't find the right words to say.

So he listened to the wheels scrape over the tracks instead until the train finally slowed and pulled into the station at Grand Island.

Mr. Perkins and Mr. Lassiter walked by him without a word and exited onto the platform. Elias came into the car and stopped by Thomas.

"They've got pretty good food at the restaurant here, sir," Elias informed him in a quiet voice and gave a quick glance at Ella's room. There had been no sound behind it since they'd stopped.

"I'll stay here until she wakes." Thomas nodded to the door. "Could you get something and bring it back for us?"

"Yes, sir."

"I'll have eggs and sausage with a cup of tea . . ." He paused. "I can't think what to order for Miss Merriweather."

"They have hotcakes and fried potatoes. Miss Merriweather has had that every other morning," Elias offered.

"Wonderful. That will do perfectly." He dug into his overcoat for his billfold, noticing for the first time an envelope sticking out of the pocket. He didn't remember it being there before, but the elegant lettering on the outside of it signified the handwriting of a lady. But it did not match Miss Howe's. Had Miss Merriweather written the letter?

He handed Elias some money, then took the page from the envelope. He skimmed to the bottom where Ella's signature confirmed his suspicions. His interest piqued, he went back to the beginning.

Dear Mr. Clayborne,

You are a true gentleman. I consider myself an independent woman and find it very hard to be in a position of dependence, but I cannot let this opportunity pass without thanking you for the example of politeness, courtesy, and protection you have set for the less gentlemanly among us.

Thomas smiled. His mother would be proud to hear him described as such, but he had only been following the example his father had set for him.

He continued reading the letter, his chest puffing out with each of Ella's compliments, though he could not help feeling some responsibility for the disagreement they'd had. As he kept reading, however, his confidence plummeted.

How could a woman know more of the cattle business than he did? And where did she get the gall to offer him advice in how to invest his money in cattle? They had only known each other a few days. It was quite impertinent of her.

But as he read the questions she proposed he ask and the sound reasoning she gave behind them, he couldn't deny that she *did* know more than he.

That was a thought he chose not to entertain. He was a man, after all. How could a woman know more than a man in matters of business?

He'd seen his own father talk to his mother about improvements needed to their property, the care of his tenants, what crops would be rotated, and more. But he spoke to her about business as a matter of conversation, not to seek advice. Mother took care of the children and household while Father managed his properties and took his place in Parliament.

But as he thought about those months his father spent in London when Parliament was in session, a memory came to him of his mother giving directions to his father's manager. Not just once but on many occasions. With the memory came a realization.

Father had trusted Mother to run the estate when he wasn't there. Furthermore, the same care and concern Ella had shown for the Indians his own mother had shown for the tenants on their estate who had been most affected by the agricultural depression.

Thomas tucked the letter back in his coat pocket and stood just as Elias walked through the door. He carried a large tray with two covered plates and a teapot and stopped near Ella's door.

"Will you be joining Miss Merriweather in her room, sir?" he asked.

Thomas didn't know how to answer other than to knock on Ella's door. "Ella?"

He was anxious to speak to her over breakfast about her suggestions, so when she didn't reply, he said her name again. "Miss Merriweather? I've ordered you breakfast, and it's arrived."

She opened the door, now fully dressed. Their eyes met, and she quickly looked away, but not before an awkward tension settled between them.

"I've read your letter and would very much enjoy discussing the points you've raised," he rushed to say as Elias carried the tray into her room. "Could I possibly join you for breakfast?"

She answered with stunned silence and slow blinking.

"Of course, if you'd rather be alone . . ." Thomas turned to leave, but Ella's words stopped him.

"You're not angry?"

"No." He shook his head. "Should I be?"

"I may have been more blunt than I'd intended." She opened her door wider, inviting him in. Elias quietly set Thomas's breakfast on the table next to Ella's before leaving.

"I'm grateful for your bluntness." As Thomas took the seat she offered him, he understood why he wanted to spend more time with Ella Merriweather; being in her presence made him crave something he only now realized he'd been missing—the company of an intelligent, kind woman—someone like his own mother. His conversations with Ella had been far more invigorating than the flirtatious, empty-headed ones he'd had with Clara Howe.

"Well you are certainly the first person to appreciate my somewhat sharp tongue," Ella said with a smile before taking a delicate bite of her hotcakes.

They spent the next few hours discussing the possible pitfalls of his investment. Thomas would have liked to discuss less worrisome things, such as Ella herself; unfortunately, every time he ventured too close to the personal, Ella swung the conversation back to him. Once they had thoroughly covered every question he should ask Howe, she stood.

"Thank you, Thomas, for a lovely breakfast," she said pleasantly, but her smile was forced.

He took her cue and regretfully returned to the corridor where Elias had moved one of the swivel chairs from Thomas's room. Thomas remained outside her door, hoping to speak to Ella again, but she did not emerge until they reached Cheyenne. When she did step out of her room, she somehow looked more beautiful than when they had begun their journey.

"Goodbye, Mr. Clayborne," she said, offering him her hand. "I wish you the best of luck in your venture."

He'd so been looking forward to seeing her again that her formalness took away his words until the only thing he could think to say was exactly what he felt. "I hope this isn't the last we will meet, Ella."

"I'm afraid so, Mr. Clayborne." She walked quickly past him, descended onto the platform, then disappeared. Had he known she could vanish so quickly, he would have gone after her immediately.

CHAPTER SIX

HOW FOOLISH I'VE BEEN, ELLA thought as she stepped off the train, her shame manifesting in the heat of her cheeks. Ella exited the depot quickly in order to face Thomas as little as possible. He had been a friend when she'd most needed one, but her feelings toward him were in danger of moving beyond friendship. And how could she possibly compete with Clara Howe?

Even if there were no Clara Howe, Ella knew she was not the type of woman someone of noble birth could—or would—court. As she'd conversed with Thomas, she'd had to keep reminding herself of that fact in order to not drift too far into his questions about her or the questions she had about him. Perhaps things would have been different if her father had lived to pursue his business ventures or if Aunt Beatrice had not squandered the inheritance he'd intended for his daughter.

The thought of her parents—their love and kindness and the life she could have had—only dampened her spirits further. If not for their deaths, Ella would have still been in New York surrounded by the buildings and streets she knew so well and not in the wild territories beyond America's civilized borders.

She had thought she was ready to leave New York City and start a new life, but after breakfasting with Thomas, each mile that brought her closer to the Wyoming Territory had changed her mind. By the time they'd reached Cheyenne, she could hardly hold back her tears and couldn't bear a long goodbye with the only person close to a friend she had in this new world.

As Ella walked out of the depot, she spotted the blue carriage Clara had promised would be waiting for her. It was not just blue but bright blue, standing out against the squat buildings and muddy streets like a single egg in a robin's nest. She climbed into the carriage with both relief and disappointment. Her new life was about to begin, but she would be taking her journey alone while Thomas would have companions, even if those companions were the Howes.

Once Elias had the luggage loaded and Ella had thanked him with the last few coins in her purse, she leaned into the seat and closed her eyes. She waited for the carriage to lurch forward, but instead, the door opened, and a familiar voice greeted her.

"Well, Miss Merriweather, it seems we are to be thrown together again."

Ella opened her eyes to see a smiling Thomas climb in with his valet close behind.

"Why—wh-what are you doing here?" Ella could not hold back her own smile.

"Miss Howe told me there would be a carriage waiting to take me to Le Manse." Unless she was mistaken, Thomas was pleased to see her. And though she didn't trust herself to not be taken in by his charms, she could not deny her happiness at being with him again.

Her pleasure, however, quickly became humiliation as the sudden motion of the carriage threw her into Thomas's lap. She quickly scrambled back into her seat, trying not to think of where her hands had landed on his legs.

The corner of Thomas's lip twitched with amusement. "I didn't mean we should literally be thrown together, but I'm grateful to you for lessening my own embarrassment at having toppled onto you yesterday."

Ella laughed, then glanced at Thomas's valet, who looked straight ahead as though he'd neither seen nor heard anything.

"Imagine the shock of the Howes if we keep toppling into each other while we're their guests." His eyes danced as though he were thoroughly pleased with the prospect, though she wasn't sure which pleased him more: the idea of shocking or of toppling.

Her smile fell. "I wasn't invited to the Howes'."

"Oh." Thomas's mouth curved into a frown. "Miss Howe spoke so highly of you. I'd assumed you would also be her guest."

Ella shook her head and considered how to respond. She hadn't held back the truth from him, so that seemed the best approach once more. "I am nothing more to Clara Howe than a poor orphan she can use as an example of her charity. I have no family or name to speak of and, therefore, can offer her nothing in return." She took off her gloves and laid them in her lap, then quickly added, "However, I am grateful for her help in procuring employment for me. She has been very kind in that." Kindness, after all, need not be genuine to be appreciated.

Thomas's brow wrinkled as though he were trying to sort out a complex mathematical problem. "I suppose she has." He cleared his throat and pulled back his shoulders. When he spoke again, his tone had changed from one of concern to that of detached politeness. "Where are you going?"

"To Miss Nelson's. I'll be living at her school." Ella took on the same tone of politeness that he used. Perhaps her words had reminded him that she was not his equal, at least not in his mind or Miss Howe's.

"Do you mean it's a boarding school?"

She shook her head. "I believe I'll be sharing a room with another maid in the servants' quarters." Ella had always had her own room at Aunt Beatrice's, a small one but private nonetheless. It would be strange to share.

"Surely they're providing you with comfortable accommodations. Your aunt's seminary seemed quite . . ." he searched for a word but landed on the same one, "comfortable."

"Looks can be very deceiving." She offered him a tight smile. "Comfortable surroundings are not what makes one *comfortable*. I don't intend to stay a maid in Cheyenne. As soon as I find a teaching position, I'll leave. Wherever in this territory it might be, I'll be providing the isolated children of ranchers and homesteaders with an education they wouldn't otherwise have. That's all the comfort I need."

Mr. Clayborne didn't offer a reply, and Ella directed her attention out the window. The carriage rattled down the muddy Main Street interspersed with patches of dirty snow and piles of manure. There were some fine brick buildings lining the street, but the whole city looked as though it were a house servant who had suddenly found herself the hostess and hastily put on her mistress's finest clothes.

Cheyenne was a new city with new money and would never be considered as important as places like New York or Boston. Ella felt an immediate kinship with Cheyenne and its hastily-constructed buildings dressed up in finery.

Mr. Clayborne said little else until they reached the large red-brick house at the edge of town. It was nicer than Ella had expected, and Miss Nelson emerged from the front door upon their approach.

"There's not much to you." The sharp-featured woman eyed Ella as she stepped from the carriage, then with some resignation, ordered, "You can take your things around back."

Thomas and his valet climbed out of the carriage behind Ella, and Thomas told the driver he would take care of the luggage. The driver merely grunted and threw Ella's things to the ground.

Thomas and his man hefted her trunk between them while she picked up her carpet bag. Miss Nelson disappeared into the house. Ella assumed a back door served as the servants' entrance, but as she rounded the corner of the house, a ramshackle lean-to came into view. As she neared it, Miss Nelson popped out of the back door of the brick house.

"You're in there. Take the empty bed," she said before disappearing again.

Ella felt the weight of her carpet bag for the first time as she neared the building. She had to put all of her weight against the weather-warped door to force it open. Very little light came through the shack's one window, and it took a moment for Ella's eyes to adjust to the dimness.

"This is where you'll be living?" Thomas asked behind her.

"Apparently so." Ella unpinned her hat and laid it on the bare straw tick mattress she assumed would be hers. The room had only enough space for two beds and a small Franklin stove between them, but there were plenty of hooks for things.

A cold draft came from the window, which lay directly above her bed. She would have to get something to stuff in the chinks surrounding the window, but otherwise, the room was quite cozy. Her roommate had even hung a picture of a cathedral.

"Why, that's St. Paul's," Thomas said as he examined it. "Whomever you're boarding with has good taste." His face glowed, and she longed for home, perhaps because his eyes were the same shade of blue as the sky in the New York countryside.

She had no coffee or tea to offer him, and with her luggage unloaded, there was no reason for Thomas to stay any longer. Yet as the silence grew between them, Ella couldn't bring herself to wish him well. Saying goodbye felt like saying goodbye to the last relic of her old life, though she'd only known him a few short days.

"Thank you again for your kind service, Mr.—Thomas." She held her hand to him, and the warmth of his gloved hand surprised her.

"Thank you, Ella, for your advice . . ." he hesitated a moment, as though unsure of his words, "and your company. I shall take your suggestions under consideration."

"I hope so," she said earnestly. She'd never met a man before who willingly heeded the advice of a woman, let alone thanked her for it, but then, she knew very few men at all.

"Well, then, I'll take my leave." Thomas went the few steps to the door but turned as he opened it. "I do hope we'll see each other again."

Ella smiled. She hoped so too, but it seemed such an impossibility that she couldn't return the sentiment. He closed the door behind him but not before the room filled with cold air. Ella rubbed her hands together and went to the stove to start a fire.

With a small fire burning, Ella made up her bed, then lay upon it. She had inherited a feather mattress from her parents but had sold it with everything else to pay off Aunt Beatrice's debts. The straw tick would take some getting used to. And though the little stove did its best to warm the room, an inescapable coldness hung in the air.

CHAPTER SEVEN

THE HOWES' ESTATE ALSO LAY on the outskirts of Cheyenne, only a short drive from the school where Thomas had left Ella. Though Jasper Howe made his money from cattle, he spent very little time on the remote ranch where he kept his herds. As the carriage came to a stop in the circular driveway, Thomas could not help but feel the house's immensity in contrast to the small room where he had left Ella. Surely the Howes had enough rooms to accommodate someone as small as Ella Merriweather. It had pained him to leave her behind in such a place.

Miss Howe did not greet him in the drawing room as he'd assumed she would. Rather, he was led to his room and told to dress for dinner. His only glimpse of Clara had been in a painting of her family that hung at the top of the grand staircase. Either the artist had not done her beauty justice or Thomas had remembered her as being more beautiful than she actually was.

Smith helped him dress, and though Thomas's thoughts should have been on Clara, they kept drifting back to Ella.

"Miss Merriweather's room was rather dark, wasn't it?" Thomas asked Smith while lifting his chin so the valet could tie his cravat.

"Yes, sir." Smith pulled the knot tight, then loosened it. He understood how much Thomas hated feeling restricted. Then he held up Thomas's dinner jacket, and Thomas slipped it on.

"Do you think she'll be all right there?"

"She seems a very determined young lady. I suppose she will find success wherever she lands in life." Smith brushed lint from Thomas's jacket, then stood back to examine his work.

"I like that about her." Thomas smiled, remembering the letter Ella had given him.

"It's a very good quality for a young woman to have in this far-flung place." Smith took his brush to Thomas once more. "A necessity even."

"Yes," Thomas mumbled and dipped his chin into his chest as Smith brushed his shoulders. "Miss Howe has that same quality . . . doesn't she?"

If there was one thing Thomas could count on from Smith—besides his impeccable ability at dressing him—it was his honesty. Smith did not say much, but the truth usually takes very few words.

"I'd say she is determined but in a different way from Miss Merriweather." Smith, satisfied with his work, turned his back to Thomas to put away his grooming tools.

"How so?" Thomas's voice took on a defensive edge he hadn't intended.

Smith took his time answering the question, being careful with his words. "I'd wager Miss Merriweather's determination will benefit more than just herself." A bell chimed outside the door as Smith's eyes met his employer's. "It's time for dinner, sir."

Thomas stared past Smith into the full-length, gilded mirror hanging on the wall, mulling over what his valet had said. He wanted to defend Miss Howe, but the only thing he could think to say made little sense. "It was her father who made sure she never had to tie her own shoes."

Smith's face went blank, and Thomas took a deep breath. He'd asked his valet to speak the truth, and he had. Thomas had no right to be angry at him.

Laughter drifted up the stairs as Thomas made his way down them. Despite his hunger and the smell of meat and onions filling the air, he walked slowly to the drawing room. Smith's words mingled with Ella's advice in his mind, and he felt more trepidation than eagerness at joining the Howes and their guests.

It would be impolite to bring up business at a social gathering, and so he would have to wait to ask the questions Miss Merriweather had suggested. However, he was anxious to get answers to those questions and would be hard-pressed to keep his mind and words off business.

Thomas entered the ornately decorated room filled with guests in as fine of silks as he'd seen in London. Indeed, he felt as though he'd been transported out of the American wilderness and back to England to any of the estates of his titled friends. He should have felt at home.

Instead, his mind drifted to Miss Merriweather in her small room, and he wished that he could be in close quarters with her again.

Jasper Howe was the first to greet him, giving him a hearty handshake that momentarily renewed Thomas's confidence in their venture. He hoped to speak with Howe long enough to casually bring up his questions, but too soon, they were interrupted.

"There you are, Mr. Clayborne." Miss Howe's voice drew his attention to the opposite side of the room, and he put on a smile as she walked toward him with her hands outstretched. Jasper clapped him on the back and left Thomas to his daughter, who clutched Thomas's hands in hers and kissed the air on either side of his cheeks.

"Come, let me introduce you." She looped her arm through his, but the thrill he expected did not materialize. Miss Howe had doused herself in a scent that made his eyes itch.

She led him first to a group of young women. "This is Thomas Clayborne, Baron of Northbrook."

The girls smiled and curtsied, but before Thomas could correct Clara, he was being whisked to another group.

"Miss Howe," he hurriedly whispered as they approached three men smoking cigars. "There's been a misunderstanding. I am not the Baron of Northbrook."

Clara stopped and took her arm from his. "Pardon?" Her smile remained, but she did nothing to keep her voice discreet.

"That title belongs to my eldest brother." He glanced side to side. They had drawn some attention, and Thomas feared for a moment that Clara might publicly accuse him of being a liar. "I should have corrected you sooner. I apologize." They were far from the roaring fire, but he felt very warm.

"Then how shall I introduce you?" The coldness in her voice increased the warmth under his collar.

"Thomas Clayborne is sufficient." In fact, his name was more than sufficient. It was she, not he, who obviously thought his name needed a title in order to be worthy of her notice.

"I'd planned a ball in the Baron of Northbrook's honor. I suppose I will have to change the invitations." She glanced behind him at her reflection in a gilded mirror much like the one in his room—it seemed mirrors were the decoration of choice for the Howes.

"Again, I apologize for whatever confusion I may have caused." Thomas wondered if Clara was a different person when not surrounded by her own reflection—if she could see something besides herself.

She tucked a loose curl into place without reply. He would have left her side and her silence if Mr. Perkins and Mr. Lassiter had not approached.

"Mr. Clayborne." Mr. Perkins held out his hand. "Nice to see you again." Thomas doubted his sincerity but shook his hand and that of Mr. Lassiter.

"Where is your traveling companion?" Mr. Lassiter asked with a nasty grin. "The redhaired one."

Thomas knew who he meant. "I don't believe she was invited." His eyes drifted to Miss Howe's, and the other men followed his gaze.

"Well, I do hope you'll invite her to the ball you're planning, Miss Howe," Mr. Lassiter said.

A look of surprise passed over Clara's face, which she quickly hid with a tight-lipped smile. "Certainly. We have a shortage of women in the territory, so rules of decorum aren't as strictly followed as they are in New York or European society. Perhaps the Earl of Lambeth will not mind having someone of Ella's station in attendance. I'll defer to his wishes, however, as he is nobility." At this, she gave Thomas a pointed look. Then, with a toss of her head, she added, "I'm sure I would love to see dear Ella again."

"As would I." Mr. Lassiter bit the tip off a cigar and grinned.

Miss Howe smiled and looked over the man's shoulder. "Speaking of the earl, I should return to his side before it's time to go in for supper. We'll be leading the procession." She curtsied a goodbye but then turned to Thomas. "Mr. Clayborne, would you please escort Miss Jones at the end of the line?" She pointed her fan toward a young girl who looked no more than fourteen.

Without another look at her less-noble guests, Miss Howe crossed the room to the overstuffed gentleman whose eyes were fixed below the bare shoulders of the young woman with whom he was conversing.

Thomas knew he'd been slighted but could hardly work up the energy to care. He gave a parting glare to Mr. Perkins and Mr. Lassiter, then found a corner for himself. He sunk into the upholstered chair and rubbed his temples. What had he gotten himself into? He'd come to America to escape England's class system, and he'd walked right back into it: the jockeying for a favored position, stepping in line behind someone because that man had more money or a better name, Thomas coming in last before the race even started.

The bell rang for dinner, and he took his place at the end of the line with a giggling Miss Jones, who clearly had little experience in society. Yet he would be stuck at the end of the table seated across from her and next to Mr. Perkins, as far away from the Howes as possible. He wondered if that had always been Clara's plan or if she'd formed it after learning he was not a baron.

Either way, it didn't matter. He'd come to America to be his own man—to be judged on his own abilities, not on a title he had inherited. His father had taught him that the Barony of Northbrook was an important part of the Clayborne heritage, but ultimately, it was just a title. It would open doors for Thomas's brother that would be closed to Thomas, but the Clayborne name itself was the greater inheritance as it had long been associated with honesty and integrity. Those were attributes that could only be learned and developed, never bought.

Though Thomas had been careless with his money, he had never been dishonest in his dealings with other men. The Clayborne name would be known for its virtues on this side of the Atlantic as it was on the other side. He would make sure of that.

Even if it meant ending his association with the Howes.

CHAPTER EIGHT

WITHIN TWO WEEKS OF HER arrival, Ella had settled into her new life. While she wasn't exactly happy with the conditions she lived and worked in, she wasn't unhappy either. Though the work was hard and her room cold, her roommate, Sally, was warm and welcoming. They became fast friends.

"Miss Nelson looks like she's chiseled outta the Rockies, but she's soft inside," she'd said to Ella on their first night sharing a room. "Mr. Howe don't give her enough money to run the school. Keeps all her pay back for the 'investment' he talked her into."

Sally's dark hands were cracked and calloused from years of scrubbing laundry, but she thanked God every day that she now got paid for the washing instead of being whipped if it wasn't done fast enough. She wanted more for her grandchildren though, and Miss Nelson provided her with books for them.

"So Miss Nelson doesn't own the school?" Ella's interest had been piqued by Sally's talk of an investment.

"She owns the house, but she invested all her inheritance with Mr. Howe. Only way she could keep ahold of the house was to open a school. Mr. Howe claims the expenses eat up all profits, and that he'll put more money into the school when his cattle pay out. Keeps promising her the money is coming. It never does." Sally's breathing had grown heavy, and she was asleep almost as soon as she'd finished talking.

Ella, however, pondered Miss Nelson's predicament through much of the night. It was too similar to Aunt Beatrice's story to forget. A few days later, she brought Miss Nelson a cup of coffee when she saw her worrying over a ledger.

"Thank you, Ella." She didn't look up, but Ella caught her first glimpse of the softness Sally had told her about.

"I can help you with those, Miss Nelson," Ella offered tentatively. "I used to keep my aunt's books when I taught at her boarding school."

Miss Nelson set down her pencil and glanced toward the door, then waved Ella to shut it. Only then did she speak. "Mr. Howe warned me not to let you do anything but housework," she whispered. "But could you? I wanted to hire you as a bookkeeper or teacher with your credentials, but Mr. Howe said we could only afford a maid's salary."

Ella suspected Jasper Howe didn't want her looking at Miss Nelson's books for reasons beyond what it would cost him. This suspicion was confirmed when she found inconsistencies in the amount of tuition Howe was likely collecting and the amount he was reporting. At that moment, she decided if she ever had the opportunity to confront Jasper Howe for preying on vulnerable women, she would not hesitate to take it.

Aside from Miss Nelson's mistreatment at the hands of the Howes, Ella's thoughts were often occupied by Thomas Clayborne. Her housework was monotonous, leaving her plenty of time to recall every interaction she'd had with him. Though it would have been easier on her heart to forget Thomas, memories of him were bright spots in her days.

Her mind had drifted to him again a few days before Christmas as she hung a holly wreath on the front door. As she was about to hammer the nail into the door, someone spoke behind her.

"Is that you, Miss Merriweather?"

She startled at the sound of Thomas's voice, toppling from her stool into the snow piled next to the door. Even when she looked up to see his face, she was still unsure if her mind was playing tricks on her.

"Are you okay, Ella? I apologize for surprising you." He was by her side in seconds, helping her back to her feet. At his touch, she knew he was real.

"That's all right," she said after catching her breath. He'd exchanged his suit for canvas trousers and a duster, though he still wore a vest and tie. He looked—almost—the rancher he would soon be. She found it more appealing than she cared to admit. "I hadn't expected to see you again."

Ella glanced down at her own heavy coat and mittens. Underneath she now wore no bustle, nor a corset, only an old calico dress one of the students had left behind. Miss Nelson had given it to Ella after seeing her "too fine for cleaning" day dresses.

"I came to deliver this." He handed her a folded and sealed invitation. "From Miss Howe."

She took it, expecting him to leave, having accomplished his task. When he didn't, she remembered her manners.

"Would you like to come in? I don't think Miss Nelson would mind my serving you tea." She opened the door, and he followed her through. "She's been quite good to me, though I don't enjoy the work." Nerves made her blurt out sentence after sentence.

"The work is beneath you," Thomas said curtly.

"It's honest work, Mr. Clayborne." She glanced at Sally, who'd come in. "The people who have treated me the best have all worked as domestics. I'd rather be teaching, but I don't mind this work."

A slow smile spread across Thomas's face. "Miss Merriweather, once again you've taught me something I should have already known." His hand went to his puff tie, a much simpler accessory than the cravats she'd seen him wear. "My valet is irreplaceable. Domestic service *is* honorable work."

"Not often will a man admit to being wrong," Sally said to Ella before looking Thomas up and down. "Would you like me to bring in some coffee?"

"Would you? Thank you, Sally." Ella watched Sally leave in order to avoid meeting Thomas's eyes, afraid her face would give away how pleased she was to see him.

"Have you been able to find a teaching position?" he asked gently, pulling her attention back to him.

"I have a few prospects. I hope to have something by the time school is back in session in January." She clutched the invitation, not sure she should open it in front of him.

"Somewhere close, I hope."

Ella shook her head. "Laramie is the closest, but other opportunities are as far away as Rawlins and Evanston. There are a few other smaller communities, but all are at least fifty miles away."

"Oh. I'm sorry to hear that." He took off his hat and duster and sat in the parlor seat she offered him. His navy vest accentuated his blue eyes, making them even more brilliant.

She sat on the sofa across from him and remembered Clara's invitation. "Shall I open it now?"

He nodded.

After breaking the seal, she unfolded it and scanned the words. "Clara's holding a ball?"

"Apparently so." He paused. "Will you attend?"

"I have nothing wear." Ella stared at the invitation. She had no desire to go, other than to see Thomas. "She's only inviting me to be polite or at the behest of someone." She looked pointedly at him.

"Mr. Lassiter asked her, but my reasons for wanting you there are more honorable than his."

Ella shuddered. "I'd rather not see that man again. I'm afraid my answer will have to be no."

"That's disappointing." Thomas spun his hat—a Western version, not his usual derby—before looking at her. "I'm surprised you would let someone like Mr. Lassiter keep you from what could be an entertaining diversion from your work." He looked down again, giving her a view of the tips of his ears as they grew pink. "I would take it as a great honor if you did attend."

Ella felt her own ears and cheeks filling with color. "I do hate to disappoint you, but I spent many years being pitied by Miss Howe. I won't have her pity me for something as silly as not being dressed appropriately."

"That's a problem easily solved," he blurted.

Ella lifted her eyebrows. Every time she thought Thomas might be different from the men of privilege she knew, he proved her wrong. "Perhaps for Miss Howe, but my salary doesn't allow for silk ball gowns."

"I understand," he said quickly. "But you've solved some problems of mine, and I'd like to return the gesture. If you'll accept her invitation, I'll take care of the dress." He sat back against the chair, and his mustache lifted with his smile.

"What problems did I solve?" Her eyes narrowed. She was not so naïve that she hadn't heard of Prince Bertie's numerous love affairs or those of other British nobility. Was Mr. Clayborne trying to seduce her with dresses and compliments?

"*Solve* is the wrong word. You made me aware of some serious problems in Mr. Howe's proposal." At this, he withdrew some papers from inside his coat. "I took your advice and asked him your very pointed questions."

He spread the papers on the sofa, then sat beside them. "I'm hoping I can impose on you again for your advice. The numbers aren't adding up for me."

She looked from the papers covered with tables and figures to Thomas, whose face had turned redder than his ears had been.

"Could you look at these and tell me if I've miscalculated the expected return on my investment? It seems to be far below what Mr. Howe promised . . ." He sucked in his breath. "I don't know who else to trust to advise me."

Ella met Thomas's gaze wordlessly. Did he really trust her to advise him? She did have a mind for numbers, that was without question, but the only bookkeeping she'd done was for her aunt. Perhaps that was more than he had ever been called upon to do.

"Of course. But you're under no obligation to me. You did me a great service accompanying me on the train." She didn't want to speak of the gentlemen from Chicago or the danger she might have been in had Thomas not been there. In fact, without his persuasion, she might not have gotten on the train in the first place, and though she missed New York, she shuddered to think where she would have found work if she'd stayed.

"And you would be doing me a great service by attending the ball." He smiled again, but it didn't reach his eyes. "The truth is Miss Howe had planned the ball in my honor until she found out her mistake in believing I am the Baron of Northbrooke rather than my eldest brother. She has been, shall we say, decidedly less enthused about my presence since."

"Oh, dear." Ella didn't want to laugh, but a giggle slipped out. It was so like Clara Howe to set her sights on a man simply because she thought he might fulfill her dreams of being invited to Queen Victoria's court. "I'm sorry to say that I'm not surprised."

"Neither should I be." Now his smile did reach his eyes. "Perhaps the harsh reality of the environment I find myself in now has helped me see the pretense in the Howes. A falseness you detected long ago."

Her pulse quickened, and she could not keep his gaze. Had he seen what she'd seen in this territory? That its rawness didn't allow it to pretend it was something it was not? Did he find it as freeing as she did?

Ella longed to ask Thomas all those questions, but her courage failed her. She offered him sympathy instead.

"I was once taken in by Clara Howe's charms too, but it only cost me my pride. I'm sorry it may cost you more than that." She let her eyes drift to the figures on the pages. Even a cursory glance told her they weren't good.

"Miss Merriweather—Ella, you and I are outsiders here. Dancing will make what is plainly a difficult situation for both of us a bit more fun. At least for an evening." There was a pleading in his blue eyes that she couldn't resist. She nodded her answer before her brain could talk her out of it.

Thomas stood with a smile across his face. "Wonderful! I'll find a dressmaker and send her to you."

Ella shook her head. "There's really no need, Thomas. I can wear something that I already have. It will be far plainer than the other ladies' gowns, but I will feel more comfortable not being in your debt or dressing in a way that doesn't suit me."

Thomas's shoulders dropped.

She rose and placed a hand on his arm. "Truly, I appreciate your offer and your generosity, but I would be more uncomfortable putting on airs than going as the school marm I hope to be."

He laughed.

"I'll look at your figures in exchange for a dance," she added, her fingers still resting on his elbow.

He picked up her hand and held it between both of his. "I look forward to seeing you a week from Saturday."

Heat rushed through her body as he bent over her ungloved hand and brushed his lips across her knuckles.

"As do I," she murmured.

She had not expected the thrill that ran through her when he kissed her hand.

CHAPTER NINE

THOMAS INSPECTED HIS REFLECTION IN the mirror. As usual, Smith had done an impeccable job dressing him, but Thomas could barely form a thank-you around the nervous pounding in his chest. He'd spent the past eight days vacillating between excitement at the prospect of seeing Ella at the ball and fear that she would change her mind. He had been too forward in kissing her hand but had not been able to resist when he saw her ivory fingers against the black of his coat. She was too genuine, too real.

And he needed something—someone—genuine at the moment. The more time he spent with the Howes in their house of mirrors, the more he was convinced they were living a charade. His successes in gambling had always come from being able to read other people. He'd also spent too many years living beyond his means not to recognize the same habits in the Howes.

Even if his own observations hadn't been enough to convince him, the exchange he overheard between Jasper and a banker would have been. The banker had hand-delivered a debt collection notice to the house in order to "keep the matter private." The following day, Smith had reported that the servants had gone unpaid for weeks and were on the verge of leaving until Howe had promised them they would be paid their wages plus a bonus by week's end.

The next day, Jasper had pressed Thomas to sign over the investment money Thomas had collected from his peers in England. Every day since, Thomas had found a new excuse to put off giving Howe any more money. He couldn't get his own money back, but he could keep his friends from losing theirs.

Of course, now he was faced with the problem of what to do with seventy Hereford bulls, which were currently pasturing on Howe's land, eating the hay Howe was providing them. It would take some doing to extricate himself from Howe's clutches, but Thomas had already taken steps to do so. The challenge lay in doing it without Howe finding out.

"Ready, sir?" Smith asked, pulling Thomas back to the present.

He nodded and proceeded to the door, pausing for a deep breath before opening it. The music traveled from the ballroom up the stairs, accompanied by the smell of pine from the boughs wrapped around the banister. Despite the festivities, sadness washed over him. His family had always decorated the Christmas tree together, but the Howes left the task to their servants. Thomas had missed his family terribly over the holidays.

As he walked down the stairs, he caught sight of Ella in the foyer, and home didn't feel so far away. Her navy dress was much plainer than those of the other ladies, yet she looked more beautiful than any other woman there. Perhaps more beautiful than any other woman he'd ever seen.

Her eyes drifted upward to where they met his. He breathed again when she smiled.

He hurried down the stairs to meet her, but Miss Howe reached her first.

"Ella, what a surprise! I didn't think you'd come!" Clara kissed Ella on each cheek, then stepped back and unabashedly examined her. "How are you? Is it very hard working as a maid?" Her voice rose with the question, and the guests surrounding them turned to make their own examination of Ella.

Thomas quickened his step, hoping to intervene between the two women. Ella, however, spoke before he could whisk her away to safety.

"No more difficult than teaching girls such as yourself basic math facts." She pasted on a smile, and Thomas held back a laugh. Clara, meanwhile, pinched her brows together, looking as if she were trying to work out whether she'd been insulted.

"I would so like to thank your father for my job," Ella continued with the same false smile on her face. "Could you take me to him?"

"Certainly," Clara said with obvious uncertainty.

She led Ella into the ballroom overflowing with guests while Thomas followed closely behind. Clara seemed intent on losing Ella as she weaved through people, but Ella managed to keep up.

"Miss Merriweather." Thomas's loud whisper was drowned out by the cacophony of noise. "Miss Merriweather," he tried again before resorting to almost yelling, "Ella!"

She stopped long enough for him to catch up but kept her eye on Clara.

"What are you doing?" he asked as she started after Clara again.

"Getting even."

Thomas nearly tripped. He wanted to ask her what she meant, but she'd pulled ahead of him again. She pushed a man out of the way who'd come between her and her target, then suddenly, Jasper Howe was ahead of them, encircled by a group of men.

Clara tapped her father on the shoulder, and he turned around. "Father, you remember Ella Merriweather . . . from my school."

Jasper Howe dipped his chin and looked down his large nose until his eyes rested on Ella. She held her chin high and met his bored gaze. Thomas had forgotten how tiny she was. She could have been mistaken for a child next to Jasper Howe's immense build. Instinct urged him to protect her, but her scathing words to Howe stopped him.

"I wanted to thank you, Mr. Howe, for my employment at Miss Nelson's." Her voice bubbled with anger rather than gratitude.

"You're welcome." He turned back to the men.

Ella, however, was not done with him. "Yes, without my job, I would have never known just how much of a swindler you really are." She spoke loudly, and this time, it was not just Jasper Howe who turned.

"Excuse me." He growled.

"Yes. I've had many opportunities to discuss with Miss Nelson her 'investment' with you and the funds you've withheld from her school. Funds paid by many of your guests here." She swiveled her head side to side, and Howe's guests moved closer to her. "They might be interested to know that their tuition payments are going into your pockets and not toward educating their children."

"How dare you!" Howe's face flared red bordering on purple.

Clara's went white.

"Is this true, Howe?" one of the gentlemen asked, stepping between Ella and Howe.

"Of course not!" Jasper tore his eyes from Ella.

"I have the investment agreement signed by Miss Nelson and Mr. Howe right here." Ella pulled a paper from the chatelaine bag clipped to the ribbon about her waist. She unfolded it and showed it to the men who now surrounded her. "He did something similar to my poor widowed aunt. Left her destitute." Ella held the agreement up for all to see.

"Give me that!" Jasper grabbed for the paper, but Ella pulled it back and clutched it to her chest.

"I've seen your signature enough to recognize it," one of the men said. Thomas recognized him as the banker who had brought Jasper the collection notice. "I pay good money for my boy to attend that school."

Ella kept her eyes on the men and ignored Howe's muttered threats. "Miss Nelson has had to borrow money for coal to heat the school rooms."

"Leave my house now." Jasper pushed the words out through clenched teeth. "And then collect your things and leave Miss Nelson's before I remove you myself."

He looked ready to wring her neck and might have if the men hadn't gathered more tightly around him, peppering him with questions.

Jasper tried to appease the men with platitudes that only made the men's voices grow louder. One man drew back his coat to reveal a six-shooter. Jasper went quiet.

This was the Wild West Thomas had read about.

And Ella Merriweather was the hero of the story.

He turned to tell her so, but Clara had Ella by the arm and was pushing her through the guests who had been too far from Mr. Howe to hear all the excitement.

Thomas caught up with Ella just in time to see Clara thrust her out the front door, throwing Ella's cape at her. "I hope you're happy with yourself!" she screamed. "You'll never work in this territory again as anything other than a—"

Clara stopped herself and looked around at the guests staring at her. She smoothed her dress and stepped away from the door.

"I am quite happy with myself, Clara," came Ella's confident voice from outside. "And I hope someday you can say the same."

Clara slammed the door shut. Her eyes bounced around the guests standing in the foyer. Their eyes did not meet hers as they whispered to each other.

Her ire landed on Thomas. "I suppose you'll follow after her. Well, go ahead. You're a nobody just like her, and you'll both end up in the poorhouse."

Thomas glanced at the door, then smiled at Clara. "Perhaps so." He stepped toward the door and opened it. "But likely not. After all, we can both tie our own shoes."

CHAPTER TEN

ELLA'S ONLY REGRET AS SHE walked the long drive from the Howes' estate to the street was that she hadn't had the chance to thank Thomas for hiring the cutter that had picked her up. She wished for that cutter now and not just because it had a much easier time getting through the deep snow than she was having. She wished for it because, perhaps, Thomas would be in it. The sight of him would warm her, even if they met only long enough for her to say goodbye. This time, undoubtedly, forever.

An offer had come from the newly built high school in Laramie, and she would be leaving in the morning. Though she didn't have to be there for another week, she hadn't been able to resist the opportunity to confront Jasper Howe before leaving Cheyenne. Even if, as she had predicted, his response would force her to leave Cheyenne earlier than she needed to.

She only wished she'd been able to dance with Thomas first. She hadn't anticipated Clara greeting her or taking her to Howe moments after she'd arrived. Then Howe had told her to get out, and she didn't doubt he'd meant it. Would she have time to offer Miss Nelson and Sally a proper goodbye before Mr. Howe sent someone to carry out his threat? She hoped so. Ella felt they would miss her as much as she would miss them.

Ella reached the street and turned toward Miss Nelson's. Her boots and stockings were soaked through from the snow, and she still had another mile to walk. There were no hansom cabs to hail, and she had no money even if there had been.

Thoughts of Thomas returned, and she pulled her cape tighter against the cold wind. Eventually, she would be able to forget him. She was sure of it.

Horses sounded behind her, and Ella moved to the far side of the sidewalk to avoid being sprayed by snow coming off the cutter's runners. The driver, however, slowed as he approached her. Before he came to a full stop, she heard her name and a "Whoa."

"Thomas?" She turned, hardly daring to hope the voice she'd heard actually belonged to the man who'd laid claim to her thoughts and wishes. "What are you doing here?"

"I'm taking you home." He took her gently by the elbow, and she allowed him to lead her to the cutter. "It's far too cold for you to walk all the way to Miss Nelson's."

Ella climbed into the narrow seat, and Thomas tucked a buffalo robe around her before pulling it over himself too. With his body pressed next to hers, she could think of nothing but his nearness. Heat coursed through her veins, causing her to shiver.

"Are you warm enough?" he asked as he urged the horse forward.

She nodded, not trusting herself to use words without stammering. Truthfully, she was warmer than she should have been on such a cold night.

Some time passed before Thomas spoke again. "You were very brave back there." His voice blended with the soft sound of the runners cutting through fresh snow.

"Thank you." Ella drew her eyes from the road ahead to his face. Tiny icicles hung from his whiskers. She resisted the urge to brush them away. "Do they know you came after me?"

A conspiratorial grin spread across his face. "They know."

"You're not concerned what our . . . *association* may do to your business venture?" She tore her eyes from his face to the outline of Miss Nelson's house, which they would reach all too soon.

Thomas pulled the horses to a stop. "I told you when we first met that I didn't gamble anymore. Business with Howe has become too much of a gamble. It's time for me to take my losses and walk away while I still have something to walk away with." His eyes drifted to hers.

"What's your next move?" Her voice quivered. She dared not hope, but his closeness tempted her to believe she might be part of whatever he had planned. At the same time, his words reminded her that, at heart, he was a gambler, even if he'd sworn off gaming.

He took a deep breath. "I'd like to cast my chips in with you if you'll have me."

Ella couldn't hold back a gasp. He was asking so much more than she'd ever imagined.

"I know we don't know each other well," he hastened to add, "and our backgrounds are worlds apart." Glancing at her hands laying atop the buffalo robe, he reached for them. "May I?"

She dipped her chin, too hopeful of his touch to speak.

Thomas wrapped his large hands around hers. "You're freezing," he whispered and rubbed his palms back and forth, filling every part of her with warmth. "I'm not asking for an answer right now, only that you'll allow me to prove myself worthy of you."

Prove himself worthy? She had never thought of him as unworthy of her, but at his words, she knew that he would have to do just that. For so many years, her life had been at the mercy of fate and family. She would not gamble with the independence she had fought so hard to gain.

"I'm leaving for Laramie in the morning," she blurted and pulled her hands from his. What were they to each other? Little more than strangers. Yet, as he let go of her fingers, an empty space opened inside her, and she wished her words had sounded more like a yes than a no. "What happens then?" she added tentatively.

"I have no reason to stay in Cheyenne, particularly after I sever my ties with Howe." He paused, his chest rising and falling slowly. "I could follow after I've settled things here and write to you until then." His words were soft and pleading.

Ella wanted to say yes, but she also had to play her own cards carefully. She thought of Maggie back in New York and the many days the girl had come to work crying because her father had gambled away her and her mother's earnings. How could she be sure Thomas had actually sworn off gambling? Letters might allow her to better know him, but why allow that intimacy if she wasn't first certain he was the kind of man she could rely on? He had come to her rescue in times of need, but what about in times of want?

"What kind of employment would you seek in Laramie?" She wouldn't be saddled with a man who could not pull his weight.

"I don't know cows, but I do know horses, and there are plenty of people in this territory who need them." He sat straighter, his face brightening. "I've already found a buyer for most of my Herefords—a competitor of Howe's." He smiled at this, and Ella could not help doing so herself. "The money I collect will be used to pay off my debts, and the remaining will go toward a down payment on a place of my own and a dozen horses to breed."

"You plan on running a horse ranch?" It seemed a sound prospect, and Ella had always liked horses.

"I do." He cocked his head toward her. "What do you think?"

The sincerity of his question drew her closer to him. "I believe there is some very nice land outside Laramie, and its proximity to both Cheyenne and Rawlins will provide a strong customer base. And the railroad will allow you to ship horses to further destinations."

Ella stopped abruptly. Had she just told him he should move to Laramie? Her face grew hot, but as she lifted her eyes to Thomas, his smile reassured her.

"I think, Mr. Clayborne, that I would very much like to be kept abreast of your plans by letter . . ." She returned his smile. "Or in person."

Thomas leaned toward Ella. Mere inches separated them. He touched her cheek, and everything else stopped. He cupped her face in both of his hands, and she drew closer to meet his lips.

Though she'd never been kissed before, Ella couldn't imagine a kiss gentler than Thomas's. Nor could she imagine not betting on their kisses lasting a lifetime.

ABOUT THE AUTHOR

Brittany Larsen loves a lot of things, but yoga, Jane Austen, and the beach are all at the top of her list. At the very, very top are her husband and three daughters, who share her yoga, Jane, and beach love, in varying degrees. The placement of her white dog and black cat on that list depends on what "surprises" and/or animal carcasses they've left for her to find. She lives in Orange County, California, and is the author of three contemporary romances: *Pride and Politics, Sense and Second Chances*, and *The Matchmaker's Match*.

OTHER BOOKS AND AUDIOBOOKS
BY JEN GEIGLE JOHNSON

THE LIBERTY SEEKERS

The Nobleman's Daughter

"Mistletoe Memories" in A Christmas Courting

A Lady's Maid

THE PIMPERNEL

Scarlet

STAND-ALONE NOVELS

His Lady in Hiding

ROYAL REGENCY ROMANCE

A Foreign Crown

A Torn Allegiance

PRAISE FOR JEN GEIGLE JOHNSON

"This story reminded me of the old Western melodramas I watched on Saturday afternoons as a kid in the single movie theater in Arco, Idaho. There's a newly arrived doctor and his daughter, a train robbery, a threatened hanging, and a long-lost love; plenty to keep the reader turning pages."
—Jennie Hansen, author *When Tomorrow Comes*

"With numerous Regency romances in her portfolio, Jen's Jane Austin-type style came through in her first set in the American West, making for a fun read."
—Carolyn Twede Frank, author *His Accidental Bride*

"Jen Geigle Johnson has done it again! Another light-hearted love story to melt your heart with just enough action to keep your pulse racing."
—Brittany Larsen, author *The Matchmaker's Match*

her frontier bandit

JEN GEIGLE JOHNSON

CHAPTER ONE

REBECCA BAILEY PRESSED HER PALM against the cool of the glass on her train window as a trail of her heart strings stretched into the blurring landscape. Did they reach all the way to Boston? Would a part of her heart always reside in her home of twenty-two years? For days now, with every passing tree, Boston fell farther away.

She watched the people on the train platforms in every station where they stopped, wondering about her new home. The farther west they traveled, clothing became less fine, manners and speech diminished in equal amounts, and everyone seemed cloaked in a layer of dust. Would Grant's Landing hold anything nearly as dear as Boston?

With the views discouraging, she turned to her reason for being so far from home, knowing that she'd find her courage. "Father." She adjusted the book in her lap. The smile she attempted felt tremulous, shaky. But she kept it in place. "Father."

He was studying the local Boston paper.

She sat up, trying to see what had caught his attention. "Reading the last semblance of home before we arrive at our adventure?"

"Hmmm." He nodded. "Such a tragedy; the Harrison brother is still missing. What's his name?"

Her throat caught, swallowing suddenly impossible. She shrugged. *Ray. Her Ray.* He'd left without a word, and she knew why, but she could never tell her father. "Oh, that is sad. I'm sorry to hear it. Can they find no clues as to what happened to him?" She didn't know where specifically he'd gone, just that he'd probably moved forward with his plan alone, even after she'd turned him down.

Her father turned the page. "No. Two years and nothing. Are they really looking, I wonder? From what I understand, the Harrisons have always been private sorts of people. Perhaps they simply hold their grief close."

She thought it more likely they were embarrassed and hiding the truth from as many as they could. The Boston elite could be somewhat unforgiving.

"Have you ever met him?" her father continued. "I don't believe we know the Harrisons, do we?" He laughed. "Besides the back of their heads on Sunday mornings."

She shook her head. "No." The lie burned like acid on her tongue. But what they had was over. No reason to admit anything to her father now.

He studied her face a moment longer than she thought necessary, then said, "Nor I." Her father's medical methods were on the cutting edge of research in Boston and much called upon by the research teams there. She'd enjoyed being Dr. Bailey's daughter in Boston. But still, some of the more elite doors were closed to them.

"We definitely socialized with different groups, and I don't think he participated much in the Seasons." Although the Baileys were respected, the Harrisons were in another social status entirely.

"Hmm." Her father had likely already moved on to whatever the next bit of news was in his paper.

She couldn't help but think more on the Harrisons and their plight. A son gone missing must surely be devastating to them. If only Ray's father had listened to his son, had given him some kind of recourse, another option. One minute, Ray seemed to be preparing to follow his father's footsteps and study at university. The next, no one knew where he was. Including Rebecca.

"Did I share the most recent letter from the sheriff of Grant's Landing?" Their new home.

"No, you haven't." She reached for it from his outstretched hand.

"He seems particularly pleased we're coming." Her father's smile lifted his mustache and curled up the ends.

She scanned the letter. "He says here that the town has not been made aware we are coming. Even his own deputy doesn't know. Why is that?"

"I think he was nervous to tell them in case we didn't make it."

"Did he think we might change our minds?"

"No." Her father shifted in his seat and avoided her gaze. "Well, that's part of it. Things can be dangerous, the travel especially. So I guess they've learned to wait until a person is actually in their town before counting on their presence." He folded his paper down. "And there have been a few instances of doctors coming part of the journey and then changing their minds."

"Have there?" A vague feeling of unease sat heavy in her stomach.

"Yes, it appears so, but we are made of tougher stuff. And the people of Grant's Landing need us."

"You will be a blessing to them, I'm certain. At any rate, we're almost there, and nothing has dissuaded our journey so far."

A loud screeching sound pierced the air, followed by the train jerking to slow its progress. Rebecca fell forward onto her father's bench. He reached a hand out to steady her. Though not young, he was still strong. She sat down at his side and clutched his arm as the train continued a long, screeching halt. "What's happening?" The pressure to remain seated, the dust that arose from the track, and her father's pinched face all made her breathe faster. "Father?"

Gunfire coming from somewhere out the window sounded close. She gasped. A group of ten horses tore past. Men with covered faces, all with their guns in the air, made their way toward the front of the train. And then others showed up on a ridge above. These men had their faces uncovered. Perhaps they were local lawmen? Shooting commenced between them near the train. Rebecca looked from group to group, her eyes growing wider.

When a stray bullet hit the train beside their window, her father pushed her to the floor. "Get down!"

The floors of their private berth were dirtier than she realized, and she kept her face lifted, but her white gloves suffered. The front of her new blue dress was likely now covered in dust. Perhaps situations like these led to everyone's overall unwashed appearance. The sounds continued outside. "I wish I could see. What's happening?"

Her father's smile held a spark of pride. "Always curious. But stay put. Though the gunmen are not aiming at us, that's a very dangerous situation." Her father crouched beside her, his face close. He whispered, "I guess we spoke too soon."

"About nothing in our journey dissuading us?" She searched her father's earnest expression. He didn't seem scared, and something about his calm helped her to feel better.

"They're after money or attention. Since we offer large amounts of neither, we should be safe, as long as we wait it out quietly."

She tried to smile, but the tightness of her face didn't allow for something so relaxed as a smile.

When her father first expressed a desire for a change of scenery, for a drastic change in lifestyle, she'd panicked inside. Moments just like this one had played through her mind. But when she saw the hopeful hesitancy and the obvious boyish excitement in his face, she had agreed immediately. What else could she do? But the awful irony of her father's desire to go west had chipped away at her peace every day since Ray's proposal. Every day in silence. She'd turned down her only love so that her father could stay in Boston, only to find out—too late— that he desired to travel west. And even though the idea terrified her, she would not be left in Boston alone. First Ray and then her father? No. She'd chosen this new adventure, train robbery and all, over being alone.

The shooting paused. When the train at last came to a standstill, the sound of horses thundering past made Rebecca curious. She crept forward.

"Stay down."

She waved at her father. "I'll just peek out the corner." She got up on her knees and lifted her head so that an eye could look out.

Two wide, filthy-looking, bloodshot eyes stared back in return. The man's greasy hair stuck to his forehead under the brim on his hat. A handkerchief covered his nose and mouth, but his eyes were laughing.

She screamed and fell flat to the floor.

Laughter outside made her cringe.

"We have to hide."

When she sat up, the same man was staring in at them from atop his horse. She scrambled for the blinds and pulled them shut against his leering, laughing face.

Her hands shaking, she turned to her father. "What shall we do? He's seen us. Where shall we go?"

"With any luck, he'll move on." Her father's hands belied his calm tone. Their subtle shake did more to increase Rebecca's nerves than anything.

Then thunderous running footsteps pounded past their berth in the train car.

She sucked in her breath. "They're inside! Can we lock the doors?" She stood up to fumble with the lever, but the door pushed back into her.

Her father stumbled back onto their bench. "Rebecca."

A large man with a handkerchief over his face stepped inside, a wide hat covering his head, and there was a general smell of prairie dust about him. He stood with his back to her, in their berth, listening at her door.

Rebecca sneezed.

"Hush now." He turned to her for a half second only. One familiar eye winked before he opened the door a crack while feet stomped past again. Then he rushed back out the door, closing it behind him, but not before he'd dropped a handkerchief in her hand.

She sucked in her breath. "What?" She unfolded it. The initials in the lower left corner, *RH*, could have been any name, referred to any person in the world with those initials if they hadn't been stitched by her own hand.

Ray Harrison.

CHAPTER TWO

THE TRAIN STARTED TO MOVE again. Rebecca breathed out in relief. "Does this mean they've gone?"

She clutched the handkerchief in her fist, not sure what to think about Ray. She hadn't seen his face. It was too dark, a black handkerchief covered most of his skin, and his eyes were darkened by the hat and shadows, but there had been no mistaking his voice or his wink. And the handkerchief proved it. Ray Harrison was here near Grant's Landing? Robbing trains?

Her head shook involuntarily, even though no words came out of her mouth. He left his father's wealth and offers of schooling to come out west and rob people, to become a . . . a bandit?

She couldn't believe it. Even though she'd seen him with her own eyes, she didn't believe it.

Before long, the train had at last pulled into the station. She opened the curtain and then clenched a hand at her stomach.

Bleak. Dry. Gone were the bustling beautiful streets of Boston with fine carriages, beautiful horses, and women in lovely dresses. Grant's Landing had no landing. She would step out of the train onto the dirt. Dust swirled wherever people walked. She leaned against the glass to see farther in any direction. The town seemed to be small, likely one strip of stores. And there was a well pump. A woman, hunched and tired looking, placed a bucket beneath the pump and started working the lever up and down.

Rebecca held her breath, counted to five, then let it out.

Her father's hand on her shoulder reminded her to be strong, if only for him, and she turned to leave their quarters with some semblance of a smile.

The sun beat down on the top of her bonnet so strongly she was immediately heated through. And she blinked a hundred times to try to see something through the brightness.

"The good news is nothing can survive this heat. I bet the town is healthy as can be." Father wiped his brow with a handkerchief, which reminded her to tuck Ray's away. Her eyes searched the few people out and about. No Ray here. Did he ride with a gang? Live in caves? She couldn't fathom what she saw. What was his life now?

A portly gentleman, wide in girth, guns at his hips, approached with a large smile. "You Dr. Bailey?"

Her father smiled. "I am indeed."

"Glad you're here." He wiped his hands on the front of his trousers and held one out. "I'm Sheriff Stanford." While he pumped her father's hands an excessive amount, he turned to her. "And you must be Miss Bailey."

"I am." She didn't offer her hand, just nodded.

"Well, let me show you to our doctor's office here in town."

Her father followed, but Rebecca waited by their trunks. Surely her father would not consider just leaving all their earthly belongings on the side of the tracks.

But as he and Sheriff Stanford walked farther away, she realized he was planning exactly that. Well, she most certainly would not. She sat down on the top of her trunk with a huff.

A part of her wished to rest her chin in her hands as she had when she was younger, but instead, she adjusted her posture, sat up as straight as her governess had taught, and waited for her father to recall he had belongings and a daughter. His absentminded, or rather single-minded, nature, was something to be amused with most of the time. However, not in this moment.

It took a rather long time. She watched him continue walking down the street and enter the front of what looked like the sheriff's office. She let her gaze wander along the street. Just what sort of place would she now call home? Across from where the train stopped was a saloon and what looked like an inn. Would they be staying in the inn above the saloon? She hoped not. Wasn't that where questionable things happened? She had no idea where they would be staying. Father had promised a homestead, a bit of land, a house. But of course, that would take some time.

He had not exited the sheriff's office yet. Next to the saloon, a large man, built with muscle across the shoulders, stood in the doorway of what looked like a blacksmith shop. He took a handkerchief out of his pocket and wiped his face. She couldn't make out his face, but his body was turned toward her. Something about him seemed familiar.

She chided herself. Would every man she ever looked at remind her of Ray? That man seemed much larger, broader across the shoulders, more a man than her Ray had been.

"Hey, pretty lady."

Rebecca smelled a man before he came into sight. Whisky on a man's breath was one of life's most abhorrent smells. She closed her eyes, hoping that whoever was approaching from behind would keep on walking.

"I said hello." A shadow fell across her face. She lifted her eyes. A short man swayed in front of her.

"Whatcha got there, Moe?" Another man approached, this one taller and younger. Rebecca sat very still. But when ignoring didn't seem an effective deterrent, she cleared her throat and stood. "I'm waiting for my father. He's with the sheriff . . ."

"Oh, with the sheriff, is he?" The man called Moe stepped closer, and Rebecca regretted standing because now she had nowhere to go with the backs of her legs pressed up against the trunk.

The lines in his face were red with dirt. He opened his mouth in a grimace, and she cringed against the sight of rotted teeth. "How's about you and me go for a walk?"

"No, thank you." He reached for her hand, but she pulled it away. "I said no."

"Well, now I don't understand that word. I say you and I are going for a walk. Come now, it ain't gonna hurt anybody."

"The lady said no."

Rebecca gasped and whipped around. But Ray wasn't looking at her. He was staring down Moe and the others who were approaching. She hadn't noticed, but she and Moe had attracted quite an open curiosity.

She held her hands together at her front and inched over until she stood at Ray's side.

When Moe finally shrugged and walked away, the others gave up too. Ray waited until the last of them had turned their backs, and then he hooked his thumbs into his belt buckles, rocked back and forth twice, and said, "Welcome to town, Miss . . . ?"

She tilted her head, knowing he recognized her. It was written all over his face and in the happy twinkles in his eyes. She barely restrained herself from flinging her arms around his neck and squealing a great happy hello.

"Bailey. And thank you for your assistance, Mr.—"

"Trundle." He nodded briefly, watching her.

"Ah, Mr. Trundle. Have you a first name?"

"Well now, I do, but out here in Grant's Landing, we wait until we've known a person for a while before we go starting to call them by anything other than their last name."

"Really!" She put her hands on her hips, done with his odd charade. "And just what are you doing all the way out here? Your family—"

He laughed to drown out her next words and then sent her a half-warning, half-pleading look. "Can I give you a hand with your things?"

"I'd be much obliged, honestly. I think Father has forgotten all about me."

"Not surprising."

She let her mouth drop.

"Meaning that he tends to do that, doesn't he? Forget things?"

She forgave him at the first hint that he might acknowledge their years of familiarity. She was full of curiosity. What was he doing all the way out here? Why had he changed his name?

"Any idea where the new doctor in town will be staying?"

"Really!" He tipped his hat and lowered his voice. "The Baileys coming all the way out here. Your father is gonna be Grant's Landing's one and only doctor."

"Is that so hard to believe?" She regretted her words the moment she said them, for she knew what was coming.

His jaw tightened. "Well, as a matter of fact, yes. I've heard it said that some ladies in Boston—that is where you said you're from?—some ladies would proclaim to never wish to come to such a place. I've heard it said that they would rather stay in Boston than even get married." His tone had started out joking and light but now seemed almost bitter. He reached down and hefted her trunk up on his shoulder. "Come. The doctor and the sheriff share a building."

"Oh, they do?" She reached down and lifted her sack onto her shoulder and then picked up a small handbag and a larger bag. But she hesitated to follow him.

He'd gone about twenty steps before he turned. "Coming?" His eyebrow lifted. His mouth turned up. He hefted that trunk as if it weighed nothing.

"Are we just going to leave the other trunks?"

"Do you think they will walk off?" He laughed.

"No, but someone might be interested in them. Perhaps? I don't know. Where I come from, people don't just leave their trunks laying around."

"Well, out here on Grant's Landing, we aren't too concerned about anyone taking our belongings right in front of our eyes, especially when we're right across the street, and I'm the assistant sheriff."

"Wait, what?"

"Which part?"

"You're the assistant sheriff?"

He bowed. "I am."

"I saw you on the train."

"Yes."

"So, you defend and break the law?"

He held up a finger, almost shook his head, then shrugged. "It's complicated, little lady."

She hurried to keep up, looking back over her shoulder twice at her father's trunks. "I'm not afraid of complicated." And she wasn't, but what did she want? To align herself with a train robber? Even if it was Ray, he'd left home, hid, and changed his name. As she caught up, she whispered, "I'm beginning to think I don't really know you. Do I?"

"That's another complicated question. Do I know you?"

"Apparently neither one of us knows the other."

"And that's how I'd like it to stay." His eyes turned serious. A hint of pleading stemmed the complaints she would have sent his way, and the questions. "As far as any of us know, you and I just met."

They approached the front of a small building.

Ray dipped his hat. "This here's the sheriff's office. I work in here with him part of the time. And that over there is the doctor's office."

A door off to the side looked like it could use some new paint. No sign welcomed anyone. "Are there apartments upstairs?" She stepped back to take a look at the building.

"There are." He reached for the door. "I'll be putting these trunks up here, then?"

"Yes, thank you."

She turned to glance at her father's trunks. Her arrival was drawing attention from every direction. But as of yet, no one else had approached. Their surreptitious glances, their open curiosity, and their suspicion told her they didn't get many newcomers, or perhaps it was just new doctors they weren't accustomed to.

Ray came down the stairs and headed back across the square toward the other trunks.

Where was her father? She stepped into the sheriff's office, where she heard voices.

A man called from the back. "I'll be wanting my breakfast!"

She moved toward the sound. But when the owner of the voice stared at her through bars in a cell, she wished she hadn't.

"Well now, if you're the one bringing breakfast, that's a right positive change." He licked his fingers and wiped down a large, drooping mustache.

But she didn't answer. She backed away and returned to the front. Voices came from the side office.

"We will get you your pay, but with the bank being robbed and the trains unreliable, we don't have much around here. But the folks'll pay with what they have. A good meal, a side of beef, a chicken." The sheriff's chuckle made her step closer. "If you get one of Marybeth's apple pies, count yourself twice blessed."

Paid by apple pie and chicken. She turned away from their voices. All at once, she became tired. Tired from their journey, tired to find out her best friend—the man she had at one point considered marrying—was hiding out in a small town robbing trains, tired that she had left everything she was used to, tired to learn she might be living in a run-down bit of a town for the rest of her life. Just plain tired. Now that she'd found father, she stepped back outside to check on the trunks.

Ray approached with the last of them, and she hurried to open their door again. "Thank you."

He grunted; she knew the trunks were heavy. This time she followed him up a narrow set of stairs.

"Will his office be up here do you think?"

Ray didn't answer. As she hurried up after him, the musty smell of the place made her sneeze. Just as she reached the top stair, Ray had turned to come back down, and she ran into him. His chest was so much larger than when she had last embraced him, since his lips had last captured hers and her knees had gone weak beneath her. She kicked herself for thinking such things while he was standing so close.

"Well, come in for a minute." She lifted her chin.

"I've got to get back to work." He indicated the stairs.

"That's it? No explanation about any of this?"

His eyes hardened. "What is there to say? I'm here now, making a life for myself. And I'd appreciate it if my old life didn't catch up with me."

Tears welled in her eyes, but she looked away and said only, "Understood." Then she stepped aside and let him pass.

The sound of the door closing told her sound carried in that building. She hoped she'd not have to hear the prisoners next door. Sharing a building with the jail? She shook her head. This whole situation just kept getting worse.

CHAPTER THREE

REBECCA HAD GONE IN SEARCH of a broom and bucket. Before her father joined her, she'd made quick work of their living space and begun cleaning the office downstairs. It wasn't perfect by any means, but she at least felt that she could sleep that evening in a room without dust.

The jail next door was louder than she would have liked. Horses arrived and left. For a moment, men were shouting. She hoped she and her father would be able to find a homestead soon and get out of town. She pushed large piles of dirt, dust, and twigs out the back door to start clearing out their office space. Then she moved back up the stairs, wondering where she would sleep.

Their front door banged open. She gasped and returned to the top of the stairs. Her father walked in the door, leading a man who was hunched over and clutching his shoulder. "Quick, Rebecca, we need a table cleared."

At the first sight of blood seeping through the man's clutched fingers, she jumped into action, splashing water up on the table, wiping it down, grimacing at the dirt.

"Fetch my kit, please." Her father's voice was calm. She could tell his mind was already turning with possible solutions, already analyzing the problem.

She rushed upstairs. The sounds of horses clopping outside registered, but she grabbed her father's satchel and ran back down the stairs.

Loud shouts from next door startled her. A quick glance out the window almost made her stumble over the last few steps. A crowd of men stood not ten feet from her front window, some on horseback, many dismounted, and others were arriving. Ray. He caught her eye through the window and looked away.

She rushed to the back of their office and handed her father his kit.

They worked side by side. She'd been trained somewhat to be his assistant as they were preparing to travel west. But nothing she'd done with him up to this point prepared her for the sight of a man's open bullet wound. She stopped herself from gagging, but only just.

When her father was finished digging out a bullet, a loud knocking startled her. "Heavens." She'd said nothing up to this point, not wanting to disturb her father.

"That would be the sheriff. You can let him in."

"What's going on?"

"I'll explain all of this in a moment."

"He's come to throw me in jail for something I ain't done. That's what's going on." The man's hand clutched at her skirts as she turned to leave. "The doc here is fixing me up for my own hanging."

"What?" Her eyes widened, and she looked at her father's face.

"That's up to the law, isn't it? Would you rather spend the night in jail with a bullet in your shoulder?"

He grunted.

"That might be all I get as far as gratitude or payment, so perhaps you should just say you're welcome. What say you, Miss Bailey?"

She shook her head and headed toward the door. The sheriff pounded again.

But when she opened it, Ray's large form blocked the sun.

She said nothing, just opened the door wider.

He nodded at her as he passed. Ten of the men still stood on the front stoop outside the jail. All of them turned to her as she shut the door. She looked down and locked it.

Not for the first time, she questioned her father's choice to come out here and live in these circumstances. Were there any people here more genteel in nature? Did they have social events or gatherings? Would she have other women to tea?

She stepped back into the office just as her father began to stitch up his patient.

The man called out and started to squirm.

"Help me." Her father held him down with one hand until Ray held down the rest of him.

"You, sir, would do well to sit still unless you want your skin left open."

"That hurts worse than taking out the bullet."

Rebecca stepped back in, her skirts swishing all around her. "Here, bite this." She put an old strap of leather in his mouth. "And hold on tight to my hands. You can do this. It hurts, but it'll be done before you know it, and then you'll be much, much better. My father knows what he's doing." She looked deeply into their patient's eyes.

He stared back, a sort of desperate hope tugging at her sympathy. Then he nodded, grabbed hold of her hands, and closed his eyes.

She stood with Ray pressed up against her and her father on the other side of the table, and they watched while stitches went in and out.

Ray shifted so that they weren't touching. The air between them drew her closer. It crackled like a dry piece of wood in the fireplace and felt just as warming. But she kept her eyes down.

The man started to squirm. Her father was sewing together the most tender spot.

She leaned over him to get his attention. "Stay with me. Look. Look into my eyes."

He turned, and she smiled into him all her energy, all her confidence that he would be able to handle the situation.

He calmed. His hands clutched hers but not in the same desperate manner. And she started to hum.

"Amazing Grace" came to mind without a thought, and as she hummed, she was taken back to her days in Boston at church on Sundays. Her father always sat at her side. Ray and his family sometimes came, sitting way up at the front of their huge cathedral. Did her father recognize him? He'd shown no sign, and Ray was no longer the young man Father might have noticed two years ago. On the last Sunday she'd seen Ray, he'd whispered as they were filing out, "Can I come calling today?"

Her father had been consulting with a woman of the congregation about her husband's ailments. When she'd turned to Ray, their eyes were inches apart. She'd nodded. "Of course."

He had seemed distracted.

If she'd known then what he'd planned . . . she shook her head. What would she have done? Prevented his proposal? Or would she have said yes now that she knew the whole of it?

How could she have left her father?

Fate could be a cruel master. For here she was, between the men she loved, far from Boston anyway, only everything was a mess. The patient's grip tightened again, and she stumbled.

Ray used a hand to steady her, and he stepped nearer so that his body could keep her balanced.

When his eyes met hers, the tenderness that flashed quickly between them stole her breath. "Oh." She swallowed and then looked back at the man.

"Almost finished." Her father seemed as nonplussed as always. She watched him complete the last few stitches, and then he nodded to her and Ray. "Thank you for your assistance here."

Ray stood taller, rotating his shoulders. "The sheriff needs him back in the station."

Her father nodded, placed a dressing on the wound, wrapped it up, and then sent the man on his way with Ray at his side.

Loud noises, calling and jeers from the men outside, met their exit.

Rebecca leaned back against the wall. "Whew. Father, what happened?"

He wiped his brow. "This is certainly not our typical Boston customer."

She shook her head. "No, nothing about Grant's Landing reminds me of home."

Father wouldn't meet her eyes. He started cleaning their table, and she picked up the broom to finish cleaning the floor while ignoring the drops of new blood from their first patient.

"Apparently, he's part of a gang around here that robs trains, banks, and stores. They just caught him and brought him in while I was over in the sheriff's office."

"And this is to be our life?"

"I don't know, Rebecca. I just don't know."

CHAPTER FOUR

As THEY TUCKED INTO BED that night, Rebecca tried not to hear the noises from the jail next door. The cellmates were arguing with each other. Outside, sounds of a rough crowd near the saloon made her nervous. She pulled the blankets up over her head, but every sound still penetrated. After many hours, she finally drifted off but jerked awake again to the sounds of guns firing. She sat up and ran to the window.

The moon was out, and the square well lit. A team of about ten horses galloped around in a large circle in the center of the street with guns firing in the air. She pulled her nightdress tighter around herself. "Where's the sheriff? Where's the sheriff?" Her eyes searched the area while her heart hammered inside. One of the riders paused and noticed her.

She stepped away from the window, her hand on her heart, breathing quickly. "Oh no, oh no." She peered back out. The man was still there; he tipped his hat to her, his face leering.

The others kept circling, firing their guns. One of them smashed the window of the general store. Rebecca sucked in her breath. She wrung her hands together. The man closest to her swung his pistol around in the air and fired. A stray bullet smashed through her window and hit the wall on the other side of the room.

She screamed.

Her father ran into the room. "Are you all right?"

"No!" She held her face in her hands. "No, I'm not. They're crazy, firing guns, this place." She started to shake.

Her father moved closer to the window.

"Be careful!"

He waved a hand back. "Someone's finally come. That assistant."

She crept closer. "Ray?"

"Ray?" Her turned to her, both eyebrows raised. "You know this man?"

"Oh, yes." She stammered. "He's the man who helped us with our luggage and then with your patient."

He watched her for a moment, but then they were both distracted by the scene outside.

Ray had a hand on his holster and stepped out into the square. He looked strong, powerful. And even though he seemed to want to have nothing to do with her, she was filled with relief he was there in her same town.

The intruders approached. They all seemed to be having some kind of a conversation, and then one of the men on a horse nodded, waved his hand, and led the group out of town.

Rebecca exhaled and leaned back against the wall.

"Daughter." Her father reached for her, and she fell into his arms. "I'm sorry. I didn't know how this would be. Should we go back to Boston?"

She wanted to shout *yes*, to tell him she'd had enough. But the hope in his voice stayed her tongue.

Then a loud pounding on her door made her yelp. She ran to the window and peeked out a corner. She could see nothing as the door was outside her line of sight. "Oh, who could it be?"

"It's Ray!" he shouted up to them from the street.

"Oh!" Her face heated, and a smile stretched across her mouth. Ray could protect them. She ran from her father.

"Wait, Rebecca."

Though he called, she ignored him. She had to hear the news. Who were those men? Why had they come, and why had they left? Something about being near Ray made her feel like everything would be fine.

She flung open the door, ready to usher him in.

But he stood at the sheriff's side. And his eyes moved over the whole of her, warming even her toes before he frowned. "Becky, cover yourself." His eyes jerked to the sheriff and back, then he cleared his throat. His fellow lawman seemed not to notice the slip.

She looked down at her nightdress, which was open at the neck, thin, and wholly inappropriate, and she yelped, placing hands at her neckline. "I do apologize. But the men. I'm . . . I'm frightened. Have you news? Come in. Please."

Her father stepped up behind her with a robe, which she gratefully donned while wishing to hide in her room.

"Yes, do come in."

"We have work to do." The sheriff nodded. "We're just checking to see that no harm came to either of you. There's a bullet hole through your window."

"Yes." Her father's arm encircled her as he stepped closer to her side. "Thankfully, she was unharmed."

"Glad to hear it. The general store can help you order new glass for repairs." The sheriff nodded again.

They were turning as if they might leave, but Rebecca called out, "Wait! What happened? Who were they?"

Ray shook his head. "This is nothing for you to be worrying about." His eyes held a warning, but suddenly, his dismissive response burned off some of her fear. She stood taller.

"I'll be worrying about what I want to worry about. A bullet went through my window." She crossed her arms and stared him down.

But he just shrugged. "Welcome to Grant's Landing." He turned from them and made his way back onto the street. Then he stopped and called over his shoulder, "Sleep in the back room." His eyes caught hers for a second, and then he moved with decided purpose to the saloon, where it seemed half the town was still inside.

The sheriff paused a moment, and his mouth turned up. His eyes were kind. "A gang of outlaws from around here. They usually leave us alone." He looked over his shoulder at Ray. "But I guess they had a bone to pick."

"Thank you, Sheriff." Her father shook his hand and then closed the door.

His face sagged a bit, and the lines around his eyes seemed more prominent. But when he met her gaze, the loving sparkle she always saw tugged her lips up in a smile. He patted her hands in his own. "What an adventure we're having." The soft exhale told her he was concerned. "Should I write to my associates in Boston and see about returning?"

She opened her mouth, wanting more than anything to run from that place, but Ray's face, his eyes looking into hers, her father's hope to make it work in Grant's Landing stilled her heart. "Let's give it a month." As the words left her lips, she felt a new resolve shore up some courage from deep inside, and she stood taller.

His responding smile told her all she needed to know about his real wish to stay and make this work.

She tried to muster up a smile of her own. "Now, since I highly doubt either of us will be sleeping, should I get some tea on?"

"We can continue your studies this morning perhaps. I think that back room should become our new library."

"Or my room. Perhaps we can move the library up to the front. And I'll sleep back there."

He nodded. "Yes, that would be wise." His face lined with concern again. "If you had been hurt . . ."

She shook her head. "But I wasn't. I think I shall sleep better back there at any rate. It appears the night life around here never ceases."

"Just so." He seemed cheered by her willingness to make do. They moved to the small corner kitchen area, and she put the pot on to boil.

With tea in front of them and a new feeling of security, she took a sip. "Tell me about that man you stitched up today."

His eyes lit with interest. "His name is Johnny Dunworthy. And he's wanted for robbery in every county near here."

"Hmm." She thought of Ray. "Is he . . . violent?"

"I have no way of knowing, but he's not wanted for murder."

"But they might hang him?"

"Sounds like it. The law around here is harsh, immediate, and certain. If the judge finds him guilty, he'll hang."

Her heart clenched.

"Does that bother you?"

"I think it does. When we help someone, when you heal them, I feel a sort of protective feeling . . . like I'd want your stitches to serve a purpose."

He nodded. "I share the same feeling. I felt a bit odd learning of his potential fate. But like I said, he could have suffered his last days in pain, likely catching an infection or . . . now he might die in comfort?" He winced. "It does sound so violent. But what did we expect?"

She exhaled. "I don't know what I expected. But this whole place is nothing like I dreamed."

"We've been here so short a space of time. Perhaps we will find once we are here a few weeks that there is a gentler side, a group of friends, perhaps?"

She shrugged. "I hope that is the case. I do want it to be nice here. I want for you to be successful. Heaven knows they need a doctor."

"That they do. I can't explain my feelings. As soon as I heard tell in the papers that the frontier needed doctors, I wanted to use my skills among those of desperate need."

"We haven't even fully moved in yet, but I've seen evidence you will have your wish."

"I think I might speak with the folks at the general store to see if there is a piece of land, perhaps a small home with a stream, where we could live. Perhaps a quieter life just outside of town."

The thought at first made her smile. "I could have a bit of a garden." She hummed. Life outside of town might be much more pleasant. "Is there a row of homes where some families might live closer?"

"I don't know. I think we should find out. For now, we must start up our practice here, but as I get to know all our new patients and we have a firmer footing here, we can see what is possible."

"That sounds nice."

He pulled some of his books out. "Shall we talk about local herbs and their uses?"

"Yes. I am most interested in what I can plant in a garden and what I might collect for us."

He opened up to a page. She leaned over to see the drawings, and they discussed their supplies and what they could use more of. As they settled into familiar conversations and ways to be most prepared for any patient's needs, her heart calmed, and after a time, she felt almost as if they were at home in Boston.

The next morning, when the light started to peek out over the horizon, she stood at the window to witness the glowing sky. "Perhaps we will have a moment to unpack a little bit today and clean and decorate." She started to imagine her yellow curtains up in the windows and a rug on the floor.

For a moment, things looked like they might improve. The town was asleep. She thought it lovely with a new, sunny glow lighting the rooftops. A man stepped out of the blacksmith shop and stretched. Ray. He moved to the water pump, filled a bucket, splashed water on his face, and then carried the bucket back to his shop. Why was he here? What was he up to? She was determined to find the answers to her questions, even if he didn't want them revealed.

CHAPTER FIVE

DAYS PASSED, AND LIFE SEEMED more of the same, each day filled with predictable cleaning and unpacking, making the place a home, and unpredictable patients arriving with all manner of odd ailments. Rebecca had put off a visit to the general store for too long. So today, as soon as she saw signs that the store was open, she stepped outside and headed in that direction. Today she was pleased to see a few splashes of color down at the other end of the street. The town boasted a small church with a cross steeple. Several women gathered in front of it, and she was immediately drawn in that direction. But first she had some purchases and a conversation about broken glass to attend to.

The door jingled when she walked in, and for the first time since arriving in Grant's Landing, she felt a sense of order. Each shelf was labeled and carefully stocked. The floor was swept. The counter was cleared. Bolts of fabric were stacked in one corner. Bins of grains, supplies, and dried herbs all had a place. Every shelf made her smile; every space filled with purpose brought a lighter step. By the time she reached the counter, her heart had filled with an open and happy expectation. "Hello."

The man behind the counter turned, and he dropped the bin he held. He was younger than she'd expected. And now he was very obviously flustered. "Oh, hello. Yes. I'm terribly sorry." He stooped to gather the many spools of ribbon that had now unraveled and fallen everywhere.

"Oh, dear. Might I help?" She moved to walk around the counter, but he held up a hand. "No." He shook his head, scooping up ribbon while he tried to speak. "No one is allowed behind the counter. I'm sorry."

"What's that? Is someone trying to come around the counter?" A large, red-faced woman stormed forward, wiping her hands on the front of her apron, but when she saw Rebecca, her mouth lifted in a smile. "Well, hello to you." She wacked the young man at her side, who was still trying to gather the ribbon. "Don't worry about that now. You have a customer."

He eyed the woman twice before straightening and pushing on the front of his glasses. "Yes, how can we help you?"

Her grin grew. "I'm Miss Bailey. My father and I have just moved here, and we live over there." She pointed. "Our window was shot this past week, so . . ."

"Ah, you'll be needing to order a new pane of glass."

"Yes, I would like that, and I need to make some purchases."

He nodded, pulling out a thick book. "Let's see." His finger ran down a column of numbers and then stopped. He looked out the window toward their home and then back to the column. "You'll likely need this size right here."

He put in the order for her while she walked about, making a list of all the things she would need.

The woman watched all the while, and after a time, Rebecca almost forgot she was there until she said, "So are you with the new doctor?"

"Yes, Dr. Bailey is my father."

"Her father." The woman winked and elbowed her associate. "Hear that?" Then she turned back to Rebecca. "I'm Mrs. Halstead, and this is Henry, my son."

"Yes, welcome to town." Henry might be a pleasant-enough fellow if his mother wasn't nearby. He jerked forward as though she'd nudged him. "And I would like to let you know about our activities coming up."

"Activities?"

"Yes, we meet at the church, a group of us, for games and a social now and then. This Friday is the next one."

"Oh, thank you. I've wanted nothing more than to meet some of the good people here. I was hoping just such a thing existed."

He jerked again as though pushed this time. "Would you like to go with me?"

"With you?" The activities were located at the church, an easy walk down the street.

He eyed his mother and then swallowed. "Yes. I can come pick you up at seven."

"Oh, well, thank you. Yes, that would be lovely."

He nodded. "Great. I'll see you then."

They gathered all of her things, and Mrs. Halstead commanded Henry to help her bring her supplies home.

As he followed, her packages under one arm, the other pulling a wagon behind, Rebecca broke the silence. "Have you lived here long?"

"Yes. My parents were early settlers and are the first owners of the store."

"That's incredible. Do you like it?"

His gaze flitted to her and then away. He seemed a bit skittish if she were to define him as anything so soon after meeting. "I do like it most of the time."

"Does the incident from last week happen very often?"

"Last week?"

"Didn't you hear it? All those men and the guns?"

"Oh no. We don't live here in town. But that's the first time we've had to replace your front window, if you can believe it."

She nodded. "Well, have you heard anything? I'd love to know more about what's going on here."

He shrugged, "Nothing for us to worry about, I'm sure. We let the sheriff take care of things like that."

She huffed out a large breath. "But don't you ever wonder? You *live* here."

He started to breathe heavier. The supplies were obviously heavy. "Not really."

They arrived at her front door. "All of the supplies can go through here to the back. We have the office and our kitchen back here."

He grunted, and she held open the door.

Eyes watched her. She could feel them, and she turned to see Ray with his arms crossed standing out in front of her building. "Hello."

He nodded. "I see you've met the Halsteads."

"Yes. Are you going to the activity on Friday?"

He raised his eyebrows and then smothered a smile. "Are you?"

"Why the tone of surprise?"

"No, no surprise here. I just might make an appearance." He stepped closer, and her stomach jumped, but then he headed to the sheriff's door. "Have a nice day, ma'am."

"Thank you."

Henry came back.

"Oh, I'm sorry I didn't follow you inside. Thank you for helping me with the delivery and purchases." She stood at his side. "And thank you for the invitation for Friday."

"You're welcome. The activities are a lot of fun. We have some good families here. I think you'll be glad you met us all."

"I know I will. I was beginning to worry when I hadn't seen hardly anyone come in to town, just a few women today in front of the church." She blushed thinking of the girls coming in and out of the saloon but didn't want to mention them.

"I'll see you Friday then. Your window might not come for about ninety days. But we will let you know as soon as it gets here." He turned to leave, then paused. "I can let you know if we ever get any berries." His smile was genuine, and his eyes full of caring.

"I would love that, thank you. And lemons. If you ever get lemons, I would like some."

His face glowed with pleasure. "I can do that." He stepped closer as if to divulge a grand secret. "Our shipments come in on the first of the month, usually by Thursday early morning."

"Oh, excellent. Thank you, Mr. Halstead."

"Call me Henry."

She smiled, unsure she wanted to be on a first-name basis with him. But it sure helped to be friends with the owners of the general store, she decided, and he was a nice enough sort of person. His mother made her a bit nervous perhaps, but Henry seemed harmless.

Ray came out of the sheriff's office, and Henry jumped and then smiled. "Ray!" He held out his hand, which Ray pumped in his own.

"Good to see you, Henry. Did any hammers come with the last shipment?"

"Not yet. But the minute we get some, I'll deliver one."

"Thank you."

"Henry!" Mrs. Halstead called across the street and waved her hands.

"Oh, I better get back." Henry's ears turned red. "I'll see you Friday, Miss Bailey."

"See you then." She smiled and held her hand up to wave.

As soon as Henry was out of earshot, she turned. "So you still go by Ray?"

He considered her, his eyes sparkling. "I do. Ray Trundle."

They stood side by side for a moment while the incredible irony washed over her. Oddly, despite all that had passed between them, the feeling was not unpleasant. A part of her was just plain happy to be back in Ray's presence.

"So are you coming Friday, really?"

"I will."

"Don't you usually?"

"Attend the socials? Not usually." He tipped his hat to her in a mock bow. "I reckon I'll come to see the new girl in town though."

She held her breath, unsure if he was mocking or flirting. "Henry has offered to come walk with me."

"Ho ho! Interested in the store owner's son?" His face mocked her for certain. And for some reason, she found it irritating.

"At least he isn't found robbing trains."

His eyes flashed. "You would be surprised what some of our townsfolk do and don't do." He stood closer, his tall form protective. He looked like he might have said more, but then he squinted off in the distance over her shoulder. The alert tension that filled his frame, stiffening right in front of her eyes, made her nervous. He rested a hand on her shoulder and stared into her face. "Get inside. Go to the back of the office, and don't come out."

"What?" She whipped her head around to see what he saw. A puff of dust rode in their direction.

Ray had taken off running toward the blacksmith's. "Do it, Becky," he called over his shoulder.

She tore into the house, her hands locking the door.

"Rebecca?" Her father peered his head around his desk.

"Lock the back door!" She shouted with enough urgency that he did so.

She ran up the stairs and to the window. *Ray.* She searched the area, desperate for any sight of him. Then a horse whinnied and tore out from Ray's shop. As he rode off, she saw him tie a handkerchief around his face.

"What's going on?"

Rebecca jumped. "Father, the deputy told me to come inside, lock all the doors, and hide." She peered out. "He's concerned about whoever is coming in that dust cloud."

"Will there be something dangerous and life-threatening every week in Grant's Landing?"

"I don't know." The dust cloud grew closer. "But I was invited to a social at the church on Friday night with the shop owner's son."

"Oh?" His pleased smile made her happy.

"Yes. He's an interesting sort of man."

"With a mother like his . . ." He whistled.

"Have you met her?"

"I have. Apparently, she's single. She's acquired her toughness through grit and frontier living."

Rebecca laughed. "You sound like a novel."

"Do I?" He stood taller, then frowned. "But look there."

The dust had materialized into real people on horses, heading straight for town.

But as they grew closer, Rebecca could see no masks at all. Their horses pounded the dirt, growing the cloud around them, and as they came over the next crest, a sheriff's badge glinted in the sunlight.

She leaned forward. "I think . . . that they're good guys?" Her mind spun. But she stayed inside.

"Let's see how this all plays out." He stood partly in front of her, and Rebeca knew he was ready to shield her. She would have done the same for him. She hoped no guns would be fired and that there would be no further need to dive onto the floor this week.

The riders arrived in town, the horses circling in a group while they slowed their pace, snorting and stomping their hoofs.

At last, the men stopped in front of the sheriff's office. "Sheriff Stanford!" a man called out. He was tall. When he took off his hat, his blond hair shone in the sun. His jaw was chiseled, his clothes clean, and when he spoke, Rebecca saw a row of straight, white teeth.

"Who is this?" Her father searched her face, and she looked away.

"Just curious."

"Hmm."

"He wears a badge," Rebecca said.

"I see that." He frowned.

At last, Sheriff Stanford stepped out of his office.

"You have a prisoner here that interests us," the newcomer said.

"I'm sure I do."

"We're here to take him and make him answer for his crimes."

"He'll have a trial," Sheriff Stanford said firmly. "Judge is scheduled to get here one week from Tuesday."

Rebecca turned her head. "Are they talking about our patient?"

"I think so," her father muttered.

"We saw him do it," the newcomer continued. "He robbed the train. More than one man saw him."

Sheriff Stanford folded his arms across his chest. "Tell that to the judge. You're welcome to wait for him."

The new man with the blond hair, who seemed to be the leader, got off his horse and approached the porch. "Stanford." His voice was quieter, but Rebecca heard every word.

He tipped his hat and caught her eye. She almost stepped away from the window but instead stayed. As he stared for a moment, his mouth curled up in a smile. It filled his face, almost reaching his eyes. Then he bowed and winked at her before turning back to the sheriff.

Her father moaned. "I wish that hadn't happened."

"What?" She turned to him. "He's one of the good guys."

He shrugged. "How can we be sure of anything like that out here?"

"Doesn't he seem like a good guy? He's clean and everything."

Father laughed. "Well, he does look as though someone cleans his clothes. I'll give him that. And he takes a stick to his teeth now and again."

"Oh, stop. You know what I mean."

"Hmm."

The men conversed in hushed tones, and then the new man pulled out a piece of paper and put a nail through it on the post in front of the sheriff's office. He turned and hopped on his horse. As the horse circled in place while he finished some kind of conversation with Stanford, he turned to look at Rebecca again, nodded, and then rode away. His whole group of men rode with him.

She exhaled in a long woosh. Who was this new man?

And where was Ray?

CHAPTER SIX

REBECCA BUSIED HERSELF PUTTING DRAPES in windows and unpacking a few more of her personal items. They set up a lovely office and library in the front room that used to be her bedroom. And she found she enjoyed using it as a sitting room. The sun shone brightly in that room, and she was drawn to the window more often than not.

She told herself she wasn't watching for Ray, but he hadn't returned, and she had noticed.

More than once, her thoughts moved to the other sheriff—a strong man keeping the law. It seemed a bit unfair of him to hang a man without trial, but nevertheless, she appreciated someone working for justice. It felt nice, like a blanket of protection had been laid across her shoulders.

Her father had come to join her, and she looked up from her needlepoint. "What do you think of Sheriff Stanford?"

"Stanford? He's a good man. I appreciated very much how he stood up for our patient."

"Because he's our patient?"

"I suppose, yes. But also because it was the right thing to do. It can't have been easy to stand in front of that group of men and deny them what they wanted."

She nodded and considered his words. Soon Father left and readied himself in his office.

Once she'd made things more pleasing to the eye around their new home, she hummed to herself. Her father had a steady stream of patients start to show. Mostly they needed simple fixes, and she hadn't yet been needed to assist in a single one. So she decided to step outdoors for a bit—not to look around for Ray, but just to perhaps take a look at the church. She wasn't even certain of the denomination of the quaint-looking white building.

The warm sun shone on her, and she welcomed the accompanying breeze. She squinted her eyes against the grit that came with every rustle of wind that blew through. Perhaps she too was now covered in a layer of dust. She walked along the front porch of their shared area with the jail to see the paper that other sheriff had posted on their pillar.

Wanted. Ray. But luckily a handkerchief covered his face, a hat covered his hair, and only his eyes peered out. Was it Ray? She felt as if Ray's own eyes bore into her soul. Surely no one else would see it, but to her, the bandit on the train, Ray, stared back at her from the poster.

She looked over her shoulder at the blacksmith shop. She admitted that if she saw Ray, she certainly wouldn't complain. Her feet dragged her in that direction and picked up their pace the closer she came.

But the shop was silent. And when she approached, the bellows was a glowing ember. She walked on past, pushing forward, although disappointed, toward the church. No activity surrounded that building either, but she supposed it would be open.

She pushed the door and blinked several times until her eyes grew accustomed to the dim interior. The church was basically a one-room sanctuary with perhaps some offices behind the sanctuary. Charming stained glass filled the front and gave the pews an ethereal rainbow glow that she found calming. She sat in a pew. The hard wood felt cool, and the room was blessedly quiet and clean.

Memories of her life in Boston flooded her mind. Her sitting room, her friends, her charities, her socials. Ray. Her mind always turned to Ray.

When he'd asked to come call that final Sunday, she'd expected them to meet in their place behind the tree in the very back of her property and go for a walk as usual, but that day, he'd seemed nervous. She closed her eyes and remembered.

"Becky, I can't do it. I can't be what he wants." His gaze had flitted about, a desperation in them she'd not seen before.

"What is it? What can't you do?"

"I just don't want anything to do with Father's business. I learned some things about him I'm not proud of. I don't want his life, his friends, his money, any of it." Then he'd grabbed hold of her hands. "I'm leaving."

"What?" The shock of his statement had hammered through her. "No! Don't do that. You can just tell him what you want, explain yourself. Stay."

He shook his head. "I can't. I just have to go. I've got enough money for a start, but we'd have to start on our own."

Her heart had jumped to her throat. "We?" Her head shook before she could even respond.

"Yes, Becky. I can't leave you. You're all I care for in the world right now."

She'd barely found space for breath; her chest felt so tight.

"Come with me." He got down on one knee. "Please, Becky, come with me. Marry me. We'll go west as far as we can, run from here, and make a life for ourselves, a happy one." His eyes had pleaded with her, large and full of love.

But she'd panicked. "But, Ray, I can't just leave my father. Ray, please. Can we talk about this?"

His hope had dimmed. He stood. "Is that your answer?"

"I can't go with you." The words had come out in a strangled whisper. If she'd had even another day to consider his proposal, she might have taken it, Father or no, but the thought of leaving her only family, the dearest person in her life, all alone in Boston was too much. She shook her head. "I can't leave him here." Her vision completely blurred with tears that fell from her face. "I'm sorry."

He kissed her on the head and then ran from her yard.

She'd never seen him again.

She'd pined for him every day since, until that day on the train.

How could a woman be in love with a bandit? But she didn't know what more to do with her love.

She stood and paced. The awful, terrible irony of it all was that her father had brought her out here anyway. Had she mentioned to him her wishes then, would she have married Ray and still traveled with her father? She hugged her middle. And if she had, Ray certainly would not have become a bandit.

The door in the front of the sanctuary opened, footsteps approached, and Rebecca dove down behind a pew. Being caught thinking her most vulnerable thoughts made her feel bare. But now that she'd ducked low, she felt foolish. How was she to explain a hiding and skulking behavior in the church? She was about to stand again when Ray's voice surprised her.

"They've cut off communication. Judge Willis won't be here for another fortnight at least."

"Can we keep him alive until then?" A voice Rebecca didn't recognize spoke from the front of the room.

"I don't know. Not when they're after my head as well." Ray's voice sounded tense, tight.

"Don't worry about it. No one knows what you look like except me. You're safe."

Ray didn't respond, and Rebecca wanted nothing more than to see his face, but she kept her head down.

They moved away, their voices muffled and quiet until a door shut at the front of the church, and the sanctuary was once again quiet. She waited a moment more in her crouched hiding place.

"Becky." Ray's voice, warm and inviting, surprised her.

She sat up.

He stood only a few pews ahead of her.

"How did you know I was here?"

He grinned, and for a moment, she felt like she was with the old Ray, the one who picked her flowers on the way to their secret meeting places. He'd always been a bit of a contrary person, comfortable hiding from his parents. Perhaps she should have seen the bandit future long before now.

But she could only see him as charming when he smiled the way he was doing right now.

"How did I know you're here?" He stepped closer. "Now, if I answer that question, it might reveal more about me than I'd like you to know."

She moved toward him. "Did I breathe overly loud?"

He shook his head.

"Did I cough or sigh?"

He shook his head.

"Did you see me underneath the pews?"

"No, and I'm certain Haws didn't know you were there."

She crossed her arms, standing right in front of him, almost touching.

And then he leaned forward and rested his face on the top of her head and breathed in. "This." He smiled and stepped back. "You smell of violets. The whole sanctuary smells like you right now."

Her face heated. Her toes heated. Her smile grew before she could stop it. "Really?"

"Yep." He reached for her hand and tugged her to the front pew. "Come on. Let's sit."

She hurried next to him, trying to ignore the million tingling pathways rushing through her hand. Was he going to explain himself?

They sat side by side. He stared up at the front. "Some of my best memories of Boston are with you at church. Even though we never really sat together, I knew you were there. I used to pretend we sang side by side." He shrugged. "Listening to you hum 'Amazing Grace' brought it all back."

Was he feeling repentant? Perhaps ready to straighten up his wayward ways? "You can always come back. No matter how far we've fallen, there's always a path to return." She thought she'd heard their pastor say that a number of times. She imagined it would be true for Ray as much as anyone.

He chuckled. "Do you think me fallen?"

She waited and then sighed. "I don't know. How could I know anything about you? You dropped off the face of the earth. No one at home knows where you are, and then I see you on the train, riding with the bandits? What am I to think?"

"I could ask you the same question. I've never been so afraid as I was the day I came to you, begging you to come with me. And you said no. You said you loved me. You just couldn't live out here, couldn't leave your father." He crossed his arms, still facing the front.

"All of that was true."

Then he turned to her. "And yet here you are." He pressed his lips together. "And with the worst imaginable timing." His eyes turned wide and pleading. He reached for her hands and held them in his own. "I'm in a bit of a bind."

"I saw the wanted poster."

He blinked, and then realization crossed his face. "Exactly. I'm in some trouble. And things are going to get dangerous around here and . . ." He dropped her hands, took off his hat, and ran a hand through his hair. "I need you and your father to leave Grant's Landing."

"What?" Nothing he could have said would have surprised her more. "Why?"

"Because things are about to get bad, really bad. That bullet through your window? That's nothing. Imagine the whole front of the jail and office burning to the ground. It's just not going to be pretty, and you are in the absolute wrong place for what's about to go down."

"What is about to go down?" She sat facing him on their pew. "I think I'd like a bit more of an explanation."

"No. There's nothing more I can tell you. Trust me? Please. Get a place just outside town. There are homes there, some of them abandoned. Just until this trouble passes."

"You're not making any sense."

"It's you I'm worried about. Look, I saw you through the window on the train when I was riding with the bandits. My heart nearly ripped in half. I tore in there as fast as I could. I had to make sure you would be safe. I haven't been able to let you go, Becky, not for one second. But we can't be together, even if you wanted us to be now. It won't work. I can't. But I can't have you in danger either. So please leave."

Rebecca was stunned. "Wait, Ray. I don't understand any of this." Her smile grew. "But you're saying you still have—"

The door at the back of the sanctuary opened, and the hot sun poured in.

"Well isn't this just precious?"

"Don't say anything," Ray murmured to her and then stood and turned.

Rebecca joined him and then gasped. It was that other sheriff—the man who'd put up the wanted poster with Ray's picture.

She looked from Ray back to him. Had the sheriff figured it out?

"What are you doing here, Travis?"

"I'm checking on our prisoner."

"My prisoner."

"Whatever. And I saw something yesterday that interested me." He tipped his hat to Rebecca. "Howdy do, ma'am. I'm Sheriff Travis Milner from Huntcreek."

"Hello. Rebecca Bailey." She smiled.

"Well now, see how friendly our new Miss Bailey is, Ray? Hopefully you're in here taking some lessons, 'cause I sure don't believe for one minute you was praying."

"Miss Bailey was just getting on home." Ray flicked his fingers behind his back, telling her to leave, but every part of her bristled. She stood her ground, looking from one to the other.

"Perhaps I should come calling," Travis said. "Do you think the good doctor would mind?"

"I'm sure he'd be pleased to receive you."

Ray stiffened beside her. Then he moved toward Travis. "Let's go make sure your prisoner is still here."

"Excellent."

Ray tried to get him to move, but Travis turned and waited for Rebecca. And then he bowed for her to pass them out the door first.

The power of the men and their burning competitive intensity almost fired up the ground beneath her. She felt their gazes on her back, so she paused. And then she stepped in between them and placed one of her hands on each of their arms. "Come now. Let's be friendly. Who is this prisoner we're talking about? The nice man my father and I stitched up?"

Travis snorted. "Nice man? He's got a stash of loot 'cause he's robbed so many trains and banks, including yours here in Grant's Landing."

"Has he?" She already knew most of this. "And is he a violent sort?"

"No." Ray's voice was firm.

"Violent enough to threaten everyone around him."

She considered their words as they walked down the street and approached the front of the jail. She stood in front of Ray's picture, her knees shaking. "That's some reward."

"He's the most elusive of them all. He is rumored to have taken a satchel from a woman while she was out walking her baby. He's stolen from the church collection boxes, and he takes from every bank and train we've heard of. Not a stage has passed through our area without a hold-up from the Bullseye Bandit. And he tends to ride with our prisoner inside. We're gonna torture the name of the Bullseye Bandit out of him." Sheriff Travis poked a finger at the Wanted poster. "I will find this bandit if it's the last thing I do, and then the plains of Grant's Landing will once again be safe for pretty ladies like yourself."

She smiled at him while her knees shook. He was incredibly determined. "Well, I, for one, am grateful for the both of you, risking yourselves like you do to keep all of us safe." She curtseyed. "I'll let you go now. I don't much like visiting the jail." She moved toward the doctor's office door, but Travis jumped ahead of her and opened it. "I'll be seeing you later." He winked.

She shared a gaze with Ray, who kept his expression completely blank, but his eyes could have burned a hole in Travis's head. Then she went inside.

The door shut behind her, and she leaned back against it, clutching her stomach. What had just happened?

Ray was the Bullseye Bandit, the most notorious and sought-after criminal in the area? Travis wanted him dead. Ray still loved her? Had he said that, or had he said something more like he couldn't stop thinking about her? Was that any different? He needed her help. To leave? No. She was not leaving.

Her heart hammered in her chest. Every time she saw Ray, her reaction to him grew stronger. She was not going to let him die. Or the man in the prison either, now that she knew they'd ridden together. If he'd ridden with Ray, she could trust him, couldn't she? She shook her head. Nothing was clear or certain any more.

"Everything all right, Rebecca?" her father's voice called out to her.

"Yes, I am well. I'll be upstairs."

She was definitely not well.

CHAPTER SEVEN

ALL DAY SHE'D TRIED UNSUCCESSFULLY to push Ray from her mind, but he showed up amidst the most random thoughts until, while working again on some needlepoint, she decided to stitch him a new handkerchief or two. Would he ever receive these gifts? Probably not, but it would still her mind if her fingers were working on something for him. At least, she hoped so.

When the air turned cooler and she thought it pleasant enough to be out of doors, she grabbed a shawl and went for a walk. She needed to take a turn down the street and back up before dark—when things got a little questionable—and then settle inside with a good book. She headed in the direction of the store. Perhaps Henry had a shipment of books. She'd never considered such a thing before now.

As she approached the door, Henry exited. "Hello, Miss Bailey."

"Why, Mr. Halstead! I was just coming in to see you."

"To see me?" He stood taller. "Well, I've just been given time off from Mother. Would you like to stroll with me?"

"Oh, I'd like nothing more." A sense of relief eased her nervous fluttering. "Thank you."

"How have you been?"

"I've been well. I'm looking forward to Friday when I can meet some others here in Grant's Landing."

"I think everyone is looking forward to meeting you." He nodded.

They walked along and talked of nothing important. He shared with her the woes of working in the store.

"And you wouldn't believe the long tabs we keep for people. Already Mother has said if old Calhoun asks for another pint of anything, we're to say no until he pays off what he owes us."

"Oh, that might be a difficult conversation. Wouldn't it?"

"I don't mind. That man's as mean as a bull, and it's about time he got what's coming." Henry's eyes flashed with anger.

Rebecca was shocked to see it. So, the mild-mannered Henry had a stronger side to him.

They made their way along in front of the church and then turned down the opposite side of the street. The saloon and inn were up ahead, but the noise level was low, and there didn't seem to be a large crowd. Perhaps she'd get some sleep tonight.

But as they made their way in front of the building, the doors flung open, and the two men she'd met when she'd arrived stepped in front of her with a third who looked equally undesirable.

"Excuse us." Henry stepped aside to go around them, wrinkling his nose.

But they moved and blocked her path. "Where are you going in such a hurry?" Moe held out his arm, swaying a little bit. "We still haven't had that stroll."

"I'm with Henry, thank you." She nudged him to try to move again.

But the three men stepped in their path again. "But Moe and I want to introduce you to our friend Cougar." The third she hadn't met yet, Cougar, grabbed hold of her arm.

"This one needs a trip inside the saloon. That'll help her see what's what."

She yelped a little as he dragged her through the swinging doors. The saloon was dark, and it smelled of beer. And other things. She brought a handkerchief up to her nose and tried not to see what went on in such a place. She'd been roundly forbidden from entering all her days and had no desire to see why. But she couldn't very well place a hand over her eyes. The man who'd dragged her in was still dragging.

"My name's Cougar. And you and I are going to sit right over here and get cozy."

"No, really. Cougar, I don't want to be here. Let's go back outside and talk." She yelped again as his grip tightened.

She nearly tripped as they made their way toward a corner table. Cougar was old, but he had a steel grip. Nevertheless, when she was pulled into another girl, only partly dressed, he'd pushed her too far. She wrenched her hand free. "Leave me alone."

His face turned red. When he came closer to try to grab her again, she shoved against him and then doused him with a half-full cup of someone's whisky on a nearby table.

While he was sputtering and fuming, she turned to hurry from the saloon, hoping to never step foot inside again. Checking over her shoulder one time, she picked up her pace and ran right into Ray, Henry at his side. She knew it was him without looking. His smell, his feel, the solid width of his chest. Shame burned inside at being caught in such a place.

"What are you doing in here?" he asked.

"I was invited in. Rather abruptly."

"What does that mean?"

"Someone forced my hand."

His eyes turned steely. "Well, I think it's time you be heading out that door."

"Don't mind if I do."

"What if I say she's staying?" Cougar approached, flexing his hands.

"You can say whatever you want." With a tired sigh, Ray turned toward Cougar. "Don't mean any of us is gonna listen."

The man swayed on the spot, placed his tankard down on the table, and wobbled toward Ray, who used two fingers to knock the man down. Everyone laughed, which made him jump to his feet with a red face and run at Ray.

"Go home and dunk your head in the rain barrel."

"You dunk your head." He swung and missed, circling Ray.

Rebecca, who was halfway out the door, gasped.

Ray glanced at her. While he was looking away, the man took a bottle from the bar and swung it at Ray's face. Ray ducked to miss the connection with his head, but beer sprayed all over him. "Get her out of here!"

Henry jumped and reached for her arm, but she shook her head, refusing to leave.

Ray picked up Cougar by the shirt at his chest, stared up into his face, shook him a little bit, and then shoved him onto the ground. "We finished?"

Cougar started to get up and then fell back down.

"Oh, give up, you old codger."

He turned away.

Ray nodded to the room and then pushed open the saloon doors. He walked in her direction, full of power. His shoulders seemed broader. His eyes were flints of steel.

Rebecca hurried out onto the street, following Ray. Rebecca tried to swallow, but her mouth was suddenly so dry it felt like all the dust from their whole town had come to settle on her tongue.

Ray nodded at Henry. "I'll take it from here. Thank you for coming for me."

Henry turned away with a small smile in her direction.

Ray placed a hand on her arm and hurried her away from the saloon. "It's almost dark."

"I can see that."

"Then what are you doing out here?"

"I was taking a quick stroll with Henry."

He grunted and picked up the pace. "Attending church socials with Henry? Taking strolls with Henry? Mrs. Halstead is going to think you're courting."

She stopped and pulled herself free.

He turned. "Can we keep walking?"

"No."

"No?" He looked around. The square was starting to fill up, the saloon getting more customers. Horses were tied to the front, and more people were coming in.

"I don't like to be dragged places, and so far today, it's happened too many times."

He looked about to argue, but then his face softened, and he stood taller. "I'm sorry. You are absolutely correct. I forget at times where we've come from." He bowed to her and then held out his arm. "Miss Bailey, would you allow me to escort you home?"

He looked so much like the old Ray, the genteel and kind, funny man who'd courted her for years back home in Boston. So much so that she almost forgot where they were for a moment and readily took his arm. "Oh, Ray, why can't it be like it was?"

He didn't answer, and when she looked up into his face, he ground his teeth, his jaw tense and unhappy.

"What is it?"

"I don't know, Becky. You being here is doing all sorts of things to me."

"Like what?"

"Well, like that. How am I supposed to answer a question like that? Why can't it be like it was? Because you said no."

They arrived at her front porch, and he opened the door, waiting for her to go inside.

"But you gave me no time to think. It was all so rushed. You were desperate and in a panic." She stepped closer. "I couldn't leave my father. It was unfair of you to ask."

He closed his eyes. "You didn't even want to talk it through. You said no, and that was it. And I was left to find my way on my own." He shook his head.

"I'm sorry I brought it up, but there you have it. Don't ask questions like that if you don't want the truth."

"The truth? I'd love the truth. Why don't you tell me the truth about what you are doing here?"

His face clouded, and he gestured for her to go inside. "Good night, Miss Bailey."

Once he closed the door, she whispered, "Goodnight, Ray."

"Was that the nice deputy sheriff?" Her father stepped out of the shadows, coming from his office.

She jumped. "Oh, Father, you startled me. Yes, that was Mr. Trundle."

He nodded. "It's late. Shall we make our way upstairs?"

"Yes. I'm tired and wish for bed."

Her father seemed to have much on his mind, and she had no desire to talk about anything, so they separated with nothing more than a quick embrace.

Once she'd climbed into bed and pulled the coverlet over her face, she moaned to herself. Nothing was simple. Nothing. But one thing worried her more than any other: she was falling in love all over again with Ray. Only this time, he was wanted by the law. And he wanted nothing to do with her.

CHAPTER EIGHT

Loud clanging noises from down the street told Rebecca that Ray was in his shop. She tried to work on a bit of ground behind their office. They'd purchased some new seeds through Henry, and she was anxious to get them planted to increase their medicine supply and to give them vegetables to eat. But every clang, every pause was so full of Ray that she almost couldn't bear not being at his side.

Once all the seeds had been planted and watered sufficiently, she stood, wiped her hands, and walked through the center of town. The clanging grew louder. Her heart hammered along with the rhythmic sound of Ray's hammer.

She approached slowly and peeked in at the corner, hoping to remain unobserved for now. His foot pumped a bellows. Fire grew up in front of him. His face was lined with perspiration. His shirt clung to him and was open at the neck. Every muscle of his rippling arms and chest tensed as the hammer went down. The heat from his shop billowed out in waves. She was drawn to him. Pure power moved with those arms, and she wanted to step within them, feel them circle about her. His face was focused, full of concentration. She wanted it focused on her. His mouth pressed together. She wanted it once again, soft and caring, moving over her lips in love. Her whole body moved closer without permission. Ray. She wanted Ray, and at once, she didn't care if he were bandit or sheriff.

As soon as her movement caught his eye, he paused, hammer in the air.

From standing in the heat, sweat now lined her face, her hair was falling flat, and her shirt was sticking to her, but still, she approached.

His face was intense, his eyes searing into her like the fire, and she kept walking. Was he happy for the visit? Annoyed at her presence? She couldn't tell. She stepped around the fire and stood at his side. "Hi." Then she placed a hand on his hammer. "May I?"

He nodded and moved to stand beside her.

She tried to lift it and lower it with the force necessary, but she didn't have the strength. "Would you help me?"

He nodded, then guided her hand on the hammer. She brought it up and then down on a horseshoe. The red-hot metal flattened more with her swing. She raised it again, and with Ray's arms around her, she worked as a blacksmith. The power of each hit vibrated through her arms. The power of the man behind her shook her core. Hit after hit, the glowing metal began to take better shape. They swung with a new unified rhythm, and she was lost to the beauty of it. Ray paused her next motion and put the hammer on the table. His hands went up to her shoulders, and his lips touched her temple.

The cool wave of pleasure rippled through her as his lips pressed against her skin. She leaned into him. Then his arms fell, and he left her standing at his anvil by herself in his shop.

As his figure slipped out a side door, she felt weak, weak with longing for the only man she'd ever loved. And she knew she was his. Come what may, she would be Ray's for the rest of her breathing days, even if he would no longer have her. Even if he was a bandit. She smiled. Maybe she liked bandits. She shook her head. She made her way toward the door through which he'd left and passed a pile of black handkerchiefs. She grabbed one and stuffed it deep inside an apron pocket.

When she stepped outside into the cooler air, Ray was standing on the front porch of the sheriff's and doctor's offices, talking to Stanford. She felt his eyes on her the moment she saw him, but he did nothing more to indicate he'd seen her.

She has halfway across the street when a loud clanging and horse hooves made her run for the general store front. Henry came out to stand beside her as a stagecoach pulled into town.

"Your next shipment."

"Yes." His face had lost some of his usual interest, or perhaps he was distracted by the coach.

"I saw you go into Ray's."

She nodded.

He didn't say anything more. Then his mother shouted, "Go get our shipment, Henry!"

With a tired sigh, he nodded to her, then stepped closer to the coach. "You there! Anything for the store?"

"Yes, we've got a few things."

Henry waited at the base of the coach while a man on top sifted through things.

The coachman gave a loud whistle. "Ray!"

Ray ran across the street and down toward the coach without a glance in her direction. He tucked a package under his arm and headed back to his shop.

Try as he might to push her away, she knew he was affected, and she'd forever be his. He wanted her to leave, but she wasn't going to do that. And there might be a way she could help. She couldn't be sure, but she'd watch for one.

That night, after she'd washed up and changed into a pretty blue dress for the social, she met Henry at her door, and they walked the distance down the street to the church.

Horses and carriages were arriving, and Rebecca was so pleased to see other colorful dresses and families, even a few children. "Oh, look! Where do they all come from?"

Henry smiled. "They have their land, their homesteads here about. We boast the only church for many miles."

"I'm pleased to hear it."

"Yes, most come Sundays. The past two have been disrupted, but it's a sight, one that gives me hope all through the week." He eyed her. "There are good people here in Grant's Landing. They just don't visit town as often as some of the others."

She wanted to laugh at his obvious reference to the saloon crowd, but at the same time, she was grateful for it. "Henry, I'm very happy to hear you say that."

"I thought you might be."

They continued in pleasant conversation until they reached the door of the church. The pews had been moved to the side, a table of food set up along one wall and some instruments ready to play along the back. "What's all this?"

Henry grinned. "Tonight we're having a dance."

"Oh! How wonderful." She turned to him. "Thank you. Thank you so much for bringing a bit of the familiar back into my life."

His cheeks turned crimson, but he held her gaze. "You're welcome."

A group of ladies approached, obviously looking forward to talking with Henry. Rebecca smiled at the realization that he was a sought-after man in these parts.

After he greeted their smiling faces, he turned to her. "Rebecca Bailey is the doctor's daughter. She's new."

"I'm so happy to see other ladies and families. How do you do?"

"Are you staying here in town?" The closest lady had the lightest blonde hair Rebecca had ever seen.

"For now." She pointed back over her shoulder. "We live above the doctor's office."

Their eyes widened.

"So you can see why I would be so relieved to learn of a social. And friends?" Her eyebrows lifted.

They studied her, and the woman closest to her in age nodded. "Most definitely. I'm Joanna. People call me Jo."

Rebecca smiled at that.

"And this is Sally and Melanie. We're sisters."

"It's lovely to meet you. I am looking forward to meeting everyone."

A man stood up at the front.

"That's Pastor Sorenson."

"Welcome neighbors!" he shouted.

Everyone cheered, and Rebecca joined along, feeling much better about her situation. Good people and families filled the space. Men were scarce, but there were some. She craned her neck, looking for her father, and smiled when she saw him enter in at the back.

The pastor waved toward the back. "We have some new folks in town. Dr. Bailey, will you wave?"

Father smiled and lifted his hand.

"Here's our new doctor. He comes with his daughter." The pastor's eyes searched the crowd, and Henry lifted a hand, pointing to her.

"Ah, yes, and there's Miss Bailey. Welcome to you both."

Curious, friendly eyes sought her out, and she smiled.

The pastor finished up his welcome, and the music started.

Henry led her to the middle of the floor. Everyone had cleared a space, and people stood in a line. It looked much like the dances she would do in Boston.

"Just watch the lead couple." Henry smiled.

Her heart felt light. She tapped her feet, waiting.

The door at the back opened again.

Several of the women gasped near her. Chatter began all around.

She peered against the bright sunlight at the back of the newcomer and then smiled. Ray. The widespread reaction to him would have been comical if she hadn't had the same reaction. Her face warmed, but she looked away.

The door shut again, and Ray made his way to the drink table. He greeted many as he went. In his wake, women were left watching after him, some fanning their faces. Rebecca could only laugh. He wore a nice shirt and trousers. He'd washed up, and his hair was combed, his face newly shaven. Rebecca grinned. He looked almost like he had in Boston, except now he was so much more. She could hardly finish her dance as the beacon to stand at his side pulled strongly.

Henry cleared his throat. "It's almost our turn."

"Oh yes." When they moved up to the top of the line, she reached for his hands, and they moved to the center, circling around, then backed up. She did the same with the next man, and the dance went on.

After a time, she felt Ray's eyes on her. Her gaze flitted up to his face. He'd moved to the corner, but as their music came to a close, he stepped forward to make his way toward her.

She turned back to Henry, and they finished their movement down the line. She curtseyed to him. "Thank you."

His grin was contagious, and soon he was surrounded by hopeful women. She laughed. How fitting that he should be so sought after.

Ray stood at her side. Somehow, he'd made it to her as the music for the next song started. It had the three-step beat of a waltz but with plenty of fiddle and country flair. She smiled.

He bowed as if they were in Boston, though they'd never attended a dance together. "Would you like to dance?"

She held out her hand. "I would love to."

When he encircled her in his arms, cradling her hand out to their side, she felt everything in her world shifting into place. He led her about the room in their limited space as one would expect a Boston-bred man to do. She felt almost as if she were flying. "Oh, I've missed this."

He raised an eyebrow. "By *this*, do you mean dancing? Or do you mean dancing with me? Since we've only danced the one time . . . and not in a ballroom."

A thrill rose up inside that he would mention their past life. "The moonlight was perfect."

"Everything was perfect." His mouth smiled, but his eyes looked fatigued. And the lines on his face became more prominent to her view.

"Are you well? What can I do?"

He held her closer. "Right now, this is all I want in the world." He smiled down into her face. "But tomorrow, I need you on the stage out of here."

She started. "I cannot."

"What? Why, Becky? Please."

"I won't. I lost you once. I won't again." She lifted her chin, a sudden stubbornness strengthening her resolve. "You and Father are all I have."

His eyes lit with the spark of happiness she used to see when they met. "While it means everything to hear those words, you must hear me now: you must go. Things are not as they seem."

A couple danced near them, laughing loudly. Rebecca was jarred into the realization that she and Ray were not alone. "Can we talk about this? Meet me tonight. Come to the back door."

He hesitated, but the yearning in his eyes told her he would agree. "I cannot tell you what hour."

"I'll wait."

He sighed.

"Again, I see you two together. Perhaps I should be jealous?" Sheriff Travis Milner leaned closer to them while his dance partner laughed, obviously delighted to be in his arms.

Ray stiffened but then let a mask descend. "We have found the prettiest girls in the room no doubt." Ray's smile was a perfect façade, and Rebecca was astounded he managed it when moments before he had looked as though the world would end. He pressed fingers into her shoulder, gently, and she jumped in. "Oh, you are a tease. And here I was thinking we've found the handsomest men in the room." She laughed overly loud. Too much? But Ray's amused expression put her at ease.

The music sounded as though it was wrapping up.

"Then we should switch? If the ladies are willing?" Travis looked at his partner, who nodded dreamily into Ray's face.

Rebecca almost snorted, but instead, she said, "Sounds good to me." She left Ray's arms unwillingly, the air feeling colder the farther she moved from him.

Sheriff Travis's face smiled down into hers. "And now everyone will wish to be standing where we are."

She laughed but was not really amused.

He lifted his chin, his gaze sweeping the room. Then he turned to her. "They say this bandit lives among us. He could be in the room right now."

Her heart hammered, but she scoffed. "There aren't many men here. Perhaps he is in the saloon though? I find that more likely."

He nodded, thoughtful. "You are right. Here we have lawmen, the clergy, a shopkeeper, and a few landowners. But all the same, we must seek him out."

His eyes turned, calculating. Instead of saying more on the subject, he smiled down into her face. "And how are you liking Grant's Landing? Much different from Boston, I gather?"

"Oh, very different." She shook her head. "This gathering is the first similarity to home I've experienced."

"But there are positive differences. How many times in Boston can you ride out on a horse over the countryside?"

"Never, but I confess I haven't done such a thing here either."

His eyebrow raised. "We can remedy that tomorrow if you'd like. Would you want to go riding with me?" His grin started slow, and she could see how many a woman would be lost in his charm.

"I'd like that. Thank you."

"I'll be by with a pretty mare in the morning while it's still cool."

He led her around the room in a fun country-type shuffle. She smiled and laughed and joked with others as they passed. But her heart longed for Ray, and even though she did not look for him, she always knew where he was in the room.

When they were finished, Sheriff Travis brought her to her father. Impressive. If he wasn't trying to hunt down Ray, she might have been interested in knowing this man more. He reached out a hand. "Doctor Bailey, I'm Sheriff Travis. It's good to meet you."

"Yes, you too. Thank you for your work keeping us all safe."

"You're welcome, sir. And thank you for yours helping us stay healthy."

He nodded.

"I'd like to come by and take Miss Bailey riding, if that would be all right with you, sir?"

Father appraised him for a moment and then nodded. "I know she'll be in good hands."

"The best, sir. I'll keep her safe."

"I appreciate it."

Henry returned, asking for a dance, and Rebecca went back out to the floor. She didn't talk with Ray again in the church, but she was already counting the moments until he would come by that evening. She had no way of knowing what time, and they had much to discuss. Something told her she wouldn't be sleeping very much.

CHAPTER NINE

THE NIGHT HAD GONE QUIETLY; even the saloon seemed to have gone to sleep before Ray's soft tap brought Rebecca to the door.

He slipped inside, and she fell into his arms.

His hands were hesitant, but after a moment, they cradled her and ran up and down her back like they used to.

"Ray." She buried her face in his chest.

"Mmm?" He rested his chin on her head.

"What are we going to do?"

He held her closer, as if he would never let go, and then he held her hand in his and led her to the chairs at their table. "Is your father sleeping?" His voice was hushed, his eyes full of caring.

"Yes, he's been quiet up there for hours." She slid a plate over to him—tarts she'd made yesterday to remind her of Boston.

"Now this I've missed." He took a bite and closed his eyes with a smile. "There are times when I kick myself. To think of the life I could be living in Boston. Tarts every day if I wanted, my horse, my car." He shook his head. "I had a car."

She watched him, holding her breath. "I miss the parks. They were so green." She smiled. "Am I covered in dust?" She lifted her arms to look at her gown.

"What? No, I don't think so."

She shook her head. He wouldn't see it. Everything around them was covered in dirt, the very grit that blew across the plains every day. Then she smiled. "And the breeze off the ocean." She breathed in as though to smell the sea. "All that water."

He studied her. "Are you happy here?"

Surprised at his question, she paused. "I think I could be. We could build a life for ourselves, find a cottage with a stream, plant our herbs." She lifted her eyes, "With you here, happiness is easier to imagine." She held her breath, waiting for his response. She'd never felt so bold before. But she'd never felt like this before either.

He closed his eyes, pain clearly visible, and she wanted more than anything to wipe it away. "You're killing me, Becky. Where were these declarations when I most needed them?"

His words hurt, but she could do nothing about the past. "Perhaps now is when you most need them."

He shook his head. "I don't know how that would ever be the case." He toyed with the plate. "What did you think of Sheriff Travis?"

A bit unsettled by the change in conversation, she thought through her response carefully. "I can see why many a woman would fall for his charms."

He studied her.

"But I can never truly trust the man who so desperately wishes to hang the Bullseye Bandit."

"Even when the Bullseye Bandit is a known criminal caught in the act of robbing?"

"Not caught." She reached for his hand and held it in her lap, studying his fingers.

"True, never caught." He held very still.

She brought his hand up to her mouth and pressed her lips to his knuckles. "I cannot believe it. I refuse to believe that the bandit is what people say he is." She stared into his eyes, dared him to challenge her.

But he said nothing.

When she kissed his second knuckle, his eyes lowered to her face. Before she could press her lips to the third, he tugged her to her feet, gently cupped her face in his hands, and then brushed his lips against hers.

She responded immediately, as if she'd been waiting for this moment her whole life. Her arms went up around his neck. She kissed him back, over and over, soft, urgent, pleading. *Stay. Be mine. Stay. Marry me.* "I love you," she mumbled.

He paused. "What?"

She sucked in her breath. "Did I say that out loud?"

"I think you did." His mouth curved up in a smile. Then he kissed her again, two times, long, drawn out, as though he never wanted to quit. "I love you too."

"Then stay. Or let's go. Just don't leave me again."

He shook his head, a long exhale draining out. "Again, words I longed to hear at any other time." He closed his eyes for a moment and then lifted her hand to his lips. "Listen to me. Please trust me. I must finish what I've started here. I have to see it through. I took a great risk. If I make it through . . ."

She gasped. Fear filled her heart.

"If . . . then I'll come for you. You, me, and your father will make a life for ourselves. Even if I have to go back to Boston, we will find a way." His eyes spoke his sincerity. His hands gripped hers. She didn't understand. She couldn't accept anything but his constant presence at her side. "Why can't we run now? Ride the next train?"

He shook his head. "Your words are torture to me. Please. Cease." The lips he pressed to her forehead were soft, pleading. Then he stepped away and out the door before anything else was said.

She decided then and there that Ray was going to make it through whatever it was he had to do. And she was going to help him.

Sleep came slowly, and when she finally closed her eyes, it felt but moments later that the general store rooster was waking her up. Really? Did they need a rooster? Perhaps she would offer to buy the creature and cook it up for dinner.

But she arose, readied herself in riding clothes and prepared a bit of food for her father. After a moment busying herself, she made a rash decision. Stepping outside her front door, she made her way to the Wanted poster, tore it down, and stepped back inside her home. Then she tossed the poster into the fire. Step one to outright war against anyone who would dare to capture Ray. She laughed to herself. What had come over her?

As she closed her eyes and remembered his soft mouth on hers, she knew exactly what.

Her father was up and in his office with a patient before Sheriff Travis came knocking on the front door.

She stepped out into the light. The early-morning hours were still cool, and she was grateful. "Hello." She smiled. "I'm so excited to be up on a horse again."

He tipped his hat to her. "We will be off in a moment. But first I have to take care of something." He reached in his satchel and pulled out a paper, then walked to Sheriff Stanford's door. When the man stepped out, rubbing sleep from his eyes, Travis held up the paper. "Please see that this gets posted once again." He pointed to the post where the other had hung.

Rebecca hid her smile.

Stanford just took the paper and closed the door, mumbling to himself.

When Travis returned, he lifted the reins from the post. "This is Checkers. She's the sweetest, softest ride I've ever seen."

"Oh, thank you." Rebecca grinned and allowed him to lift her up in the saddle. She adjusted her seat. The horse tapped her hooves a few times, and then she followed Travis out in a walk. He led her right down the center of their street. And when he waved at Ray in his shop, she suspected the reason.

Ray's eyes followed her. She casually put a hand over her heart, and then they were out of sight.

As soon as they had left town and there was nothing but open prairie all around, Travis turned back and grinned at her. "You ready?"

"So ready!" she called.

And he took off.

Checkers jumped to follow with the tiniest nudge of Rebecca's foot, and both horses were racing across open land.

For a moment, Rebecca forgot her suspicions, her worries, even her move to Grant's Landing, and just enjoyed the air, the beauty around her, and the feeling of flying across the prairie.

"I love this!" she shouted with arms stretched wide to her sides. The horse's smooth gait beneath sent a wave of exhilaration through her.

Sheriff Travis turned, and his face lit with a look of appreciation, the kind she would just as soon avoid. He guided his horse to ride beside her. "There's nothing more beautiful to a man than a woman who loves to ride."

She smiled and looked away, then vowed to keep her moods more temperate for the rest of the outing.

He pointed up ahead, and they both slowed as they arrived at what looked like a delightful oasis amid the waving grasses of the prairie: a cluster of tall trees, shade, a bit of green, and a stream.

"This is beautiful."

He stood at her side, reaching up to help her down.

Oh, help.

She reached her hands down to the tops of his shoulders.

When he lowered her, though, he was a gentleman and soon offered her his arm. He led her closer to the trees and the stream. Then he dug around in his satchel and pulled out a blanket and a wrapped parcel of food. "It's not much, but perhaps we can enjoy a small picnic before riding back."

"This is really special. Thank you, Sheriff Travis."

"Please just call me Travis. I'm not always the sheriff."

"Aren't you?"

"Well, I suppose I am. But to you, I could also be Travis?" She didn't respond to his hopeful expression, so he continued. "There's good news about riding with a sheriff; you will always be safe with me." He organized the things he brought.

"My father and I were talking about just how much we appreciate knowing we are in good care. You really take your job seriously. I've never seen such a commitment to finding one bandit."

"And we'll find him." He handed her some breads and cheeses. "Now, I don't want to alarm you, but I've confirmed he's in your community like we thought."

She swallowed a large lump of cheese and winced as it pushed its way down her throat. With watering eyes, she pressed on her chest. "Do you think it's someone I see every day?"

He shook his head. "I doubt you would be in any of the places he would spend his time." His eyes sharpened. "Although, if you wouldn't mind keeping your ears open, sometimes men say things around a pretty lady, thinking that she's harmless."

She nodded. "If I hear or see something, should I just tell Sheriff Stanford?"

He shook his head adamantly until he'd swallowed his bit of bread. "Tell me and only me. I don't want to further alarm you, but I don't trust Stanford. He's so hesitant to hang a man who's so obviously guilty that I have to wonder if he's delaying, waiting for a rescue plan. Could he be in league with the robbers?"

She opened her mouth in disbelief.

"I'm not accusing the man. I think he's a decent-enough sort of person but misguided and soft. You're new to these parts, but the good folks of Grant's Landing are tired of cowering in fear. Why do you think you never see anyone in town?"

She nodded. "It's a shame. I was so pleased to see so many good people at the church social."

"All those people used to walk the streets of town, but the town attracts an unsavory group now."

The more he talked, the more she suspected him to be a decent-enough man, though misguided as far as her Ray was concerned.

"Well, as loathe as I am to end such a moment with a beautiful woman, duty calls."

"Oh yes, of course." She dusted off her hands.

He stood and offered his hand.

When she stood, he was closer than she expected. "Thank you." She stepped back.

"I'd like to call on you again if I might?"

She lifted her lashes. "Come call on Father and me anytime." As they packed up the remains of their lunch, she smiled. "What are we going to do to trap this bandit?"

"Now, I'm happy you're aware and keeping a look out for me, but that's all I want you to do. This rascal is dangerous. He's proven himself able to get out of the worst scrapes, steal whenever he wants, and leave destitution and unhappiness behind. He's not to be trusted."

She nodded. "I understand. Thank you for being so strong in the face of danger."

He stood close, ready to help her back up on her horse. "One thing we hope to do is attend more social gatherings around town—try to catch him when his guard is down. Sometime, somewhere, he's gonna slip up, and one of us is gonna be right there listening."

A slice of fear tore through her. How close were they to overhearing a conversation between her and Ray? As soon as she could, she'd warn him.

The sound of horse hooves interrupted them. She craned her neck, and Travis stepped in front of her with a hand on his gun belt.

She peeked around his shoulder and smiled.

Ray rode up. He dipped his head. "Travis."

"What is it?"

"The judge has arrived."

Travis started and leapt up on his horse. He was about to take off, then he turned back to Rebecca. "Would you mind if Deputy Sheriff Trundle escorted you back? I need to return to ensure a criminal gets his due."

"I shall be in good hands, I'm sure." She nodded and gave what she thought was an encouraging smile, and then he took off at a gallop back across the prairie.

As soon as he was gone, she turned to Ray. "He's got spies everywhere, looking for you, especially at socials, hoping you slip up." She clasped her hands together.

He hopped down off his horse. "And why should that concern me one whit?"

She tipped her head. "What if you slip up?"

He lifted an eyebrow and then reached for her hand. "I won't."

As her fingers laced through his, she almost believed him. When they were together, it seemed as though the world would wait and nothing could ever go wrong. But she knew she'd spend half of tonight worrying for him.

He led her along the riverbed.

"What are we doing?"

"What do you mean?" He chuckled.

"Shouldn't we be getting back?"

"To see the judge?" He snorted.

"Is he not there?" She opened her mouth, shocked that he would make something like that up.

"Oh, he's there, but he's tired. He went straight to his bed and refuses to hear the case until early tomorrow."

Her smile grew. "You knew."

"Of course."

"And you sent him off."

"Again, of course."

She shook her head, her grin growing. "But what if I was getting some good information out of him?"

"I was more worried about you watching him with starry eyes. Left too long in such a romantic place with his charming mug talking at you, who knows what you might start to think. What if he came off as the good guy all of a sudden?"

She stepped nearer, looking up into his face. "I've already decided."

"What's that?" He tucked a flyaway hair behind her ear.

"Bandit or not, I'm with you."

"Even if I'm the bad guy?" His eyes crinkled in part amusement, part worry.

"I will never believe that."

He nodded in relief. "Very good." He led her along, then he turned. "Look. The trial tomorrow—it might get bad."

"I'm not leaving."

He sighed. "Of all the stubborn . . ." He ran a hand through his hair. "Well, at least move yourselves away from the jail cell. Stay in my place, you and your father." The pleading in his eyes gave her pause.

"What do you expect to happen?"

"I can only guess, but we can't let that man hang. If it comes to it, I'm riding out of town with him on my horse."

She choked and for many moments couldn't speak. "Are—Are you certain?"

"I am." He shook his head. "I know I'm asking a lot of you here. I know I'm giving you nothing to go off of. You've got no reason to trust me at all. But you'll help me and keep me safe if you just stay put in my place until this whole thing blows over, no matter what." He held up a finger and gently touched the tip of her nose. "No matter what. I can't have you thinking you need to go rescuing any bandits."

"What if I like bandits?"

"Even so. And I sincerely hope there is only one bandit on all this Earth that you like."

She considered. "True enough. I have discovered my taste in bandits limited to the worst, most-wanted bandit of all time, the Bullseye Bandit."

"Nothing could make me happier." He grinned. "One day, I hope to be able to explain all of this to you."

"I'll be waiting for that day."

He led her back. "I won't hold you to that. Things are going to get a whole lot worse before they ever get better, if they do." His eyes caught hers, and she saw the seriousness of his situation. She knew he was expecting a great risk, and she didn't even know what the risk was.

"Tell me."

He shook his head. "I've said all I can." He pulled her close. "But this is something I never expected. Having you back in my life has made me happier than I knew I could be. I go into this not knowing how it will turn out, but happy that at least before I go, I held you once more. Thank you for that."

Her heart clenched in fear, but she said nothing more, just stood up taller to meet his lips on their way to hers.

She pulled him as tightly to her as she could. He kissed her again and again until her legs hardly held her weight, and then he led her back to her horse.

As he lifted her up into the saddle, he shook his head. "I'd like to send my fist into Travis's face for thinking he could help you up on a horse."

She laughed. "I barely endured his hands."

"That's what I like to hear." He threw his leg up onto his horse, and they both began at a walk. "I do have to get back, but I'd like this time to never end."

"I feel the same way." She winked. "But . . ." She kicked at her horse and took off across the meadow, shouting, "Wooooo!"

"Hiya!" he shouted behind her, and their horses raced, side by side, egging each other on, flying faster and faster. She felt free. And strong.

His grin could not get any wider. She laughed into the wind. And if nothing else made them happy ever again, she would treasure this moment forever.

As they arrived at Grant's Landing, the town seemed as sleepy as ever. She dismounted and tied Travis's horse to the post outside the sheriff's office. His horse was still there. Loud voices inside made her wince, but Ray just shook his head and winked. "I'll see you later. I'll find you. If I'm free, I'll find you. I promise."

The finality of his words brought the fear up into her throat, but she refused to heed it.

CHAPTER TEN

THE NEXT MORNING, REBECCA AROSE early. She had decided to keep her word to Ray and move into the blacksmith shop as soon as it got dangerous. In order to convince her father, she'd spent the evening explaining to him the whole situation with Ray except for his true identity: the Bullseye Bandit, the other man in prison, and Sheriff Travis's fixation on capturing Ray, though Travis didn't know it was Ray he was fixated on.

When she had finished, her father had stared at her for one very long moment and then asked, "And how do we know that this Ray person is trustworthy? There seems to be a lot going against him, all of it from appropriate legal channels."

She sighed. She hadn't told him who Ray really was or of her original relationship with him. And she wasn't quite sure how to explain it to him now. "Honestly, Father, I don't entirely know. But I have feelings for Ray, and I support him, even if . . ." She swallowed. "Even if he is the Bullseye Bandit." For a long moment, she couldn't look up, but when she forced herself to look into her father's eyes, she saw only compassion.

He nodded. "Thank you for your honesty. He does seem an honorable man even on his Wanted poster." Then he chuckled. "How odd the frontier is turning out to be." Then he leaned forward. "But you mustn't put yourself at risk. We are here to mend and heal, and we will continue to do so."

"Father, Ray wants us to leave early tomorrow morning and spend the day above his shop. He doesn't think the jail or our office will be safe places during the trial."

His brows had furrowed, but then he nodded slowly. "Very well."

Early the next morning, thinking over their conversation, she was amazed at how well her father had taken the news of Ray. She was about to wake him. The sun had just barely made an entrance, and just a glow of light, at that. They still had four hours until anyone else would be awake.

Movement down the street caught her eye. A figure snuck around Ray's shop. She looked closer—Ray.

She grabbed her shawl and slipped out her front door without thinking. Shadows hid her somewhat from others' view. She slipped along as quickly as she could after Ray. She knew where he was heading on foot: the church.

Her heartrate picked up the closer she got to the building. He moved along the side to the opposite door.

She waited so he couldn't turn around and see her, and then she slipped after him, hurrying as fast as she could.

The other side of the small chapel had an entrance. It looked like it was meant for the pastor or other workers or staff. It was a small door, almost unnoticeable.

She slipped inside and closed it as quickly as possible. Voices carried to her—hurried, urgent sounds.

As soon as she moved close enough to hear, she froze.

She peered around the corner. Ray spoke with two other men in badges.

One of the men clasped Ray on the shoulder. "You've done good work here. We have what we need, and you can step aside, build a life for yourself."

"General, sir, with all due respect, the situation has become urgent. We have no more time. We need to move in on Travis or we'll lose a good man already in jail too long." The hint of pleading in Ray's voice clenched Rebecca's heart.

The general said something, but his back was to Rebecca, so she couldn't make out the words. Then the general and the man who was with him exited out the front of the church. She watched Ray for a moment. He stood tall with purpose. She was so proud of him. He was working for a general? To bring in the real bad bandit—Sheriff Travis? She sucked in her breath. To think she'd been out riding and dancing with a real bandit. And Ray hoped to bring him in? The man had power, and he had the entire county fooled. It was a dangerous prospect, just as Ray said. Fear filled her, fear for Ray. She stepped forward, ready to run to him, to beg him to run away instead of face this day. But just as she was about to reveal herself, a door on the other side opened, a door she didn't know existed.

Ray whirled around, tied a black handkerchief around his face, and raised a hand in greeting.

A group of five mangy-looking men in handkerchiefs similar to Ray's circled around, and he did some kind of secret handshake with them all. Then he said, "Sheriff Travis is your man. I have our proof. He's your traitor."

Rebecca gasped.

"He's double-dipping. We have enough evidence. He runs our gang, and he's out for blood. He knows I know too much. He just doesn't know it's me."

A hand clamped over her mouth. "But I do now." Travis's whisper in her ear sent panicked screams into his hand. But he effectively stifled any sound. "He doesn't know what he's talking about. I'm no bandit. But hush now or your boyfriend dies." He held up a gun, pointing it at the cluster of men in the chapel.

She held her breath, willing Ray to say nothing more that would incriminate him further.

He shook hands with the men and looked like he might be walking in her direction. Travis pushed her back through a door behind them. They were in the praying room for the pastor. A step and an altar of sorts with a large Bible were all the room had space for, but Travis pressed them inside while they waited for the men to pass. He leaned forward over her body as her back pressed into the Bible behind her. "Someday I'd like to repeat this closeness." He winked.

She looked away, suddenly ill.

Sounds of the outer door closing sent Travis opening their small door. He exited the prayer room. She ran after, but he pushed her back inside and then closed the door on her before locking her in. She pounded on the door and tried the knob, jerking it with all her strength. But her efforts were futile. Resting her forehead on the door, she forced herself to think. Travis was the true bandit. Ray was trusted by a gang of bandits and the local general. Someday he would be revealed. Travis was leaving to reveal Ray. She pounded again, crying out at the pain in her hands.

Her heart pounded. She refused to give up. She turned. The room had nothing . . . but there was a drawer under the Bible. She pulled it open and dug through the papers and the quill, hunting. Nothing. She slid down to the floor, knees to her chest, staring up at the ceiling. Time passed. She had no idea how much. The sound of horses racing by filled her with a new panic. Had they come to get Ray? Her eyes lifted to the desk. Surely there was a key somewhere. She twisted her body to see beneath it, and there! A key hung on a hidden hook under the drawer. Relief coursed through her. Her fingers shook as she lifted it and fit it in the lock in the door. It turned. She breathed out in relief and ran from the room, stumbling out the back door and around the front of the building.

She lifted her skirts, racing down the street and through the center of town. A crowd had gathered in front of the jail. She raced to the edges, pushing through the bystanders until she stood in front in time to see Ray, tied up, being shoved out in front of a man dressed in a black suit. The judge? The man she and her father had healed stood at Ray's side.

Then Travis exited the sheriff's office. "I have just received evidence with my own eyes that this man here, this Ray Trundle, is none other than the elusive Bullseye Bandit!"

The crowd gasped.

The judge frowned. "I came to hear the evidence for one man, this Johnny Dunworthy. Not to judge a trial for the Bullseye Bandit."

"But how provident that you are here now to judge both." Sheriff Travis smiled, and Rebecca wanted to punch him.

"What evidence do you have? Is it sufficient for a trial?"

"My own eyes and an admission from his own mouth."

The crowd gasped again.

The judge frowned. "With only one man to witness, we would need something else. Has anyone else seen the Bullseye Bandit who can testify? Or have you confiscated anything from his person? Any evidence? Any items stolen?"

"No, nothing."

"He's a liar!" Rebecca shouted.

Ray's eyes immediately met hers, and he shook his head, subtly but enough. She didn't care. She was not watching this judge rule against Ray.

"Ah, the other witness." Travis beckoned her forward.

She shook her head and realized her mistake. "I'm no witness. This man is lying to save his own skin. He's the bandit."

The crowd laughed.

The judge called her forward. "Those are tall accusations. Have you any proof?"

She opened her mouth and then closed it. "I don't."

"But she does have a knowledge, just as I, about the identity of this man, Ray," Travis said.

She shook her head. "I don't."

"But you do know him?" the judge asked.

"As does everyone else in this town. He's our deputy sheriff and blacksmith."

"And you have no reason to believe he's the Bullseye Bandit?"

Her heart hammered. She panicked. Nothing came to mind. She knew he was the bandit.

"Rebecca, what is going on out here?" Her father stepped forward, next to the man they'd healed, Johnny Dunworthy.

"Father, they're trying to put Ray and Johnny on trial for being bandits."

"Why, that's ridiculous. Sir, if you need a character reference for this man, Ray, here, I've known him and his family since he was a young boy."

She gasped, and Ray couldn't have looked more surprised.

"Oh, that's excellent. Tell me about him."

"He's the son of Randolph Harrison."

He knew! Rebecca couldn't think another thought. Her mouth went dry from hanging open. He'd known all this time.

"Renowned barrister and businessman in Boston. He's known all over that part of the country. Well respected. And here, Ray's been nothing but upstanding and helpful. He's our assistant sheriff. He's fair, and he's a hard-working blacksmith. There is no way this man is a bandit."

"And the other man?"

Her father shook his head. "Him I know nothing about. But if Ray vouched for him, I'd believe him."

The judge considered her father.

Sheriff Travis stood in front of the judge. "We don't have a courthouse, but we could use the jail and the sheriff's office for our official proceedings." He gestured inside. "If you'd like to follow me."

"I thought you'd preferred to have the proceedings out here."

She pointed her finger. "It's because he's lying, and he doesn't want to hear the truth from anybody else."

Ray shook his head at her, more obviously this time.

The judge turned to her. "Young lady, while I appreciate your defense and your energy, you are speaking out of turn. And since you've already stated that you don't know the suspect any more than the next person, you can have nothing further to add." He stepped forward. "Perhaps it would be best to proceed inside."

Sheriff Stanford held the door open for them, and everyone moved inside. Sheriff Travis narrowed his eyes and then motioned to two men from the crowd. They stood on either side of Rebecca and ushered her inside with them. She resisted, but then her father joined her at her side, so she allowed herself to be ushered in.

Once inside, Sheriff Travis's men stood on either side of her and her father, who turned and gave her a warning look. If Ray didn't come out on top here, he would be hanging from a noose. And now Rebecca had endangered her own life and her father's as well by betraying Travis, by revealing she knew his true motives.

She sought Ray's gaze, but he was conversing rapidly and intensely with the man at his side. She had no idea how they were getting out of this mess, but she had something else to discuss with her father.

"Father," she whispered, "you knew he was Ray Harrison?"

"Of course."

"Why didn't you tell me?"

He clucked, and she turned to look him in the face. The sadness she saw there clenched in her throat. "The question is why didn't you tell me?"

He knew.

"How long have you known?" she asked.

"Since your first meeting behind the tree in our backyard."

"What?" She couldn't believe it. "Why didn't you say anything or invite him in?" She laughed.

"I thought you would tell me. I thought there would come a time, but then he disappeared." His eyes held hurt, enough that it tore at her.

"I'm sorry. I'm so sorry I didn't confide in you. I lied to you so many times." She felt so ashamed to think of all the times she'd deceived her father.

"But he is a good man."

"Yes, he is." She turned to Ray. Their eyes caught. For a moment, she was brought back to their last moments together in Boston. She placed her fingers at her lips. Then he turned away, and the impossibility of their situation crowded back around her. She wrapped her arms around herself and shivered.

Sheriff Stanford, Johnny, Ray, Travis, and the judge conversed together.

They spoke in undertones she couldn't make out. But at length, they must have come to a decision, for the judge stood taller and, in an official voice, said, "I wish further deliberation and further witnesses before I can make any decision about one Ray Trundle or Ray Harrison as has been presented. Verifying his identify from Boston might take several weeks."

"And the other prisoner. Surely you've had witness enough to sentence him?" Sheriff Travis looked as though he might explode.

"I do not. For as the doctor suggests, if Ray vouched for him, he might have a case for himself. But the veracity of Ray's testimony is dependent upon verification of his identity, which, again, comes from Boston."

Travis frowned. "Very well." He waved a hand. "Until then, these men are staying in a jail cell."

Sheriff Stanford stepped forward. "You don't have jurisdiction here. You can't make those kinds of decisions."

"But I do." The judge nodded. "And I'd like Ray confined to this building, if not the cell, and Johnny Dunworthy, of course, back in his cell."

Stanford nodded. "Yes, sir."

The judge stood up to leave.

Ray cleared his throat. "Before you leave, Your Honor, if I might?"

"Yes?"

"I think the young lady and her father need some protection tonight."

The judge considered Rebecca, turned back to Ray, and then nodded. "Sheriff Stanford, see that they have a man."

He raised an eyebrow. "Done."

Sheriff Travis clenched his fist and stood as close as he could to Ray.

Rebecca stood closer to her father.

"You're going down, Ray Harrison. Don't think you can double cross me and get away with it. Let it be known this is what will always happen to those who double cross me." He turned his eyes to Rebecca.

She cowered behind her father.

Where once his eyes had been warm and charming, they were now cold and ruthless. Looking back at Ray, he continued. "There is no guard that can protect you from justice when it is at last delivered." He turned on his heel and left the room, his men following.

She let out her breath and leaned on her father's arm. "What will we do?"

Ray nodded to Sheriff Stanford, then turned to her and her father. "I'll be staying with you."

"What?" she half protested with a half-smile.

Stanford hooked his thumbs in his belt loops. "I was told to assign a man to protect you."

"And I was told to stay in the building." Ray shrugged. "But this doesn't help Johnny, and tonight, they're coming for all of us."

CHAPTER ELEVEN

ONCE EVERYONE HAD LEFT THE jail-turned-courthouse, Ray, Rebecca, and her father slipped out the back door of the jail and into the doctor's office. Father led them through the place, up the stairs, and into their library.

"If you two will please take a seat."

Rebecca sat, and Ray moved a chair to sit right beside her. He reached for her hand. "Sir, I would like to apologize for not coming to you to court Rebecca properly."

Her father nodded.

"I can't believe you knew," Rebecca said. "I'm sorry too, Father. Ray wanted to keep it a secret from his family. He thought it would have harmed your business if the Harrisons didn't approve of our relationship."

Her father cleared his throat. "Ray, I wasn't certain what kind of man you were, hiding about with my daughter. But when you left, the light left her eyes, and even a year later, it had not returned. So I conducted my own search for you. It took some time, but once I found your location, it was simple enough to seek a position as Grant's Landing's doctor. They were in desperate need, as I'm sure you know."

"What? Father, you moved out here to be by Ray?"

"Naturally." His eyes welled up. "When you turned down happiness with the man you love so that I wouldn't be left alone, you thought you were doing the right thing, but squelching your own path to please mine would never do."

"And what about you? Do you not prefer to be in Boston?"

He smiled. "I do. But this life on the frontier has been eye opening in many ways and has improved my abilities. When we return, I shall be all the better for it."

Her mouth dropped. "Return?"

He turned his perceptive eyes on Ray. "Why did you leave?"

"Sir, if I may, I want to thank you for coming out here, for bringing Becky, but I'm afraid you may have put yourselves greatly at risk."

"Yes, we'll talk about that. First, your reasons for leaving Boston."

He looked away. "The more I think on them, the more I realize I could have fought Father and created my own path in Boston."

"I'm not sure you could have then. Now, certainly, with the courage and grit of two years on the frontier, you will have no problem, but then?" Father shook his head.

Ray sat taller, seeming to gain strength from Rebecca's father's support. "Father had my life all mapped out, including negating any choice I might have in marriage. I felt restricted, trapped, unhappy. Once I met Becky, I knew I couldn't marry anyone but her, but even then, I tried to find a way, any way to remain. Then I stumbled upon a meeting Father was having with some local disreputes. I learned of his shady dealings, and then I learned of the depths to which he has stooped to maintain the Harrison wealth. Some of his most lucrative clients are crime bosses and worse." He looked away. "When I told him I refused to work with them, he became angry, struck me, and then threatened my life." He sat back, the pain etched in his face. "I had to leave."

Father nodded. "And I'm proud of you for doing so. It takes great strength in a man to walk away from wealth and power."

Rebecca squeezed Ray's hand. "I can't believe it. You never told me. That's just awful."

"If you'd known, I was worried your life would be at risk, even if it was by a small amount."

Father frowned for a moment and then stood to look out the window. "And now? What problems are we facing?"

Ray sighed. "For the record, I asked Becky to take you and run. I don't see an easy way out of any of this."

"Hmmm."

Rebecca would have laughed at his typical distracted response were their situation at all humorous.

Ray ran his thumb along the back of her hand. "I work for the federal military. I report to General Decker. My assignment in Grant's Landing has been to discover the identity of a known bandit boss who is controlling several gangs all over the frontier."

"Sheriff Travis."

"Yes. I discovered his identity just recently, and we have an arrest planned, but because of a dumb move on my part, Johnny—my partner and another spy for the government—was captured and is about to be sentenced to death."

Father nodded. "I knew our patient to be a good man."

Rebecca smiled. Caring for patients was a little like having children, she imagined, and perhaps her father was blind to their faults.

"And now?" Rebecca hoped there was a plan.

"Now, I'm unsure. We wait for the general to come and arrest Travis. But he doesn't know yet of my capture, and Travis will come tonight, now that he knows both of us are here. He will burn the building or shoot us by bandit mob."

"Your fellow bandits would shoot you?"

"Well, they wouldn't have. But he will tell them that I'll squeal. I don't believe he knows my connection to the general."

"He came to the church after the general left."

"What?"

"We were there. I saw your meeting with the general, but Travis showed up while you were with the bandits."

"So that's how he knew." Ray frowned. "And how did you come to be in the church?"

"I saw you and followed."

"With Travis right behind."

She sat back. "Well, I didn't know he was right behind."

"I told you to run away."

"Are you saying all this is my fault? That I led him to you?"

Father held up his hands. "So we leave tonight."

Rebecca sat forward. "Yes! We leave now." She stood.

"I'm not leaving Johnny."

"Then let's break him out of jail."

"Stanford is tougher than you think. He's in on some of this, but the man believes in due process of the law, and he's bound and determined it be carried out." Ray cleared his throat. "So, some of the bandits know already that I've been captured. I saw a couple of them watching in the crowd."

"Would they break you out?"

"Yep. Me and Johnny. But they're not going to have any patience for you or your father, and they're a rough crowd. I'd just as soon not involve you with them. But even though you're not wanted by any law at all, you are at great risk because of your betrayal of Travis. I don't feel comfortable with you anywhere but near me or near Stanford when I leave.

"But then what? You go ride with the bandits again and never show your face here in town? Then you'll really be wanted by the law."

"We hope the general would clear him." Father stepped away from the window. The sun had set.

"What is it?"

"We've got company."

The door downstairs banged.

"Who is it?" Ray was on his feet, hand on his gun belt.

"It's Henry." Her father grinned.

"Oh, bother." Rebecca stood and made her way downstairs.

But when she opened the door, Henry's urgent expression made her heart pick back up. "What is it?"

He held out a basket. "From mother. We saw what you did to defend the prisoners. We don't like Sheriff Travis. No one around here trusts him."

"Thank you." She smiled.

"I've a trapdoor behind the store. I'll leave it unlocked in case you need it." He stepped away and hurried back across the street.

His mother watched from the door. Rebecca lifted a hand, and she nodded.

She brought tea and the goodies from the store up to her father and Ray. For a moment, the atmosphere felt quite cozy. Her father and Ray got to talking about all sorts of things—the study of medicine, the people in Boston, the news since Ray had left. She sat back and watched the two men she loved most. A feeling of almost peace settled around them. After a time, as the night grew darker, she picked up their things.

Father stood. "I don't know if any of us will sleep much tonight, but you are welcome to take a bed in my room."

Ray nodded. "Thank you, but I'm going to keep watch."

"We could take turns." Rebecca called out as she went downstairs.

If there was no incident during the night, they would all have a trial first thing in the morning. The general and his men would be there, and hopefully, Ray would be cleared. And then what? Would they really be heading back to Boston? Everything was happening so quickly.

As Rebecca cleaned up their tea and put away the leftover supplies sent from the store, she considered her life in Grant's Landing. It had been lovely in many ways, but she felt her father would agree that their purpose was to come for Ray. She smiled. And all this time . . .

"Rebecca." Her father stood in the doorway.

"Oh, Papa." She embraced him. "You came out here to the frontier for me." She squeezed him tighter.

"I did." He wrapped his arms around her. "But I, too, have benefitted."

"I'm sorry I didn't confide in you."

He nodded against her head. "All will be well, I hope, and we will still have many years to practice confiding all manner of things."

She laughed. "That sounds heavenly."

Rebecca and her father went to their rooms. Ray stayed by the window. But she suspected no one slept. She lay fully clothed with her boots on and a satchel by her bed. Neither she nor her father wished to leave Ray by himself. He hadn't complained, but she knew he was worried.

Hours later, she was startled from a doze by the crashing of glass and a rush of sound. Crackling and burning sounds made her leap from bed. "Father!"

He stepped out into the hall. "I'm here."

A line of men stood at the front of the jail with guns out. Behind their backs flickered light from a newly started fire.

"They're going to burn the whole thing down."

Ray joined them. "Those are Travis's men."

Gunshots came from down the street, and a bunch of men on horses arrived. Bullets went flying. Ray shouted, "Get down!" He waved at them, then dove forward, crouched down, used his rifle to break their window, and started shooting through it.

Rebecca and her father raced down the stairs. Men blocked the back door as well. Rebecca felt her heart in her throat. "What about the roof?"

"What?" Her father's eyes widened.

Someone had to get Johnny out, get them all out. "I'll get the sheriff and bring Johnny back here." She nodded and raced back up the stairs, lifting her skirts. They had an attic space. She opened the space in the ceiling and, while standing on a chair, climbed up inside. It was dark. She waited for her eyes to adjust, then she crawled along the boards that spanned the space. It looked as though it might go the length of the structure. But as she got closer, the heat increased. Smoke started to rise, and she knew her efforts were futile.

She was about to turn back when the boards beneath her crashed through, and she felt herself falling.

Smoke caught in her lungs. The heat was almost unbearable, but she saw no immediate flames. It looked like she had fallen into a back storage room. The entire ceiling above her had crashed through on the jail side. Loud crackling and burning sounded almost everywhere around her. But hanging on the hook was a set of jailer keys.

"Yes." She stood, grabbed the keys, and reached for the knob. With a cry of pain, she withdrew her hand, cradling it. The knob was scorching hot.

A pile of folded linens on a shelf might do. She wrapped her hand in one and grabbed the knob, turning as quickly as she could. Flames rose up in the hall to her front. She clutched the linens to her face and ran toward the front, toward the cries for help.

Sheriff Stanford lay on the floor unconscious, a line of blood on his forehead. "Help!" The men in the cells were coughing. Johnny reached out a hand. "Save us!"

"I've got keys!"

His fingers widened. "Toss them."

She did, and they missed his hand but landed nearby on the floor.

"I've got them."

She turned to Stanford. "Oh, wake up. Wake up!" He was alive. She coughed, starting to feel dizzy. Sweat dripped from her forehead. She could no longer hear shooting outside. She didn't know what that meant. Were they safe to simply walk out the front door?

She lifted the sheriff's arms to drag him, but the way to the front door crashed down around them. They must make it to the back.

She blinked. Stanford was not moving one inch no matter how she tugged. The linens fell from her face, and her arms were not responding. The world faded to a gray, then black, as thicker smoke filled the air around them. Someone lifted her. Voices didn't make sense to her ears. And then a sudden cool air. She gulped in deep breaths of it. They'd made it out the back.

"Ray. Father."

"I'll get them." He nodded.

The other prisoner, who had been there for weeks on end, grabbed hold of Stanford's arms. "Where're we taking him?"

Rebecca pointed. "Behind the general store. There's a trapdoor."

He nodded and grunted.

"I'm Rebecca." She tried to help by lifting Stanford's legs, but the man was just too heavy.

"Clint."

Footsteps came around the back of the jail.

She and Clint froze, but the man paid them no mind and ran to the other side, ducking and hiding. All the commotion came from out on the street, from the front of the jail, while the men faced Ray's bullets from the window and watched the jail burn to the ground. In no time, the doctor's office would also burn. Rebecca's heart clenched.

They moved along at what seemed too slow a pace behind the jail, but at least they were making progress. Soon, the back of the store rose up in front of them.

The door opened and candlelight shone out. Henry's mother frowned. "I'll take Stanford. The prisoner, no."

Rebecca nodded. With her help, the sheriff was soon laying inside their kitchen.

Clint nodded. "I'll be off then." Before they could so much as thank him or say goodbye, he had disappeared in the darkness.

"Get in here, child. This is no place for you." She ushered Rebecca in.

"Thank you." Rebecca started to shake. Her whole body trembled. "I—I don't know wh-what's wrong with me." Tears fell.

At once, Mrs. Halstead encircled her in her arms. "There now, dove. There."

Rebecca clutched her, melting into the softness of a woman's hug. Was this how it might have been to have a mother?

The shots stopped, but a loud cracking and crushing sound brought both women to the front window.

Rebecca gasped. The jail was no more. The flames were spreading. And a line of buckets had begun being passed from the pump. "Oh, they are so dear." She wiped her face. "I have to help."

"Yes, we all do. As long as they've stopped shooting."

It seemed they had.

"Henry!" Her shout made Rebecca jump.

"I'm here, Mother."

"Oh, yes. Let's join them."

He already had three buckets. "We've more in the back."

CHAPTER TWELVE

REBECCA STOOD BEHIND RAY, PASSING one bucket from behind to him in front over and over for what felt like hours, until every muscle in her arm quivered and burned from the exertion. His man, Johnny, had been shot in the fight to get Ray free. Rebecca didn't know much more than that. Her father was with Johnny right now, tending to his new injuries.

Ray said very little.

When the last bit of flames had been doused, some of their office and rooms remained. They would have to sift through their things and see if any of it was salvageable. But she was too exhausted to care.

People made their way off the street, smiling weakly when they passed one another. Rebecca thanked as many as she could.

"Go get some rest." Ray pointed to his rooms and handed her a key.

She nodded and walked in that direction but then turned.

"I'll see to Father," Ray said.

Father. Not *your* father. Father. Family. That was more comforting than anything at the moment. But she couldn't think clearly any longer, and she couldn't summon the energy to do much more than shuffle across the street, enter Ray's apartment, smile at the certain Boston feel to the place, and then fall into his bed, surrounded by smells of him. She smiled herself into a deep sleep.

Days went by with little to no contact from Ray. She didn't know where he slept. One night, she thought she heard him and might have seen evidence he spent some hours on a chair, but he was gone all the next day. She and her father had collected some things that were salvageable. They had one trunk between them packed, and they had a scheduled train early next week. But no word from Ray. Would he go with them? Was he staying on? She sat at morning tea with her father.

He put down the book he was reading. "I like Ray's apartment. He has a good life here." His eyes searched hers.

"What are you saying? Is he planning to stay here?"

"He hasn't said."

"But you will be returning to Boston."

"Yes. I've had my adventure. I wish to return to lecturing and seeing patients and conversing with my university colleagues."

She smiled. "That sounds so foreign, like a different world than what we've been living."

"Yes."

Johnny had been saved again, though he might be weak the remainder of his days.

Horses whinnied, and Rebecca moved so that she could see outside the window. "It's Ray with the general."

"About time that man showed his face."

Rebecca shook her head. They'd fought off Travis's bandits with friends of Ray's and the local townsfolk with no general in sight.

Within moments, Ray's footsteps sounded up the stairs. Rebecca stood, her smile growing.

Her father chuckled.

She ran to meet Ray.

His face looked tired, but when he lifted his gaze to her, he smiled.

"Have you news?"

"I do."

She reached for his hand.

He kissed her quickly, and the contact sent warmth all the way to her toes. When they were seated with her father again, Ray drank his entire cup of tea in one swallow and then stared at them both in turn. "You're set to leave on the next train?"

Father nodded.

She held her breath. He was coming with them, right? She watched him. But he avoided her gaze.

Finally, he cleared his throat. "I have some things to tie up here."

"What?" She sat forward.

Finally, he looked in her direction. "The general was delayed because of a run-in with some of Travis's men. He needs my assistance cleaning up more of these bandits. Some of them have been helpful and could be recruited lawmen. Some of them are truly the bad sort of men."

"And you want to help differentiate?"

"I do. And things won't be safe here for a few weeks yet. As much as I hate to see you leave, you need to leave."

"So you've been saying." She looked away. Panic started to rise. "So, are we to just leave without you?" She heard the rise at the end of her question, heard her voice shake.

Ray looked from her father back to her. "Might I have a word with you?" He stood and held out his hand.

She nodded and followed as he led her down the stairs.

They moved to the back of the shop so that any who passed on the street would not see them. When at last he stopped and turned to her, she blinked back blurry tears to no avail.

"Will I never see you again?" Her hands shook, so he pulled her into his arms.

"You aren't happy out here. It's dangerous. And it's obvious your father prefers Boston."

"But I prefer you, wherever that is." She pulled away and looked up into his face. "I chose you, bandit or no." She fell back into his arms. "But how can I watch my father leave on a train?"

"I don't want you to watch him leave. I want you to go with him."

She searched his face.

"I don't have a life for you here. I can't guarantee when I'll be finished rounding up the bandits or helping keep the peace. Stanford is a mess right now. We are without a sheriff . . ." He looked away. "I can't look at you when you stare at me like that."

"I'll stay."

He shook his head. "You can't. Your father is leaving."

"And you . . . won't have me?"

His smile started small and soft. "Is this a proposal?"

She turned from him. "You know it isn't, but all the same, you would turn me away? Send me off to Boston?"

"I would."

"With no promise? I might never see you again?"

"When I clear things up out here, when I manage my own family affairs back home, then we might have a chance, but until then? What do I have to offer you but a life full of danger and unsavory relationships in either location?" He shook his head. "This is not what I had hoped for you."

Her tears fell freely, but she had nothing more to say. She reached for him, pulling him as close as she could and then broke away, running back up the stairs.

And he didn't follow.

They prepared the rest of their belongings. She stopped in at the general store and left her seeds with Henry with instructions on how the herbs could be used for healing. And then she and her father made their way back to the tracks, which were just outside of the main street of town. As she looked back over her shoulder at the burned-down jail, the church, the store, she knew she would never ever forget this strip of land that had been home for so short a time. She prayed that whatever more Ray had to do would finish quickly and peacefully and bring him home to her. But she had no way of knowing if such a thing could be.

Ray had said farewell last night. But just as the smoke from the coming train made an appearance far out past the hills, Ray rode up on his horse. She ran to him, and he pulled her up in front of him on his horse. "I love you." His whiskers were rough on her cheek, his voice thick in her ear, his eyes full of pain.

"I love you too. Come to me." She turned as much as she could to face him. "Come to me, Ray. I shall not live a day of happiness until we are together."

He pressed his lips to hers in a fierce response.

She clung to him. The train pulled into town, and he slid her down off his horse, nodded one time, and then took off at a gallop.

She sobbed in a breath and turned back to join her father.

They stood in a compartment much like the one they'd been in on their arrival. Father held her close as the train pulled away, this time trailing strings from her heart in Grant's Landing.

She turned away from the window and kept the blinds closed for much of their first day of travel.

An attendant stopped by one morning offering newspapers, which her father hungrily scooped up.

"We find them as people leave them at different stations. They aren't always the most current."

"To us, they will be. We've heard nothing from home our whole time away." Father paid her some coins. "If you find more, please know you have willing readers in this berth."

Rebecca opened the blinds. "Oh, look where we are." Rebecca shook her head. The very land on which she'd seen Ray.

A cloud of dust rose up on the horizon. "I don't believe it."

"We should believe it. Nothing can be a surprise to us any longer."

The cloud moved closer. Soon figures were clear. They wore masks. Her heart picked up. A couple shot their guns in the air. Soon they were riding alongside the train. This time, instead of hiding, she watched them. Is this what Ray did all that time?

And then one of the riders turned to her and tipped his hat. "It's Ray!"

Father came to peer out beside her. "Are you certain?"

"Of course."

The train jerked to a stop, sending Rebecca toppling forward onto the bench. She righted herself and moved again to the window, bracing against the constant strain of a long-slowing motion. The riders had moved on ahead. She stuck her cheek on the glass to see what they were doing. "I have to go to him."

"You cannot."

"Father, why not? He's out there! It's Ray!"

"Think, daughter."

But she ran to the door, ignoring her father and all sense. When her hands reached the handle, it flung open, but a hand reached out to stop her from stumbling backwards. Ray's hand.

He stepped inside, searching the passageway outside their berth, closed the door, and then got down on one knee. His eyes shone at her, the only part of his face she could see.

"Becky, I'm an idiot for involving you in my life. But I can't live without you. Please, please marry me."

Father cleared his throat. "I admit the mask is unsettling. Perhaps if you lowered it."

He chuckled and was about to, but Rebecca got down on one knee and shook her head. "No, I like it." She tipped off his hat. "Am I to live the life of a bandit?"

"I'm not sure." He cleared his throat. "Although, Johnny knows every bandit as well as I and can easily assist the general in rounding them up. So perhaps not." He looked up at her father. "Very shortly, I realized I was not needed in the bandit roundup; I asked a favor, and we stopped your train." His sheepish grin was almost too much for her.

"Are we to live in Boston?"

"I don't know that either. Not if it's unsafe."

She nodded. "But we are to be together?"

"Yes. That I have every surety, for I cannot live without you a moment longer."

"Then, yes. Yes, I will marry you, and we shall live on our horses." She lowered his mask.

He pressed his lips to hers, once, and then turned to her father. "Might I have her hand?"

"Yes. However, there are many options to living that don't involve your father's ways or the life of a bandit." He cleared his throat. "Or simply on the back of a horse. Will you join us on our way to Boston?"

He tipped his head to the side. "I don't understand."

Then her father held up a newspaper.

Rebecca gasped, and Ray reached for the headline as he read, "Ralph Harrison dead, nationwide hunt for the Harrison heir underway. Reward for any who has news." Ray's picture was in the center of the page. "Dated just this week. Wow, wanted on both sides of the country now, I guess."

"But this is excellent, isn't it?" Rebecca looked over his shoulder to skim the news.

"I think so." One corner of his mouth lifted in such a charming half-grin that she wanted to kiss it and tease his lips into a larger grin, but with a glance at her father, she stood and motioned that Ray sit beside her.

Gunshots out the window drew their attention. A group of the bandits waved, and Ray saluted. "Johnny will take care of them with the general." The bandits took off again, back to where they'd come from, and before long, a cloud of dust rose once more. The train picked up speed again, and they were on their way. Rebecca wasn't sure what to think, except that happiness was at the center of every plan, every path her life could take, because now Ray would be a part.

"Might we go for a stroll?" He stood and held out his arm, Boston style.

"Why, Ray Harrison, I'd be delighted."

He led her from car to car, past the dining car, past the cars for sleeping passengers, past the group cars, even past one with glass on the ceiling, until at last they'd reached the caboose, and they stood out in the air at the very back of the train, watching the landscape fall away behind them. He stared for many minutes before turning to her.

"Are you happy, Ray?"

He wrapped her in his arms. "I am happier than I have ever been." He searched her face. "Are you?"

"So very happy. Standing here with you, I don't care what happens as long as we're together." She stuck out her bottom lip. "There is just one thing."

"And what's that?" His gaze lowered to her mouth.

"If we're in Boston, does that mean the Bullseye Bandit is lost to me?"

"Oh no. He can make an appearance should we ever need a bit of a rascal in our lives."

Her smile grew. "Good, because I've taken a liking to him."

"Have you now?"

He pulled her closer and pressed his lips to hers. She was lost in a delicious warmth. She knew in that moment that no matter what they made of their life, she would never ever get enough of her bandit.

ABOUT THE AUTHOR

Jen Geigle Johnson discovered her love for British history while kayaking the Thames as a young teenager. Now an award-winning author—including the Praiseworthy Award for romance and the Foreword Indies Gold in romance—and mother of six, she loves to share bits of history that might otherwise be forgotten. She has become a prolific author with more stories in her heart than can possibly be told.

Visit https://www.subscribepage.com/y8p6z9 to receive Jen's newsletter for free books and new-release notifications, and follow her on social media.

jengeiglejohnson.com

Facebook: facebook.com/AuthorJenGeigleJohnson
Instagram: instagram.com/authorlyjen/
Pinterest: pinterest.com/AuthorlyJen/
Twitter: twitter.com/AuthorJen

OTHER BOOKS AND AUDIOBOOKS
BY JENNIE HANSEN

Abandoned

All I Hold Dear

Beyond Summer Dreams

The Bracelet

The Emerald

The Topaz

The Ruby

Breaking Point

Chance Encounter

Code Red

Coming Home

High Stakes

Macady

Some Sweet Day

Wild Card

High Country

Shudder

If I Should Die

The Heirs of Southbridge

Run Away Home

Journey Home

Where the River Once Flowed

The River Path

By the River

When Tomorrow Comes

PRAISE FOR JENNIE HANSEN

"A good story filled with cattle rustlers, gun fights, and of course, handsome cowboys. Reading it is like stepping into an old John Wayne western. Best of all, Sally ends up with the guy you'll be cheering for all the way through."
—Carolyn Twede Frank, author *His Accidental Bride*

"From the title to the fun premise of the story to the engaging characters, Jennie's inclusion of English characters trying to fend their way in the Western Frontier was just what I wanted to read."
—Jen Geigle Johnson, author *A Torn Allegiance*

"Jennie Hansen knows how to pack a lot of story into just a few pages. Her descriptions of sagebrush and desert had me missing my hometown in Idaho."
—Brittany Larsen, author *The Matchmaker's Match*

sagebrush sally

JENNIE HANSEN

CHAPTER ONE

"THERE IT IS!" PAPA'S VOICE aroused Sally enough from her heat-induced stupor for her to crawl to the flap at the back of the wagon and peer out the narrow opening in the canvas.

Sagebrush! As far as Sally could see, there was nothing but gray-green brush and dry, sandy dirt baking in the bright sunlight. Not even a lizard or jackrabbit broke the monotony. Surely Papa couldn't be serious. Ever since they left England, he had spoken in glowing terms of the forests and cold mountain streams they would find in the American West. He'd even hinted at the possibility of discovering gold in one of those streams. So far nothing had measured up to her expectations.

Sinking back down on the narrow bed that occupied a large share of the wagon and was where she'd slept the previous two nights, she stared at the canvas above her head, blinked her eyes, and struggled not to cry. She recognized they'd had no choice but to leave their home in the hills of northern England when the landowner had opted to raise sheep instead of continue allowing tenant farmers to raise their puny crops on the steep hillsides. Evicted from the farm where she'd lived all her life, and where her father had spent all of his, they had nowhere to go and seemingly no one who cared. Their neighbors faced the same eviction and were too involved in their own problems to show concern for her and Papa. Pastor Jones had brushed off their concern with a brief admonition to seek jobs in the city or emigrate to America. Still, it was hard to trade the rich green hills and forested slopes of England for a desolate sea of gray and a relentless sun that dried her pale skin and formed wavering mirages in the distance.

"I don't think I can face this wild, gray land," she whispered to herself. She had always been timid.

When Uncle John's letter arrived, inviting them to travel to America to work for him, it had seemed like a miracle, an answer to their prayers. Uncle John, Papa's older brother, had run away to America after their parents had died, refusing to spend his life on the cramped farm, though the brothers had stayed in touch through the years. Papa had stayed on the farm because he had a wife who was ill and a young daughter who needed him. With the passing of time, Sally had become a young woman with no marriage prospects. She and Papa had been grateful for their only relative's invitation, though, secretly, the prospect of moving to America had terrified Sally. Now that she was on American soil, she was still terrified by it.

She wondered if she could survive in such a harsh land if they ever reached Uncle John's ranch. It seemed as though they'd been traveling forever. First they had walked to the stage line, carrying their meager belongings. They'd sold what they couldn't carry to raise the necessary funds for the trip, then they'd taken the stage to the coast, where they'd boarded a ship for the long voyage to New Orleans. That was followed by a journey aboard a paddle wheeler to St. Louis. In St. Louis, they had purchased tickets with part of their small hoard of funds for seats on a great, roaring train that carried them to Ogden, Utah, then another train north to Eagle Rock, Idaho. There Papa had purchased a rickety wagon and two emaciated horses to pull it. They had loaded their meager supplies inside the canvas-covered wagon and begun what was supposed to be the last leg of their journey.

"Sally! Sally, come up here beside me!" Papa called. "You don't want to miss this."

Sally dried her eyes and stood, her head barely clearing the canvas wagon top. She didn't want Papa to see how disappointed she was in their new home. Slowly she made her way to the front of the wagon. As she seated herself on the flat board that served as a wagon bench, she lifted her eyes and was surprised to see a few slight structures ahead. They looked like sheds of some sort, made of weathered boards that blended into their gray surroundings. What interested her most was the massive mountain that rose behind the shanties. It looked odd. It wasn't a mountain range—just one large mountain peak standing by itself in a sea of gray sagebrush. Papa had told her much of the area where they were going had patches of ancient lava rock scattered about and an occasional butte formed by long-ago volcanic action. The mountain was surely one of those long-dead volcanoes. She shivered, wondering if the volcano might not be as lifeless deep inside as it was believed to be.

Watching the ramshackle buildings grow larger as they drew closer, she became aware the road wasn't as flat as she had thought, and that they were actually moving at a slight upward angle. From her place on the wagon seat, she could see a green haze some distance behind the wooden buildings they were approaching. To her eyes, tired of the monotonous gray sagebrush, that hint of green was a lift to her spirits. As they drew nearer, she could see a wide, serpentine stream bed, almost devoid of water, wending its way a little lower than the flat plain. In one spot there appeared to be a small clump of willows along its bank. She couldn't help comparing the scant bit of greenery to the lush green of her old home.

It didn't take long to reach the first of the wooden buildings. Its appearance offered no clues to its function. It looked like a regular-size door sticking up in front of a cellar-like structure half-buried in the dirt. It was followed by several small wooden sheds and several more doorways leading into mounds of dirt. Two larger wooden buildings came next. Both had hitching rails and horse troughs in front of them. Across the street was the largest of the wooden buildings. None had signs indicating their purpose. All in all, there were fewer than a dozen structures. Her spirits dropped further as she contemplated whether these few shabby piles of dirt and boards made up the "nearby village" Uncle John's letter had mentioned.

A number of horses were tied to the rail in front of one of the larger buildings, and as Papa and Sally made their way down the short, narrow street, a cluster of men spilled out of the building. Papa pulled his team to a halt as the crowd blocked the street. Amid a great deal of shouting and milling about, two of the men drew apart from the others. They stood in the street, facing each other. Sally couldn't hear their words, but it was clear there was a great deal of anger between the two. Suddenly, both men pulled guns from holsters strapped low on their thighs. A sudden gunshot startled Papa's team of horses, causing them to bolt and the crowd to hastily scramble to the boardwalk.

In a cloud of dust, Sally and her father's wagon started careening down the road toward the steep stream bank. Sally gripped the side of the board bench until she noticed Papa bouncing ever closer to the edge of the wagon seat, a look of panic on his face. Reaching out, she grasped the back of his shirt with one hand while gripping the narrow seat with the other. Her action slowed her father's movement toward the edge of the seat but brought her nearer to bouncing off with him.

A thicker swirl of dust passed the wagon, and a firm voice shouted a command for the horses to stop. A rider bent low to grasp one of the draft horses' bridles. The tired animals needed little encouragement to slow their mad dash and lumber to a halt. Peering through the dust, Sally spotted a rider beside the team. She noted dust-caked pants, a leather vest over a worn shirt, and a wide-brimmed hat pulled low, almost hiding dark eyes set in a deeply tanned face. Damp, dark curls could be glimpsed beneath the hat. The rider suddenly smiled, revealing a flash of white teeth, and Sally found she could barely breathe.

"Howdy!" He addressed Papa. Without releasing his hold on the horse, the man who had come to their rescue spoke. "Best back 'em up a few steps before tryin' to turn 'em. They're awful close to pitchin' into the river."

What river? Sally certainly hadn't seen any river in the sea of gray sagebrush. She gasped as she turned her head far enough to see a deep gorge directly in front of the wagon. Partially standing, she glimpsed a shimmer of water at the bottom of the gorge.

Their horses had bolted; they had almost plunged into a ravine; a handsome stranger had rescued them at the last minute; and yet her mind seemed to only be able to focus on the absurdity of calling the trickle of water at the bottom of the gulley a river.

Papa's awkward attempts to back up the team were assisted by the stranger's firm hand until they once again faced the sorry little town they'd just passed through.

"Thank you, Mister . . . ?" Papa wiped his forehead with a handkerchief.

"Just Gabe, short for Gabriel Jenson."

"I'm Arthur Cranston, and this is my daughter, Sarah Elizabeth." Papa gave a vague wave in Sally's direction. She ducked her head, unable to acknowledge their rescuer.

Gabe touched his hat with two fingers in greeting. Was it her imagination that his eyes seemed to linger on her? "Where you folks headed?"

"My brother, John Cranston, has some land around here."

"I know the Cranston ranch well. It's not far from my family's place. If you don't mind, I'll ride along with you as far as the cutoff. I'm right sorry for that ruckus in town. When Pete Taft and Frank Prescot get drinkin', there's always trouble. Those two can't abide each other."

Was it just her imagination, or did the cowboy glance her way when he offered to ride along beside them?

"Sounds good to me," Papa replied and slapped the reins across his team's backs, urging them into motion. A plume of dust billowed behind the wagon, almost obscuring the small cluster of buildings that passed for a town. A pang of disappointment struck as Sally contemplated doing her shopping in the dreary little place. It was nothing like the cluster of small shops and friendly faces she'd grown up with in England.

Papa and Gabe carried on a sporadic conversation as they moved steadily toward the large butte. Sally pretended to have little interest in their conversation or in the young man riding beside their wagon. She took care to hide her surreptitious glances at him. He certainly could do with a bath and a change of clothing, she decided. Then honesty compelled her to draw the same conclusion concerning her own appearance. Under all the dust, he appeared to be quite handsome and not much older than her own nineteen years. Once or twice she caught him glancing her way, and she couldn't help wondering if he liked or found fault with her average height and slender build. Too bad he couldn't see the waist-length coils of auburn curls tucked beneath the bonnet she wore to protect her pale skin from the blazing sun.

They came to what appeared to be a wide stream bed, though it was now reduced to a few muddy puddles. The high banks seen near the small town they'd passed through had disappeared, and Gabe informed them that in the spring, when the river ran high, it was one of the few places where they could ford it. She almost burst into laughter when he referred to the almost-dry stream bed as the "Lost River." In her opinion, the river was well and truly lost.

On reaching a point where the dusty road they followed split into two narrow trails, Gabe announced, "I'll be leavin' ya now. The Cranston spread is a short piece straight ahead. I'll be headin' for the Double J. It was mighty fine meetin' ya." Though the brief farewell speech was clearly intended for her and Papa, the look he sent her seemed to be a message intended for her alone.

Sally watched Gabe touch his heels to his horse's sides and depart in a cloud of dust. She wondered if they would meet again. She couldn't help hoping they would.

"Seemed like a fine young man," Papa observed. Sally merely shrugged, not willing to admit she agreed completely.

The scenery changed a small amount as they proceeded. Along with the sagebrush, an occasional short, squatty tree Papa said some folks called cedar and others called juniper, began to appear. She didn't care what they were called; she was simply happy to see something green. At last, the shapes of several buildings appeared. As they drew closer, it became clear one was a house, and she assumed the taller building was a barn of sorts.

"It looks like there's a welcoming committee waiting for us." Papa lifted one hand from the reins he held to point ahead to where a large group of men and horses were milling about.

As they drew closer, Sally noticed that every man seemed to be dressed much the same as Gabe had been: wide hats, sturdy pants, vests, and boots. Her eyes widened. These men each carried a rifle and had a pistol strapped to his thigh.

One man noticed the wagon and ran toward them. He was followed by one of the men already mounted on his horse.

"Art!" the first man called. "Glad you made it. Just go on inside and get settled. Mazie will see to you."

Papa jumped from the wagon, and the two men embraced.

Sally quickly surmised the man was Uncle John, and she knew Mazie was John's wife's name. She had no idea who the man on the black horse hovering behind Uncle John might be, though she did notice he was mighty easy to look at. He held the reins to Uncle John's horse and was clearly impatient at the delay.

"No time to talk now. We've got an emergency on our hands." Uncle John waved them toward the house.

CHAPTER TWO

UNCLE JOHN SWUNG INTO THE saddle of the big bay horse led by the broad-shouldered cowboy, who sat high atop a beautiful black stallion. The stallion's prancing indicated he was anxious to be on his way. Uncle John shouted something as he gathered up his horse's reins, but his words were drowned out by the restless stomping of horses and shouts of men. With Uncle John and the man on the black horse leading, the riders left in a flurry of shouts and dust.

As the dust settled and the troop of riders disappeared, Papa climbed back to the wagon seat and snapped the reins, signaling the tired team to draw closer to the barn. There Sally helped him unhitch the horses from the wagon and lead them inside the sturdy log structure, where they could remove their harnesses. Papa found a brush and gave each of the animals a cursory brushing.

She had almost finished hanging up the harnesses on crude pegs when she noticed a woman with a small child. A rag doll dangled from one of the child's hands as she peeked from behind the woman's skirt, watching Sally. Sally hadn't heard them enter the stable.

"You must be Aunt Mazie." She spoke nervously, then hurried to introduce herself before her courage failed. "I'm Sally Cranston. Over there is my father, Arthur Cranston."

"I thought as much." Mazie offered a smile. "We've been expecting you. If you've finished here, come on up to the house. Lunch is ready."

"Thank you."

"Feel free to wash up at the pump." Mazie returned to the house. As she turned, it became obvious Mazie was expecting an addition to their family. The little girl clinging to her skirt sent Sally a tentative smile before following her mother.

A few minutes later, Papa, seated at a large table, set down his fork and addressed Mazie. "John and a good number of men left just as we arrived. He mentioned an emergency. Is there anything I can do to help?"

"No, John and his foreman can handle it. Some of the ranch hands discovered a half dozen cows and calves missing this morning. They calved early this spring and were recently put out to graze alone in a sheltered area. They should be relatively easy to follow."

"Does John think they wandered off, or does he suspect rustlers?" Papa sounded concerned.

Mazie was silent for a few minutes before continuing the conversation without answering Papa's question directly. "John has a natural corral formed by lava rocks on three sides. For years he's put cows with nursing calves there. It gives the calves a good start before they join the herd on the open range. They have never wandered away before."

Following lunch, Mazie put her daughter down for a nap, though five-year-old Mary Beth made it clear she considered herself much too old to be required to take a nap. While Aunt Mazie was occupied with her daughter, Sally tackled the dishes. When Mazie joined her, Sally couldn't help wondering aloud, "Will you be required to prepare dinner for the men who rode away with your husband?"

"No," she assured her. "There's a cook shack out by the bunkhouse where the men eat. John hired a man called Chen Le five years ago to keep the men fed. Sometimes the foreman, Marvin Streck, joins us for dinner if John has important matters he needs to discuss with him."

Sally couldn't help wondering if the handsome man on the black horse was the foreman Aunt Mazie referred to.

When the dishes were finished, Mazie led Arthur and Sally to the wide veranda that stretched across the east side of the house. From there, they could see a seemingly endless view of low, sagebrush-covered hills reaching toward the lone butte Sally had noticed earlier. She was amazed by how far she could see from Uncle John's and Aunt Mazie's porch with its unobstructed view. Turning her attention toward the north, she spotted the range of mountains she had glimpsed earlier. They appeared closer than she had previously thought them to be. Curious to see what else she might have missed, she turned her head toward the west, where the sagebrush stretched for a long distance, then disappeared in a sea of blackness. She couldn't help wondering if the blackness was due to a recent range fire.

It was growing dark when the men returned. It was obvious at a glance that their search had been unsuccessful. Some of the men looked downcast and discouraged. Others, like the foreman, appeared angry. Horses were quickly stripped of their saddles, given a quick brushing, and led to the corral, where one man was pumping water into a large trough. Two others pitched a shower of hay into the corral from the upper floor of the barn. When the other men made their way to the pump to wash up before heading to the cook shack, the broad-shouldered man stayed behind with Uncle John. Together they walked slowly toward the ranch house, stopping on the veranda, where Uncle John introduced his foreman, Marvin Streck, to his brother. The men shook hands.

"And this is Art's daughter, Sarah Elizabeth." John introduced Sally.

"Most people call me Sally." She was surprised by her own boldness and immediately felt shy, almost tongue-tied. She hadn't expected to formally meet the foreman, nor for him to be smiling at her. He had appeared stern and unyielding when she'd glimpsed him earlier.

"And most call me Marv." He smiled, and she felt a flush rise up her cheeks. She couldn't help noticing he was at least six feet tall, with blond hair and striking hazel eyes.

"Dinner is ready." Aunt Mazie ushered them toward the table. "You can discuss business while you eat or after, but Sally and I have kept your dinner warm for almost two hours, and that's long enough."

Sally had enjoyed the afternoon spent with Aunt Mazie, preparing dinner and talking. She liked that Aunt Mazie was a strong, take-charge kind of woman with firm opinions she didn't mind sharing. Sally had few memories of her own mother, who had passed away when Sally was not much older than little Mary Beth, but from the little she remembered and the stories she'd been told, she suspected her mother had been much like her aunt.

While Aunt Mazie carried a huge platter of roast beef to the table, Sally followed with a basket of rolls, which, by some miracle, were still warm. Setting them between Uncle John and Marv, she quickly retreated to the kitchen to retrieve a heaping bowl of mashed potatoes. She'd been a little surprised to find the Irish staple an ocean away and so far west. As she set the potatoes on the table, she realized the only seat left was the one next to Marv. As she started to claim it, Marv quickly rose to his feet and held her chair for her.

"Thank you," she spoke in a soft voice, almost a whisper, while trying to appear at ease. He smiled and returned to his own chair.

Sally helped Aunt Mazie keep bowls and plates filled as the men ate and discussed the loss of cows and calves. She tried to listen to their discussion but missed portions as she made frequent trips to the kitchen. She did learn that

Uncle John's ranch was not the only ranch that rustlers had struck. Most of the surrounding ranches had suffered losses as well.

"It's time to call the ranchers together to discuss the problem and come up with a plan," Uncle John said. "I can't afford to lose any more stock, and working together, we might be able to prevent further loss."

"As you share information, you may put pieces together and discover you know more than you think you do at this point." Papa added his perspective.

"That could backfire," Marv pointed out. "If one of the ranchers or some of the hired cowhands are involved with the rustlers, it might not be wise to advertise what we know or alert them to steps we're taking to keep from losing more cattle."

"The risk would be greater not to work on this together." John was adamant. "I'll send riders out first thing in the morning to arrange a meeting."

Mazie stood to begin carrying dishes to the kitchen. Sally gathered up a large bowl and followed her aunt. The men rose from the table, and Sally was surprised to find Marv right behind her as she stepped into the kitchen. His hand patted her shoulder, and he spoke in a low voice. "I'm glad you've come, and I hope we'll have a chance to get better acquainted." Without waiting for a response, he stepped past her and exited through the back door.

For several minutes, Sally stood bemused, staring after him.

Later that evening, as Sally lay on the mattress hauled inside from the wagon and snuggled beneath a heavy quilt Aunt Mazie had provided for her, she recalled all that had occurred that day. Her mind flashed quickly past the two men who faced off on the street of the dreary little town, their faces seared into her memory. Turning to more pleasant thoughts, she recalled the handsome young man who had come to their rescue as her and her father's horses raced from town. She drifted to sleep picturing Uncle John's foreman leaning toward her as he bid her goodnight.

The following night, Sally knelt on the floor beside a grate cut in the floor of the attic room she'd been given. It was directly over the wood stove that spread its heat to the large room below and allowed a bit of warmth to reach the small room above. From her position, she could see directly into the room below. She watched as nine men and one woman filed silently into the house with grim expressions on their faces. She hadn't expected to see a woman among the ranchers, and this woman was unlike any other woman she'd ever seen. She was dressed in britches identical to the men around her and wore a cotton shirt and leather vest. With her hair pulled back in a tight bun, only her feminine curves revealed her gender.

Uncle John ushered his guests to the sofa and chairs clustered together at one end of the main room, where Papa and Marv were already seated. When everyone had found a place to sit, John went straight to the point.

"Every ranch represented here has lost some of its best breeding stock in recent weeks. Yesterday I lost another half dozen cows with their calves."

"I lost four of my best cows and calves. I was countin' on those cows to build my herd," said one rancher.

"Ain't no way those cows wandered off on their own," piped up another.

Others added comments too. "They must have been snatched in broad daylight. This land's too rough to drive cattle at night."

"Hanging's too good fer them blasted rustlers!"

"What's your plan for puttin' a stop to losin' our cows?" asked the woman.

"There's no tellin' how many more of our cows and calves are missing on the open range. None of us can afford to keep a guard watchin' every minute, and we can't keep our herds close and feed them hay all summer."

"Why are they takin' a handful of cows at a time, 'stead of a whole herd, like rustlers generally do?"

Sally listened to a chorus of similar statements until Uncle John called the meeting back to order. Once he had the group's attention again, he reminded them they were all familiar with the way the animals were disappearing and that none of them could afford the loss. "It seems to me we need to send a man to Eagle Rock to keep an eye out for cattle with changed brands being shipped by train to other places. The same goes for the routes trail drives make from here to Montana or Oregon. We could combine forces to send out a couple pairs of lookouts every day to sweep the area."

A lanky rancher with long gray sideburns stated his opinion. "Doesn't seem to me whoever's takin' the cows could get very far in the short time between when he snatched them and when they was missed, considerin' he's takin' calves that ain't more'n a month or two old. Takin' calves means he's probably not plannin' to sell to a slaughterhouse. Since he's only takin' cows with calves, I figure he's holin' up in one of them canyons or caves in the lava rocks until he's collected enough to make a nice herd for himself. Seems to me we need someone out explorin' that area."

"Good point, James," John agreed. "That's what we need to decide: how many places we need to check out and how many ranch hands we can each spare to do the checking."

Sally shifted her position, taking care to make no sound that would alert the guests below to her presence. Most people would probably think she had no cause to be eavesdropping and that the matter wasn't any of a woman's business anyway. Her eyes caught sight of the woman rancher. Maybe it was different in America or at least in the West. The female rancher was taking part in the discussion, and none of the men seemed bothered by her participation. Sally leaned closer. Anything that caused a financial loss for Uncle John was her concern. She and Papa would be without anywhere to turn if Uncle John's ranch failed and he couldn't afford to provide a job for Papa or a home for them.

"Seems to me someone's starting up a new ranch. We've all—except for the Double J and the Prescots—lost half a dozen or more of our best breeders and their calves," the woman rancher spoke up. "The Prescots ain't been here long enough to have anything worth stealin', but I think James Jenson and his Double J," she pointed a finger at the previous speaker, "best be setting a guard around his fancy new bull that just arrived a few weeks ago from one of them British islands."

"Been thinkin' along them lines myself," the rancher, who Sally assumed was Jenson, said.

The men got down to business, working on a schedule outlining which ranch would provide scouts on each day of the coming weeks. All agreed the land was too vast to cover it all every day, even with two sets of scouts riding across opposite sections, but with the routes varying each day, the riders would increase their odds of finding anyone who shouldn't be on the land.

"I propose we send my brother, Arthur, to Eagle Rock to check the cattle being transported by train."

Sally was surprised to hear Uncle John offer Papa's services. Assuming she would be expected to go with him, she felt a surge of disappointment. Though they'd only been on Uncle John's ranch a few days, she wasn't anxious to leave it for the raw railroad town they'd passed through briefly on their way to the ranch.

"I 'spect I should go with your brother," a bewhiskered old man spoke up, "seein' as how I worked with assigning and inspecting brands in Kansas before comin' here. My boys and their ma can manage just fine while I'm gone."

"I appreciate your offer, Clark." Uncle John thanked the man.

Perhaps Sally wouldn't need to leave the ranch after all, but would she be comfortable knowing Papa was so far away?

Others spoke up, most offering to send riders. Only one rancher seemed reluctant to send riders to serve as scouts. "It's just me and my two boys," he said.

"I can't afford for either to lose a day's work. My ranch is new and ain't doin' well. I 'spect I should have taken up land farther up the Lost River 'stead of on this miserable, sagebrush-covered desert."

"My boys will be anxious to help," the female rancher spoke up. "We Tafts ain't got no hired hands, but the lads will be rarin' to do their share."

CHAPTER THREE

SALLY STOOD ON THE WIDE porch that ran across the front of the house, enjoying the view that stretched to the mountain peaks. The air was filled with the rich aroma of sagebrush. Papa had been gone three days. She missed him. They'd never been apart before more than a few hours since Ma had died. Aunt Mazie found plenty to keep her busy, though, and Sally was enjoying her new experiences. Yet she felt restless, as though something was missing. Missing Papa didn't account for the vague emptiness.

Aunt Mazie startled her by interrupting her musings. "Sally dear, would you mind taking Mary Beth to the corral? I'm not feeling well this morning, but I don't want to disappoint her."

"To the corral?" The request made little sense to Sally. Most of the time, she and Mazie both took pains to make certain the little girl didn't wander into any area where she might be injured by horses or cattle.

"Oh." Mazie laughed. "I forgot you aren't familiar with our routine. We, John and I, want Mary Beth to learn to ride. John doesn't have the patience to teach her, and with me expecting a little one, we thought it best for one of the ranch hands to do it. Twice a week, Marv sends Clarence Hoops to fetch Mary Beth's pony and help her learn to ride it. She loves the pony and the lessons."

"I can take her there," Sally agreed.

Mazie went on. "Oh, you might want to change into a riding skirt. If Clarence takes her for a short ride outside the corral, you'll want to go along."

"I-I don't have a riding skirt." She didn't want to admit that she knew nothing about riding. At their old home, they'd never owned a riding horse, just an old, broken-down plow horse, and there had never been a need for her to learn to ride.

"Mine is too tight for me now. You might as well use it until we can make one for you. Come. We'd best hurry. Clarence will be waiting."

Minutes later, Sally stood in front of an oval mirror in Mazie's bedroom examining herself in the strange skirt her aunt had insisted she wear. Made of heavy fabric, the full skirt was split up the center, dividing it almost like a pair of trousers.

Twenty minutes later, she discovered the purpose of the odd skirt.

"You expect me to ride astride?" She stared doubtfully at the elderly cowboy who had waved vaguely toward a mare standing docilely nearby. The animal was saddled just like the pony he'd set Mary Beth and her ever-present rag doll upon and the larger horse she assumed he meant to ride. She didn't know much about horses or riding, but the ladies from the large estate near her old home had always ridden on saddles designed to keep both feet on the same side of their mounts. She'd always thought they looked elegant with their wide skirts spread across their horses' sides.

"We ain't got any of them fancy lady saddles. Good thing, too, 'cause they ain't safe in this country. Best you get to it. Daisy's a patient little pony, but she won't take kindly to bein' kept waitin'. Neither will the little miss. She's rarin' to git goin'."

"Come on!" Mary Beth called, impatience clear in her voice.

Sally warily eyed the reddish mare that Clarence had saddled for her. He'd assured her Daisy was docile and patient. She stepped closer to the animal, heaved a sigh, then attempted to place her foot in the stirrup as she'd seen Clarence do. Her foot didn't come even close to reaching the stirrup. Mary Beth had scampered up the corral poles and slipped one foot across her pony's back, then slid into the saddle. It appeared Sally would have to employ the same technique.

Climbing from one pole to the next wasn't too difficult, but when she reached the top pole, she found herself clinging to a post and wishing the horse was a little closer to the fence. She wasn't a quitter. She'd do it. She eyed the gap between herself and the horse, took a deep breath, and swung her foot toward the far side of the saddle just as she'd seen her small cousin do.

Daisy chose that moment to sidle a bit farther away. Sally clutched frantically at the saddle, attempting to halt her fall. It was no use. In moments, she found herself flat on her back looking up at the underside of the mare. Fearful of being stepped on, she attempted to roll away. That's when she felt hands lift her to settle her against a rock-hard chest.

"Are you hurt?" She felt the words rumble against her cheek.

"I'm fine. I think." Actually, she wasn't certain, but she couldn't pinpoint any one place that hurt more than another. Suddenly remembering her assignment to watch over Mary Beth, she squirmed to free herself from the strong arms that held her. "I need to get on that horse."

"That can be arranged." She heard a masculine chuckle and suddenly found herself hefted up and then plopped down in Daisy's saddle. Startled, she glanced up and caught a quick glimpse of the ranch foreman's grinning face before her eyes settled on the twitching ears of the mare. She was sitting on a horse! She clutched the knob at the front of the saddle with one hand and the reins with the other. Marv slapped the horse's rump, and the mare lurched forward to settle into a slow, but jarring pace behind Clarence's and Mary Beth's ambling mounts.

Riding a horse was both exhilarating and frightening, but Daisy seemed to know what was expected of her. She moved at a slow, plodding pace, following behind the other two horses without any direction from her rider. Sally found she wasn't comfortable so far from the ground, and it didn't take long for her posterior and her legs to become decidedly uncomfortable. Fear that she might slip from the saddle and land once more in the dirt kept her clutching the saddle and scarcely daring to breathe. She noticed that neither Clarence nor little Mary Beth bounced up and down as she did.

The air was sharp and clean, with a faint aroma of sage. The seemingly endless vista of the gray-green brush and the abrupt mountains in the distance held more appeal than she'd first expected. The western saddle cradled her securely, lessening her fear. Still, she'd enjoy the ride more if every step the mare took didn't pound her bottom against the saddle.

It was a tremendous relief when the circular route Clarence led them on angled back toward the corral. Sally's dismount wasn't as graceful as Clarence's casual swing from the saddle. She slipped and slid until her small boots touched solid ground. She staggered and nearly lost her balance as she attempted to walk toward Mary Beth. But before she could reach her small cousin to assist her, Clarence scooped the little girl from her saddle.

"Seems you'll be needin' ridin' lessons more than the little miss," Clarence spoke to her, making it clear he'd observed her disastrous attempt at riding. "Come a bit early next time, and I'll give you a few tips." He gathered up the horses' reins and sauntered toward the barn, leaving Sally staring after him.

She glanced around, hoping Marv hadn't seen her less-than-graceful scramble from Daisy's back. Not seeing anyone, she hurried to catch up to her cousin, who was skipping toward the house. They had almost reached the porch when the thunder of running horses reached them. Glancing behind her, Sally saw half a dozen horses in a cloud of dust racing straight toward her.

Snatching up Mary Beth, she scrambled to safety on the porch. The door slammed, and Mazie stood beside them. She caught a quick glimpse of Clarence, Marv, and two other ranch hands running from the barn toward the riders, who stopped in front of the porch.

Two men she quickly identified as Uncle John and Gabe Jenson dismounted before their horses had come to a complete halt. They hurried to ease an unconscious man from the arms of a tall, thin man seated on a big chestnut horse. The other men swarmed around them and hustled to support the man's weight as they carried him past the women and into the house. Mazie quickly followed them.

Sally wasn't certain what she should do. Should she stay with Mary Beth or try to help Mazie? She didn't know a lot about caring for the sick or injured, though she'd administered simple aid as needed on the farm. The decision was taken out of her hands when a Chinese man slipped into the house carrying a leather bag and wormed his way between the men crowded around the cowboy stretched out on Mazie's sofa.

Getting her first good look at the injured man, Sally noted his ripped, blood-soaked shirt and the blood and grime on his face and hands. His pants were torn as well, revealing scrapes and scratches.

The Chinese man flapped his arms as though shooing flies, and Marv immediately began ushering most of the ranch hands out of the house. Uncle John and Gabe remained kneeling beside the man on the sofa. Mazie rose to her feet from where she'd been kneeling. She looked around, then hurried to Sally.

"Take Mary Beth to the kitchen. Find her some lunch, then put her down for her nap," she whispered, then led the way. While Sally followed Mazie's instructions, Mazie scooped water from a bucket to fill two large kettles she had set on the stove.

Sally set a biscuit and a glass of milk in front of Mary Beth and was reaching for a plate when she heard an odd sound from Mazie. Turning, she saw Mazie sink onto a nearby chair. Sally hurried to her side. "Are you all right? Is it the baby?"

"I'll be fine in a moment," Mazie murmured. "I shouldn't have tried to lift the tea kettle, but Chen Le will need the hot water."

"I'll do it. You sit here beside Mary Beth."

Without waiting for a response, Sally picked up the hot pads Mazie had dropped, snatched up the heavy kettle of steaming water, and marched resolutely into the other room.

Her eyes went immediately to the group surrounding the outstretched figure on the sofa. Chen Le hovered over the cowboy while Gabe and the man she now recognized as the owner of the Double J ranch held the unconscious man's arms as though they expected him to suddenly thrash about. Uncle John and Marvin stood near the window. They appeared to be in deep conversation.

Chen Le motioned for Sally to set the teakettle near him. Hesitantly, she approached, feeling awkward in the presence of the group of men. The cowboy's bloody shirt had been removed, leaving his chest bare. As she bent to place the heavy teakettle on the floor, Gabe rose to his feet and took it from her. As he did so, his hand briefly covered hers, sending an unexpected jolt to her hand and upward through her arm. Stunned, her eyes met his as he smoothly transferred the weight of the kettle from her hand to his. His eyes seemed to be conveying a message of recognition and assurance that all would be well.

"Shouldn't we send for a doctor?" The words came out in a hushed whisper.

"The nearest doctor is two days' hard ride away," he replied. "Don't worry. Chen Le is as good as any doctor I've ever met."

"How . . . ?" She didn't know what to ask, though she'd wondered since the men rode into the yard how the man had been injured.

Gabe's face darkened. "He was shot."

CHAPTER FOUR

IT WASN'T UNTIL HOURS LATER that Sally learned more details about the shooting. A buckboard escorted by six Double J riders arrived shortly after the cowboy regained consciousness to transport him back to the Double J. After the wagon disappeared from sight, Chen Le returned to the cook shack, and Uncle John and Marvin made their way to the kitchen looking for dinner.

Once they were all seated around the table, Uncle John explained that he and some of his men had been working on a fence line alongside several Double J men, including the rancher and Gabe, when they heard shots. Shortly after, Gabe and one of Uncle John's ranch hands had discovered one of the Circle C cowboys frantically trying to staunch the blood flowing from a Double J man's shoulder. The two cowboys from neighboring ranches had been paired together to watch for the cattle thieves. They were crossing the far end of Uncle John's ranch near where the ancient lava flow ended when they were ambushed by an unseen assailant.

Sally shivered. She and Mary Beth had ridden with Clarence toward the lava beds that morning. They had stopped more than a mile from the field of black rocks, but she had no idea how close they had come to where the shooting had taken place. She couldn't help feeling a stab of concern for her father as well. He'd been gone a week, and she had no way of knowing if he'd encountered trouble too.

"Is something wrong, Miss Sally?" Marvin interrupted her thoughts.

"No." She was quick to assure him. "I was just feeling sympathy for that poor cowboy, then found myself hoping Papa doesn't encounter any such trouble."

"I'm sure Art is fine," Uncle John said. "It's not likely the cattle rustlers are anywhere near Eagle Rock. They're most likely holed up somewhere out in the lava rocks where there are plenty of caves and tunnels to hide in."

"How long can the cattle stay hidden in a cave?" Mazie asked. "They have to eat."

"I don't think the rustlers would attempt to keep the cattle in a cave more than a day or so," Uncle John replied. "The lava field is huge. It would take a couple of weeks just to ride around it, and some places are near impassable. There are many areas where the ragged edge of the old lava flow left small inlets where grass and brush grow. The cattle could be hidden in one of those natural corrals, and there aren't enough cowboys in Idaho Territory to find and check them all."

"That cowboy getting shot near the lava beds makes one think the outlaws are hiding out there, but the fact is they might have moved the cattle north to one of the mountain canyons and are just keepin' a lookout out there in the lava rocks," Marvin added.

As the men continued to discuss the possible whereabouts of the rustlers, Sally noticed that little Mary Beth's head was nodding and she was close to falling asleep. The little girl's afternoon nap had been much shorter than usual. Sally rose to her feet and hurried to the kitchen to retrieve the cobbler she'd baked that afternoon while nervously waiting for the injured cowboy to awaken. After returning with generous servings for everyone, she seated herself. Moments later, she saw that even dessert wasn't enough to keep the child awake. Mazie noticed too and was soon lifting Mary Beth in her arms to carry her up to bed.

Seeing that both Uncle John and Marvin had finished eating, Sally began clearing the table. She was surprised when Marvin gathered up a couple of serving bowls and followed her to the kitchen. He further surprised her by picking up a dishtowel, then standing beside her.

"You don't need to do that," she told him.

"I think I do." He smiled.

She returned the smile, and together they finished the dishes and straightened up the kitchen.

Lifting the dishpan, she prepared to carry it outside. Marvin took it from her hands and emptied it over the porch rail. Then setting the pan aside, he took Sally's arm and led her toward a faint path that led past the two scrawny trees Mazie had planted in hopes of one day having a shady refuge. Releasing her arm, Marvin indicated that Sally should precede him along the path.

As shadows lengthened, they wandered together to a rocky knoll. Sally wasn't certain what she felt. She'd never been alone with a man before except for Papa. Truth be told, she'd had very little experience being around men at all, even though she was nineteen and knew plenty of girls in the village who had married before they reached her age. With Papa having no sons and Mum being gone, she had needed to help Papa and care for their cottage. There had been no time for potential suitors or even male friends.

They reached a rocky outcrop that looked out over miles of brush with the butte far in the background. She noticed the rock beneath her feet was the now-familiar lava rock. It seemed strange to her that chunks of black lava rock protruded from the ground on hills miles from the lava beds.

"You ever ride a horse before this morning?"

Marv's question took her by surprise. She'd been half expecting something romantic following a stroll at dusk through the fragrant brush. At the same time, she couldn't help feeling a mite relieved.

"No," she admitted. "I watched some of the estate ladies ride, but I never had a need or a horse to ride."

"I could give you a few pointers next time you take little Mary Beth to Clarence for her riding lesson. Out here, it's a good idea for everyone to know how to ride."

She gladly accepted his offer.

They talked a few minutes longer about horses and her journey from an English village to the American West as a round, full moon rose in the southeast. Marv stood close, and she wondered if he might try to kiss her. Feeling unsure whether she wanted that to happen, she took a step back. He smiled and brushed her cheek with the tip of two fingers, then slowly he led as they strolled back to the ranch house. He tipped his hat as he wished her a good evening.

Later, as she lay in bed replaying the day's events in her head, she found herself wondering if she might be just a little bit in love with Marvin Streck. Oddly, it wasn't Marv's handsome face that appeared in her mind as she drifted off to sleep. She relived the moment Gabe's hand had brushed hers as he relieved her of the heavy teakettle.

"Mama says we have to wash the windows."

Three days had passed since Marv had promised to teach her to ride when Mary Beth approached Sally with a bucket and an armful of rags. It was hard not to laugh at the child's woebegone face as she presented the items to her cousin. Mary Beth, like everyone else on the ranch, had her assigned chores, and she made no secret of preferring outside tasks to housework. She cheerfully gathered eggs, bottle-fed orphaned calves, or chased crows from her mother's garden but grumbled over dusting or washing dishes.

Sally filled the bucket with water and a handful of soap shavings.

It took most of the morning to wash the first-floor windows inside and out. They were almost finished when Aunt Mazie urged them to finish quickly and come in for lunch.

While eating lunch, Mazie informed them they would be going to town to shop right after Uncle John came in for his lunch. Sally assumed her aunt was referring to the cluster of dirt soddies and unpainted board shacks she and Papa had passed through on their way to the ranch. She couldn't force herself to feel as excited as Mazie and Mary Beth appeared to be over the outing.

"Wear your blue dress," Mazie called after her as she climbed the stairs to her attic bedroom.

Sally pondered her aunt's advice. Her blue dress was her nicest gown, the one she usually reserved for dress-up occasions, such as church, but ranch life provided few opportunities to dress up, and she hadn't attended church since she and Papa left England. A shopping trip just might be the closest she would find to a dress-up occasion. She pulled the dress from the hook where it had hung since she'd unpacked her trunk.

Mary Beth fell asleep on a pile of blankets her mother had placed in the wagon for the little girl and Sally to sit on. Sally sat beside Mazie while Uncle John drove, and she found herself enjoying the ride more than she'd expected. She relived the trip with her father and being escorted by Gabe from the little town to the ranch. She knew more now about the cowboy who had stopped their runaway team. He was the son of rancher James Jenson and the acting foreman of James's Double J ranch. Then her thoughts turned to her uncle's handsome foreman, Marvin, and their evening stroll. There had been nothing improper in his actions, and in her inexperience with men, she'd likely assumed more than she should have, but the event had taken on romantic overtones in her mind. She smiled. Never before coming to this sagebrush-covered land had she imagined meeting two such handsome eligible bachelors.

As they approached town, Sally experienced the same disappointment she'd felt the first time she'd seen the tiny cluster of shacks and soddies. Uncle John halted the horses in front of the structure she assumed to be the general store. He assisted Mazie in alighting from the wagon, then Sally passed the sleeping child to him. She was preparing to jump or slide from the wagon when two hands reached up, circling her waist to lift her from the wagon.

Swallowing a gasp, she looked up as her feet touched the dusty street. Her eyes met a familiar face, and she felt a blush grow on her own cheeks.

"Gabe!"

CHAPTER FIVE

"This must be my lucky day." Gabe laughed. "What brings you to our grand metropolis?"

"Aunt Mazie invited me to come along while she does some shopping."

"Let me escort you inside the best and only store in town." Gabe crooked his arm, inviting her to take it. Together they followed Mazie and John inside the tiny general store.

Sally released Gabe's arm once inside and let her gaze wander around the interior of the store. She could see Mazie was losing no time collecting an armful of items to deposit in a box John carried. Thinking she should offer to help, she approached them.

"We're fine," Aunt Mazie told her. "Just look around. You might see something you want."

It didn't take long to explore the store. Shelves lined three walls of the square structure, with a double-sided row of shelves down the middle. A couple more shelves rose behind the counter that extended along the fourth wall to the door and a window. Under the window was a row of barrels. Food items, harnesses, tools, rope, hats, a few shirts, a small number of bolts of cloth, thread, and many other staple supplies vied for space on the shelves or in the barrels. None of it struck her as anything she needed to spend her few precious coins on.

Catching sight of Mary Beth eyeing a jar of lemon drops on the counter, she changed her mind. Mary Beth should have a paper of the candies. When she reached the little girl's side, she discovered she was too late; Gabe had already reached the same conclusion. He gave the man behind the counter a coin and handed Mary Beth a paper twist of the sweet-tart candies.

Mary Beth shared her candies with both Sally and Gabe. Somehow the three of them wandered outside the store. They stood chatting until Sally became aware of wagons beginning to gather across the street and people entering what appeared to be the largest structure in the village.

"What's happening over there?" She motioned toward the people entering the building she had assumed was a school or church.

"You don't know?" Gabe grinned. "On the last Saturday of each month, the community center becomes a dance hall. I suspect that's the reason John and Mazie chose today to do their shopping."

"They didn't say anything to me about staying for a dance." Sally couldn't believe her aunt and uncle would plan to attend a dance without telling her, though a dance would explain Mazie's suggestion that Sally wear her blue dress.

John and Mazie left the store, and Sally watched her uncle stow their purchases in the wagon. He reached under the seat, pulling out a basket she hadn't been aware had been placed there. Mazie approached her, looping her arm through Sally's, and spoke in a nonchalant voice. "We'll eat supper at the community center. It'll give you a chance to meet some of the neighbors."

"There's a dance after," John boomed. "There aren't many young single gals around these parts, so Gabe here better get in his bid for a dance early." He laughed and nudged Gabe with his elbow. "You'll eat with us, won't you?"

Gabe glanced at Sally, then nodded his agreement.

Sally could feel her cheeks flush. "What about Mary Beth? Isn't she too young to attend a dance?" She avoided looking at Gabe.

Mazie laughed. "There will be quite a few children present. When they get tired, the mothers will spread blankets under a table, and the little ones will curl up on them to fall asleep. When it's time to leave, their fathers scoop them up, blankets and all, and put them in their wagons or buggies."

While they talked they moved closer to the building across the street.

Soon they were seated on rough wooden benches around equally rough tables placed against the walls of the room she learned really did serve as the school, church, and community center. She noticed the middle of the room had been cleared, presumably for dancing.

Several couples stopped to talk to John and Mazie, and Mary Beth slipped away with three other children to play a game on the soon-to-be dance floor. Gabe stayed attentively beside Sally, and she found it easy to tell him her experiences of traveling to America and to admit that she missed Papa. She was surprised by how easy it was to talk to Gabe. She learned his upbringing had been quite different from hers. He'd started out life in Virginia and lived there until his father decided to try his hand at ranching in the West. There had been no formal education in his life, though his mother, a former teacher, had done her best to teach him and his six younger siblings the basics of reading, writing, and arithmetic. She'd succeeded so well that he had become an avid reader who purchased every book he could find on his infrequent trips to Eagle Rock.

It wasn't long before the squeal of a bow across someone's fiddle announced the band was warming up and dancing would soon begin. Gabe took her hand and drew her to her feet.

It soon became clear the little bit she'd learned about dancing in her English village hadn't prepared her for the rowdy, stomping beat that filled the hall. She'd never heard of a dance where someone called out instructions, instructions that made no sense to her. Only Gabe's whispered promptings and gentle pushes saved her from making a complete fool of herself as she stumbled from him to someone else, then back to him.

When the dance ended, and before Gabe could return her to the bench where they had been seated earlier, another cowboy claimed Sally for the next set. She lost count of the number of partners who claimed her and was getting fairly good at understanding the caller's instructions when she suddenly looked into a face she recognized: Marvin stood before her. She smiled, and he grinned as though secretly amused. When he assumed a dance position she remembered from her brief acquaintance with dancing prior to coming to America, she breathed a sigh of relief, expecting a more sedate tempo. Instead, Marvin swung her about as though she weighed nothing. The dance seemed to consist of a great deal of boot stomping and being twirled off her feet.

When the dance ended, Marvin didn't release her. He whispered, "I suspect you could use a drink about now."

She nodded, and they slowly made their way to one end of the hall where a couple of ladies stood behind a table laden with large kettles and a crazy assortment of cups and glasses. The cup he handed her proved to be a lukewarm, watery punch. She couldn't identify the slight, fruity flavor.

Holding the cup in one hand and taking occasional tiny sips, she visually surveyed the room. She spotted Mazie in conversation with an older woman. Gabe was standing a few feet away. He caught her eye and winked. Flustered, she looked away. She noticed there were far more men than women present, and most of the women she did see seemed to be the wives of various ranchers. There were fewer than a dozen young women in the crowd, and they appeared to scarcely be out of the schoolroom. Each was surrounded by a cluster of ranch hands. One woman who caught her eye looked only slightly older than Sally.

Noticing her attention focused on the woman, Marv leaned forward to whisper, "That's Linda Reynolds. She's the schoolmarm. I'll introduce you."

Before he could make good on his promise, a disturbance erupted near the door, drawing most people's attention. Sally turned her head to see a group of rowdies explode into the room. Whooping and shouting, they began dragging reluctant partners onto the dance floor while shouting for the musicians to get back to their music. A lone harmonica and a single fiddle began a simple tune.

Suddenly two of the rough, drunk cowboys shot across the room toward Sally. Before she could devise an escape plan, two solid bodies blocked her view. Gabe and Marvin formed a barricade between her and the approaching duo.

"Outta my way," the first man shouted and tried to shove Marvin aside. Marvin shoved back, and the man landed on his backside. As he hit the floor, he reached for the pistol he wore strapped to his thigh.

"No you don't!" Gabe stepped forward, his boot landing on the man's wrist. Sally couldn't be sure whether the sound she heard was the gun hitting the floor or the bone in the man's wrist cracking.

An arm slid around Sally's waist, and the second ruffian began dragging her, not toward the dance floor but toward the open door. She kicked at her captor's legs and struggled to free herself from his steely grasp.

"Let me go!" she shouted.

"Now, girlie," the man sneered, "don't go actin' like you're too good fer ol' Pete. I'm just aimin' to have a little fun."

"Let her go!" There was a ring of steel in Gabe's voice.

"You ain't man enough to make me." The man who called himself Pete continued to drag Sally toward the door. Shouts and screams filled the hall as the other rowdies began dragging their dance partners toward the door too. As they passed the lit lanterns on tables or windowsills, they shoved them to the floor. The men trying to free the captives ceased their pursuit and rushed to stomp out the flames.

From the corner of her eye, Sally saw Gabe's fist land a powerful blow to the side of Pete's head. For just a moment, her captor continued to hold her with a thick arm; then he slowly crumpled to the floor. The momentum of his fall freed her from his grip but thrust her toward the floor. As she fell, she heard something whistle over her head. Fearing it was a bullet, she lay still, scarcely daring to breathe. After a few moments, she opened her eyes and looked around. She couldn't see much, but she could hear a great commotion and was aware that Gabe and the intruder were wrestling on the floor. Most of the lanterns that had lit the hall had been extinguished or smashed, leaving the room filled with moving shadows. She could make out the picnic table where she'd eaten dinner not far from where she lay. It was the only protection she could ascertain within her grasp. Slowly, she edged her way toward it until she could slip behind the overturned bench. When she attempted to sit up, the top of her head brushed the underside of the table.

She stiffened as fingers touched her arm until she recognized Mary Beth's frightened voice. "I prayed someone would come. I can't make Tommy stop crying." Looking down at the child, Sally became aware the little girl cradled a real baby in her arms, not the doll she tended to drag about with her.

Mary Beth thrust the infant toward Sally, and as Sally's arms instinctively closed around him, she felt almost as much at a loss to know what to do as the little girl did. "Shhh," she whispered in the baby's ear. Her fingers touched the small face, and without her knowing quite how it happened, the baby latched onto one of her fingers and began sucking vigorously. She wasn't certain that was a good thing, but it stopped his screaming cries. Mary Beth snuggled closer, leaning against her shoulder.

She wished she could see what was happening but was grateful to be hidden from the drunken man who had tried to force her to go with him. She said a quick prayer, pleading for the protection of Gabe and Marvin, Uncle John and Aunt Mazie too. Shots rang out, and something thumped hard against the bench she and the children sheltered behind. Once she thought she heard Uncle John's commanding voice above the tumult.

Gradually, the sounds reaching Sally's ears changed. Instead of men's voices and the rough and tumble of scuffling men, she heard the desperate cries of women seeking their children and attending to their men. Through the thin board walls, she caught a sound like a hundred horses stampeding past the dance hall.

Poking her head above the bench, she attempted to ascertain whether it was safe for her and Mary Beth to emerge from their hiding place. She noticed at once someone was relighting or replacing some of the lanterns that had been snuffed out. Several men were wandering about as though lost or confused. Women knelt beside a couple of men who lay sprawled on the floor. Neither one was the man Gabe had rescued her from. Half a dozen women huddled with their arms around small children. There was no sign of Gabe or Marvin. Not even Uncle John was among the few men in the hall.

"How did you get this baby? Do you see his mother?" Sally whispered to Mary Beth who was still snuggled against her side with her thumb in her mouth.

Lowering her thumb, the little girl mumbled, "That man took Mrs. Gardner. He threw Tommy under the table, and I catched him." Her thumb went back in her mouth.

Sally was still trying to make sense of the child's words when the little girl screamed, "Mama!" Mary Beth flung herself from beside Sally toward Mazie, who was frantically searching among the overturned tables and benches. After a tearful greeting for her daughter, Mazie hurried toward Sally with Mary Beth clinging tightly to her skirt.

"You're safe!" Mazie said, and Sally wasn't certain whether her aunt was stating the obvious or asking a question. "I was afraid you were among the hostages."

"Hostages?"

"When those ruffians left, they took some of the young women with them." Mazie's eyes dropped to the baby now sleeping peacefully in Sally's arms. She brushed against tears streaming down her face. "I'm afraid young Tommy's mother is among those kidnapped."

CHAPTER SIX

"WILL THOSE MEN BE BACK?" Sally voiced her fear aloud.

"No, they won't be back." Mazie, Sally sensed, wasn't as confident as she attempted to appear. "Almost every able-bodied man here at the community center has gone after them."

"They was those Taft boys!" A voice came from the back of the cluster of women that had gathered around Mazie and Sally. "They're always startin' trouble, but they ain't ever gone this far before."

"Those Taft boys are always causing trouble. Their ma insists they're 'good boys, just a little rambunctious.'"

"They was more than rambunctious tonight!" Another indignant voice joined the conversation.

The name *Taft* sounded familiar, but at first, Sally couldn't place it. Then she remembered the outspoken female rancher who'd helped to formulate a plan for catching the cattle rustlers. To Sally, the woman had seemed to make sound and reasonable suggestions. Could she have been wrong about the woman? Might she and her sons be responsible for the cattle thefts as well as the commotion stirred up this evening?

"Who all is missing?" another questioned.

It was soon determined that in addition to baby Tommy's mother, two thirteen-year-olds, a fifteen-year-old, and the schoolteacher were missing. The mothers of the teenagers had frantically searched everywhere for their daughters.

The baby Sally held made a snuffling noise and twisted his head against her bodice. She feared he'd soon be awake and begin screaming again.

"I'd better take him." A young woman reached for the baby. "He's waking up, and when he does, he'll be hungry. My baby is asleep under the far table," she added by way of explanation as she waved vaguely toward one of the few tables still upright. It took a moment for Sally to understand the woman's meaning. Grateful, she transferred the sleeping infant to the other woman's arms.

Time seemed to drag as the women set about doctoring the men who had been injured in the fighting and straightening up the room. Children were once again snuggled in blankets under the tables. The women separated into smaller clusters to watch over the children and speak together in hushed tones.

Sally found her head nodding as she sat on the bench in front of Mary Beth, waiting for the men to return. She learned only one woman in the group lived near enough to walk home. Sally recognized her as the storekeeper's wife. Though she could have returned home, she chose to remain with the other women. There were a few teams and wagons left behind by the men, but their owners' wives chose to wait for their husbands' and, in some cases, daughters' return.

At last, thudding hoof beats and jangling harnesses heralded the return of the men. Mothers were the first to dash toward the door.

Uncle John strode into the hall. Following like ducklings behind their mother were the three teenagers. Several ranchers and cowboys followed, then came Marvin with one arm around the schoolteacher, assisting her in limping into the room. The last captive to stagger into the room was a young woman with her hair loose and straggling almost to her waist. Her dress was ripped, the skirt almost separated from the bodice, so it dragged behind her. Her face and arms were scratched and dirty. A young man walked beside her, his arm around her and a worried expression on his face.

"My baby! Tommy!" The woman sobbed. She turned toward the table where Sally and Mary Beth had hidden earlier. Before she'd taken many steps, the woman who had relieved Sally of the infant rushed forward with the baby in her arms.

"He's here, Florence. He's fine. I fed him so he wouldn't cry."

"Tommy!" The mother began to cry as she reached for her child. The young husband wrapped his arms around them both. His shoulders shook as though he, too, might be crying.

The ride home seemed endless. Sally lay on the heavy quilt beside Mary Beth, who seemed to have no trouble sleeping. Both the Double J and the Circle C cowboys, including Marvin and Gabe, chose to escort the wagon back to the ranch. Uncle John spoke in a low voice. Even so, Sally heard him tell Mazie how they'd caught up to the Taft boys, all eight of them, before they reached their ranch. The cool night had sobered them, and they'd put up little resistance, with the exception of Pete, who was still smarting from the licking Gabe had given him. He insisted it was his right to claim any woman he wanted since Gabe kept him and his chosen woman apart.

Sally recoiled at the faulty assertion that without Gabe's interference, she would have gone voluntarily with Pete.

"Florence fought like a wild cat to free herself, and Thomas had to be held back from shootin' the bounder. It took some maneuverin', but we finally got her free. In the commotion, the schoolteacher, Miss Reynolds's, foot got stepped on by one of the horses. Marv wrapped it and carried her on his horse all the way back."

Sally shuddered. She was so glad all the victims had been returned and that she would soon be back at the ranch.

Once they reached it, she lost no time crawling into bed. Surprisingly, she didn't fall asleep at once. Instead she found herself staring into the darkness, reviewing in her mind over and over all that happened.

It was later than usual when Sally awoke the following morning. She dressed quickly and made her way to the kitchen, where she found Mazie alone.

"John and Mary Beth have finished breakfast," Mazie informed her. "John was in a hurry to join his men, and Mary Beth is in her room dressing for her riding lesson."

Sally felt a stab of guilt. She'd forgotten about the riding lesson. She'd have to eat quickly and change her clothes.

It wasn't long before she and Mary Beth walked hand in hand toward the corral. The little girl squealed and ran ahead as soon as she saw her pony. Sally spotted Daisy once more tethered to a post in the corral and swallowed a groan. She didn't look forward to once more experiencing the soreness she'd barely recovered from, courtesy of her last attempt to ride.

"Sit on the corral and watch while I get your horses ready," Clarence instructed. "I'll not expect you to saddle your own horses just yet, but you need to start seein' how it's done."

As Sally watched the cowboy swing her saddle into place, she doubted she'd ever be ready to lift it. It was far larger and clearly much heavier than the saddles she'd noticed on horses back near the village where she'd grown up. A wave of homesickness hit her, and she struggled to keep the picture of her old home and village from her thoughts.

Just as Clarence finished saddling their mounts, Marvin sauntered from the barn. "You help the little miss," he said to Clarence. "Take a couple of turns around the corral. I'll see that Miss Sally is mounted and give her a few pointers."

Marvin assisted her in mounting Daisy and showed her how to keep the horse from stepping away as she moved toward it, then instructed her in the proper way to hold and use the reins. She felt he was a bit distracted through the whole thing, as though his thoughts were somewhere else. After the previous night's experience, she felt only sympathy.

"Follow Mary Beth's pony around the corral," Marv instructed. Feeling more confident, she nudged the horse forward. When she returned to the starting point, he was shaking his head.

"Look," he told her, pointing to Mary Beth astride her pony. "See how she moves with the pony while you bounce up and down with each step?"

She felt her face turn red. It hurt to be criticized for something others took so much for granted and that even a child could do better than she could.

Clarence indicated he was ready to take Mary Beth for a short ride beyond the corral, and Marvin motioned for Sally to fall in line behind them.

"Remember what I told you," Marvin called as he stepped back and waved her on.

Sally straightened her shoulders, gritted her teeth, and followed Mary Beth from the corral. Feeling the bouncing motion with each step Daisy took, a wave of discouragement washed over her, but only moments later, she found herself studying the fluid motion Clarence made as he moved with his horse. Turning her attention to Mary Beth, she noted how the little girl's body moved with her pony as though the two were connected. Whether it was stubbornness or determination, she vowed to learn to ride as well as they did. She struggled to copy their motions and posture. At first, her efforts felt awkward and foolish. They were almost back to the corral when she began to feel she was beginning to catch on to following her horse's rhythm. Feeling triumphant, she looked around for Marvin, but he was nowhere in sight.

After a couple more riding lessons, Sally was beginning to feel confident in her ability. To her surprise, one morning when she and Mary Beth arrived at the corral, Daisy was nowhere to be seen. In her place stood a beautiful roan mare with white stockings and a white streak down the middle of her long head.

"This is Victoria," Clarence said. "John and Marvin both agreed with me that you're ready for a more spirited mount than old Daisy. You take your time getting acquainted while I get the little missy set to ride."

Sally looked around for Marvin but didn't see him. He likely had more important responsibilities that morning. Approaching the new horse, she stroked the animal's velvety nose and whispered soft words in her ears. Nudging the mare closer to the pole fence, she felt a moment's trepidation on sliding one leg across the saddle and steadying herself with one hand on the pommel. *Clarence did say Victoria was more spirited than Daisy.* Willing herself not to shake, she settled herself in the saddle, then slowly reached to unloop the reins from a nearby post. A feeling of exhilaration filled her as she sat astride the horse she'd mounted on her own. That feeling grew as she followed Clarence and Mary Beth out of the corral and down the trail leading to the creek. Somehow she felt more connected to Victoria, a name she shortened to Tori, than she had to Daisy.

Marvin didn't show up for any of her riding lessons the next week, and he seemed to be taking most of his meals with the other cowboys. She missed him but knew from Uncle John's comments that all of the men were extremely busy, and the ranch was shorthanded with one of the men needed each day to ride on scouting duty.

One morning, as she and Mary Beth approached the corral, Sally was dismayed to see Clarence limping and using a crutch for support. Chen Le stood beside the cowboy, shaking his head. Both the pony and Tori were saddled, but Clarence's horse was nowhere in sight.

"I'm sorry," Clarence said. "I fell last night and hurt my leg. Can't ride for a few days."

"We don't have to ride today," Sally said. "You should rest."

"You and the little one both ride well enough that you don't really need me. Why don't you go ahead for a short ride."

Clarence's words surprised her. At the same time, the prospect of riding without a caretaker thrilled her.

"All right," Sally agreed and turned her head to make certain Mary Beth was mounted before settling herself on Tori. Together, they moved toward the gate Chen Le opened for them.

They moved down a well-worn path toward the stream, Mary Beth's smaller pony following behind Tori. Sally enjoyed the feel of the sun on her face and the sense of freedom as they rode unescorted. She took care to begin the return trip where Clarence always turned the horses. The horses obediently followed their accustomed routine.

When they approached the corral, Chen Le met them at the gate, urging them to hurry to the house. He promised to care for their horses. As they entered the house, they found Mazie rushing around in preparation for a trip to town.

"You two will have to hurry. John and Marvin are ready to leave," Mazie warned them. "I left biscuits and jelly on the table for your lunch."

Remembering their last trip to town, Sally wasn't certain she wanted to go. Only knowing that a rider from Eagle Rock might have dropped mail—including a letter from Papa—at the general store on his way to Boise persuaded her to change clothes and find a spot in the wagon beside Mary Beth.

As the wagon rolled through the dust and ruts toward town, Sally was conscious of Marvin on his big chestnut horse riding beside the wagon. She stole peeks at him, admiring his broad chest and handsome face. She liked him—a lot. *Is this what it's like to be in love?* No, she couldn't say she loved Marvin, though she liked and admired him a great deal, and she appreciated the kindness he'd shown her in assisting with various tasks and teaching her to ride. But she had feelings for Gabe too. Perhaps in time her feelings would turn to love for one of them.

She smiled her thanks when Marvin extended his hand to support her as she climbed down from the wagon in front of the small general store. But she was surprised and a little disappointed when he didn't follow her into the store. Instead, he turned to cross the street.

As she'd done on her previous visit to the small store, Sally wandered about, looking at the various items. Spotting a box of peppermint sticks on the counter, she remembered Mary Beth's pleasure on receiving lemon drops during that trip. She quickly purchased a penny's worth of the peppermint sticks to share with her on the return journey.

It didn't take long for Mrs. Cummings to gather the items on Mazie's list or for Uncle John to begin loading the supplies onto the wagon. She gathered up one of the smaller bags and followed him out the door. They were almost finished with the task when Mr. Cummings strolled outside with the last box, and the two men became involved in a discussion concerning the Taft boys. Not wanting to spoil her day with thoughts of the frightening experience she'd endured during her last trip to town, Sally began a short stroll down the boardwalk fronting the few businesses.

Thinking it might not be wise to wander very far, Sally turned back shortly toward the store and Uncle John's wagon. A movement across the street caught her eye. Thinking Marvin might be returning, she stopped to watch. She was right. It was Marvin leaving the building that served as school and community center, but he wasn't alone. Even from across the street, Sally could tell the woman beside him was the schoolteacher, Miss Reynolds. They weren't just walking together. Their hands were clasped, and before they parted, Sally watched Marvin draw Miss Reynolds close. Perhaps he only whispered in her ear, but to Sally, it looked suspiciously like he kissed her.

CHAPTER SEVEN

ALL THE WAY BACK TO the ranch, Sally mulled over and over in her mind what she'd seen. Strangely, she didn't feel particularly sad or upset. In fact, there was something almost heart-warming about seeing something good come from the bad experience the two had shared. Clearly she'd misread Marv's kindness toward her.

Sally and Mary Beth had been riding without Clarence daily for almost a week when Sally noticed a rider moving toward them one day as they neared the corral. She felt a tremor of delight when she recognized the rider as Gabe. She hadn't seen him since the night of the dance. For just a moment, her thoughts returned to that night and how happy she'd been thinking she had two beaus. She felt no lingering disappointment on learning Marv's interest lay elsewhere. Perhaps Gabe wasn't interested in her either, and if he found someone else, her reaction would be the same. A little voice in the back of her mind seemed to cast doubt on her reasoning.

"Hello," he called. "I've come seeking your help."

"I don't know what I can help you with, but if I can, I'd be happy to help," she said, keeping her voice cool as she halted Tori beside Gabe's horse.

"I'll help too," Mary Beth volunteered as she drew closer.

"Sorry, sweetie." Gabe bent low to speak to the little girl. "I'm afraid this a job for grown-ups." He straightened again to speak to Sally, but she didn't miss Mary Beth's unhappy scowl.

"I've been assigned to scout duty for the rest of the day. My partner is supposed to be one of John's men, but there aren't any around other than Clarence and Chen Le, and they can't accompany me right now. We all agreed that the two scouts should come from different ranches. If I go looking for a partner on one of the other ranches this late in the day, I won't make it back to my assigned area in time. I spoke with Clarence and with Mazie. They both assured me you ride well enough to be my partner. That is, if you're willing to accompany me?"

Sally stared at Gabe in shock. She felt comfortable riding now, but she'd never ridden anywhere but on the trail from the corral to the bluff overlooking the creek. And what if they met the rustlers? She didn't know the first thing about what she would be expected to do. On the other hand, spending the afternoon with Gabe appealed to her a great deal.

"Are you sure I won't just be in the way?" she asked.

"That's another rule of this scouting agreement: no riding alone out of sight of other ranchers. If you don't accompany me, I can't do my job." There was a hint of laughter in his eyes, leaving her wondering if he was inventing an excuse for her to go with him or if he really needed her help.

"I'll go, but I need to return Mary Beth to her mother first."

A short time later, they rode side by side through the tall brush toward the sea of black lava rock. At the crest of each hill, they paused, and Gabe took his time surveying the surrounding land as far as he could see. Sally was intrigued by the jagged black rock that appeared more frequently as they approached the vast, rugged wasteland before them. She was equally intrigued by the picture Gabe presented with his broad shoulders and slim waist as he sat astride a horse as dark and rugged as the great lava field.

At last, the thin soil beneath their horses' feet ended. Another step would be onto the black rock that appeared to stretch on forever. She was surprised to note the many twisted shapes the rock took. Unlike the rocks and boulders of her homeland, worn smooth by wind and water, these rocks were more like the clinkers left behind by burnt coal. Before her were hills, valleys, and even mountains of the jagged rocks.

"I didn't know the lava would look like this up close." She turned to Gabe. "How could the rustlers possibly walk or drive animals across that?" She waved an arm toward the lava.

"Some spots are easier to navigate than others," he told her. "A few hearty explorers have made their way across most of it. They've even found caves and tunnels. Surprisingly, there are a few animals who make their home out here too." He slid from his horse and held out his hand to her.

"Come on. You should take a close-up peek at this strange world."

Reluctantly, she slid from Tori's back and watched as Gabe tethered both horses to a stunted juniper tree. Holding his rifle in one hand, he took her hand with his free one to lead her to the rocks, where she gingerly placed a foot on the ragged surface of the hardened lava. It wasn't as bad as she'd expected, and she was soon walking and hopping beside Gabe. As the terrain grew rougher, Gabe moved a few steps ahead of her. She paused to look around and felt a wave of appreciation for the strangely beautiful landscape.

"Don't move!"

At Gabe's strident command, Sally froze beside a rock slab that towered above her head. An ominous rattle sounded nearby. She'd heard of deadly snakes common to the West that made a rattling sound before striking. Horrified, her eyes sought the coiled threat and found it little more than a meter from her feet. Standing in frightened silence, she watched as Gabe's rifle extended slowly toward her. Then in a sudden motion, he flipped the snake far out onto the rocks.

In seconds, he was beside her, holding her shaking form against his broad chest. She didn't give a thought as to whether or not it was proper to allow him to hold her in such a way. She was simply grateful for his action in removing the snake. Once her breathing slowed and she could think clearly again, she decided she liked being held in Gabe's arms.

"Perhaps we should return to our horses." Gabe spoke in a soft voice. It seemed to Sally that Gabe was as reluctant to release his hold on her as she was to be released.

Back on their horses, they moved slowly along the edge of the lava field. They traveled some distance before Sally became aware it was long past lunch time and her saddlebags were empty. The day was hot too. She longed for lunch and a bit of shade. Thank goodness Clarence had filled a canteen and insisted she always carry water when out for a ride. She opened it and took a long swallow. Minutes later, as though he'd read her mind, Gabe pointed to a cluster of juniper trees on a small rise overlooking a vast panorama and informed her they would stop there for a short time.

Gabe shared his lunch with her as they sat on slabs of lava rock and enjoyed the meager shade of a scrubby tree. Sally's eyes slowly scanned the area before them. The lava field seemed to go on forever. A movement caught her eye. A picture of the badly wounded cowboy a few weeks earlier filled her mind. She blinked and tried to focus on the spot where she thought she'd seen movement. All appeared calm in spite of the creepy feeling crawling up her spine that they were being watched.

"Gabe," she whispered, "something or someone is out there."

His eyes widened. "Gather up your things and move slowly toward your horse. Don't glance toward whatever you saw, and don't rush."

Grateful he didn't argue or doubt her, she did as he instructed. When she reached Tori, he boosted her into the saddle before mounting his own horse, then motioned for her to precede him down the hill. The prickling sensation in her back continued, and she expected a shot to ring out any minute.

She couldn't resist a quick glance back. What she saw brought a gasp to her lips. There on the jumble of rocks where she'd seen that brief movement minutes ago stood an animal.

"What is it?" Gabe turned in the direction she was staring. He began to laugh. "That's a bobcat. He looks like an overgrown kitty, but you wouldn't want to tangle with him. See how his coloring helps him blend into the rocks? That lava field is home to half a dozen or more different kinds of rodents. Where there are rats and squirrels, you'll usually find cats, and that one is a fierce hunter."

"I didn't think anything could live out there." She waved vaguely toward the lava field.

"You'd be surprised how much wildlife is out there," Gabe went on. "When you said you saw something move, I thought at once of the shooter who shot Lee. Then I remembered reports a few years ago of a mountain lion hanging around these parts. Mountain lions have been known to stalk and attack men, but bobcats are not as likely to attack larger prey unless they're cornered."

"I'm not sure being stalked by a wildcat is any better than meeting the rustlers," Sally muttered, still feeling shaky.

"I'm glad you noticed movement." Gabe was no longer laughing. "There's no telling whether the bobcat would have attacked while we were sitting down. If cattle, including young calves, are being held by the rustlers nearby, he may be finding the calves easy prey. That might explain why he's hanging out this close to a ranch area that is consistently patrolled by your uncle's ranch hands."

Continuing their patrol along the edge of the vast lava field, Sally considered Gabe's words. Perhaps she hadn't been wise to accept his invitation to ride with him as his partner. She didn't want to meet rustlers or wild animals. Besides, she'd be of little use to Gabe if they came under attack. She wouldn't know how to shoot a gun if she had one, which she didn't, and she was too small to be of any use in physical combat.

The day grew warmer in spite of dark clouds that rolled in from the northwest. What at first felt like a cooling breeze turned to a fierce wind, and a few large splatters of rain stirred the dust at their horses' feet. Tori took mincing side steps and appeared to be as nervous concerning the storm as Sally was.

A crash of thunder was a precursor to a torrent of water pouring from the sky.

"We need to find shelter!" Gabe shouted over the roar of the storm.

Sally nodded and clung tightly to her horse's reins. Gabe led the way, and Tori fell in line behind his horse without any guidance from Sally. It was impossible to ascertain in which direction they rode, though Sally sensed they were moving on an upward slant, and the ground beneath them seemed to be growing steadily more solid, as if they were traveling over rocky terrain.

Minutes, which seemed like hours, later, Gabe drew his horse to a halt beneath a thick overhang of lava rock. Sally and Tori joined him in the protection provided by the rock. Gabe was almost instantly at her side, helping her to dismount and leading her deeper inside the shallow shelter. Leaning back against the porous rock, she closed her eyes and drew in several deep breaths in an attempt to calm her rapidly beating heart. Moments later, she opened her eyes and looked around. The shelter Gabe found for them wasn't exactly a cave. It was more like a shallow bowl set on one side, with barely enough room for her, Gabe, and the two horses. A curtain of water fell like a waterfall from the overhang, forming a miniature river as it rushed away from their refuge.

Gabe settled himself against the rock wall and gently tugged her down beside him. "Tell me about your former home and what you think of Idaho."

Somehow it didn't seem difficult to sit close beside Gabe and share her thoughts and feelings with him as the rain formed an isolating curtain around them. There was something comfortable and reassuring that seemed to flow from him to her, putting her at ease as she told him of the English village she and Papa left behind. She shared the loneliness she often felt being separated from her papa. At last, the rain slowed to a drizzle, and Sally mounted Tori for the return journey. Her clothes were damp, and she quickly felt aware of a stiffness in her legs and back. It wasn't going to be a comfortable journey. Nevertheless, she urged Tori to follow where Gabe led.

"Whoa!" Gabe said softly, and Sally heard the anxious note in his voice. She lifted her eyes to ascertain his reason for stopping. She did so just in time to see a horse and rider disappear from sight in the distance.

CHAPTER EIGHT

Tori came to an abrupt stop, then stood nervously shuffling her hooves in thick mud. Rivulets of water, like miniature rivers, flowed around them. When the mare refused to move forward, Sally slid from the saddle and moved tentatively forward, slipping and sliding in the muck. There was no doubt her shoes and stockings were ruined.

Reaching the point where Gabe had traveled out of her sight, she was surprised to find herself on the edge of a long slope, peering down into a soggy enclosure at the end of an unexpected ravine. If they had passed by it earlier in the storm, they hadn't even noticed it. Ten- to twelve-foot-high lava rocks and cliffs formed an almost complete circle at the end of the ravine. A jumble of brush completed the circle, and inside it were a few reddish-brown shapes she assumed were some of the missing cattle. They appeared to be standing in belly-deep water. Gabe, holding his horse's reins, stood in front of the rock-and-brush corral. He pointed toward the north and motioned for her to go that way.

She didn't want to leave Gabe. Besides, there was no way she could remount without a boost from him or something to stand on. Still, holding Tori's reins in one hand, she began hesitantly trekking in the direction Gabe had indicated. Tori followed meekly behind her. Mud and water slowed her steps. She hoped Gabe meant to join her and that she wouldn't have to walk all the way back to the ranch alone. More than that, she hoped the rustlers weren't nearby. She startled at every sound, fearful of a gunshot.

As she approached a grove of juniper trees, she was surprised to see a few straggly head of cattle weaving their way through the thick trees. In a moment, Gabe appeared behind them, leading his horse, which walked with a definite limp.

She approached him slowly, not wanting to startle the cattle. "Won't taking the cows alert the rustlers that you've found their hiding spot?"

"It may do, but I can't leave them to drown. Two of the calves are already dead, and the other three are struggling to keep up with their mothers. With any luck, the rustlers will think they broke out due to the high water filling their makeshift corral. In case the thieves come by to check on them after the storm, I think it best to get them as far away as possible."

"Are they Uncle John's cattle? Or yours?" Sally wondered if the cattle belonged to the Double J or Uncle John since Gabe began herding them back the way they had come.

"No. The brands haven't been changed. These clearly belong to the Gardners, from over next to Myrtle Taft's place." Gabe pointed toward the mark on the cow nearest them.

"But isn't the Gardner ranch that way?" She gave a vague wave in the opposite direction from where they were now headed.

"It is. Both the Taft and Prescot ranches are in that direction as well, but I think John should have a look at these animals. Folks around here tend to think of him as the closest thing we've got to a lawman."

Sally continued to walk beside Gabe, no longer making any attempt to keep the hem of her riding skirt from collecting mud. She pondered all Gabe had said. Finally, she spoke her thoughts. "After what happened at the dance, I understand most folks think the Taft boys are responsible for the cattle thefts. Is that really why we're headed toward Uncle John's ranch?"

"No." He hesitated. "My horse needs attention, and John's ranch is the closest. Besides, we would be in big trouble if we encountered the rustlers with only one horse and one rifle between us. Best we get to your uncle's place as soon as possible."

She conceded he was right. What he'd said in the nicest way was that she'd be useless in a fight. Aloud she said, "You're limping almost as badly as your horse. Why don't you ride Tori for awhile."

He started to protest, then changed his mind. "We could ride double until we reach the creek. It wouldn't be the first time she has carried two riders."

Sally was a little skeptical, but she allowed Gabe to boost her onto Tori's saddle. He quickly mounted behind her, and as they slowly made their way toward the creek, she found she quite liked feeling Gabe's firm chest at her back and his arms circling her waist. Something in the action went beyond the warmth and security his arms provided.

Cresting a small hill, she found she couldn't hold back a gasp. Instead of a stream, a huge river lay before them. The earlier torrent of rain, followed by gullies filled with water and rivulets trickling at their feet, should have served as a warning that all that water would make its way to the ravine. Perhaps calling the wide expanse of water a river wasn't a mistake after all. As they drew closer, an unmistakable roar met her ears, warning of a swift current. The cattle stopped their forward movement and began a restless shuffle and nervous bellowing.

"There's no way we can cross here," Gabe shouted over the roar of the water. "We'll have to follow the river to where it widens and disappears into sinkholes near the lava field. There's a place I know where it will be safe to cross."

Sally glared at the water suspiciously. She couldn't believe there could be any place where it would be safe to cross. She worried, too, about Gabe's lame horse, Tori carrying an extra load, and the cows and calves who were tired from their already long trek. Besides, it would soon be dark.

They moved slowly, following the fast-moving stream but staying back far enough to avoid slipping into the water. At frequent intervals, they were forced to wade through gullies that had become small streams rushing toward the larger river. There were places, too, where wet sand and limp grass told a story of recent saturation. As Tori seemed to move steadily slower and Gabe's horse appeared to be limping more, Sally offered to walk.

"Another quarter of a mile, and we'll both have to walk," he informed her. "We're almost to where the river disappears into the ground, and it'll be tough walking for all of the animals. It'll take both of us to lead and push them across."

"How can a stream of water just disappear?" It didn't make sense to Sally.

"Both the soil and the rocks here are extremely porous. Rain and snow seep through them. Some people believe the Lost River and the creeks and streams around here become part of a huge underground reservoir that releases some of its water into a bigger river many miles south of here called the Snake River. Some of the water collects for a time in some of the caves and basins of the lava field."

As they both lapsed into silence, Sally thought she heard a strange cry. Immediately, she thought of the bobcat they'd seen earlier. Looking around, she could see nothing alarming. Then the sound came again. This time, she noticed one of the calves shying away from a clump of brush.

"Gabe, there's something over there." She pointed toward the brush.

Without a word, Gabe slid from Tori's back. Sally held her breath as he took cautious steps toward the source of the keening wail. A rustling movement shook the brush, and she found herself praying for his protection. He made a swooping motion, and when he stood, Sally was shocked to see Mary Beth in his arms. She was crying and clinging in desperation to him. Her hair hung in tangles over Gabe's arm, and she was clearly soaked, covered in mud, and cold.

Sally slid from Tori's back and stepped toward her small cousin, remembering to hang onto the reins of both horses with one hand.

"Oh, honey, what are you doing out here?" She reached with her free hand to smooth Mary Beth's hair from her tear-covered face. At Sally's touch, the child struggled to leap into her arms. Gabe took the horses' reins as he smoothly transferred Mary Beth to Sally, where she snuggled close and Sally murmured soothing assurances in the little girl's ear. Moments later, a thick poncho settled around Mary Beth's shaking form.

"Thank you," Sally whispered.

"I'd almost forgotten that old thing was in the bottom of my saddlebag." Gabe paused, then added, "We need to keep moving. It's getting dark, and that little girl needs her warm bed. It might be best to put her on your horse for as long as possible while we walk."

He didn't mention the rustlers, but Sally felt certain they were one of his concerns. Like Gabe, they would know there was only one way to cross the creek.

CHAPTER NINE

THE GROUND GREW INCREASINGLY DIFFICULT to walk on, though Gabe kept them to the higher side of the bog-like basin they reached in a short time. He pointed out markings in the dirt that showed the water was rapidly dropping and assured both Sally and Mary Beth that the rare rainstorm was unlikely to occur again anytime soon.

Sally had no idea how long they had been plodding along with the bog on one side and sharp lava rocks on the other. Her arms ached from holding Tori's reins in one hand and steadying Mary Beth with the other. The child was so weary that she kept nodding off, then lurching to the side. Sally had caught her several times, preventing her from falling.

In an effort to keep the child alert enough to stay in the saddle, she asked, "What happened? How did you get on this side of the creek?"

"I wanted to go with you and Gabe," Mary Beth mumbled. "I followed, but I got lost and it rained. Star runned away. I couldn't find you."

"Oh, sweetie, your mum must be so worried."

"Star is losted too, and I couldn't find him." She began sobbing again.

"I understand horses usually find their way home." She attempted to comfort the child. "Oh!" Sally almost ran into Gabe when he stopped abruptly in front of her.

"If you can lead both horses, I'll carry Mary Beth across this next stretch. It'll be rough going, but I think the water has gone down enough, and there are quite a few rocks to step on for us to get across. The cattle have already moved out onto the marshland, and I think we should follow."

Sally looked ahead of her. Sky and marsh blended together in the darkness. Venturing across the sinkhole sounded to her like a frightening step, but she trusted Gabe. With a jolt, she realized Gabe was the only person she trusted as implicitly as she trusted Papa. In every interaction she'd had with him, he seemed to have her best interests at heart. She nodded, then, uncertain whether or not he could see the gesture, she whispered, "If you think it's best to attempt to cross here, I'll follow your lead."

Stepping from the slippery mud to the thick bog grass made little difference at first to her wet feet. However, walking became increasingly difficult. The rocks proved to be few and far between. With each footstep, her feet sank deeper in the thick ooze, and she could no longer be certain her shoes were still on her feet. She attempted to protect her skirt, but it didn't take long to decide there was no way to hold up her skirt and the horses' reins. The animals made their dislike of the situation clear by balking at taking a step or by lunging forward, thus jerking her aching arms. She couldn't avoid worrying about Gabe and Mary Beth. Gabe hadn't complained about his leg, but she knew it must still be bothering him.

The wind was increasing in strength, and the overcast sky made it impossible to discern how much farther the bog extended. She could barely see Gabe's form before her. She would have bumped into him if he hadn't spoken in a hushed whisper.

"Off to our left . . . I thought I saw a flicker of light."

Sally glanced nervously toward the north. She saw it too—the tiniest speck of light.

"Someone is camping out on the point. We'll have to be very quiet and head a little more to the south. Sound is amplified out here by the stillness of the night." He continued to whisper. "It could be John and some of the ranch hands looking for Mary Beth, but we can't risk it being the rustlers."

Without commenting, Sally clutched the horses' reins tighter and followed Gabe. Each sound made by the animals sounded like a trumpet blast to her ears and had her frantically searching the blackness for pursuers. She stayed as close to Gabe as possible, and as the night wore on, she noticed his limp becoming more pronounced and that the child on his back lay unmoving against his shoulder. She couldn't help wishing they were all safely back at the ranch in their beds. Fatigue gradually slowed her steps, and her mind seemed to drift into a trancelike state.

"I think we've got trouble," Gabe said.

She hadn't been aware of Gabe dropping back to stand beside her, or that they were no longer moving.

"Something is out there."

Sally listened, but she didn't hear anything. Neither could she see anything beyond the dark shapes of the two horses. Somewhere along the way, they appeared to have lost the small herd of cattle. It occurred to her that whatever Gabe had seen or heard might have been the cattle they were attempting to return to their rightful owner. But a sick sensation in her stomach told her it wasn't.

He pointed toward a dark shape to the right and behind them, then began trudging toward it. Though unsure where he was going, she followed. As they drew nearer, she could tell they were approaching a small hill comprised mostly of sharp lava rocks. It wasn't much higher than the soggy basin they'd been traveling through, but the horses seemed to welcome a respite from the swampy ground. At Gabe's urging, they settled close to the ground.

"Get down as far as possible," he whispered. "We can't afford to have our silhouettes visible to anyone."

Sally and Gabe took shelter behind a couple of the larger rocks. Sinking gratefully to the ground beside Gabe, Sally heaved a sigh of relief. Her life had been filled with hard work as long as she could remember, but she didn't believe she'd ever before been as tired as she now felt. She watched as Gabe gently settled Mary Beth beside him with her head resting on his lap. She felt a lump in her throat seeing the tenderness this big, strong cowboy showed the small girl.

"Hungry," the child muttered.

"We don't have any food," Gabe whispered back. "Perhaps this will help." He offered her a drink from his canteen. She took a few sips, then settled back to sleep.

Neither Gabe nor Sally spoke as they leaned against the large rocks, their shoulders touching, and simply watched and listened for movement or sounds. Small, unidentifiable noises were reminders that the swampy ground was home to many small animals and some not so small. Fatigue gradually overtook fear, and Sally slept. She wasn't aware when the hard rock behind her head changed to a more comfortable shoulder.

A gentle movement against her cheek startled Sally awake. She had no idea how long she had been asleep.

"Shh," Gabe whispered. "It's almost dawn, and we should be moving on."

Looking around, she was surprised to be able to see distinct shapes and even a few stars in the sky. The small mound where they huddled was like an island in a sea of bedraggled grass and brush.

"Whoever or whatever I heard last night has gone. If we hurry, we can make it to your uncle's ranch in about two hours."

"I want my mama," Mary Beth whimpered. The child raised her head and looked around.

"We're going back to your mama now," Sally assured the child as she scrambled to her feet and helped Mary Beth to stand. Gabe assisted her in mounting

Tori, then set Mary Beth in front of her. She didn't need his explanation for leaving his own hands free to use the rifle if needed. She held his horse's reins too.

As they left the mound, she glanced around apprehensively. All seemed to be well, but she couldn't shake the feeling more trouble lay ahead of them.

The ground felt firmer than it had the night before as they made their way to the edge of the bog. Nevertheless, Sally felt a greater sense of urgency as they left the swampy area behind.

It wasn't long before she noticed Gabe making frequent glances to one side. The set of his shoulders warned her he was anticipating trouble. She followed his gaze but couldn't see anything alarming. The sun was now sending its first wide beams across the sagebrush-covered land in a dazzling display of light. Perhaps he was concerned the light would make them visible to the rustlers if they were about.

"What's that?" Mary Beth sat up straight and leaned forward.

Sally couldn't see what had caught Mary Beth's attention, but as they started down a shallow arroyo, a flash of color caught her eye. Moments later, a large, reddish cow lumbered into view. Not far behind it, a second cow appeared. Was it possible they'd caught up to the stolen cattle they'd rescued earlier? Her heart raced, and she almost shouted in jubilation before remembering they were on open grazing land, and the cows could be anyone's cattle.

Feeling her horse jolt forward, she felt a moment's confusion before realizing Gabe had slapped Tori's rump to urge her to a faster pace across the dip in the ground. He placed one finger across his lips, urging silence. His rifle was in his other hand, and he was using his knees to urge his lame horse forward.

Suddenly scared, she clasped Mary Beth tighter and used her heels to encourage Tori to climb the low embankment. From the corner of her eye, she was aware of Gabe keeping pace beside her. Looking back, a quick count showed five cows and three calves being driven by two cowboys. The cowboys spotted her and Gabe at almost the same moment she saw them. One raised his head, looking directly at her. A momentary flash of recognition flitted through her mind. He was one of the gunfighters she'd seen the day she and Papa first arrived. The man's eyes hardened, and she saw him reach for his rifle. She crouched low, determined to provide Mary Beth as much protection as possible. Sally dug her heels into her horse's sides, and the animal surged forward. The crack of the rifle and the whistle of a bullet passing too close for comfort intensified her fear.

As she crested the small rise, her heart sank. Coming toward them were at least six more riders.

CHAPTER TEN

SALLY DIDN'T KNOW WHICH WAY to turn. They were trapped, but she couldn't stop. The man with the rifle was surely right behind her. Another shot rang out just as she realized Gabe was no longer beside her. Looking around frantically, she saw him kneeling beside a rock with his rifle pointed at the man who had fired at her. He turned his head just enough to shout, "Go!"

How could she leave him? What if he was killed? A fierce stab of pain tore through her, telling her she didn't want to live in a world without Gabe. But there was Mary Beth! She couldn't let the rustlers murder an innocent child. Pulling on Tori's reins, she turned the horse, hoping to outrun the oncoming riders. Too late, she realized she was headed straight for the sinkhole, and her efforts were futile anyway since Tori was exhausted from the previous day's long ride and much too short rest without even being unsaddled.

She could hear the pounding of hooves behind her drawing closer. "Faster!" She shouted as she frantically tried to push the weary mare to greater speed.

A dark flash passed her, and she saw the rider lean down to grasp Tori's halter, bringing the horse to a stop. Holding the bit of leather, he twisted to look up at Sally.

"Where you going so fast, little lady? Or should I say, *ladies*?" Grinning up at Sally was Pete Taft, the last man she'd ever wished to see again.

Before she could say anything, Mary Beth sat up straight and glared.

"You was mean to Tommy. You aren't supposed to throw babies under tables!"

"You're right, missy. That warn't what I shoulda done, and I'm right sorry fer doin' it." He glanced back at Sally before adding, "Best we stay back here until the boys finish havin' it out with them rustlers."

"Aren't you one of them?" Sally's voice was filled with scorn. She remembered too well the obnoxious man who had tried to force her first to dance with him, then to leave with him and his brothers.

"Look, Miss High and Mighty, I apologize fer ever'thin' that happened that night. The boys and me had too much to drink, and everyone mistook our attempt to have a little fun fer somethin' more. We bin tryin' to make up for our behavior that night by helpin' our neighbors. When we heard you and the little miss were lost in the storm, we came to help."

Sally sniffed. She didn't believe he was sorry for his crude behavior at the dance or that he'd actually come to help.

Gunshots sounded, sending darts into her heart. There were too many for Gabe to fight alone. If only she had a gun—and knew how to use it. If she hadn't already discovered her feelings for Gabe, she would love him now for his willingness to sacrifice himself in order to give her and little Mary Beth a chance to escape. The least she could do would be to make certain his sacrifice wasn't in vain.

A sudden jab of her heels into Tori's sides sent the horse lunging forward. Clasping Mary Beth with one arm, she gave the horse its head. A glance over her shoulder brought a surprise. Pete Taft wasn't even following her. Neither had he raised his rifle. A second glance showed his horse with him astride trotting back toward his brothers. Good! She had a solid head start, and with any luck, she'd reach the ranch and be able to send help back for Gabe. She prayed he'd be able to hold on until help arrived.

Mary Beth clung to her, and she felt Tori gradually slow. The horse was exhausted, but still, she pressed on. Surely it couldn't be much farther to the ranch.

Seeing a cloud of dust rising in the air and moving rapidly toward her, she felt a moment's panic. There appeared to be a number of horses and riders charging toward her. Surely the Taft brothers hadn't gotten ahead of her. Praying she wasn't riding into more trouble, she continued toward the oncoming group.

Suddenly Mary Beth sat upright and shouted, "Papa!"

The little girl was right. The big horse in the lead was the one Uncle John usually rode, and keeping pace with him was Marvin's big black stallion. Just behind them came Clarence and half a dozen or more of the Circle C cowboys. As they drew closer to the approaching group of riders, Sally heard John's jubilant shout. In mere moments he was beside her, reaching for Mary Beth, who practically leapt from Sally's arms to her papa's.

"Are you all right?" Marvin drew closer to ask. "And . . . ?" He cocked his head toward Mary Beth.

"We're both fine, but Gabe and his horse both have injured legs and are being shot at!"

"Let's go!" Marvin shouted. He dug in his heels, and his horse leaped forward.

John thrust his daughter back toward Sally. As he did so, he shouted over his shoulder to the older cowboy. "Clarence, see that these two get back safely to the ranch." He then spurred his horse into action.

"I want to go with you," Mary Beth protested. Ignoring his daughter's cries, Uncle John urged the big roan stallion into a run to catch up with his men.

A silent prayer winged its way heavenward as Sally watched the rapidly disappearing riders. Was it possible that Gabe might have held off the rustlers this long? She couldn't bear to think of anything bad happening to him.

"This way, miss." Clarence pointed in the direction they should travel to reach the ranch. His voice softened, and he looked directly at the whimpering child. "Your ma is sure going to be happy to see you. Hold on tight, and we'll be there in no time."

Mary Beth sat up straighter and wiped at her tear-streaked face. Turning to Sally, she whispered, "Mr. Clarence knows where my mama is. He'll take us to her."

Sally couldn't stop worrying. It had been some time since she'd heard any gunshots. Were they too far away to be heard, or was the fight over? Was Gabe still alive? If Gabe was dead, would she ever recover? She knew she had to concentrate on her mission to return her small cousin to her mother, but her thoughts and her heart remained behind in that dark unknown with the man who had become her confidant, her partner, her rescuer.

Mazie burst into tears when she saw the three riders make their way toward the barn. She met them before they could dismount and relieved Sally of Mary Beth at once. Both mother and daughter sobbed as they hugged each other. Clarence motioned for them both to accompany Mazie to the house and assured Sally he was just fine with caring for both horses.

At the mention of caring for the horses, Mary Beth cried harder as she choked out, "Star ran away. I couldn't catch him."

"Don't you worry about that little horse." Clarence smiled and spoke in a comforting voice. "He came wanderin' in late last night. He's kinda banged up, but Chen Le fixed him up and says he's gonna be just fine."

Mazie took Mary Beth inside the barn to see her pony before leading the way to the house, where she assured both Mary Beth and Sally that warm baths and breakfast were waiting for them.

Darkness had fallen again by the time Sally at last heard the jangle of spurs and the steady plodding of horses approaching the barn. She closed her eyes and prayed for strength before dashing from the house to confront the returning riders. Her gaze landed first on Uncle John. Behind him trailed a horse on a lead rope. Her heart almost stopped beating when she recognized the riderless horse as Gabe's.

Desperately, she searched the crowd of men and horses without seeing the one person she longed with all her being to see. She was pleased to discover the small herd of cattle she and Gabe had attempted to rescue. As her eyes slid past Uncle John once more, she noticed Marvin dismounting from his big stallion. He reached up to assist someone who had been riding double behind him. Two men whom she quickly identified as James Jenson and Pete Taft emerged from the melee of men and horses to add their assistance.

"Gabe!" It was almost a scream. She flew toward him. For just a moment, his eyes lit up, and he smiled, then his body went limp.

Sally hovered nearby as Uncle John and Marvin carried Gabe inside the house and placed him on the sofa. She stared in horror at the blood smeared across his face and down his shirt. She started toward him, but Mazie held her back as Chen Le bustled into the room. She watched in a daze as the man daubed at the stream of blood on Gabe's cheek, then applied smelly ointment to the wound that creased his cheek before disappearing into his hair. Next he slit Gabe's pant leg. Sally gasped, seeing how swollen his leg was from ankle to knee. She cringed, remembering how far he'd walked and the long distance he'd carried Mary Beth. Tears came to her eyes as she recalled each action he'd taken to protect her and her small cousin. Gabe would forever be her hero.

"Sally, you need to come with me." Mazie placed an arm around Sally's shoulders and attempted to draw her away from the spot she'd claimed at Gabe's side. "John will help Chen Le clean up Gabe and put clean clothing on him. He assured me the wound isn't deep and looks worse than it is because head wounds bleed more than other injuries."

"He be fine. You go and come back soon," Chen Le added as he motioned for her to leave with Mazie.

Reluctantly, Sally followed Mazie from the room where Gabe lay to the kitchen, where she paced the floor and silently prayed for his recovery.

"I can tell you care about Gabe Jenson," Mazie said quietly. "He's a good man, and I think he cares about you too."

"Neither Mary Beth nor I would have survived out there without his care."

"I think it's more than gratitude you're feeling."

Sally nodded without speaking. A sound caught her attention, causing her pulse to accelerate. Footsteps were approaching. She turned expectantly toward the door just as Uncle John stepped into the kitchen.

"Chen Le says Gabe will be fine. He just needs a good night's sleep and to stay off that leg for a week or so," John spoke without waiting to be prompted. "I just peeked in Mary Beth's room to see she's sleeping soundly. Both of you need to find your beds as well, since neither of you got much, if any, sleep last night." His gruff words sounded like an order.

Before Sally made her way upstairs to her bedroom, she stopped beside the sofa where Gabe lay. He appeared to be sleeping peacefully. Behind her she heard Gabe's father bidding Uncle John good night. "I'll be over tomorrow with a wagon to take him home. I appreciate Chen Le's doctorin' and you lookin' after him tonight."

"It's no trouble. I owe him. Without him, it's doubtful my daughter and niece would have made it back here safely. Either the storm or those Prescot boys would've got them. Seems they camped within a mile or so of each other last night."

"It's hard to believe it was the Prescots all along stealin' our stock."

"They were planning to start a new ranch farther north where there's more grass. Some of us will have to go up there in a day or two to fetch our cattle back."

"Speakin' of them boys, what's to be done with their bodies?"

"Pete Taft and my foreman volunteered to deliver them to their pa. I expect Marv had two reasons for volunteering. He'd want to make certain the Taft brothers don't shoot the old man too, and it gives him a good excuse to stop at the Weatherbys on the way back to visit a bit with that schoolteacher he's sweet on."

Her room was dark, with only a sliver of light making its way into the room, when Sally awoke from a restless sleep. Her thoughts went at once to Gabe. Knowing there was no way she'd be able to go back to sleep without checking on him, she slid from bed and donned her robe, tying the sash securely about her waist. She stealthily opened her door and proceeded to make her way silently down the stairs. When she reached the living room, she went straight to the sofa where Gabe lay.

For several minutes, she stood watching him sleep, then, kneeling, she lightly touched his chest and felt a sense of comfort as it rose and fell beneath her hand, assuring her he was breathing. Settling more comfortably on the rug beside the sofa, she leaned toward him and was both surprised and pleased to feel him lift his arm and settle it around her shoulders.

"Sally?" His voice was little more than a breath of air.

"I'm here beside you." She leaned closer.

"I want you beside me always." His fingers pressed more firmly against her arm, sending flickers of heat all the way through her. He paused long enough that she began to wonder if he'd gone back to sleep, but then he spoke again. "As soon as your father returns, I'd like to ask him for permission to court you. That is, if you're agreeable."

Tears sprang to Sally's eyes; this time, they were tears of joy. "I think he'll say yes, and that's my answer too." She couldn't imagine anything she wanted more than to be courted by Gabe, then become his wife.

Gabe's arm tightened, drawing her closer. A delicious warmth filled her as his lips touched hers. Tiny shivers of pleasure swept from her head to her toes. The brief kiss was her first, but it left her convinced she would happily spend the rest of her life practicing and perfecting the skill with Gabe.

Whispered words of endearment, plans, and dreams passed between them. Kisses were exchanged, each one longer and more delicious than the one before. Tension from their earlier ordeal dissipated, and they slept.

The sun was rising when John and Mazie entered their front room to find Sally sitting on the floor asleep with her head on Gabe's chest and Gabe's arm encircling her shoulders. A smile brightened his sleeping features. They both seemed to radiate an aura of peace and love. John and Mazie exchanged their own smiles and silently crept from the room.

ABOUT THE AUTHOR

JENNIE HANSEN GRADUATED FROM RICKS College in Idaho, then Westminster College in Utah. She has been a newspaper reporter, editor, and librarian. In addition to writing novels, she reviews LDS fiction in a monthly column for Meridian Magazine.

She was born in Idaho Falls, Idaho, and has lived in Idaho, Montana, and Utah. She has received numerous writing awards. Jennie and her husband, Boyd, live in Salt Lake County. They have five married children, twelve grandchildren, and another six "almost" grandchildren.

OTHER BOOKS AND AUDIOBOOKS
BY CAROLYN TWEDE FRANK

The Hitler Dilemma

Trapped in East Germany

CRAIG, COLORADO, SERIES

Heart of the West

Saving Susannah Jones

Under the Stars

His Accidental Bride

PRAISE FOR CAROLYN TWEDE FRANK

"On a rare break from the constant work to establish their family's homestead, two sisters rescue a seriously wounded stranger. In the ensuing weeks, the older sister and the stranger develop strong feelings for each other, but she already has a commitment to someone else. Divided loyalties, honor, and gratitude lead to an unforgettable Fourth of July celebration. Readers will love this Western tale."

—Jennie Hansen, author *When Tomorrow Comes*

"I was immediately drawn in to 'Celebration for Celia.' Carolyn crafts an engaging story with interesting tidbits keeping me reading until the very last page. She has an impressive grasp of the time period and characters of the western frontier."

—Jen Geigle Johnson, author *A Torn Allegiance*

"Carolyn Twede Frank's took me back home as she described the areas of Idaho where I grew up. I could picture her characters visiting the City of Rocks just as I used to!"

—Brittany Larsen, author *The Matchmaker's Match*

celebration for celia

CAROLYN TWEDE FRANK

CHAPTER ONE

"I wish Pa would have let us leave sooner." Celia would have liked more than just an hour or two for their outing. To have the entire day would have been nice. She tilted her chin up, enjoying the late-spring breeze on her face and enjoying the freedom of riding Copper for sheer enjoyment's sake. It had been too long since she'd done this.

"Don't complain." Sophia nudged Celia's back. "It was nice of Pa to let us out of chores for the *afternoon*."

"You're right," Celia responded, knowing she should be glad for what time she had to share the saddle and explore with her twelve-year-old sister. "Let's stop here first."

They dismounted and tied Copper's reins to a straggly juniper. For several minutes, they walked around Registration Rock, as it had been called by the pioneers who'd written their names on this huge stone formation sitting at the edge of their family's homestead. How many wagon trains had passed by this remote spot of the Idaho Territory before the transcontinental railroad was completed thirteen years ago? That was ten years before they'd moved here. Sophia ran her fingers over the faded names written in axel grease upon the stone surface in reverent silence.

"Maybe Pa's feeling generous because it's my birthday." Celia broke the hush, still thinking about him letting them come. She motioned for Sophia to step away from the towering rock. They needed to get going to be back by suppertime. "And it's his way of letting me celebrate."

"Pa?" Sophia laughed and followed her.

"I know, I know. It made me smile too, just imagining Pa indulging us with a little fun." Celia swore her pa didn't believe in special occasions. At least not since that Fourth of July four years ago when Pa's old Civil War buddy had run into him at the parade. Celia would give anything to know what he'd said to Pa that day. Fourth of Julys hadn't been the same since. Neither had Pa. Maybe it was simply because they'd moved out West, leaving Massachusetts behind them.

She climbed onto Copper, not bothering to pull her full skirt down to cover her bare shins, just tucking it around her thighs. The air felt good on her legs, and Sophia wouldn't care. Her sister climbed into the saddle and settled in behind Celia in similar unladylike fashion.

"You'd better hold onto me while I take Copper off the main trail." Celia thought about their family's other two horses; they were probably grazing in the pasture behind their log cabin at this very moment. "It's too bad Pa didn't let you take Pepper so you didn't have to share the saddle with me."

"It's all right." Sophia's hands locked together around Celia's waist. "I'm just glad we got to come. Paul and little Abby didn't."

Celia nodded, though she doubted the constant hinting that special days deserved celebration finally got through to her parents. Most likely, they had noticed her melancholy. It had plagued her since receiving Wesley's letter last week. His words had felt cold in spots, like spring soil dotted with drifts of snow, most certainly weary of being weighed down by the chill of winter. Was Wesley feeling weighed down by the prospect of marrying Celia and it showed through in his letter? The thought rose goosebumps on her arms, as if she were sitting in a spring snowdrift. Ma and Pa had their hearts set on her and Wesley getting married—as did Celia. Did Wesley no longer feel the same?

She refused to taint the day by thinking about the letter and turned from side to side, taking in the beauty of the June grass and the gray stone rising up from the fresh-green hillside in the distance. She'd grown to love the wide-open expanse of raw land Pa was turning into alfalfa fields. And she'd more than warmed up to the people of Almo. True, the town wasn't much more than a general store, a telegraph office, and a blacksmith shop, but it was home now.

So much so that she wasn't sure she wanted to leave next year when she turned twenty and Wesley finished medical school. Maybe she could convince him to move out here . . . if his letters warmed up again. Almo needed a doctor. Right now all they had was Pa—a medic from the Civil War. Gracious be, it'd been three years since she'd seen Wesley. But she hadn't forgotten the deep sound of his voice or the spark in his light-brown eyes when he told her she was beautiful.

"I wish we could have ourselves a town celebration or something," Celia spoke up to divert her thoughts, "like we used to back in Springfield. Parades, picnics in the park, sack races, and fireworks. Oh, wouldn't that be grand?" She sighed.

"Wow, all of that for your birthday?" Sophia's voice held a note of disbelief. "I thought it was dandy enough of Pa to let us go exploring." She pointed up ahead at the multitude of stone formations that dotted the rising meadow like a community of rounded, misshapen gray homes and shops. "I've never seen them up close—only from the wagon as we've passed by."

"I was speaking of a Fourth of *July* celebration, not a fourth of *June* celebration. This little adventure looking at rocks is fine for my birthday, more than I'd expected. But don't you think it's high time we celebrate *Independence Day?*"

"What's In Depend Dance Day?" Sophia snickered.

"Goodness gracious, it's been a national holiday for well over a hundred years." Celia blew out a breath. "Just because we're living in a territory, that doesn't mean we're not part of the United States of America. How could my little sister be so ignorant of history? For sure Ma and Pa will see how important it is to celebrate the Fourth of July now." She turned and looked at Sophia over her shoulder. "Surely you remember the parades down Main Street in Springfield and *all* the fun we had?"

"I was teasing." Sophia hunched her shoulders. "Independence Day is just another name for Fourth of July."

"Of course it is." Celia wished her family could remember the Fourth of July this year. "And in this next month, I want to convince Almo—well, at least Ma and Pa—that we need to have a celebration."

"I doubt Pa will want to."

"The problem with you, Sophia, is that you'd never complain about anything. You could have the plow horse step on your toes, and you'd not say a thing."

"That's 'cause Ma says you complain enough for both of us."

Celia sucked in a quick breath. She'd only been trying to make her parents understand her daydreams; that was all.

As she guided Copper up the stone-pocked slope, the barren ground rumbled. Copper reared up on his hind legs. Celia struggled to rein him down. Sophia's hold on her waist tightened. No sooner had Celia grabbed the saddle horn with both hands than Copper settled down and everything fell silent. Not even the chirp of a bird or whistle from a breeze could be heard.

"What was that?" Sophia held tighter to Celia.

"I'm not sure," Celia responded. It all happened so fast. "But something spooked Copper—maybe that strange noise. Did you hear it? Or was it my imagination?"

"Yeah, I heard it. Do you want to turn around, go back home?"

"No," Celia said. This was a rare day. It didn't matter what the noise was. She wasn't going home. "We might not get another chance to go exploring for some time."

"You're right." Sophia let go and pointed toward a wind-carved rock protruding from the ground that looked like a huge elephant. "We're here now. Copper seems fine." She leaned around Celia and gave the horse a pat.

"Yes, he does." Celia prompted Copper past the elephant.

"Aren't we gonna stop?"

"If we stopped and looked at every interesting rock in this place, Sophia, it'd take us days. I'm going where Mr. Durfee down at the mercantile told me about. We'll dismount then and hike around. We'll have our fill of elephants and giant turtles and scary rock monsters without having to ride any farther."

"How will you know when we're there?"

"There's a stream and trees that run along the most interesting rocks of all."

They rode for another half mile or so. All the while, Sophia oohed and aahed at each formation they passed. The tiny trail faded into nothingness. Celia would have preferred riding in the well-worn tracks all those wagon trains had cut into the rocky ground. She loved the history of this area—and history of any kind for that matter. "If you were to go to a regular school, rather than have me and Ma teach you lessons, you would know all about the significance of the California and Oregon Trails."

"You already teached me that."

"*Taught* you that," Celia corrected.

"Yeah, taught. And about how the stagecoach used to run through here on its way from Boise down to Kelton." Sophia bounced in the saddle. "Ma says this fall they're gonna have a real school in Almo. Maybe you could apply for the job and be the teacher. You know so much; you'd be really good at it."

"Thanks, but they want a teacher that's going to be around for longer than a year," Celia said flatly. She was about to say that Meg Durfee already got the position—because she could promise she'd be here for two years in a row—when she saw a man on horseback. He'd come into view where the trail curved and disappeared behind a massive rock. He approached them such that she could now clearly see the red bandana at his neck.

"Who's that?" Celia exclaimed. Very few people ever traveled this trail.

"I don't know," Sophia responded. "Only that Ma'd skin me alive if I ever got that dirty."

Celia didn't care that his trousers appeared more brown than blue from caked dirt, sweat stained his shirt under each arm, and a careless meal or two left spots where the buttons lay only halfway done up on his chest. He could have just been too busy working to tidy up. But the fact that he was on this trail at all and didn't hail from Almo gave her cause for concern.

He continued to saunter toward them on his horse.

Should she turn Copper around and hightail it for home? *No.* She wanted to finish their outing. If he meant them harm, surely he could outrun docile old Copper and her unpolished riding skills. Running would do them no good.

Was it possible he was destitute and was merely approaching them because he needed food and water? His appearance certainly fit with *that* story line, his face being unshaven and as dirty as his clothes.

"Stay calm," Celia whispered to Sophia as she pulled her skirt down to cover her legs. "We'll just ride past him with a simple 'howdy-do' and be on our way. If he needs some water, give him our extra canteen, but that's all we can spare. Understand?"

"All right," Sophia responded, her voice now sounding frightened.

"Good afternoon, miss." He lifted his hat as he approached and focused on Celia. He was close enough she could tell his eyes were blue. Not that grayish shade that Pa and Paul had, but a brilliant blue Celia had only ever seen in the sky those rare times when the morning was ripe and the sun bounced off the white clouds just right. It was a shame; those eyes seemed out of place on such a dirty face.

"Afternoon," Celia responded, trying not to stare at his eyes but to keep her attention on the trail. From the abundance of trees ahead, she assumed the spot Mr. Durfee had told her about was close.

"What brings you ladies out this way?" he asked.

Might I ask the same about you?

"We're on an afternoon outing," Sophia spoke up rather shakily. "I've never really been out here, you know, to go exploring and such. Pa said we could come today, it being my sister's birthday and all." She rambled like she often did when she was nervous.

"Well, that's as good a reason as I could ever think of." The man plopped his hat back on his head. "Have a good day, girls." He gave them a nod and rode by.

Relieved about being wrong about his intent, Celia kept riding, letting that dirty-faced man and his dusty horse ride away from her and her thoughts.

She kept her eyes and Copper pointed toward the tall backbone-like ridge of stone Mr. Durfee had described.

Sophia squealed with delight when they finally dismounted. Celia was quite giddy herself, this particular spot being blessed with a trickling stream and the shade of aspens combined with that of towering walls of stone. She gazed at bizarre shapes Mother Nature had carved in the rock while she tied Copper's reins to a tree.

She climbed alongside the stream, feeling as though she'd been transported to another world, one where the people stood like statues along a boulevard, all without arms or legs, some with heads that appeared ready to fall off.

"Look at that one!" Sophia pointed to a particularly thin-necked rock person and ran toward it.

"Hold on. Wait for me," Celia called out but to no avail. Sophia kept running. Then she saw a flash of red. *The man's bandana!*

She held her breath. Had that dirty-faced man returned, ready to do some unseemly deed now that they were all off the trail and tucked away where no one could see them? She spotted the bandana and dirty clothes again. He approached on foot.

Sophia stared up at a rock formation, standing between Celia and the dirty-faced man.

Not wanting to alarm her sister, Celia mustered what courage she could. "What are you doing here?"

"I came to warn you," he said in an innocent-sounding voice.

Celia walked briskly toward Sophia and the man. "Please leave. This is my pa's property." It wasn't really, but he didn't need to know that. "He knows we're here and wouldn't be too keen on you being here with us."

The man held up his hands as if she'd pulled a gun on him. "Hold on there, miss. I was just trying to do you two a favor." He rubbed his whiskered cheek like he had a toothache. "You'd think a fellow like me'd learn by now to quit doing favors. It only gets me in trouble."

Celia stopped. She was close enough to see into the man's eyes. There was not a hint of darkness or malevolence there, only that calming shade of blue. "What do you mean by *favor*?"

"I saw you two get off your horse and hike into this spot."

The fact that he'd been watching them did not make her comfortable at all, despite his eyes. "Yeees?" she said, urging him to continue.

"A buddy of mine used to come here all the time. He's the one who told me about the—" He cleared his throat. "Never mind about that. He told me about a friend of his who got killed in this part of the City of Rocks." He pointed to a round stone perched precariously atop another. "It was his misfortune to have one of those darn things fall right on top of him while he was digging below it.

I just thought, what with that little tremor we just had, that it might not be safe for you girls to be in here."

"So that's what that was." Celia straightened her back, determined to continue their outing. "Well, thank you kindly, sir, but we'll be fine." She'd never heard of anyone getting killed in this place by a falling rock. Good gracious. Hundreds of pioneers had camped here on their trek to the California gold fields. And Pa would have told her so if that was true—and he certainly wouldn't have let her and Sophia come today if that was the case. "If you'll kindly be on your way, we'd appreciate it." She motioned for Sophia to come to her and move away from the dirty-faced man.

The man backed away. "Fine, fine, whatever you say, miss."

The ground rumbled again, and a loud cracking sound drew Celia's eyes up. The man looked up too. A shower of small rocks tumbled to the ground. A boulder teetered on the edge of a column of stone. It gave way.

Celia screamed.

The man dove toward Sophia, knocking her out of its path, and scrambled to get himself to safety.

He didn't move quickly enough.

A boulder the size of Ma's steamer trunk fell on his leg, pinning him to the ground.

CHAPTER TWO

PAIN SEARED BRUCE'S LEG LIKE a thousand banding irons all at once.

He screamed in agony and stared in disbelief.

A boulder as big and heavy as a cast-iron floor safe pinned his leg to the ground, his worst nightmare now playing out before his eyes. No amount of safe-cracking skills would do him good here.

Was he going to die? Lose his leg? He held to the hope that the smattering of small stones lying on either side of his leg would keep the boulder from doing either. Still, it hurt like Hades.

"Help!" he cried, wincing through his teeth. His gaze met that of the striking young woman he had come to warn. "Get it off! Get it off!" He knew her slender frame could never budge that boulder, but the pain—*oh!* He couldn't help it. Screaming helped. A little. "Make the pain stop. Please!"

She knelt by his side, slipped something soft under Bruce's head, and then gathered his hands into hers. "I'm here. I won't leave your side until help comes," she said in a voice so sweet and gentle he swore she actually cared. That in itself brought a measure of comfort. She looked up at the young girl at her side. "Sophia, take Copper and go fetch Pa and Paul. And hurry!"

Her eyes returned to his. He read sincere concern pouring from those kind brown eyes that reminded him of his mother's.

"How long?" he asked, jerking his head toward the young girl who had just left. Speaking took such effort breathing like he was, short and quick.

"Soon," she assured him. "Our cabin is just before you enter the Almo Valley." She let go with one of her hands and pointed. When she returned her hand to his, he took hold of it and squeezed. She held hers firm, allowing him that liberty—more like a bullet to bite on.

He nodded in response, grateful for her strong hands to latch on to, her very presence as well. He'd always feared he'd die alone, what with no friends and hardly a family to call his own.

"Don't worry. Pa will drop everything and come. He's the closest thing we have to a doctor in these parts," she continued as if she thought her rambling would take his mind off the pain. "He became a medic in the Civil War. One of the best. He'll take good care of you. I know he will."

Gritting his teeth now, he nodded again in response. His head felt light and dizzy.

"My brother is strong as an ox." Her sweet voice carried past the fog in his head. "So is my pa. They'll get that rock off your leg faster than you can say 'Bob's your uncle.'" She smiled. "Probably faster because you're not doing too good with talking right now, are you?"

He shook his head, wishing he could smile back, but he couldn't. He felt like throwing up and passing out. He closed his eyes.

"No, stay with me," she murmured and placed a hand on his forehead. It felt warm. "You're sweating, but your head is cool. You've got to try to relax. Concentrate and take longer, slower breaths."

He tried his best. Gripping her hand helped, as did her stroking of his forehead and cheek.

"That's good. Keep doing that. I'll keep talking to you. Don't worry about responding. Just listen and try to stay conscious. At least until Pa gets here. He's the one who'll know best what you need."

Bruce nodded his response, leaning his head into her soothing hand. He listened as she carried on a one-way conversation, telling him her name: Celia Edwards. Her family had moved to the outskirts of Almo three years ago as homesteaders. That much came through rather clearly. Then, whether it was because he didn't quite understand what she was talking about or because his mind grew foggier, he didn't grasp much more of what she said. There was something about her pa getting three hundred and twenty acres rather than one hundred and sixty because it was a special kind of homestead. She mentioned words like *Desert Land Act* and *irrigation*, then the subject made an abrupt change to the Fourth of July. He wasn't sure if she loved Fourth of July celebrations or disliked them, or just disliked the way Almo celebrated, or rather *didn't* celebrate, the holiday. In either case, she seemed to spend a lot of time on the subject.

He kept his eyes closed, allowing himself a glimpse here and there at her face, a face that, under normal circumstances, he could have gazed at for hours.

But in this moment, he didn't care to. The only thing he wanted was for the boulder and the pain to be gone.

He felt her hands let go of his. He opened his eyes to see her stand and run toward a horse and its riders: a boy, younger than Celia but almost a man in stature, and the younger girl he'd seen earlier.

"Paul," Celia called out, "where's Pa?"

"Not too far behind. He's bringing the wagon."

Celia pulled the young man toward Bruce the moment he dismounted. "That was quicker than I'd expected."

It had felt like an eternity to Bruce. He tried to sit up so he could help the one named Paul push the boulder off his leg. His arms stretched toward the granite surface.

Celia rushed to Bruce's side and gently coaxed him back down. "No, please, you must save your strength for healing." Once she'd gotten him still, she motioned to her brother. "Paul, see if you can move the boulder."

Paul leaned his shoulder into the boulder. Celia came around and pushed with her hands. Bracing his feet in the ground, Paul grunted and pushed. "It's no good." He motioned for Celia to step away. "Even with Pa's help, we're going to need a lever."

Bruce closed his eyes, listening to the scurry of footsteps and constant mention of a lever. Then came a deeper, unfamiliar voice. *Their Pa.* Bruce opened his eyes to glimpse the man on whom his life depended. Dressed in dusty overalls and with a graying beard covering his jaw, the man they all called Pa stood a few inches shorter than his son, but his shoulders spread a few inches wider.

Their pa walked with confidence toward Bruce with a crowbar in hand, took but a moment to survey the situation, and then spoke in a commanding voice. "Let's get to work."

Amazed, Bruce watched as their pa pressed down on the lever, Paul pushed against the stone, and Celia and Sophia grabbed him by the armpits and pulled him free. His leg felt immediate relief from the pressure. A new, sharper pain took its place. He cried out, cursing like his pa. He'd tried not to but couldn't help it.

Their pa was at his side in a flash. "He's bleeding pretty badly now that the pressure's off. Celia, bring me those bandages and the splint. And some laudanum."

The next moment, Bruce felt someone lift his head. The touch was so gentle. He opened his eyes to confirm his hope. Celia, with her arm around his neck propping him up, lifted a bottle to his lips. "Here, take a drink of this. It will help the pain," she said and then lowered him back down.

Between the pain, nausea, and dizziness, Bruce slipped in and out as the old man worked on him. He was vaguely aware of being moved onto a stretcher of sorts, carried down the hill, and then loaded into a wagon.

Every good-sized bump in the road sent a jolt to his leg, and he momentarily relived the torture of that boulder. Sophia rested his splinted leg in her lap while Celia cradled his head in her lap. Celia held one of his hands in hers as well, squeezing it each time the road got rough. In between the bumps, he surveyed the two girls. Each wore a simple but clean calico dress, their dark-brown hair neatly braided down their backs. Driving the wagon, their pa was dressed in well-worn, but neatly patched, overalls. Same for the boy on the horse, who was leading Celia's horse and Bruce's horse, Lucky, behind him.

Who were these people? Why were they so kind to him? They didn't know him at all. If they had, surely they would have left him there to die. Or would they have? They didn't seem to care who he was as they'd helped him. He knew he must look a sight, having been digging for that darn treasure for the past few weeks without a bath or a shave. He grimaced when they hit a particularly bumpy spot, then returned to wishing for a bath when the worst passed. It wasn't like he had a home to go to where he could clean up. There were not many good streams around here to bathe in. And a bathhouse cost money. That's why he was looking for some of that gold that had been recently cached by stagecoach robbers in the City of Rocks. Hundreds of thousands of dollars' worth was the rumor. Heck, he'd be content with a mere sliver of it.

Oh, what he'd give to be part of a family like Celia's. He gazed briefly at Celia and her sister, wondering what their ma was like. Wonderful too, he was sure. And she was most likely very proud of each of her children.

Bruce's thoughts went to his own mother, and then to how disappointed she'd be if she knew where his life had ended up. That's why he hadn't seen her or gotten a letter to her in years. His past would need to stay hidden while the Edwards family nursed him back to health. If not, he could be turned out like so many had before. At least he *hoped* these people would take care of him until he could ride away on his own. Surely they wouldn't have gone to all the trouble they had to free him from that boulder just to abandon him once this wagon stopped.

Hope. He had to cling to it. He had little else he could lay claim to.

CHAPTER THREE

CELIA RAN INTO THE CABIN ahead of the others.

"How much laudanum did you give him?" Pa yelled at Celia as he and Paul hefted the man's unconscious body into the smaller bedroom she and her sisters shared. He glanced up at Paul. "Get back to your work now but grab me a kitchen chair first."

"I handed him the bottle and told him to take a swig." Celia hurried and pulled off the covers of her bed. "But he took three."

"He's really out." Ma spread the mattress with two old quilts, then some ratty but clean dishcloths on the lower part of the bed.

"That many quilts?" Celia raised her eyebrows, yet she knew this man was in a bad way.

"I know how messy the healing process can be." Ma touched Celia's arm. "And I'm glad it's you who will be helping your pa. You've got the constitution for it, dear. And the compassion—giving up *your* bed as you did, *offering* to sleep in the barn. Wesley is fortunate indeed to be getting you for his wife."

Celia chose not to respond but straightened the poor fellow out so Pa could work on him easier.

"Okay, so maybe it was good you gave him so much," Pa said gruffly and stepped out of the room. The sound of water sloshing from the bucket into the sink told Celia that Pa was washing his hands. Paul brought in a chair and the man's saddlebag, then left. Pa stepped back into the room and sat himself at the bedside. "It'll be best he's out for this next part anyway." He looked to Celia. "Go wash your hands. I need your help."

By the time Celia returned from scrubbing her hands all the way up to her elbows, Pa had the splint and bandage removed and was dousing the gaping wound with whiskey. The dirty-faced man jerked his leg away.

"Hold him down," Pa barked. "We best hurry; the laudanum will be wearing off soon."

Celia sat on the man's thighs while Pa pulled on the injured lower left leg and set the bone. After checking the bone through the open wound, Pa stitched him up, all the while mumbling that he hoped he could save the leg. Celia knew Pa had amputated more legs than he'd ever wanted to or thought necessary. During the war, there'd been too many casualties and too little time to give those soldiers the attention they needed. She appreciated the attention Pa gave this stranger, especially with all the work he had to do on their farm. Her pa had a heart of gold. She just wished his tongue had a little of that gold. Better yet, she wished his heart hadn't gotten buried somehow the past few years.

After the leg had been bandaged and the splint put securely in place, Pa stood. "I've done all I can. His life's in your and your ma's hands now. You clean up the mess. I've got work to do," he said in the gruff voice he used when frustrated and then walked out of the room.

The dirty-faced man began to stir. Celia figured she should be by his side to lend comfort when he came to, so she'd best hurry. "Ma," she hollered through the door, "can you grab Sophia and get her to help you move her and Abby's bed into the front room? Gracious, I've got to clean up this blood while this fellow's still out."

While Ma and Sophia moved out the bed, Celia removed the bloodied rags and top quilt and cleaned up all signs of Pa's surgery. As she headed for the sink to wash her hands, she looked at the man's face before she left the room. To keep referring to him as the dirty-faced man didn't set well with her. When she came back, she brought a bucket of clean water, some clean rags, and soap. She'd also sneaked into her parents' bedroom and brought Pa's shaving supplies.

She started at the bottom of the bed, removing the one boot that remained on his foot, along with two nearly black socks. As she washed his feet, breathing through her mouth as she worked to avoid the odor, she wondered if it had been this disgusting when Jesus had washed the feet of his disciples. Surely not. But then again, Jesus would have never complained, even if it were disgusting. *I'm not complaining—I just don't like this.* But it needed to be done. Unsure how to deal with his legs and his trousers, which Pa had cut the mangled pant leg off, she left them alone and moved to his upper body. She told herself to let go of decorum and remove that filthy shirt. In order to clean him properly, it needed to be done. As his nurse, surely that would be acceptable. It was not like she had any feelings for the man other than brotherly love.

She dug through the man's saddlebag only to find one change of clothes that was dirtier and more ragged than what he had on.

"Ma," she called out as she unbuttoned his shirt, "do you know where that old blue shirt of Paul's is, the one he's outgrown?"

"Yes."

"Would you mind if we lent it to this fellow while we wash his?"

"But of course." Ma hurried into the room a minute later with shirt in hand and surveyed Celia's work. "Good idea. Nothing like being clean to help a person feel better."

Ma stayed and helped Celia wash layers of sweat and grime from the man's shoulders and chest. Seeing his smooth skin and firm muscles, Celia realized he was much younger than she'd imagined him to be.

Shaving his face after Ma left served to verify that. His whiskers had not been gray as she'd originally thought but a sandy blond. Smattered with dirt, his whiskers had given him a look of age he didn't deserve. When she rinsed off the shaving soap and cut whiskers and toweled his face dry, she caught herself staring at his face. He didn't look that much older than her. And he was rather pleasant to look at, what with his firm jawline, distinctive yet softened cheekbones, and a cleft in his chin. He stirred again. She hurried and washed his stringy hair, not wanting to leave her task unfinished.

"Ohhhh," he moaned and slowly thrashed from side to side.

Celia grabbed his hand, which was noticeably cleaner now. Not that it repulsed her before—her only thoughts had been on lending him comfort—but now the touch of his hand in hers gave her a feeling she couldn't exactly describe, only that it was good. Most likely because he needed her right now.

"Try to stay still. Pa's fixed you up the best he could. But if you don't want to lose your leg, you'd best do as I say."

His eyes flew open. "No, that's my digging foot. I can't lose it. Don't let him cut it off."

Celia gathered his other hand into hers and squeezed them both. Though unsure what he meant, she sensed his fear and ached for him. "He's not going to."

"Where am I? Where's my horse?" He struggled to sit up, propping himself on one elbow as his eyes darted around the small room, then groaned and collapsed into the pillow.

"You're in our cabin, and your horse is in our corral." Celia said. "You're going to be fine now. I'm your nurse, and I'll take care of you. Trust me."

His eyes met hers. "You?" The hope she saw within them bolstered the color despite the pain she also saw. "You're going to nurse me back to health?" His voice trembled. "W-why would you do such a thing? You don't know me from Adam."

Had this man never received a kind deed before in his life? Celia swore that's what it sounded like. Yet he'd performed an amazingly kind deed for them. "Yes,

I am going to nurse you back to health. You saved my sister." She paused. "And because I want to." Her feelings tumbled from her mouth before she had time to understand them or rein them in.

The wider awake Bruce got, the more agony he felt. But the burning pain in his leg was more bearable than having that blasted boulder sit on it. Still, he would have preferred to remain knocked out—except for one reason. Her.

She held his hands in hers without the least show of disgust. And her voice may as well have been singing her words of encouragement. That's how sweet they sounded. He glanced at her hands. And then his—his were clean. At least cleaner than they'd been for ages. Without thinking, he pulled them from her grasp and examined the lack of dirt under his fingernails. "My hands." He rushed them to the shirt he wore, and then to his face. "Whoa, you've been busy, girl." A throb of pain made him wince.

"I washed you up the best I could," she said, sporting a sheepish smile.

Dang, that just made her heart-shaped face all the more beautiful. Her dainty mouth gave life to her full cheeks, and her brown eyes sported a hint of a spark. He leaned forward and looked at the neatly done-up splint on his leg so as to not stare at her. "Your pa's been busy too, I can see." He laid back down, wanting to continue talking with her—to take his mind off the pain— but he was exhausted. "How can I ever . . . say . . . enough thanks?" He tried to sit up again.

She gently eased him back against the pillow. "By resting. So you can heal."

That came across like a scolding, the kind his ma used to dish out. He loved the sound of it. And he'd loved the sentiment behind it when his ma had spoken that way. He heaved a sigh, sweeping aside the memory—and the foolish hope that Celia meant anything by it other than not wanting him to take any more time than was needful to heal up and hurriedly get out of their hair.

"Yes, ma'am," he responded instinctively like he'd done with his ma and then gave her a mock salute—the one he'd always given his ma once she was safely out of sight.

"Excuse me," she said as if she'd been offended. Or had she been teasing? He chose to dwell on the latter. With the pain he was in, he'd better darn well grab all the pleasant thoughts he could. "It's not *ma'am*; it's *miss*." She pinched her dainty lips together as she brushed a strand of dark-brown hair from her eyes.

"That's . . . good to know," he responded, meaning every word and tiring himself further with each he spoke. But he cared not to stop. "So, do I call you miss? Miss Celia Edwards? Or may I simply call you Celia?"

She sucked in a quick breath. "How'd you know my name?"

"You told me." He mustered a quick smile while he winced. "Back there in the dang rocks, when you were trying to keep me hanging on 'til your pa got there. You did a good job. Thanks. So, can I call you Celia?" This time, the desire to smile was stronger than the pain. His mouth spread wide into a grin.

"Depends." It appeared it was her turn to smile.

"Depends on what?"

"Depends if Pa is listening. Then it's got to be Miss Edwards." She heaved out a sigh, then her demeanor lightened again. "What should *I* call you? I have yet to learn your name. If I am to spend night and day taking care of—"

"Night and day?" he interrupted. "Perhaps a boulder falling on one's leg has its silver lining."

"Yes, night and day." She smiled. "But it's hardly continual, mind you. I have plenty of other chores to tend to. Good gracious, it's not like you need my attention every minute."

Oh, but I would like it.

"Now, as I was saying." She wagged a hand at him. "If I'm to be spending time taking care of you, I can't keep calling you, 'That,'" she cleared her throat twice, "'Man.'"

He wasn't sure what she'd meant by that. She wanted to know his name, and he'd give it to her. For some reason, the fear wasn't there like it was most times people asked. But then, he usually associated with people like his two bank-robbing brothers and no-good Pa. Celia had probably never even heard of Tom or Will Pickett—Bruce's older brothers. Bruce didn't even know what his brothers were doing nowadays. Bruce just knew that they were out of his life now, and he wanted to keep it that way. He'd never intended on getting mixed up in their bank-robbing schemes when Ma had begged him to try to talk them out of following in Pa's footsteps. But then, he was never that good at standing up against his brothers, nor could he stand up to his pa back in Boston where Ma still lived, widowed ever since Pa got shot by someone he cheated. Oh how he wanted to turn out better than his pa and brothers.

"My name's Bruce Pickett," he said, hoping bad luck didn't come his way like it usually did from giving out his real name. He had to take a chance so as to shake off the past—his family's past. Ma deserved one son she could be happy with.

CHAPTER FOUR

CELIA CAREFULLY HOISTED THE CHAMBER pot outside, not allowing it to slosh even a little bit. She had enough work on her hands and didn't need a mess to clean up too. The sun warmed her face as she headed toward the privy. A chickadee sang in the background, and the morning sun lent the sky, their rows of crops, and even the barn an appearance of freshness. She had the urge to set down the bucket and run through the June grass to celebrate this lovely day. Her patient was finally feeling better.

"What you doing just standing there?" A voice pulled Celia from her daydream.

Celia turned to see Sophia approach with hoe in hand.

"Just enjoying the day for a minute." Celia lifted the chamber pot slightly by its handle to justify her whimsicality. "Then I'm emptying this pot."

"Well, when you're done, we could *more* than use *your* help in the garden." Sophia overemphasized some of her words. She scowled and pointed the hoe across the barnyard where Ma pulled weeds while little Abby picked up the limp leaves and put them in a bucket. "It feels like you've done nothing but tend to that fellow ever since he got here."

"Sorry. I'll be there in a minute to help," Celia said. For the first time in the week since Bruce had arrived, Celia felt guilty for the time she'd given him.

Had she given him more attention than was warranted? She hadn't thought so. After the laudanum had completely worn off that first day, and that conversation she'd had with him, he'd really suffered. His pain had since made such conversations near impossible for the following three or four days. And the agony in those blue eyes had nigh unto crushed Celia's heart. He needed extra attention, for Pa had no more laudanum and didn't care much to give him whiskey as a painkiller. "It'll only serve to delay the healing process," Pa had told her. And Pa didn't want that. So she thought her family understood: she was giving extra attention in the place of medicine. But apparently Sophia didn't understand.

After an hour in the vegetable garden, and at least two in their potato crop, her hands and back begged for relief from weeding. Mid-day came, time for dinner, and she gladly headed to the cabin along with Sophia, Paul, and Pa. When she stepped inside the cabin, Ma had the table set with six bowls and spoons and a loaf of sliced bread. A seventh bowl sat on the cupboard. Celia knew that was for Bruce, and she appreciated her ma's thoughtfulness. If Ma felt like complaining about having another mouth to feed, she certainly didn't show it.

"Thanks, Ma, for setting this out for Mr. Pickett." Celia ladled a healthy portion of beef and potato stew into the bowl as Paul and Sophia walked into the adjoining front room. She could see Pa heading in from the barnyard through the open door. "I'll hurry and take this to him now." She grabbed a slice of bread, balanced it atop the bowl of soup, and scurried into the small bedroom.

Bruce's eyes lit up as she walked into the room. He propped himself on his elbow. "Where you been all morning?"

"Good gracious, I can't tend to you all day," Celia said, though apparently Sophia thought she did. "Besides, you're starting to feel better."

"So you're punishing me now for my quick recovery. That ain't hardly fair." His eyes twinkled with merriment as he sat up all the way and accepted the bowl of soup.

"Of course not." Good gracious, why did Celia feel the need to defend her actions with everyone? "I stayed longer than I usually do *last* night. And read and helped you to read from one of my books. Don't you remember?"

She wondered if Ma and Pa noticed the extra time she'd spent with him yesterday evening. Did they have the same thinking as Sophia? Ma had seemed a little distant when Celia dished up Bruce's soup a minute ago.

Well, if they did, that was ridiculous. Celia knew darn well that she only tended to Bruce three times a day for meals, and once in between meals to see if he needed more water or the chamber pot taken out—thank heavens he could handle his own bed pan and emptied it himself into the pot. Oh, she forgot that she did always check on him once at night to make sure all was in order before she went to bed. And lately, she read to him then and taught him a few words because, after all, how could she do anything less after discovering he could barely read?

"Of course I remember," Bruce said. "I could tell you really disliked that book, what with the way your eyes kept twinkling." He dipped his bread into the soup and bit off the soggy corner. With an impish look in his eyes, he asked, "Will you punish me again tonight and read to me some more?"

"I'll think about it." She couldn't hold back a smile. "But only because I know I'd go stir-crazy if *I* had to lie in bed all day with nothing to do." She felt justified, and she most assuredly would read to him that night.

"About that. It'd do me good if you could bring me a scrap of wood and a sharp knife. I love to whittle."

"Sure—"

"Celia!" Pa yelled from the kitchen. "We're waiting on you. I'd like to thank the Good Lord for our food before winter sets in."

"Sorry. Pa's in a mood." Celia patted Bruce's hand and hurried from the room.

It was late afternoon yet not quite suppertime. Celia had finished weeding the last of the potatoes and headed to the barn to put away her hoe. She wondered how Bruce was doing. Her chores were done for the day. The supper dishes would not be ready to do for some time. Surely no one would have reason to complain if she were to spend a little time with him now.

She slowed her steps as she reached the barn, thinking. Ma had checked on him and the chamber pot, or so she had said when she'd joined Celia in the potato field an hour ago. She had no real reason to see how he was doing. Why had Ma done that and made such a point of telling Celia? Celia had taken on that responsibility. She didn't need anyone else's help.

The patter of feet prompted Celia to turn. Ma approached with Abby three steps behind. Abby held onto Ma's hoe like it was a shepherd's staff. A stray hen pecking in the dirt caught Abby's attention, and she used her staff to corral the poor chicken back into the coop.

"Abby, you put that hoe away for me when you're finished with that hen, you hear me?" Ma hollered across the barnyard. "I'm going in to get supper started."

"Yes, Ma," Abby answered in her sweet five-year-old voice.

Ma's eyes caught Celia's, and she grinned. "Looks like you and Sophia both finished your chores early today. What are you going to do with a whole hour to yourself?"

"I'm not sure," Celia responded, suddenly uncomfortable with telling Ma her plans. Since when did Ma concern herself with what Celia did in her free time?

"Sophia's in the cabin right now grabbing a book. She's going to read in the shade of the big cottonwood tree. I thought maybe you'd like to join her. Or you could help me with dinner." She smiled wryly.

Ma hadn't mentioned Bruce, the option Celia preferred. If only the books were stored in their bedroom. Then Ma wouldn't think twice at Celia going in there. Celia could take her time browsing for one.

Wesley's letter. It lay in the bottom of her dresser drawer, where it had sat untouched since she'd received it two weeks ago. "Thank you, but I think I'll reread Wesley's last letter. I haven't yet had a chance to write him back." She beamed—it was a great excuse.

"I think that is an excellent idea." Ma smiled like she meant every word. "You do that," she said and headed for the cabin.

Celia placed her hoe in the barn and followed Ma inside, thinking about Wesley's letter and how she hadn't written to him earlier because she was still trying to decipher its meaning. Yes, she should write a letter rather than visit with Bruce. Of course, she would say hello to Bruce, but that would be all. Perhaps she could merely sit in the room with him and pen her letter there. At least he wouldn't be alone.

Bruce was whittling away at a stick but set it down and perked up when Celia walked into her old bedroom—his room for now. She bedded down on the couch where Paul normally slept. Her brother, bless his heart, now slept in the barn. Bruce's eyes held that spark they always did. If she were to sit in a room alone for hours like he did, she'd likely complain to each and every person who walked through the door, not send them such a charming greeting. "Doing some whittling, I see."

Bruce grinned. "Yep."

"Why is it you always look so cheerful when I walk in this room?"

"Because I'm happy to see you."

She loved how he teased. "Well, sorry I can't stay and visit long." She walked over to the dresser. The old kitchen chair they only used when company came had taken the spot where Sophia's and Abby's bed used to be. She'd moved it in here so as to have a place to sit while she tended to her patient's needs, which were growing less and less by the day.

"I'll take what I can get," he said.

A wave of guilt hit her. He might not require much nursing as of late, but he had need for companionship. No wonder she'd felt such a need to spend time with Bruce.

But Wesley deserved a letter. She couldn't neglect her future simply because she had a patient who needed her at the moment.

"I have a letter to write . . . that's long overdue." Celia opened the drawer and pulled out Wesley's letter. "I realize I won't be very good company. But if you don't mind, I can sit in here to compose my correspondence."

Bruce laughed. "I don't mind one bit." He sat up, propped himself in the corner with pillows, and gazed at Celia as she sat down in the chair. "Hey, I'd rather look at you than at these blasted log walls."

She wagged her empty hand at him, thinking he said the sweetest things. None of the other patients she'd helped over the years while assisting Pa had ever really thanked her. "You are very kind, Mr. Pickett."

"Hold on there. What happened to you calling me Bruce?" He exaggerated his movements as he looked around the room. "I don't see your pa nowhere."

"You are right. Pa's not here." Why had she reverted to calling him Mr. Pickett? She glanced at the letter in her hand. Because Wesley wouldn't approve? Most certainly he wouldn't. "You are very kind, *Bruce*."

"That's better." He leaned back and repositioned his leg. "And I ain't so much being kind. I'm just being truthful."

Celia wagged her hand at Bruce again. He had such a way of making her feel good. Wesley did that too. At least he used to. She switched her attention to the envelope in hand. With apprehension, she pulled out the letter and opened it.

"I thought you said you were going to write a letter not read one."

Celia sent Bruce a sideways glance. "You'll need to be quiet, or I shall have to go someplace else."

Bruce gave her a look of mock hurt.

"For your information," she continued, "I've got to read his last letter again so I'll know how to respond."

"His?" The spark in Bruce's eyes disappeared. "Who exactly are you writing to?"

"That, Mr. Bruce Pickett, is none of your concern."

"Yet I feel concerned." He grinned. "Please don't tell me he's your fiancé."

"No, Wesley Cornelius is not my fiancé. Yet." Celia straightened her back. She had not planned on speaking to Bruce about Wesley at all. But here she was. "The plan is that we will be wed in a year from now after he finishes his medical training. But as of this moment, we are not officially engaged."

"Plan? Whose plan?"

"Well, his . . . and mine and each of our parents. It was planned by all of us before Pa and Ma moved our family out here."

"How long ago was that?" Bruce looked around the room. "By the looks of this cabin . . ."

"A little over three years ago."

"And how old were you then?" Bruce asked in a cynical tone.

"Sixteen," Celia said sheepishly. "Wesley was twenty. Pa thought I was too young to get married."

"I agree with your pa this time."

Celia scoffed and put her fist on her hip. "One of my friends back in Springfield got married at sixteen. Pa said it wouldn't be such a good idea for me to be alone for hours and away from both our families while Wesley attended Harvard. So Pa wanted me to come out West with the family until Wesley graduated. That would put me at age twenty and him at twenty-four when we wed. It was a good plan. I realized it even more once I got here, for then I saw how much Ma and Pa needed my help."

Bruce stared out the small window behind Celia. At what, she was unsure. He'd not be able to see much from his angle. "So, have you seen this Wesley fellow much these past three years?"

Celia chewed on her lip and looked straight ahead into the front room. Bruce brought up a good point. Hesitating with her answer, she stared at their homemade stone fireplace and the mantle that leaned down on one side. "No, not at all. Pa's poured all his money into our homestead, so he can't afford to send me back East. And Wesley doesn't have the time to come West."

"What about his parents?" Bruce asked, looking at Celia now. "Couldn't they foot the bill for you to come see their son?"

"No, they're very stingy with their wealth. In fact, they thought Pa was rather foolish for investing all his money in this ranch." Celia felt her blood begin to boil, and she clenched her fist. This ranch was the best thing that had ever happened to her pa—and her family. She loved the fresh air, wide-open space, and the friendly neighbors—even though they were few. Most of all, she loved the feeling of having turned this arid land into something of worth. "They were wrong, though," she continued. "Pa got three hundred and twenty acres for next to nothing. He's finally a landowner—a big one, like he'd always dreamed of. And with him being an orphan, that's quite the accomplishment. Even Ma's affluent family saw the value in what he'd done."

"Oh." Bruce shifted in his bed. "I'm sorry—about Wesley's folks. The story about your folks, though, I like." He waved a hand at her. "I should let you get back to your letter writing."

Celia sighed. "Yes, that would be good." She unfolded the letter and began to read.

> *Dearest Celia,*
>   *I apologize for the time that I have let slip by since my last letter, but I have been very busy.*

"Sorry. One more question," Bruce interrupted. There was a look in his eyes other than curiosity that she couldn't determine.

Celia lowered the letter. "All right, one question. But that's all." She smiled. "I really do need to finish before supper."

Bruce stared out the window again. "Do you still love him?" His voice sounded flat, almost mechanical. "It's been three years since you've seen him, after all. People change."

Celia dropped her hands and the letter into her lap. She did not know the answer. Up until two weeks ago, she thought she did.

"That, Mr. Bruce Pickett, is none of your concern," she said again but, this time, rather snippily. It surprised her. She'd not intended to be rude.

"You are absolutely correct." He slid down in the bed and turned his face to the wall.

Feeling bad but unsure what to do about it, Celia resumed reading.

> *They have me working with actual patients now, and it has been very taxing on my nerves to say the least. I am an intern at Massachusetts General Hospital, which is not far from the tenements on Lowell St. We are constantly overrun by immigrants from that odorous housing project. They come in with cases of influenza, tetanus, measles, or some other unpleasant malady. Do those people not know the right end of a bar of soap? It must be the case. Some of the patients I have had to attend to not only reek of bodily odors, but their feet and hands are black with dirt.*
>   *Have no fear, though. When I do procure my own practice, I shall establish it far from this end of Boston and shall only*

accept patients with sufficient money and manners to make my
three years of schooling and year of internship worth my while.

Celia scanned the next three paragraphs, unwilling to reread Wesley's uppity remarks. There were more of them in this letter than in his previous one and definitely more than in the one before that. *Yes, people change.* How could she possibly respond to this letter? Only the weather seemed a safe subject. Would he find any interest in her planting the garden, nursing a dirty stranger back to health, or any of the things she had been doing? She did need to bring up the matter of their engagement again. Apparently he'd forgotten to respond to her inquiry.

Dear Wesley,   *June 12, 1882*
We've been having delightful weather here in the Idaho
Territory. I do hope the weather in Boston is nice for you as well.

Celia looked up from her sheet of writing paper, unsure what to write next. Everything she felt like saying she feared would come out sounding like a complaint. She wouldn't do that to him. Nor to herself—she was trying to curb her complaining. When she'd arrived in Idaho, the lack of running water, the cramped cabin, and her endless chores felt foreign. Of course she complained. Now she was used to her new life and felt bad about this disagreeable habit she'd developed. Sighing, she ventured into another safe subject. It had always been one of her favorites.

The Fourth of July is fast approaching. It has always been
my favorite time of the year, as I'm sure you remember. I would
like to try to bring together some sort of celebration in Almo
this year, if for no other reason than to try to get Pa to enjoy
himself at a picnic, or a parade, or a dance. Unfortunately, I
don't believe much will come of it. Will you be doing any kind
of celebrating of the holiday this year? You being so close to our
nation's capital and in an area rich with our country's history, I
would think there would be numerous festivities in which you
could take part.

Celia stopped writing and tapped the pen against her thigh. This couldn't be put off any longer; she needed to inquire again as to their engagement. Her past two letters, she'd inquired, but he had yet to answer. He probably had lots on his mind. She put her pen to the paper and then hesitated. Bruce still lay with his back toward her. His words replayed in her mind: *do you still love him?*

Did she still love Wesley?

Three years *was* a long time to go without seeing someone, and they still had one more year to go.

She looked through the door into the kitchen area this time. Pa walked in from the fields. He greeted Ma at the stove with a kiss on her cheek. Should she confide in her parents? Tell them of Wesley's indifference in his last letter? More importantly, should she tell them that he'd ignored her simple request yet a second time? She wanted to know when they would make their engagement official.

No. They'd see it as complaining. And she couldn't imagine not marrying Wesley—not to mention how it would devastate her parents if she didn't.

Celia looked at Bruce. She would simply dedicate herself to helping her patient heal to take her mind off Wesley's unsettling behavior. At least here, tending to Bruce, she could be the type of nurse she wanted to be. Unfortunately, she doubted Wesley would ever take on a patient such as Bruce. That stuck in her mind like a boil that wouldn't heal.

CHAPTER FIVE

BRUCE HAD FEARED HE'D SAID too much yesterday and had lost himself his favorite nurse. But Celia walked in with tray in hand, holding his supper. The savory aroma of fresh bread and baked potatoes delighted him almost as much as seeing her.

"Does this mean you've forgiven me and it's going to be you who brings me my meals from now on?"

Celia's brow wrinkled. "What?" She set down her tray. Her look of confusion faded, but her face sagged with what appeared to be sadness. "Oh, sorry." She sighed. "The rest of the family seems determined to help me tend to your needs."

"Is that the reason for your long face?" Bruce could hope, couldn't he?

"No, no, that's not the source of my melancholy."

"So, was it me prying into your business, asking about the fellow who sent that letter?"

"No, it's not that either."

Bruce pretended to wipe sweat from his brow. "Whew. Then it's not me that's the problem, eh?"

Celia's lips curled up ever so slightly. "No, it's not you." She laid her hand atop his.

That sent a tingle clean up his arm. Whether she'd meant to do that or not, he didn't care—he'd take it. And think about it over and over again while he sat alone for hours in this darn bed. "I'm glad," he said, placing his other hand atop hers.

She let her hand linger as their eyes met. Then she jerked her hand away, almost like she realized he came from the no-good family that he did.

A pang of pain spread through his heart.

She turned to leave and then spun back around. The spunk he had grown to draw upon during this difficult time had returned to her face.

"I almost forgot to tell you the good news. After Pa examined you this morning, he's decided to put a cast on your leg."

"What? When?" Bruce couldn't keep the excitement from his voice. "Does this mean I can finally get up out of this bed? Will you be helpin' him?"

"I don't know." Her melancholy returned. "Pa didn't tell me any of that." She walked out of the room.

Bruce dug into his supper. He didn't enjoy it as much as he'd expected. Something was bothering Celia, and that bothered him. If only he could help, do something to cheer her up. "Like what?" he mumbled to himself, glaring at his bed prison. "Like a Fourth of July celebration," he said to the walls of the tiny room. Yesterday, she'd mentioned that a second time. Her desire for such a celebration had stood out in her ramblings as she'd comforted him when that boulder sat on his leg.

Unfortunately, he was unsure how he could do such a thing in his present state.

There was something, however, he could do. She needed it every bit as much as a holiday celebration: convince Celia that she didn't love that Wesley fellow. Then again, that might very well be cause for celebration. He, for one, felt Celia was no longer a starry-eyed sixteen-year-old in love with the idea of being in love. And she didn't have a look in her eyes he'd have expected from a girl in love. It was more a look of pain. He'd be doing her a favor.

"You certainly have a healthy appetite," Mrs. Edwards said as she picked up Bruce's emptied breakfast tray.

"That's because I work up a sweat laying here all day doing nothing." Bruce winked.

Mrs. Edwards smiled. "Humor is a powerful medicine, Mr. Pickett. It's no wonder my husband is amazed at how quickly you are healing." She turned to leave.

"How come Celia didn't bring me my breakfast?" Bruce dared to ask.

Mrs. Edwards stopped. Awkwardness filled the room. With her back to him, she said, "I asked her to do something else for me this morning, something I shall need her to do probably every morning from now on."

After Mrs. Edwards scurried from the room, Bruce laid back down in his bed, ready to stare at the log walls—he'd already whittled all the wood he had. He glanced at the book Sophia had placed on the chair last night when she'd checked the chamber pot. The book didn't interest him—only reminded him of his poor reading skills and the times Celia had tried to teach him to read. "At least I got that much."

Mr. Edwards walked into the room carrying a tin bucket and a smaller wooden one in one hand and what looked like a strange ball of yarn and a stocking in the other. "Who you talking to?"

"The wall." Bruce smiled. "It has a knack for listening."

Mr. Edwards set down his buckets and plopped into the chair. "I'm going to put a plaster cast on your leg, young man. Once it's hardened, you'll be able to move around better."

"That's wonderful."

"I should've done it sooner, but this homestead takes a lot of work. There's little time for anything else."

"Like celebrating the Fourth of July?" Bruce asked without thinking. Okay, he was thinking—but about Celia's desire to do things she used to with her family.

"I have my reasons." Mr. Edwards furrowed his brow. "And don't be poking your nose where it doesn't belong, young man."

"Sorry, sir." Bruce held up his hands instinctively.

"No putting any weight on this leg for four to five weeks. You hear me?" Mr. Edwards unwound the bandages that kept Bruce's splint in place.

"Five more weeks!"

"No need to despair." Mr. Edwards's voice lost its gruff tone, and Bruce relaxed slightly. "This cast should immobilize your leg sufficiently that with a good set of crutches, you can get around." Mr. Edwards removed the splint and Bruce's leg felt a measure of immediate relief. "Let me see what I can do about getting you a set. In the meantime, I brought you these." He held up a pair of clean but worn trousers with the left leg seam torn open past the knee. "These were Paul's. Take those ghastly ones off and let's get these clean ones on while your splint is off."

Mr. Edwards helped Bruce get his old, nearly ripped-to-shreds pants past his injured leg and then pull on the fresh pair. He wrung out a rag he'd pulled from the smallest bucket and washed Bruce's leg. Then he removed the stitches and dabbed the healing wound with whiskey.

Bruce sucked in a breath through clenched teeth. He had thought the gash was healing up nicely, but dang, that stung. He watched intently as Celia's pa carefully pulled a long stocking with the toe end cut off onto the injured leg, stretching it up over the knee. Mr. Edwards extracted a strip of muslin covered in white stuff from the tin bucket and wrapped it around the stocking. He did that again and again, smoothing the strips down in between each one, struggling with holding the leg up while wrapping the strips underneath. Bruce tried to help by lifting his leg, but Mr. Edwards still fumbled.

"It appears you could use another set of hands besides mine," Bruce said. "Celia's a right good nurse. Perhaps you should have someone fetch her."

"That she is," Mr. Edwards said rather brusquely. "One who will make the perfect wife for an up-and-coming young doctor, which I plan to see happen." He looked at Bruce, his eyebrows furrowed again. "I've seen you look at her. There's way too much hope in your eyes, Mr. Pickett. You're a right decent fellow, but you can't have her. She's already taken." His eyes concentrated on his task of applying more white strips. "Let me give you a bit of advice: save yourself some heartache and just forget about my daughter right here and now."

"You're right." Bruce let his face soften.

"I am?" The furrow in Mr. Edwards's eyebrows lifted into a look of surprise.

"Yep, there *is* way too much hope in my eyes," Bruce said, "and the rest of me. But sometimes hope's all a fellow like me's got."

"And what exactly is a fellow like you?" Mr. Edwards didn't look Bruce in the eye but continued with his work. "I realize, Mr. Pickett, I know very little about you. Where are you from? Do you have a family—someone we should be contacting to let them know you are all right? I would have thought you'd ask to get a message out to someone by now, but you haven't."

"My family?" Bruce held his breath. Here was the part he'd been afraid of ever since he woke up in this cabin. He certainly couldn't tell him the truth, at least not all of it. "I was born and raised in Boston. My parents had a place on Lowell Street." *A cramped tenement.* "My ma lives there by herself now. My pa's dead." *He was shot in the back by a man he'd cheated.* "His name was John. Her name is Matilda. I have two brothers. One lives in Colorado, and the other . . . I'm not sure." *Both are likely hiding from the law.* "There ain't much else to tell. My ma would probably appreciate a letter. But she's used to not hearing much from me or my brothers, so don't fret about it." Bruce hadn't written to her, because he could only scribble out a few words at best. He used to make Tom write the occasional letter to Ma for all of them, seeing that he was the only one of them who could write. Life had worn Ma down too much for her to teach Will and Bruce.

"What brings you out this way?" Mr. Edwards rubbed a little too hard over a tender spot, and Bruce winced. "Sorry." He was gentler applying the next piece of muslin. "What in the blazes were you doing in the City of Rocks a week and a half ago anyway? Though I'm glad you were, for Sophia's sake." He offered Bruce a smile—the first he'd seen from the old man, and Bruce appreciated it all the more. "It's not as if that spot is on the road to somewhere like it used to be."

Bruce weighed his options. There was not a fib to be had that would explain his reason for being there better than the truth. "I was digging for treasure."

Mr. Edwards chuckled. "Ah, you've heard the rumors too."

"They're not just rumors. I knew a man personally who"—Bruce caught himself before he said, *robbed one of those stages loaded with gold*—"who knew someone who robbed a stagecoach coming out of one of the mines up north. The thief let it slip that he'd cached the gold somewhere in them rocks." Bruce winced back the embarrassment and added, "I'm kinda in between jobs right now, so I thought I'd try my hand at finding some of that gold."

"Had any luck?" Mr. Edwards smoothed down the last strip from the tin bucket.

"No," Bruce said, dreading what that meant once this nice family turned him out. He switched to a positive thought. "Speaking of luck, how's my horse, Lucky?" Lucky was all he had to his name and the only spot of good luck he'd ever met with. He'd won him in a poker game two years ago, and the horse was his best friend.

"Don't worry. We've taken care of him." Mr. Edwards ducked his head. "I hope you don't mind, but I had Paul ride him into town the other day for supplies."

"Naw, I don't mind at all. And I'm sure Lucky was glad to help." Bruce glanced at the man's work. Four inches above his knee down his entire lower leg, except for his toes, looked like it was encased in a cocoon. "So this is what you call a cast?" Bruce said.

Mr. Edwards washed his hands in the small bucket and then dumped its cloudy water into the tin bucket. "Yep," he said as he propped the cast up off the bed with the wooden bucket laid on its side under his ankle.

"I've heard tell of them but never seen one," Bruce said, overwhelmed by the good care this family was giving to him, a perfect stranger . . . one who had eyes for their daughter.

"This cast needs to dry for several hours before you move it around too much. You got that?" Mr. Edwards carried the old splint and the tin bucket toward the door.

"Yep. And thank you kindly." Maybe he *was* due for some kindness. Even if it came with a gruff edge. Bruce went back to staring at the wall, thinking about how every time he'd stuck his neck out for others, he'd gotten burned. First, he'd stuck his neck out for Ma and tried to talk his brothers out of their life of crime. Instead, they pulled him into their schemes. Then he'd lost his job at that ranch in Boise after he'd finally gotten away from Tom and Will. His buddy Travis had gotten himself in trouble with the law, unbeknownst to Bruce. Then Bruce had gone and vouched for him when some money had gone missing from his boss's safe. When the truth came out, Travis let out about Bruce's bank-robbing days, and Bruce lost his job too. It didn't matter to his boss that he'd never held up a bank—only held the horses for his brothers. Or that he'd only cracked one safe in his life—and that was only because his brothers knew he was handy with tools and forced him to do it.

Bad luck just seemed to follow him.

He'd ended up with a boulder on his leg because he stuck his neck out—or he should say *leg* in this case—to warn a couple girls of danger.

Should he stick his neck out again, this time for Celia? It was almost certain she would never be his to love or that he would become part of a family like hers.

But she needed to be convinced that marrying that Wesley fellow would be a big mistake. Not because Bruce wanted her for himself—though that would be wonderful—but because he feared she'd not be happy with Wesley.

CHAPTER SIX

Bruce sat up in bed and stretched the best he could. He'd slept lousy. No one had come in to take out the pot before he went to bed, and he'd had to breathe in its foul odor all night.

Well, he certainly wasn't going to complain about it or his diminishing visits from the family. He was just grateful that he was being taken care of. Having no one who cared about you, except your aging, penniless ma who lived over two thousand miles away, was dangerous business out here in the Wild West.

He threw his thin blanket back and examined his new cast, running his fingers over the smooth white surface and then knocking against it with a knuckle. It was hard as a rock. Thank heavens he didn't need to prop it on the bucket anymore. He swung his feet over the side of the bed and let his feet rest on the wood floor.

"Whoa there, don't go standing up yet."

Bruce looked up to see Paul coming through the door. He hadn't seen much of the Edwards boy—except when Bruce got loaded into that wagon. The only conversation they'd ever had was probably so laced with curse words that the poor kid was scared to death of him. Paul stepped into the room with a plate of eggs and biscuits in one hand, and in the other, he held what looked to be a pair of carved wooden crutches. The kid stood nearly as tall as Bruce himself, yet his shoulders were broader. "Kid" was not a fitting description.

"Don't worry. I'm not trying to stand. Just getting a feel for this cast your pa put on me yesterday." Bruce tapped his knuckles on it. "Pretty spiffy, eh? Oh, and thanks for the new trousers—sorry your pa had to tear them."

"Oh, those things." Paul laughed. "They aren't exactly what I'd call new. Glad you can use them." He handed Bruce his breakfast and then rested the crutches against the wall by the bed. "These are for you too. Pa wanted me to teach you how to use them. He made them for me last year when I broke my leg. I fell off the cabin while trying to fix the roof."

"Sorry to hear that," Bruce said and took a bite of eggs.

"It was nothing—at least compared to your leg." Paul pulled the chair away from the wall. He sat down on it backwards, leaning his arms over its top.

"How old are you?" Bruce asked.

"Fifteen."

"You're big for your age."

"That's what Pa says. I don't think much about it. There's only three boys my age around here to compare myself to."

"Is it hard living out here in the middle of nowhere?"

"Sometimes." Paul let out a noticeable breath. "But most of the time, I'm too busy to think much about it. And I don't mind. I like helping Ma and Pa make this land into a right nice place to call home. And come fall, when the harvest is over, there's time to have a little fun. Me and those other boys, well, we go riding. Sometimes we camp out. We have a good time together."

That sparked an idea in Bruce. "So you know the people of Almo, then?" he asked.

"Pretty much. There's not that many of them to know." Paul chuckled.

"Do they ever get together to have, say, a Fourth of July celebration?"

"You been talking to Celia or something?" Paul's face pulled to one side in a crooked grin.

"Not nearly enough," Bruce said, a heaviness weighing down his voice. "No offense, but I had kind of hoped she would bring me the crutches."

"Yeah, sorry about that," Paul said in a voice that sounded sincere. "Both Ma and Pa have gone out of their way to ask me and Sophia to replace Celia when it comes to you." Wearing a sly expression, Paul looked at Bruce. "I gather you don't like that much, do you?"

"No, not at all—not that I don't appreciate your attention today, but . . ."

"But you'd like Celia's better." Paul smiled.

"I think your parents must know that too," Bruce admitted. "And they want to keep Celia away from me."

"Only because she's supposed to be marrying this total bore named Wesley Cornelius."

Bruce smiled, liking Paul more and more. He took another bite of eggs and spoke out of one side of his mouth. "Seriously, his last name is Cornelius?"

He felt the urge to laugh and didn't hold back. "Her name would be Celia E. Cornelius? Such an awkward mouthful, even without the eggs." He swallowed. "Especially for such a wonderful woman."

"I take it you like my sister." Paul had lost his mirthful demeanor.

"Don't repeat what I say to your parents but, yes, very much so." Bruce took in a deep breath and let it drain out. "I mean, who wouldn't? She's beautiful and the kindest, gentlest nurse a person could ever hope to have. Mr. Cornelius is a lucky fellow. That's all I can say."

"And Celia's unlucky." Paul looked out into the front room where Celia could be heard talking as she ate her breakfast. "I was Sophia's age when we left Springfield, old enough to get to know my sister's suitor and see him for what he was."

"And what was that?" Bruce could see that he and Paul were going to get along just fine.

"A snob. He was very selective in who he liked." Paul grinned. "He didn't like me, by the way. That didn't hurt my feelings. The guy sat around all the time, being waited on by servants."

"What did your sister possibly ever see in him?"

"Uhhh." Paul hunched his shoulders. "A good provider, I guess. Ma and Pa wouldn't need to worry about her future." He jumped out of the chair. "I'd better hurry and get you trained on these crutches before my breakfast is stone cold and Pa heads to the fields."

Bruce's hopes sunk low to where he could trample them himself. What did *he* have to offer Celia? He had no money, no job, and no education, only a deep desire to work with his hands—not cracking safes—and make something of his life. He really should take Mr. Edwards's advice and forget about Celia right here and now. For her sake. Or at least forget his guilty hope that by some miracle they could be together.

For the next five minutes, however, as Celia's brother showed him how to use the crutches, Bruce refused to forget about his desire to give her a gift. While Paul helped him hobble around the room, he brainstormed but came up empty-handed. He could tell Paul was finishing up with his instructions by the way Paul kept looking through the door and acting antsy—his pa was most likely waiting for him. It was now or maybe never. If Bruce was to give Celia any kind of celebration, he'd need to recruit help. "Paul," he said. "Before you go, I need to ask you something."

"Sure."

"I could never ask your parents for help on this, 'cause they might see it as me trying to weasel in on Wesley's territory. But I'm not. I'm just wanting to show my thanks to your sister for being such a good nurse—and cheer her up a bit."

"Yeah, I've noticed Celia's been kind of down in the mouth the last few days." Paul nodded.

"I think it has to do with a letter she got from that Mr. Cornelius fellow. She was trying to write a letter back to him while she was sitting in my room. She was really struggling with it. I could feel it. And there was something in that letter that bothered her." Bruce wanted to recruit Paul to help convince Celia to forget Wesley but decided that might be sticking his neck out too far. He'd just stick it out a little. "I was thinking if we could give Celia some sort of Fourth of July celebration, it might cheer her up. What do you say? Could you help me do that?"

"That's right thoughtful of you, Bruce." Paul slapped him on the back. "Yeah, let's see what we can do. Celia has complained to Ma and Pa every year since we got here that we don't do nothing for the Fourth of July anymore. I haven't heard much of anything from her this year though, so I just figured she'd gotten over it. But it's a dandy idea. Especially since it'll be our last summer with her." He headed for the door, his eyes still on Bruce. "Now that you can get around somewhat, I'll see what I can do about sneaking in some ways for you and Celia to see more of each other." He turned and walked out, mumbling, "I'd quite like it if my sister was still here next summer."

CHAPTER SEVEN

PAUL CAME OUT OF THE bedroom carrying Bruce's emptied breakfast plate. Celia thought what Ma and Pa were doing was just plain and simple *not fair*. Not to her and not to Bruce.

She waited until after breakfast when she was alone with her ma, the two of them doing the dishes. "I have a bone to pick with you."

Ma calmly pumped water into the sink. "Only one bone this time?" She smiled and winked at Celia.

"Ma, I'm serious. I've tried to bite my tongue on this, but it really *isn't* fair." Celia paused and breathed deeply, wanting what she had to say to come out as a sound argument, not as whiny. "Why is it that you asked Paul to take Bruce," she cleared her throat, "I mean Mr. Pickett, his breakfast this morning? Good gracious, it was not like I was busy—I was just eating my breakfast."

"Because Pa wanted him to take Mr. Pickett his old crutches."

Celia could have easily done that. "I can see what you and Pa are doing," she said firmly.

"What are we doing?" Ma's expression was a little sly as she placed the dishes in the water.

"Ah, there!" Celia pointed to her ma's mouth. "Your smile is incriminating. You and Pa are purposely asking Sophia and Paul to take care of Mr. Pickett rather than asking me. So much so that I hardly ever get to help him anymore. I thought you and Pa *wanted* me to practice my nursing skills."

"Oh, dear." Ma set the dishes in the soapy dishwater and dried her hands. She placed them on Celia's shoulders, guided her down onto a kitchen chair, and stood firmly at her side. "We do want you to continue to train as a nurse. You have such a knack for it. One that your future husband admires greatly and will most certainly take advantage of when he opens his private practice." Ma blushed. "At least until your children come along."

"Wesley?" Celia suddenly felt concern about her future children growing up with a father with Wesley's views. She reminded herself that Wesley would be a good disciplinarian to their children. And a good provider. And he'd always been so sweet and tender with her when they were together. Medical school must be taking its toll on him, and he'd forgotten to respond to her inquiry about their engagement. That's all.

"Of course I'm talking about Wesley." Ma clamped her hands on her hips. She let out a sigh and continued. "I guess you are an adult now. And you are right. Pa and I should not have tried to restrict your time with Mr. Pickett. You're no longer a child where we need to oversee your decisions. But hear me out on this, Celia; I've never seen you so invested in a patient before. Pa neither. We are concerned that your heart might get involved. And that you possibly might forget about the man you promised to marry. You two are so perfect for each other."

"Of course we are," Celia said in a hesitant voice, wanting to believe that.

"Thank heavens." Ma let out a sigh. "Be careful, Celia. Mr. Pickett cleaned up well."

"What is that supposed to mean?"

"Your patient is a handsome, unmarried young man. You are young and a somewhat reckless young woman. We fear you might not be thinking things through because of Wesley being so far away. That's all."

"I promise you, Ma, I am thinking things through very thoroughly, more than you realize. More than *I've* realized." Celia thought about the superficial letter she'd just sent Wesley. Perhaps she should write him another letter, only this time she would not skirt the issues that bothered her. She needed that commitment from Wesley. Or a "no" and a blessing to move on.

The squeak of floorboards and shuffling sounds pulled Celia's attention away from her ma and toward the small bedroom. Bruce stood in the doorway, balancing himself with the aid of Paul's crutches. A smile spread across his face.

"Good morning, ladies," he said in a cheerful voice. "I'll wager you thought you'd never see this day come. There ain't going to be no more hauling out the chamber pot for you two—or anyone else. I'm going to try these girls out here and now." He lifted both crutches while balancing on his good foot. "So if you'd point me toward the privy, I'd be much obliged."

Ma pointed to the front door. "Turn to your left as soon as you get outside and head around the side of the cabin." She looked to Celia, and her eyebrows drew together. "You'd better go with him."

"Well, that might be a little awkward." Bruce sported a mischievous grin.

Ma's face blushed a noticeable shade of red. "Uh, I uh, I meant—"

"I was just teasing you, Mrs. Edwards." Bruce motioned for Celia to come. "Truth is, I would appreciate your daughter's escort—as far as she dares. I'm a mite unstable on these things."

Celia looked at her ma and smiled, hoping her gratitude showed through.

"Just remember what I said." Ma motioned with her head toward Bruce.

"Don't worry. I will." Celia hurried to Bruce's side.

Bruce appeared to scan the main room of the cabin. His eyes gravitated to the banjo set on the mantel of the fireplace as Celia reached his side. "Who's the banjo player?"

"Oh, that's Pa's." Celia had practically forgotten it was there. "He rarely plays it anymore."

"He's lost interest?"

"Most likely." Celia opened the front door and held it while Bruce hobbled through onto the porch. "He's too busy or tired. Back in Springfield, he played it all the time." She pointed to the east. "It's around this corner." She took the single step off the porch at his side really slow, allowing for him to maneuver his crutches.

"Are you sorry your family moved out West?" Bruce didn't look at her but kept his full attention on the placement of the crutches and his good foot. Once on the dirt, he turned east.

"Not so much anymore. But I am sorry that Pa no longer plays his banjo or likes the Fourth of July. I doubt the two are connected to moving, but they all happened about the same time, so what else can I think?" Celia held out her hand for him to slow down. "The ground gets a little rocky here, so you'll need to be extra careful. And whatever you do, try not to put any weight on your bad leg."

"Don't worry—I will. And don't worry—I won't." Bruce winked at her. "I guess that means you shouldn't worry about me at all."

Celia felt herself smile. "You think you're rather clever, don't you?"

"What I really think I am is rather lucky—a rare occurrence for me."

"You mean about your leg healing so nicely?"

"Well, yeah, that too. But mostly about being in your company right now—even if I'll have to cut it short in a minute." He smirked and eyed the weathered outhouse in the barren patch of gravel a few yards away. "I about had a fainting spell when your ma asked you to help me."

"Yes, that surprised me too." Celia thought of her ma with fondness. "Perhaps she did listen to me this time." And maybe Ma had listened to Celia all those other times she'd spoken her mind the past three years—or *complained* as her family labeled it—but this time Celia's argument had been sound.

Bruce stopped a few feet from the privy and focused his attention on Celia. "What was it you told her?"

"That it didn't make sense for her and Pa to make Paul and Sophia tend to you when I'm the one who wants to be a nurse. And that I have more time on my hands than Paul does."

"What did your ma say after that?"

"To be careful."

"You mean, be careful taking care of me 'cause she changed her mind about letting you do that?"

"She said to be careful with my heart." Then it hit Celia; she understood what her ma was talking about now, standing here like she was, staring into Bruce's face. The light in Bruce's blue eyes drew her in. It gave her a sense there was something more to this man than his exterior.

"You're heart, eh?" Bruce raised one eyebrow. "And your ma really feels like she has cause to worry about that?" His tone was teasing, but she swore it held a measure of hope.

"Well, the word 'handsome' did find its way into her discourse." Good gracious, why did Bruce look so charming as she spoke to him?

"You going to fight your ma on those points? Tell her she's mistaken?"

Celia ducked her head. She should be telling Bruce about Wesley's skill at poetry or his being top of his class or her and Wesley's plans to wed—not this.

Those words weren't there.

She raised her chin but didn't meet his eyes. "No, I quite agree with her."

Bruce slapped his good leg. "This day just keeps gettin' better and better. Another hour or so and you'll have me dancing on the clouds. Without crutches." He lifted both hands toward the sky leaving the crutches leaning against his armpits. He glanced at her. "Tell your folks you're not only a good nurse; you're good medicine. And if they'd but leave me entirely in your care, I'd be healed up and out of everybody's hair in no time."

"Oh." Was that what he really wanted, to be on his way, back to his old life? Something pricked at her heart to think of him leaving, yet she knew so little of that life—so little about him. Ma was right; she needed to be careful. She knew Wesley. He represented a secure future, one with wealth, a big home, and no worries.

CHAPTER EIGHT

CELIA STEPPED INTO THE CABIN looking for Bruce. Ever since he got his crutches, she swore she saw him almost as little as she had last week when Ma and Pa had conspired to keep her away from him. True, she saw him at meals, but she had to share his attention with everyone else around the table.

Ma stood at the sink scrubbing the remainder of last year's potatoes for dinner and turned around when Celia shut the door. "Ma, have you seen Bruce?" Though Ma and Pa had loosened up about Celia spending time with him, she still tried to keep her interaction with him to a minimum for her parents' sake—for her sake, until she knew her mind for sure. "Pa needs the plow hooks sharpened," she said, oddly grateful to Pa for the excuse to seek out Bruce.

"The last I saw him, he was with your little sister."

"Which one? I have two."

"Abby, of course."

Celia felt a measure of jealousy toward her five-year-old sister. "Yes, she quite adores our convalescing patient, doesn't she?"

"Well, who else around here has time to dote over her?" Ma rinsed her peeled potatoes in a bucket of water and placed them in the big pot. "I must say, the way Mr. Pickett keeps an eye on the girl is a godsend for me."

"Yes. And his skill with a whetstone is a godsend for Pa," Celia reminded her ma. It was funny how she was constantly pointing out Bruce's strengths, all the while trying to compare those to Wesley's refined wit and financial security. "So do you know where they might be, Abby and Bruce?"

"Try the garden." Ma set the pot on the stove. "Sophia came in here half an hour ago and took that ratty chair from Bruce's room—which, by the way, he's moving out of this evening so you girls can have your room back."

"Where's he going to sleep?"

"He insists he's ready for the barn." Ma shrugged. "Oh, and Sophia said something about needing that chair to pick peas." Ma glanced at Celia with an amused expression. "My guess is she's recruited Mr. Pickett's help."

"I'll try there, then."

"She could use your help too if Pa's done with you."

"He is." Celia hurried out the door, silently chuckling. She wouldn't doubt Sophia had gotten Bruce to help her. Bruce would be amenable. He always seemed more than happy to do anything anyone asked of him, constantly finding creative ways to work around his broken leg.

Celia walked by the big cottonwood tree at the side of the cabin and enjoyed that moment of cool shade. She moved past the chicken coop, the smell of chicken manure reminding her that it needed cleaning, and then walked around to the back of the barn. Three long rows of bush peas, with deep furrows Pa had dug on each side to irrigate them, ran down the middle of the garden. At the far end of one of the rows, Bruce sat on the old chair, leaning down and picking peas. Abby was on the other side of the row of pea vines, picking, though not nearly as fast.

A few strides away, Sophia busily stripped the pods from the middle row. She looked up from her work. "Celia! You came to help?"

"Yes, and to deliver a message to Mr. Pickett from Pa." Celia added the last part quickly, not that Sophia seemed to care anymore if and when she talked to Bruce. But Celia needed to keep up appearances—even about Wesley. At least until she wrote that letter and pressed Wesley for a straight answer concerning their engagement so she could set her own feelings straight and not be tempted to let them drift to Bruce.

Sophia appeared pleased. "Thanks."

Celia nodded and headed down the furrow to the end of the row with a bit of a skip to her steps. It could be because work always went faster when she had company, but she knew better.

Bruce gazed at her as she approached. A wide smile spread across his face. The morning sun lit his face, making his eyes appear all the more blue. "Celia!" He stood and, holding on to the back of the chair, motioned to its seat. "Come, have a sit. It's a right dandy way to pick peas if you ask me. It's a mite easier on your back."

"And your legs." Celia pointed to his cast as she neared him. "I'm not the one who's supposed to keep weight off their leg." She smiled. "I have to say, that's a rather clever idea though."

"I can't take all the credit." Bruce balanced on his good leg, lifted the chair, and moved it a few feet down the row. "It was Abby who gave me the inspiration for it." He turned and looked at Abby. "Right?"

Abby sat on the ground, nestled in the cradle of the furrow. Her eyes shone with delight. "I told him to sit down like me—that way he could help. He helps good and makes it more fun."

"Oh really now? How is that?" Celia leaned down next to her littlest sister, pulled off a handful of pods, and dumped them into the bushel basket.

"He tells stories even better than Pa." Abby pulled off a single pod and placed it methodically in the basket.

"Is that all?" Celia continued to strip pods from the vines.

"Sometimes I make her move my chair for me." Bruce winked at Abby.

Abby giggled. "No, you don't."

"And heft the basket."

"No, you don't." Abby giggled again at Bruce.

"I might have to ask *you* to do it, though, when we're finished." Bruce grinned at Celia. "Scooting it along the ground all the way back to the house with my crutch might get tiresome."

"I'll be more than glad to. For now, I'll help pick." Celia moved over to the row no one else was working on. Over her shoulder, she said, "Good gracious, I forgot to tell you; Pa needs you to sharpen his plow blade sometime today so he can hill potatoes tomorrow. He appreciates your skills," she added, wanting him to know that.

Bruce straightened up. "I'll get right on it this afternoon."

The three of them worked in silence for a minute or so until Abby stood and brushed off her dress. "You know what Mr. Pickett told me?" she said to Celia. Her sweet little voice took on a tone of bragging.

"No, what did Mr. Pickett tell you?" Celia glanced over to the next row where Bruce busily worked. By how full the peas came up in the basket, it was apparent he and Abby had spent a good amount of time together this morning.

"He told me I was pretty."

"I'd say that Mr. Pickett is absolutely correct."

Abby beamed. "He said he could only think of one thing prettier in the whole world than me."

"Oh really now?" Celia glanced again at Bruce. She could only see his profile, but it appeared he was listening in the way he kept his ear toward them. "Did he tell you what that one thing was?"

"Yeah." Abby slapped her hand to her mouth and smiled.

"Can you tell me?"

Abby nodded. Giggling, she responded, "You."

Bruce turned and looked at Celia straight on. "That's right." His lip curled up in a most charming fashion. "I might be a lot of things, but one thing I'm not is a liar."

Celia felt herself blush, but it was a blush as inviting as the kiss of crimson on their peaches come fall. It left her tongue-tied and unable to respond. She pretended to be intent on picking a large handful of pea pods.

"You're too quiet," Abby said. She turned around and started picking off Bruce's row. She jabbered to him about their chickens and then their old tomcat as the three of them worked and moved toward the end of the garden. Bruce usually responded with something that made Abby giggle.

With each burst of her little sister's laughter, bittersweet emotions churned inside Celia. She couldn't possibly keep her mind and heart focused on Wesley when Bruce was right here, making her little sister so happy. And brightening everyone's day, it seemed. Wesley had never interacted with any of her siblings the times he came over to visit Celia. If they ever did discuss their families, he dominated the conversation with talk of his sister's wonderful singing voice, his brother's new law practice, or his father's inherited wealth.

Maybe time has matured Wesley.

She really did need to write that letter. She needed to know if Wesley was still committed to their marriage. After all, Ma's future inheritance had all but dried up two months ago when Grandpa Bentley's shipping line quit running—their wind-powered ships were unable to compete with the new steam-powered ones. Ma had seen that coming for some time, and it was part of the reason Celia's parents had decided to move out West. Could it be possible that Wesley's parents had become privy to this fact, them being good friends of the Bentley family, and Wesley was bothered by the fact that Celia's family would now be considered poor?

No, surely Wesley wouldn't be that shallow.

After they'd picked all the ripe pods, they sat under the shade of the big cottonwood and shelled peas. Celia sat on the ground next to Bruce, leaning her back against the trunk. Her two sisters sat in the dirt across from them.

"Thanks again for helping, Celia." Sophia pushed a string of peas from its pod into one of Ma's big bowls.

"What about me?" Abby pouted. Her bowl was the smallest and least full.

"Thank you too, Abby," Sophia said.

"Hey, what about me?" Bruce attempted a pout, but it came out as a crooked grin.

Sophia chuckled. "Yes, Mr. Pickett, you too . . . most of all. You picked more than any of us."

"Only 'cause you fetched me the chair." Bruce tossed a pea pod at Sophia, and she laughed. "Besides, how could I not work like a horse? Your family's been so—" His voice faltered, and he looked away. After a pause, he cleared his throat and continued. "So good to me. I'm beholden to you all—more than you'll ever know."

"You make it sound like we're doing something out of the ordinary," Celia said.

"You are." Bruce reached over and laid his hand atop Celia's.

The gentle touch of his fingers tingled the back of her hand. Her heart quickened to where she could hear its rapid beat in her ears. "Th-that's nonsense."

"No, it's not." He kept his hand on hers and gave it a squeeze. "You treat me better than my own family did. I feel I fit here better than anywhere I've ever been."

Celia gulped. Their eyes met. "You are too kind."

"It's definitely the other way around." Bruce's tone held none of the humor it had a moment ago. He looked at the girls. "Sophia, your bowl's almost full. Tell you what—you and Abby take what peas you've done in to your ma, and me and Celia will finish shelling the rest of them. Isn't that right?" He gazed at Celia with hope spilling from his eyes.

Celia's insides fluttered. He was getting rid of her sisters so they could be alone, and he hoped she would go along with his scheme. Would that be wise given the uncertain feelings she was having for Wesley? She took a deep breath, trying to decide.

"Yes," she responded, surprising herself.

Bruce nodded quickly. "And we'll gather up all the old pods and feed them to the pigs. So Abby, Sophia, go play and have some fun for the rest of the morning."

"Let's go." Little Abby looked at Sophia and jumped to her feet, and together they headed for the house carrying their share of shelled peas, most of which would be spread out this afternoon to be dried.

Celia turned to Bruce. "If I didn't know better, I'd swear you were trying to get rid of my sisters."

"Yep." His eyes held that spark that warmed her like a nice fire on a cold day.

"Uh . . ." She chewed on her lip.

He touched a finger to her chin and brought it to where their faces were mere inches apart. "I can see it in your eyes," he said, grinning like a little boy who just got exactly what he wanted. "You wanted to be shed of our audience as much as I did."

"Well . . . um . . ." She wanted to tell him yes, but memories of Wesley pulled at her.

"Celia," he said her name softly, gathered her hands into his, and scooted closer. "I realize you maybe don't share my feelings—you're just being the kind soul that you are. But still, I've got to say something, or I'll burst. I've tried to keep my distance—for your ma and pa's sake and for your sake, but I can't do it no more. Every time I'm near you, my heart ricochets around in my chest. The only thing that brings it peace is the hope that maybe, just maybe, you have feelings for me too and that I have a chance. Just give me a word, a signal, a look . . . anything that tells me I've got something Wesley doesn't—something you like about me."

Celia felt as though she'd been caught up in a whirlwind. Sitting there so close to Bruce, her hands in his, their hips touching, his brilliant blue eyes holding hers captive, her heart and her mind felt to be spinning in opposite directions. Through all the emotions being kicked up like dust by a team of horses, she managed to give him a nod.

CHAPTER NINE

Bruce thought about Celia's nod again as he spread his quilt over the pile of straw. He smoothed it out, ready to spend his fourth night in the barn—and fourth day wondering what she actually saw in him that Wesley didn't have. She wouldn't say more about it as they shelled peas again the other day, but her smile and attentive conversation was enough to keep his hope alive.

Paul stood beneath the old lantern that hung from a crossbeam in the barn. "You ready for me to turn off the lantern?"

"Yep. And it's really kind of you to keep bedding down out here, just so I don't have to fumble in the dark with this darn cast after I snuff the light."

"Aw, it's nothing. I prefer it out here during the summer." Paul turned down the flame, and the light faded into darkness.

The shifting of straw grew silent. Bruce figured Paul was settled for the night. In a week, this young fellow had grown to feel more like a brother than his actual brothers ever had. "Paul?" he called out.

"Yeah."

"We need to get going on that Fourth of July celebration. I realize it can't come close to those we both had back in Massachusetts, but it will be better than nothing."

"Hey, I didn't know you were from Massachusetts too. How come you never said anything before?"

"Uh . . . I guess most of my life's not worth mentioning." Bruce paused and ran his mind through some of his favorite childhood memories. "Except for the Fourth of July celebrations I went to in Boston, what with the huge bonfires, parades, and of course, the fireworks."

"The fourth is only a week away." Paul sounded doubtful.

"I know, but I've got to do something for her if I can."

"Yeah, Celia's still down in the mouth. This morning, though, I noticed she cheered up after she gave Pa a letter to mail. I'd like to keep her cheered up. Where do we start?"

Bruce could hope she was saying goodbye to that fellow, but no matter what, he wanted to please her. "The first thing we're going to need is a parade. I've never been to Almo. How big is it? Is there a street that would be fitting for a parade?"

"There's only one to choose from—the dirt road that heads to Elba. It's got Dumfrey's store on it, along with the telegraph office and the blacksmith's. I suppose we could have a parade march down it—if that's what you want."

"It is." Bruce tried to sound confident. He'd hoped for at least a block or two. "We'll just have the local folk line up along the road as far as they stretch. It's the thought that counts. At least, I hope Celia will think so."

"We've got a problem. If you got all the people lining the road, who's going to be in it?"

"Uh . . . you're right." Bruce heaved out a sigh. "Is this why your town hasn't done anything before—it's too small?"

"Probably."

"Me and my big ideas. Wanting Almo to throw a celebration is kind of like expecting a single bee to whip up a batch of honey to put on my biscuit."

Paul chuckled. Then he sat up, his silhouette etched by a bit of moonlight streaming through the barn door. "I know what we can do. We could have all the kids and their favorite animals be in the parade. Abby would love it! Even Sophia."

"Brilliant idea."

"Thanks."

"All right, so how we going to get folks out to watch or be in this here parade? I'm definitely going to need your help on this," Bruce said sheepishly. "I don't know anybody around here. Plus, I still have yet to climb on my horse. I'm afraid Celia would shoot me if I tried."

"Always the nurse, isn't she?"

"I suppose." Bruce wished Celia spent more time "nursing" him. Since he'd opened up to her with his feelings four days ago, he swore she'd been avoiding him—at least avoiding all opportunities where they could be alone. At mealtimes, she'd sit by him, talk about the weather, and ask how his leg was doing. But he longed for more.

"Well, I'll see what I can do." Paul's voice held a measure of hesitancy. "I know most of the folks around here, and things are slowing down temporarily around the farm, so I can go talk to them. A nice long ride on Copper sounds like fun—I could use that right about now."

"Good, good." Bruce felt a lift to his spirits.

"Don't go getting your hopes up yet." Paul stirred in his bed.

The sound of straw bunching and moving made Bruce want to do the same to get rid of the wad of straw poking his back. But concentrating on the task at hand seemed more important at the moment. "Why not?" he asked, determined *not* to give up hope.

"I don't rightly know if people around here would want to stop what they're doing—to survive—long enough to come into town and celebrate something most of them, I'm guessing, don't give much thought about. Especially Pa." Paul paused and then added, "I'll ask them anyway—the townsfolk that is, not Pa." He laid back down.

"Oh." Bruce had forgotten about that roadblock. There had to be a way around it. From what Celia had said, it sounded as if her pa had been quite fond of the holiday at one time. Why the change? "This could be a long shot, but I'm guessing your pa used to enjoy the Fourth of July."

"Yeah, he did," Paul said like it'd barely dawned on him.

"What changed?" If Bruce could get to the bottom of that mystery, maybe he could help Mr. Edwards enjoy it once more. That could make the celebration even sweeter for Celia.

"We moved out here, and Pa didn't have time for fun anymore."

"If a person really, truly enjoys something, they manage to make time for it somehow. You sure there's not something more?"

"Not that I can think of. I guess I never gave it much thought." Paul paused. "Wait a minute. Once he told me he 'didn't deserve to celebrate no more,' or something like that. I don't know what he'd meant by that, and I don't know if that helps, but that's all I can give you. Sorry."

"No, that was interesting." Bruce had at least something to start with.

"Hey, what about fireworks?" Paul spoke up. "Being from Boston, you got to see some dandy ones. Am I right? Much better than the few I got to see in Springfield, I'm sure of it."

Fireworks cost money. Bruce stared at the moonlight streaming in, knowing his little celebration would be like moonlight verses the sun when compared to the ones Celia was used to back East. "Maybe we could have a bonfire instead."

"Yeah!" Paul exclaimed. "I've got a mound of sagebrush I just cleared. It'd be smoky, but it'd make for a dandy fire if Pa'll let me burn it."

"That would be good. But how could you haul all that brush into town?"

"I don't know."

"Maybe we forget the bonfire and we just settle for a dance." Bruce did like that idea. He'd love to be Celia's first partner. And her second and third and fourth . . . He rolled over and felt the weight of his cast. The idea of the dance lost its appeal.

"A dance is a great idea!" Paul sat up again. "Mary Jane Richards might come and . . . Anyway, I like that idea. I'll talk that up in town. I'm sure folks will come to that. What about the music though?"

"Surely there's somebody in the area that plays an instrument or two."

"Not that I can think of," Paul said.

An image of the banjo above the fireplace popped into Bruce's head. "What about your pa?"

"Oh." Paul said that like he'd totally forgotten the instrument. "I'd doubt he'd do it. He hasn't played his banjo since we moved here. He's too serious. Work is all he wants to do."

"What about before you moved?" Bruce wanted to verify the pattern he was seeing.

"Pa played it all the time back in Springfield. He was even in some kind of a band when I was little." Paul laid back down. "But heck if I'm going to ask him to do that. Pa's changed since he decided to move."

"Why?" Bruce mumbled under his breath. Again, this wasn't making sense.

Paul paused for a moment or two. "Come to think of it, Pa's not going to be keen on this idea at all. Heck, the only thing he celebrates is when it rains in the summer—which ain't too often. I don't think he believes in having fun." Paul rolled over and yawned. "Maybe we should forget about this whole thing."

Bruce sat up, determined to smooth out the lump of straw poking his back and the bumps in his celebration for Celia. He pulled away the blanket and punched down the straw. "I still say we give it a try."

CHAPTER TEN

CELIA DUG TO THE BOTTOM of her drawer for the three-year calendar Grandma Bentley had sent her last Christmas. The simple gift had been Celia's first hint that her grandparents were in financial trouble. Usually they sent her a crisp five-dollar bill. She picked up the heavy card with a boy in a tree and a dog below printed along with its ad for Hoods Sarsaparilla and turned it over to check the date.

Today was June 28. She'd sent her letter off to Wesley yesterday. Somewhere during the week of July 16 to 22, it should arrive. If he responded right away, she should have her answer by the first or second week of August at best. That felt like an eternity. She wanted to know now, today, if Wesley still wanted to marry her. If he wasn't committed to their marriage, how could she possibly be expected to be? And if he was . . .

Not ready to stow the calendar back in the drawer, she gave it a second glance. Her eyes gravitated to July 4. It was a mere six days away. She quickly stuffed the calendar away. With tending to Bruce and Wesley's letter on her mind, she'd been too preoccupied to come up with any sort of celebration like she'd hoped. And her family certainly wouldn't do anything. Why would this summer be any different than the past three years? Her family seemed to have given up on the holiday alongside Pa. Oh, why couldn't Pa be like he used to be? He'd always been the first to wake up on July fourth, not merely so he could milk the cow but to salute the sunrise and the American flag after he'd hung it across their porch. Then, with a smile on his face, he'd get everyone to finish their chores early so the family could hurry down to the park to get the best spot to watch the parade. "Oh well." She sighed. It appeared yet another Fourth of July would come and go without celebration.

She proceeded outside to the garden, grabbing a hoe from the barn on her way. A glint of sharpened steel caught her eye. The hoe's blade and wood handle looked nearly new as well, having been cleaned and oiled. Her heart swelled. Was it appreciation for Bruce easing her task of weeding? Pride in his attention to detail? Or admiration in the quiet fashion he had been paying her family back for taking care of him?

On the other hand, she swore by the way he went around helping that it was just who he was. When Celia walked around the side of the barn, she stopped. She stared at Bruce's clean-shaven face, trimmed and combed hair, and shirt unbuttoned down to where she could see the beads of sweat glistening on his firm chest.

"Good morning." Bruce sat on the ratty old chair and looked up from the wagon wheel he scrubbed. He clasped Ma's old boar's hair cleaning brush with one hand and held the other above his eyes to shield them from the sun. The entire wagon looked as though it had met with that brush. Every speck of dirt and manure had been scrubbed away to where she could see the wood grain showing through the years of weathering.

"Good morning," Celia responded as soon as she steadied herself. "Are you that desperate for things to keep you busy that you've had to resort to scrubbing down the wagon?" She chuckled demurely. Part of her begged her feet to keep walking toward the garden, but a larger share of her demanded she stay put. "You can always come help me weed if you have time on your hands," she said without thinking.

One corner of his mouth lifted into an intriguing grin. "I have an ulterior motive with the wagon." His grin softened into his usual cheerful smile. "But I'll be glad to stop here and now to come help you weed. It's not like I get a heap of invitations to join you as of late."

Celia stared at her feet, at her dusty shoes without holes, unlike Bruce's. He was right. It was no longer Ma's or Pa's doing. It was her doing, her indecision's doing. She'd hoped he wouldn't notice. "Sorry. I've been busy," she said in a feeble attempt to smooth things over.

"I understand." He stood, dried his hands on his pants, and, using the old chair as a cane of sorts, hobbled toward her. "I've made you skittish. And you have every right to be with me declaring my feelings for you like I have after knowing you for such a short time."

"No, no, it's not like that—"

Bruce hushed her by lifting his hand and placing his fingers on her lips, sending a tingle through her body. "No need to explain." He removed his hand, sat down, and dunked the brush back into the bucket of soapy water. "I'd say I was sorry for declaring such things to you, but I'm not. They're my feelings, and I don't care to keep such good things buried. A man in my position has so few pleasurable moments to cling to. Thanks for giving them to me." He squinted back up at her. "And if you don't mind, my eyes'll continue to enjoy your beauty for at least another week. I'll keep the rest of me at a distance for the time I'm here—if that's your wish."

"A week? What are you saying?" She'd planned on him being here when she received Wesley's reply. The thought of him being gone tore at her heart. More pain grew there when she realized waiting for Wesley wasn't fair to Bruce. Bruce was no consolation prize, only to be considered if her first choice bowed out.

"Your pa says I should be fit for riding in about a week or so. There'll be no reason for me staying. I'll be out of your hair then." The corner of his mouth lifted again. "But not before I finish up my gift to you."

His words came like a slap to her face. "A gift? For what? I don't deserve any such thing." Her stomach soured.

"In my book you do." Bruce turned away and concentrated on the wheel. "This past month's been hell, but it's been heaven at the same time because of you. Please don't deny me the pleasure of giving you something as a way to say thanks."

Grappling for the right words, Celia placed her hand on his shoulder without thinking. She could feel the firm contour of his muscles through his shirt. She sensed he enjoyed her touch—as did she. "I won't deny you," she managed to say in a wispy voice.

He rose again from his chair and turned toward her. "You won't, eh?" His arm wrapped around her waist and pulled her close.

Surprise took her off guard, weakened her knees, and leaned her into his body. She held on to him as he kissed her full on the lips, and she instinctively returned his kiss with like passion. Her arms clung to him after he pulled his lips away, reluctant to let go.

He released her and hobbled back a step, his eyes still gazing at her. "Sorry, Celia. I'm guessing that's not what you were referring to when you said you wouldn't deny me, but . . ." His mouth curved up only slightly, but his eyes smiled. "I liked my version of your invitation better. Gosh darn it, Celia, if you weren't so all-fired beautiful and kind I could have held myself back."

Celia brushed at a wrinkle in her skirt. "It's okay," she said, scolding herself inside for being glad he hadn't held himself back—and for enjoying that kiss more than any of Wesley's.

"Don't worry." Bruce lowered himself onto his chair. "Like I said, you'll be shed of me soon. Until then, no more putting my own interpretation on your words, I promise. But I can never promise to forget you—not in a thousand years."

She took her hoe and hurried off to the garden, juggling the tool, her hand having lost control of its balance from grabbing it at an awkward angle. Her head and her heart felt just as off balance as they battled to be the one in charge, especially when she thought of the touch of his lips against hers and his promise to never forget her. He'd said it with such feeling that she believed him. Wesley, she feared, had already forgotten her. Not who she was and how vital she would be to his medical practice, but his feelings for her. Was that the kind of marriage *she* wanted, one where love and attraction were secondary?

CHAPTER ELEVEN

BRUCE DUMPED THE SUDSY BROWN water from the bucket onto some barnyard weeds as soon as Celia was gone. Placing the cleaning brush into the bucket, he set them on the old chair and headed out to find Mr. Edwards. Confronting the old man appealed to him only slightly more than having a boulder fall on his leg.

He placed very little weight on his crutches as he walked across the barnyard. Surprisingly, putting weight on his leg didn't hurt much, which was fortunate, for he spotted Mr. Edwards in a field some distance away. He stopped so as to wave his hand. "Mr. Edwards, I need to talk to you," he yelled and then walked briskly toward him, avoiding the harrowed piles of hay.

Mr. Edwards hurried toward Bruce with rake in hand. "What's the matter?"

"Nothing's the matter." Bruce came to a stop a few feet from Celia's Pa. "I just need to ask you something, before I lose my courage."

"In regards to what?" Mr. Edwards leaned on his rake's handle, cupping his hands over the handle's end.

"Not what, but who," Bruce said. "I'm asking for Celia." *And for you, to a certain degree.*

Mr. Edwards squared his shoulders. "You'd better not be asking for her hand in marriage. Forget about it here and now if that's the case. I told you, she's spoken for already."

Bruce held up his hands. "No, no, that's not what I wanted to ask." He chuckled. "She's a caring, wonderful woman who deserves more than a drifter like me could ever give her. So don't worry; I'm leaving her alone. She's all Wesley's."

Mr. Edwards raised an eyebrow. "You know about him—and her, the two of them . . . and their plans to wed?"

"Yep." Bruce breathed deep to numb the pain. "Celia told me everything, except every tidbit of that latest letter from Mr. Cornwallis." He brought his hand to one side of his mouth. "I'm not sure, but I think it made her sad."

"It's Cornelius. And that's impossible!" Mr. Edwards lifted his hat and wiped the sweat from his brow.

"Maybe . . . maybe not. Who am I to say? I'm just a nobody in most folks' book, but a nobody who wants to show my thanks to your daughter and you, too, Mr. Edwards, for saving my life. I can't think of a better way to do that for both of you than to give her something she's been pining for. She needs cheering up."

Mr. Edwards looked off to one side while nodding. "True, her melancholy has been rather worrisome. But I fail to see where I fit into all of this."

"I need your help." Bruce's leg grew tired, and he leaned on his crutches as he held out his hands toward Celia's pa. "I wanted to give her a Fourth of July celebration. Of course, it won't be like those she was used to. But I'm hoping she'll be the jewel that she is and recognize it's the thought that counts."

"Well, that's very thoughtful of you, Mr. Pickett. But I still fail to see where I fit into this."

Bruce swallowed hard, garnering every last shred of courage. "It would mean a lot more to her if her father would enjoy the celebration too. There's a spark in her eyes when she speaks of how *you* used to love the parades, the picnics, and the fireworks. Don't mind me for asking, but what changed, Mr. Edwards? A passion like that doesn't turn off overnight."

"I do mind you for asking. That, Mr. Pickett, is none of your business." Mr. Edwards cleared his throat as if he were the one who was nervous. "But because I've appreciated your help, I'll tell you—if you must know. It takes a lot of work to homestead 360 acres. Frankly, I don't have time for such frivolity," he stated like he was reading a script.

Bruce was tempted to say, "Thank you, sir," turn around, and leave without another word. But Celia deserved a celebration, one that included her pa. Backing down wouldn't solve anything—just like it hadn't when he'd tried to sway his brothers onto a better path. "Are you sure there is not another reason? Your tone betrays you."

Mr. Edwards stared at Bruce, silent and mouth gaping slightly.

Bruce gulped down a wad of spit. "I know I couldn't give up something I love so easily, especially when there's no cause to do so. Like making things with my hands. I enjoy it. A lot. It makes me happy. Even when I'm busy working, I find time to create . . . say, a whistle with a bird-feather design or a back scratcher for a friend with their initials carved into the handle."

Mr. Edwards's silence continued.

"Hey, I understand you used to play the banjo. Am I right?" Bruce asked to try to break the uncomfortable quiet.

Mr. Edwards nodded hesitantly.

"You were really good, I hear. I'm telling you, a smart man like you doesn't just throw away happiness simply because they're busy. Mr. Edwards, please, let go of what's bothering you. Either that or share it. Sometimes that can help. I'd be happy to listen. I know what it's like to keep things hidden inside where they can fester and make you cross. You'll get no judgement from the likes of me, that's for sure."

"And why should I tell you—if by chance I had something to get off my chest? I hardly know you, Mr. Pickett."

"All the more reason. After a week, you'll never see me again. You need not fear I'll share it with anyone you know—because I don't know anyone you know." Bruce grinned out of one side of his mouth. "Except your family. And I give you my word I won't say anything to them if that is your choice."

"I don't know." Mr. Edwards winced.

"Lance that boil so it can heal."

"I don't enjoy being ornery and working nonstop like I do," Mr. Edwards said in a defensive tone. "But I don't deserve to celebrate anything ever again."

"Whatever mistakes you've made are in your past now. Trust me, you've got to forgive yourself, or you'll never be happy."

"Sit." Mr. Edwards pointed to the nearby pile of hay. "This might take a while." He lowered himself onto the hay and helped Bruce to do the same. Mr. Edwards told of his time in the Union Army before he became a medic. His tone grew solemn as he described a particularly gruesome battle, how they'd fought hard, and their ultimate victory. That evening, with the help of some stout cider, they celebrated big—even though their commanding officer had told them to lay low. As soon as the officer slipped out to meet with his field commander, they commenced dancing around their fires. Harmonicas were brought out, and he'd even played a banjo they'd found in an abandoned farmhouse.

The next morning, they were ambushed, and their troops didn't fare well. Mr. Edwards had attributed their losses to horrors of war—until four years ago when he ran into his commanding officer at a Fourth of July parade. He was in Springfield visiting his daughter for the holiday. It was then he shared details he had only recently learned about himself of that fateful battle years ago.

"Because of the noise we made celebrating that night, the confederate troops discovered our location and easily ambushed us the following morning." Mr. Edwards hung his head. "Then and there, standing in the park next to my old commander, I told myself I'd never celebrate ever again—including my favorite holiday. At the time, my wife and I were merely considering homesteading out West. Meeting with my old commander cemented my decision."

"It seems to me, sir, that your mistake was not that you were celebrating but that you had disobeyed orders." Bruce struggled to his feet. "Still, I understand your hurt, your blaming yourself. But that was years ago. Please, Mr. Edwards, let it go. I just know if I was to keep beating myself up for a particular mistake I made years ago, I could never be happy."

Mr. Edwards helped him to stand. "I always did admire your happy disposition."

"Well, thanks. Speaking of happy, I know it would make Celia more than happy if you were to play your banjo for the Fourth of July dance."

Mr. Edwards leaned backward and looked away from Bruce. "Uh . . ."

"A celebration ain't a celebration without music," Bruce jumped in, a wave of enthusiasm fueling his courage. "I wouldn't have bothered you none, but me and Paul have already asked all the folks we could in and around Almo to help us drum up some music."

"Is that meant to be a pun?" Mr. Edwards's eyes were back on him.

"No, sir," Bruce said. "I'm just saying, all we've come up with is Mr. Durfee and his harmonica. Oh, and his wife did agree to strum out a rhythm on the washboard—but only if we could convince you to play your banjo."

"Why didn't Paul ask me?"

Bruce hesitated. "See . . . I don't want to get Paul in trouble none, 'cause I count him as a friend—a rather dear one."

"I promise, Paul will not be in trouble." Mr. Edwards looked earnest. "But I would like to know."

"Well, he said he'd no more dare to ask you to play your banjo for our dance than he would care to play with a badger whose burrow got buried by his plow."

"Really now?" Mr. Edwards stroked his chin.

"Plus, he said you didn't like celebrations anymore, only work." Bruce felt uncomfortable with the puzzling expression flushing Mr. Edwards's face. "Oh, I don't blame you for liking work. Look at all you've accomplished." He swept his arms wide, indicating their acres of land. "I don't know how you've managed to do such a bang-up job with just you and your family."

"It's been difficult."

"I'm sure it has. I wish I could have helped you more." He leaned back off his crutches and shook them. "Danged leg. It's feeling better though, thanks to all of you. I could really help you out once this blasted cast is gone. But that'd mean I'd have to stay around." Bruce swallowed hard. "Once I'm done with giving Celia her celebration, I promise I'll be outta here. Can I have your help, you know, with the music? Please?"

Mr. Edwards stood still and silent.

"You can think on it. If it's something you don't feel comfortable with, I'll understand. I'll convince Mr. Durfee and his wife to play for the dance without you."

Mr. Edwards rubbed his chin. "I'll consider it."

"Whatever you decide, can we keep this secret? I'd like to surprise Celia."

CHAPTER TWELVE

Celia awoke to the smell of pastries baking. The gray light of dawn barely peeked through the window as she opened her eyes wide. *Sweet rolls? Cake? Cookies?* And why was Ma baking them so early in the morning? She threw back the blanket, ready to get up. A smile came. Today was the Fourth of July. Maybe Ma was making the family a special treat—her way of giving Celia what she'd begged for these past three summers in Idaho. If so, Celia didn't want to spoil Ma's surprise, so she pulled the covers back on and snuggled into her bed. Ma would probably keep the confections hidden until suppertime. If Celia was lucky, Ma might even talk Pa into playing a hand or two of cards with the family before sunset.

She arose at her usual time. Her sisters stirred in their bed. While she dressed, Celia found it peculiar that neither Sophia nor Abby said a word to her like they usually did. She wanted to mention that today was July fourth, but somehow, the moment didn't feel right. Were her sisters sick of her pointing out what day this was every year—and then complaining that no one wanted to remember it with her? Most likely.

A hint of vanilla lingered in the air when Celia walked into the kitchen. Not wanting to spoil Ma's surprise, Celia merely said, "Good morning," and grabbed the bucket and hurried off to milk the cow. The barn looked tidy, and Daisy had a fresh pile of hay.

"It seems Paul got to his chores early today," she said to Daisy as she set the three-legged stool into place.

When she returned with her bucket full of milk, Sophia and Abby ambled out of the bedroom, sniffing the air. Celia feared they would say something about the sweet smell, but they set the table without a word. And much quicker than usual.

"What do you need me to do?" Celia asked Ma, glancing into the huge iron frypan at the almost-ready scrambled eggs and at the pot of porridge.

"Just strain the milk for the mush. Pa and Paul should be in any minute." Ma looked at Sophia. "And could you grab the honey from the cupboard and put it on the table?"

"Yes, Ma."

The door opened, and Paul and Pa filed in and sat down. Sophia and Abby scurried into their seats, and then Ma set the food on the table.

Celia was still straining the milk and felt like all eyes were on her, waiting. Everyone's but Bruce's. She wondered where he was—and still wondered about that kiss, him leaving, her feelings toward him, and her feelings for Wesley. She filled a pitcher of strained milk and carried it to the table, then slipped into her chair as Pa brought his clasped hands up in front of him.

After Pa's prayer, everyone ate without a word.

"Where's Mr. Pickett?" Celia asked to break the silence and because she really wanted to know.

Paul took a long swig of milk and wiped his mouth with the back of his hand. "He's busy. Said he didn't feel like eating breakfast."

"Is he sick?" Celia looked to Pa. "Good gracious, do you think he's coming down with something? That wouldn't be good with him trying to recover from his accident and all."

"He's just fine," Pa said a bit lower and slower than usual, like he was hiding something.

"Well, I hope you're correct." Celia took a bite of egg and chewed. "Say, what has got everyone in such a dither this morning?"

Paul's eyes skirted around the table. "Uh, we just got lots to do. That's all."

Pa nodded as he scraped the last spoonful of mush from his bowl. He popped it in his mouth and stood from the table. "Yep, and I'd best get going."

Paul finished his breakfast and rushed out the door. Then Sophia and Abby left together, Abby covering a big grin with her hand as they scurried from the cabin.

Ma finished her last bite of eggs, rose from the table, and grabbed the bucket by the sink.

Celia finished eating her breakfast alone. "What has gotten into everyone?"

Ma shrugged her shoulders and dipped her bucket into the reservoir of hot water at the side of the stove. "When you're done, clear the table. I'll get the dishwater ready."

After Celia and her ma finished the dishes and tidied up the house, Celia changed her dress that had been splashed with milk and manure. She chose her nice blue dress to wear. If no one else cared to celebrate today, other than with a cake at supper, she was not going to let that stop her from doing so.

Ma hollered into the bedroom. "When you're through changing, come with me."

"Where?" Celia couldn't keep the surprise from her voice.

"Just come."

Celia followed Ma to the barn and opened the doors to see both Copper and Pepper saddled, their reins tied to the manger. "Huh?"

"How would you like to go on an outing with me today?"

"Don't Paul or Pa need the horses?"

"They've got Zed."

"Zed!" Celia couldn't imagine Pa strapping a saddle to their plow horse, let alone riding him. Neither had Ma ever taken the time to go on an "outing" with her since they'd moved to Idaho. "Ma, what's going on?"

"It's the Fourth of July. Our homestead is doing fine. Don't you think it's about time we celebrated both of those with a little bit of leisure?"

"Oh, Ma!" Celia hugged her. "I guess my complaining has finally paid off."

"Dear, your complaints had nothing to do with it." Ma walked out of the barn with horses in tow. "The truth is, you reminding us every July fourth that we should take some time away from our work and celebrate this great nation we are blessed to have is not a complaint. There is a difference between whining about something and standing up for what you believe is right."

Celia climbed into Copper's saddle, letting Ma's words sink in.

Ma mounted Pepper. The sight only added to the excitement kicking up inside Celia—she rarely saw her ma atop a horse. What on earth did Ma have planned for just the two of them? She appreciated this immensely, but deep down, she wished she could be celebrating this day with Bruce too. Yet she was still considering marrying Wesley. She *needed* to decide—for everyone's sake.

"Where are we headed?" Celia asked when Ma guided her horse in the opposite direction from Celia's outing with Sophia.

"You'll find out soon enough."

They rode side by side down the parallel ruts of the old Oregon Trail. The clomp of horse hooves, the warble of meadowlarks, and the swish of a light breeze made for a lovely chorus. Celia breathed in the fresh air that held a hint of juniper and sighed. "Thank you, Ma. I really appreciate you doing this for me."

Ma nodded. "You've been a bit sad lately. Care to talk about it?"

Celia hesitated. "It's Wesley. I fear three years apart hasn't been a good thing."

"And you?"

"I'm not sure if I love him anymore." Celia felt a burden lift as she spoke and as she saw Ma give a nod.

They stayed to the trail through the small canyon, then emerged into the Almo Valley. "We're going into town, aren't we?"

"That's correct."

Images of the jars of peppermint sticks and licorice whips came to mind. Though that would be nice, Celia hoped for more than just a piece of candy from Durfee's store to make this day special. Good gracious. Earlier, she'd thought the horseback ride was sufficient. And there was Ma's homemade treat still to come, if that's what she'd even smelled. "Ma, what were you baking early this morning?"

"A dessert for our picnic."

"Picnic!" Celia clasped her hands together, accidentally causing Copper to slow down. "For later on today, supper under the cottonwoods maybe?" She hoped Bruce would be *there*—oh dear, she didn't want him to go away next week.

"For later on today, yes."

When they reached the curve that led into town, Celia noticed a number of people gathered outside Durfee's store and in the shade of the church's poplar trees across the street. She also saw several hitched wagons parked behind the store. Children ran about, weaving in and out of the collection of wagons. "What is going on?"

"My dear, we are about to attend Almo's first Fourth of July parade."

Celia gasped. "Oh, Ma, are you serious?"

"Completely."

As they rode past the general store, Celia noticed a man sitting outside at the checker table wearing a store-bought suit and a bowler hat. He looked out of place. And by the way he swung his crossed leg and kept glancing at his gold pocket watch, she gathered he felt out of place. Yet, he looked familiar.

"Wesley?" Celia gasped. She stopped Copper, dismounted, and ran to him. Instinctively, she readied her arms to wrap them around him but stopped. Everyone's eyes seemed focused on her, including Wesley's. "What are you doing here?" she asked instead.

"I came on the morning stage. The store owner told me if I waited for a while, chances were I'd run into you." Wesley reached out hesitantly and then quickly clasped his hands behind his back.

"Why didn't you tell me you were coming?" Celia found herself wishing she'd had more notice to prepare herself.

"It was a spur-of-the-moment decision, sorry. Your last two letters pricked my conscience. Then when I didn't hear from you for weeks, I knew I must come and apologize." Wesley cleared his throat. "Say, is the rumor true, that all of your grandmother's money is gone?"

"Well, yes, but . . . never mind. I'm—I'm glad you're here. You're just in time to join Mother and me for the parade." Celia waved at her ma, who was still on Pepper.

Ma motioned for them to follow her. Celia led her horse and walked alongside Wesley.

"This town has no hotel," Wesley said with noticeable irritation in his voice. "What am I supposed to do?"

"You can bed down in our barn with Paul and Bruce."

"Really?" Wesley shuddered.

Celia had thought it a fine offer, especially since he'd given them no warning of his arrival.

Ma stopped at the blacksmith's shop and dismounted, and Thomas, the blacksmith, took their horses and led them around back.

Thomas's wife, Maybelle, motioned to a couple of empty chairs sitting in the shade of the shop like they were waiting just for her and Ma. "You're just in time." She glanced at Wesley. "Sorry, but I only have two extra chairs."

Wesley said nothing, but his eyes said he was put out.

"You sit next to Celia," Ma said to Wesley. "I really don't mind standing. I'm sure it won't be very long."

Wesley sat, glancing up the road and then down. "Yes, I can't imagine you'd have much of a parade in a town like this."

Celia felt in a daze as she sat down—first a celebration and now Wesley. She pinched herself to make sure she wasn't dreaming. Had her parents actually convinced the town of Almo to start celebrating the Fourth of July?

"Here it comes!" the blacksmith hollered.

Celia bounced in her seat as Paul and his friend John marched by holding a banner which read: *Happy 4th of July, Almo.*

Sophia followed several paces behind Paul. Sophia pulled the wooden wagon their family used to carry in vegetables from the garden. Inside it rode Abby, holding her favorite piglet from the brood their old sow gave birth to last week. They all three wore red bows, in Abby's and Sophia's hair and around the piglet's neck. Behind Celia's sisters came an array of children decorated in similar fashion. They all marched to the beat of a catchy rhythm being played in the background somewhere. Some of the older children pulled wagons filled with toddlers. Some pushed wheelbarrows full of friends, while other children led pet roosters, lambs, and calves on leashes.

"Ma, this is wonderful."

The music got louder as their wagon pulled out onto the road from behind the store and joined the parade. Celia caught her breath. Bruce sat on its bench, flipping the reins gently across Zed's back. He wore a clean white shirt with a black tie knotted in a neat bow at his neck. His blond hair appeared freshly washed and hung in gentle curls around his smooth face. The blue of his eyes looked extra vibrant as their gazes met, and he smiled, making her heart beat faster.

The wagon moved forward, and she noticed Pa and Mr. and Mrs. Durfee, each sitting on a chair and playing the catchy rhythm that accompanied the parade.

"Pa's playing his banjo!" Celia looked up at her ma standing at her side.

"He sure is." Ma smiled wide. "Isn't that grand? I could hardly believe it when he told me this morning."

Pa was smiling too. Celia couldn't help but stare and wave. It did her heart good, seeing her pa enjoy himself so. Her eyes moved down, noticing words had been painted on the side of the wagon in crudely formed lettering.

DANCE TONITE 7 BON FIRE 8 AT THE EDWARDS PLACE

Bruce wrote that. Had he been practicing his spelling even after she'd quit teaching him? She reached up and wiped her eye. The other eye needed wiping when the message sunk in. "Ma, are we really going to have a bonfire at our house *and* a dance?"

"That's right, in the spot that Paul cleared of sagebrush. He and Pa watered and packed it down the day before yesterday. It should be perfect for tonight."

Celia grabbed her ma's hand. "This day just gets better and better."

"There's more to come."

"More?" Celia couldn't imagine this day getting any better.

"After the parade is our picnic. It'll be down by Almo Creek with all the other families." Ma swept her hand toward the spectators on both sides of the road.

"What about Br—Mr. Pickett?"

"He'll join our family to eat, of course," Ma said.

"Who is this Mr. Pickett?"

Celia jumped at the sound of Wesley's voice—she'd forgotten he was there. The day was *not* getting better—it was turning awkward.

CHAPTER THIRTEEN

"Uh . . ." Celia grabbled for the right words to say to Wesley, staring into the street as the remainder of the parade marched by.

Ma patted Celia's shoulder ever so softly as she spoke to Wesley. "My husband mended Mr. Pickett's leg after it was injured saving Sophia, and he's been staying and working at our place while his leg heals."

Thank you, Ma.

Ma turned to the blacksmith. "Thank you for the lovely spot to watch. We'll see you down at the town picnic, I presume?"

"Of course," he and his wife responded together.

Wesley offered Celia his crooked elbow, and instinctively, she linked her arm through. She chided herself when she realized she kept her eyes open for Bruce as she and Wesley walked toward the creek behind the church. But heavens, Bruce had looked so striking. Her heart warmed further as she contemplated his willing participation in the parade.

When she saw Bruce, she gasped inwardly. She steadied her arm in Wesley's and tried not to look at Bruce as he helped Paul spread a blanket in a spot of shade. Pa carried a bushel basket covered with a nice dish cloth and set it on the blanket while Sophia, Abby, and three other children played tag nearby.

"Wesley?" Pa's eyebrows rose. "Heavens, what are you doing here?"

Bruce looked up as Celia approached. His eyes spoke the same as his words. "You sure look pretty today." Then they moved to Wesley and shone of fear. "So this is your fiancé?" he said to Celia but continued to lock gazes with Wesley.

"We are not officially engaged," Wesley said. "That, Mr. Edwards, is what I'm doing here. Celia and I need to get some things figured out concerning our courtship and finances. I feared a correspondence through the mail would not be the best way to accomplish that."

"Finances?" Celia responded. That had not been an issue she'd brought up in her letters. Or ever in their relationship. Her mind raced to Wesley's words when he'd first seen her today. There had been no mention of how much he missed her or an apology for having ignored her requests to solidify their engagement in her letters. No, he had asked about her grandmother's money—or, rather, the possible lack thereof. Her back bristled, and she pulled her arm from his.

The action apparently didn't go unnoticed by Pa. His face softened as his eyes met Celia's. They appeared questioning as they met Wesley's. "What's to figure out with your finances?"

"That's between me and Celia." Wesley pushed out his chest.

"Ex*cuse* me," Pa said.

Ma interrupted their conversation in her efforts to gather the family onto the blanket. Celia sat down in between Wesley and Bruce, fearing Ma's or Pa's disapproving glance and not caring about Wesley's. None came from her parents. Pa spoke with Paul, and Ma seemed intent on unloading the picnic basket. The first thing Ma pulled out was a rectangular cake with white frosting decorated with stripes of red-raspberry jam and blue-purple lilac blooms in the upper left-hand corner.

Abby clapped her hands to her cheek when Ma set it in the middle of the blanket. "Oh, Mama, that looks pretty!"

"And delicious," Bruce said.

"And festive," Celia added.

After Ma said a prayer of thanks, everyone filled their plates with cold roast beef sandwiches and the last of the fresh pea pods. Celia left her food untouched momentarily and focused on her ma. "What a delightful Fourth of July. It's better than anything I could have ever imagined."

Wesley rolled his eyes.

Celia motioned to the numerous picnicking families and then at the makeshift corral of horses, some still attired in flowers. A lump rose in her throat. "Thanks for arranging all this."

"Sorry, we can't take the credit. It was Mr. Pickett's doing," Ma said.

Pa nodded and grinned at Bruce.

Celia turned to Bruce and stared, her insides a jumble.

A shy smile spread across Bruce's face. "It's my way of saying thanks. You folks have done so much for me." His expression grew serious. "Especially you, Celia."

Myriad words and wonderful feelings spun inside her, making it impossible to express any of them. She barely murmured, "Oh, Bruce."

After a moment of silence, where he looked as pleased as she felt, Bruce continued. "Thanks for everyone's help. I couldn't have created this celebration for Celia without you. And don't worry, Mr. Edwards. I painted that sign on your wagon with whitewash. I can either wash it off or paint the whole thing. I'll make it look dang good before I leave next week."

Celia's world slowed to a crawl—hearing it from Bruce made it feel real. But she had Wesley.

Do I really?

Pa set down his sandwich. "We're going to miss you, Mr. Pickett. You've been a tremendous help around the farm even with your broken leg. That says a lot."

Celia nibbled her sandwich. Her eyes kept staring off into the distance as she contemplated how empty the farm would feel in a week. Going about her chores would feel as tasteless as her sandwich.

A pea pod hit her on the nose. Paul laughed. "Hey, sis, brighten up. This here's a celebration, not a funeral."

Bruce touched her arm. "Are you all right?"

She forced a smile. "I'm fine. Just thinking, that's all."

Later that afternoon, Paul and Pa rode the horses back home. Ma rode in the back of the wagon with the girls and belongings. Celia sat on the bench between Wesley and Bruce, continually smoothing out her skirt so as to keep her hands busy. No one said a word, creating tightness inside her. Celia glanced at Bruce as he flicked Zed's reins. He had gone to a lot of effort to make this celebration special for her, and she was grateful. Then she thought about Bruce leaving. The uncomfortable feeling in her chest grew tighter.

Wesley cleared his throat. "So, Mr. Pickett, where will you go after you leave here?"

"Hopefully, I'll find a good job in Denver. I think that's where I'll try first after I leave."

"But there's plenty of work here—" Ma cut her words short but not before they gave Celia reason to ponder.

"Denver is a good choice for you," Wesley said, and the silence returned.

When they arrived home, everyone got to their evening chores. Celia helped Ma make a light supper and then cleaned up while the men went to prepare for the bonfire and dance.

Celia freshened up, partially removing her dress and airing out under her arms and then splashing them with a bit of lilac water. "I wish Ma had told me sooner what was going on. It would have been nice to have my blue dress clean and fresh for the dance," she mumbled to her reflection in the mirror of her bedroom.

"What was that?" Sophia bent over, brushing her hair out.

Celia recognized her words for what they were. "Nothing. I was just complaining."

"Today of all days. I declare, Celia, will you ever learn?"

"You're right. I have not one reason to complain today." *Except that I don't want Bruce to leave.* Interestingly enough, she didn't feel that way about Wesley.

Then again, according to Ma, that was not complaining. Celia realized those feelings *were* standing up for what she knew was correct.

As Celia walked with Ma and her sisters through the barnyard, townsfolk joined them. Together they headed toward the corner of their land where the evening's festivities were to be held. Ma and her sisters chatted excitedly with their neighbors. Celia kept to herself, thinking of ways to keep Bruce around. *But what of Wesley?*

The confusion returned.

Pa and the Durfees began playing their music when Celia arrived. Pa's face beamed as he plucked his banjo. Gratitude swelled in her heart for Bruce for more than just this holiday celebration he'd put together for her. Wesley would never do such a thing. Bruce's kindness made her insides warm up as she considered it. Gratitude, kindness, hardworking, and a sense of humor—qualities she would love her future husband to have. Wesley offered financial security, prestige, and refinement. At one time, she thought that was what she'd wanted. Now . . . her heart and head told her she'd rather have the prior.

Couples trickled onto the well-packed dirt of the dance floor, and then families gathered around the perimeter. Out of the corner of her eye, she saw Wesley approach.

"I assume I may have the pleasure of this first dance." Wesley extended his hand. "And the remainder of the evening with you and you alone?"

"This first dance, yes." Celia accepted his hand. But she had to tell him. "As for the rest of the evening, I have other plans. And I think it best that you make plans to return to Boston tomorrow. In my letter, I had been adamant that you make a decision concerning our engagement. You needn't worry about that now, for I have made the decision to end our courtship." She looked around for Bruce. She had to tell him she loved him. Then maybe he'd stay.

"But—" Wesley's eyes followed her scan as they danced. "Don't tell me you'd rather be with that lowlife drifter your father patched up."

"Okay, I won't tell you." Celia caught a glimpse of Bruce's white shirt and leaned to see him better. He stood at the other side of the dance floor by an enormous pile of dried sagebrush talking, no doubt, to the man he'd put in charge of lighting it on fire in an hour. Just then, two straggly looking men with holstered pistols approached them, and Bruce appeared noticeably upset.

"Fine, but if you choose him over me, that is the kind of company you'll have over to dinner. Bank robbers or bank presidents. It's your choice, Celia."

"Yes, it is." Celia didn't care who Bruce knew, just who he was.

Bruce spoke to the straggly men at length, standing firm the whole time. She noticed Pa watching the confrontation too, not missing a note on his banjo as he stared. By the time her dance with Wesley ended, the two men lumbered away. Pa set down his banjo and approached Bruce.

"Goodbye, Wesley." Celia let go of him.

"You're making a big mistake, Celia."

"No, I am not."

"Fine! It's just as well. Marrying a penniless woman would not sit well with my parents."

"Or are you speaking of yourself?" Celia asked.

Wesley huffed and stormed off.

Celia turned away from Wesley and waved at Bruce. He waved back, said something to Pa, and walked toward her, barely using his crutches.

Yes, she'd have to talk to him tonight. The way he was healing, he could be gone even sooner than a week. Celia glanced at Pa, then at Ma standing at the edge of the dance floor with Abby. She thought about the impropriety of asking them to let a single man stay with them as a farm hand, sharing their house come winter when they had an unmarried daughter. There was only one solution: marry Bruce.

Bruce continued toward her, wearing that ever-cheerful expression. The evening sun lit his face, adding to his inner glow. Yes, she had to act. Now. It would be bold. It would upset a lot of people—or maybe not.

"Good evening," she said to Bruce when he reached her. "You've come to ask me to dance, I hope?"

Bruce laughed with delight. "My dear Celia, there is nothing more I'd rather do than dance with you. But I'm afraid I'd make for a pretty lousy partner." He lifted his crutches. "I hate saying this, but you're going to want to keep dancing with Wesley."

She stepped close to Bruce and looped her arm around his. "I don't want Wesley. I want you."

The music started up again.

"Well, I'll be—if that's what you want. But I can't promise more than a little swaying to the music." Bruce let go of his crutches, letting them fall to the ground. He took her left hand in his and placed his right hand at the small of her back. "After all, this is your day."

Celia felt at home in his arms. She gave Bruce's hand a squeeze. Pa winked at her as he played his banjo. "And what a wonderful day it has been."

Bruce swayed her to the music. "The day's not over. There's more to come."

"There certainly is." Celia wondered how and when she would propose her idea to Bruce. She cringed inside at the impropriety of it all, for that was exactly what she would be doing: proposing.

"Ah, you're looking forward to the bonfire, are you?"

"Uh . . . of course."

Bruce pulled her closer and spoke softly in her ear as he continued to sway. "I'm glad. I'm sorry I couldn't give you any fireworks."

"That's all right. Say, who were those men you were talking to?" Celia asked.

"My brothers tracked me down when they heard I was looking for buried gold. They wanted a cut of it. Told them I wasn't looking for it no more— I'd found something better. They got angry and said they wanted some of whatever 'that' was because it looked like I was doing really good. I told them they'd never find it. Then I told them to leave—and leave me alone. Your pa knows the whole story. You can have him tell you someday if you want. Right now, I don't want to talk about my brothers. Only hold you."

"Bruce," Celia murmured, her lips inadvertently brushing against his neck as she nestled under the crook of his chin. He pulled her closer. She loved their closeness. Now seemed as good a time as any. "I've got something to ask you."

"Ask away. Your wish is my command."

"Don't go away next week."

"Ah, you want me to wait until you and Wesley announce your engagement. Then I leave?"

"No. Not anymore. I'm mature enough to know what's best for me." She leaned back so as to look Bruce in the face. "I don't want to marry Wesley. It is *you* who I want to spend the rest of my life with."

Bruce's eyes glossed over. His lips trembled, and a weak smile slowly grew into a wide grin. "Are you saying you want to marry *me?*"

"If you'll have me, yes."

"Well, lands almighty!" Bruce let go of Celia and snatched his crutches from off the ground. Hanging onto the hand pegs, he awkwardly lowered onto his good knee and took Celia's hand in his. "Celia Edwards, will you marry me?"

"Yes, yes, I would love to marry you."

Bruce pulled himself onto his feet. He let go of his crutches, gathered Celia into his arms, and gazed into her eyes. "I am the luckiest man on earth." He leaned down and placed his mouth on hers.

The hardships that faced them slipped away, and Celia focused only on his soft lips touching hers, her quickening breath, and the fluttering longing in her chest. It appeared Bruce gave her fireworks for the Fourth of July after all.

ABOUT THE AUTHOR

CAROLYN TWEDE FRANK LIVES IN the Rocky Mountains and has always enjoyed old black-and-white movies, especially ones depicting the American frontier and those spiced up with a bit of romance. Carolyn is not new to the genre of historical fiction. Some of her earlier works include *The Hitler Dilemma* and *Trapped in East Germany*. When Carolyn is not writing, she enjoys gardening, sewing, renovating houses, and playing with her grandkids. She also loves taking road trips in the western United States with her husband, scoping out interesting tidbits of history to weave into her next novel.